**Nora R**

bestsellin

than 300

150 *New* … to date, Nora Roberts is indisputably the most celebrated women's fiction writer today.

Visit her website at www.nora-roberts.co.uk

*By Nora Roberts*

Homeport
The Reef
River's End
Carolina Moon
The Villa
Midnight Bayou
Three Fates
Birthright
Northern Lights
Blue Smoke
Montana Sky
Angels Fall
High Noon
Divine Evil
Tribute
Sanctuary
Black Hills
The Search

*Three Sisters Island Trilogy:*
Dance Upon the Air
Heaven and Earth
Face the Fire

*Chesapeake Bay Quartet:*
Sea Swept
Rising Tides
Inner Harbour
Chesapeake Blue

*The Key Trilogy:*
Key of Light
Key of Knowledge
Key of Valour

*In the Garden Trilogy:*
Blue Dahlia
Black Rose
Red Lily

*The Irish Trilogy:*
Jewels of the Sun
Tears of the Moon
Heart of the Sea

*The Circle Trilogy:*
Morrigan's Cross
Dance of the Gods
Valley of Silence

*The Born In Trilogy:*
Born In Fire
Born In Ice
Born In Shame

*The Dream Trilogy:*
Daring to Dream
Holding the Dream
Finding the Dream

*The Sign of Seven Trilogy:*
Blood Brothers
The Hollow
The Pagan Stone

*As J.D. Robb:*
Naked in Death
Glory in Death
Immortal in Death
Rapture in Death
Ceremony in Death
Vengeance in Death
Holiday in Death
Conspiracy in Death
Loyalty in Death
Witness in Death
Judgement in Death
Betrayal in Death
Seduction in Death
Reunion in Death
Purity in Death
Portrait in Death
Imitation in Death
Divided in Death
Visions in Death
Survivor in Death
Origin in Death
Memory in Death
Born in Death
Innocent in Death
Creation in Death
Strangers in Death
Salvation in Death
Promises in Death
Kindred in Death
Fantasy in Death

*By Nora Roberts and J.D. Robb*
Remember When

# vision in white

*nora*
roberts

piatkus

PIATKUS

First published in the US in 2009 by The Berkley Publishing Group,
a member of Penguin Group (USA) Inc., New York
First published in Great Britain in 2009 by Piatkus
Reprinted 2011



A CIP catalogue record for this book
is available from the British Library.

ISBN 978-0-351-32175-7

Printed and bound by CPI Group (UK) Ltd, Croydon, CR0 4YY

Papers used by Piatkus are from well-managed forests
and other responsible sources.

FSC
www.fsc.org
MIX
Paper from
responsible sources
FSC® C104740

Piatkus
An imprint of
Little, Brown Book Group
100 Victoria Embankment
London EC4Y 0DY

An Hachette UK Company
www.hachette.co.uk

www.piatkus.co.uk

*For Dan and Stacie.*
*For Jason and Kat.*
*For all the moments.*

Seduce my mind and you can have my body,
Find my soul and I'm yours forever.

—Anonymous

It is not merely the likeness which is precious . . . but the association and sense of nearness involved in the thing . . . the fact of the very shadow of the person lying there fixed forever!

—Elizabeth Barrett Browning

# PROLOGUE

By the time she was eight, Mackensie Elliot had been married fourteen times. She'd married each of her three best friends—as both bride and groom—her best friend's brother (under his protest), two dogs, three cats, and a rabbit.

She'd served at countless other weddings as maid of honor, bridesmaid, groomsman, best man, and officiant.

Though the dissolutions were invariably amicable, none of the marriages lasted beyond an afternoon. The transitory aspect of marriage came as no surprise to Mac, as her own parents boasted two each—so far.

Wedding Day wasn't her favorite game, but she kind of liked being the priest or the reverend or the justice of the peace. Or, after attending her father's second wife's nephew's bar mitzvah, the rabbi.

Plus, she enjoyed the cupcakes or fancy cookies and fizzy lemonade always served at the reception.

It was Parker's favorite game, and Wedding Day always took place on the Brown Estate, with its expansive gardens, pretty groves, and silvery pond. In the cold Connecticut winters, the ceremony might take place in front of one of the roaring fires inside the big house.

They had simple weddings and elaborate affairs. Royal weddings, star-crossed elopements, circus themes, and pirate ships. All ideas were seriously considered and voted upon, and no theme or costume too outrageous.

Still, with fourteen marriages under her belt, Mac grew a bit weary of Wedding Day.

Until she experienced her seminal moment.

For her eighth birthday Mackensie's charming and mostly absent father sent her a Nikon camera. She'd never expressed any interest in photography, and initially pushed it away with the other odd gifts he'd given or sent since the divorce. But Mac's mother told *her* mother, and Grandma muttered and complained about "feckless, useless Geoffrey Elliot" and the inappropriate gift of an adult camera for a young girl who'd be better off with a Barbie doll.

As she habitually disagreed with her grandmother on principle, Mac's interest in the camera piqued. To annoy Grandma—who was visiting for the summer instead of being in her retirement community in Scottsdale, where Mac strongly believed she belonged—Mac hauled the Nikon around with her. She toyed with it, experimented. She took pictures of her room, of her feet, of her friends. Shots that were blurry and dark, or fuzzy and washed out. With her lack of success, and her mother's impending divorce from her stepfather, Mac's interest in the Nikon began to wane. Even years later she couldn't say what prompted her to bring it along to Parker's that pretty summer afternoon for Wedding Day.

Every detail of the traditional garden wedding had been planned. Emmaline as the bride and Laurel as groom would exchange their vows beneath the rose arbor. Emma would wear the lace veil and train Parker's mother had made out of an old tablecloth, while Harold, Parker's aging and affable golden retriever walked her down the garden path to give her away.

A selection of Barbies, Kens, and Cabbage Patch Kids, along with a variety of stuffed animals lined the path as guests.

"It's a very private ceremony," Parker relayed as she fussed with Emma's veil. "With a small patio reception to follow. Now, where's the best man?"

Laurel, her knee recently skinned, shoved through a trio of hydrangeas. "He ran away, and went up a tree after a squirrel. I can't get him to come down."

Parker rolled her eyes. "I'll get him. You're not supposed to see the bride before the wedding. It's bad luck. Mac, you need to fix Emma's veil and get her bouquet. Laurel and I'll get Mr. Fish out of the tree."

"I'd rather go swimming," Mac said as she gave Emma's veil an absent tug.

"We can go after I get married."

"I guess. Aren't you tired of getting married?"

"Oh, I don't mind. And it smells so good out here. Everything's so pretty."

Mac gave Emma the clutch of dandelions and wild violets they were allowed to pick. "You look pretty."

It was invariably true. Emma's dark, shiny hair tumbled under the white lace. Her eyes sparkled a deep, deep brown as she sniffed the weed bouquet. She was tanned, sort of all golden, Mac thought, and scowled at her own milk white skin.

The curse of a redhead, her mother said, as she got her carroty hair from her father. At eight, Mac was tall for her age and skinny as a stick, with teeth already trapped in hated braces.

She thought that, beside her, Emmaline looked like a gypsy princess.

Parker and Laurel came back, giggling with the feline best

man clutched in Parker's arms. "Everybody has to take their places." Parker poured the cat into Laurel's arms. Mac, you need to get dressed! Emma—"

"I don't want to be maid of honor." Mac looked at the poofy Cinderella dress draped over a garden bench. "That thing's scratchy, and it's hot. Why can't Mr. Fish be maid of honor, and I'll be best man?"

"Because it's already planned. Everybody's nervous before a wedding." Parker flipped back her long brown pigtails, then picked up the dress to inspect it for tears or stains. Satisfied, she pushed it at Mac. "It's okay. It's going to be a beautiful ceremony, with true love and happy ever after."

"My mother says happy ever after's a bunch of bull."

There was a moment of silence after Mac's statement. The unspoken word *divorce* seemed to hang in the air.

"I don't think it has to be." Her eyes full of sympathy, Parker reached out, ran her hand along Mac's bare arm.

"I don't want to wear the dress. I don't want to be a bridesmaid. I—"

"Okay. That's okay. We can have a pretend maid of honor. Maybe you could take pictures."

Mac looked down at the camera she'd forgotten hung around her neck. "They never come out right."

"Maybe they will this time. It'll be fun. You can be the official wedding photographer."

"Take one of me and Mr. Fish," Laurel insisted, and pushed her face and the cat's together. "Take one, Mac!"

With little enthusiasm, Mac lifted the camera, pressed the shutter.

"We should've thought of this before! You can take formal portraits of the bride and groom, and more pictures during the ceremony." Busy with the new idea, Parker hung the Cinderella costume on the hydrangea bush. "It'll be good, it'll be fun. You need to go down the path with the bride and Harold. Try to take some good ones. I'll wait, then start the music. Let's go!"

There would be cupcakes and lemonade, Mac reminded herself. And swimming later, and fun. It didn't matter if the pictures were stupid, didn't matter that her grandmother was right and she was too young for the camera.

It didn't matter that her mother was getting divorced again, or that her stepfather, who'd been okay, had already moved out.

It didn't matter that happy ever after was bull, because it was all pretend anyway.

She tried to take pictures of Emma and the obliging Harold, imagined getting the film back and seeing the blurry figures and smudges of her thumb, like always.

When the music started she felt bad that she hadn't put on the scratchy dress and given Emma a maid of honor, just because her mother and grandmother had put her in a bad mood. So she circled around to stand to the side and tried harder to take a nice picture of Harold walking Emma down the garden path.

It looked different through the lens, she thought, the way she could focus on Emma's face—the way the veil lay over her hair. And the way the sun shined through the lace was pretty.

She took more pictures as Parker began the "Dearly Beloved" as the Reverend Whistledown, as Emma and Laurel took hands and Harold curled up to sleep and snore at their feet.

She noticed how bright Laurel's hair was, how the sun caught the edges of it beneath the tall black hat she wore as groom. How Mr. Fish's whiskers twitched as he yawned.

When it happened, it happened as much inside Mac as out. Her three friends were grouped under the lush white curve of the arbor, a triangle of pretty young girls. Some instinct had Mac shifting her position, just slightly, tilting the camera just a bit. She didn't know it as composition, only that it looked nicer through the lens.

And the blue butterfly fluttered across her range of vision to land on the head of a butter yellow dandelion in Emma's bouquet. The surprise and pleasure struck the three faces in that triangle under the white roses almost as one.

Mac pressed the shutter.

She knew, *knew*, the photograph wouldn't be blurry and dark or fuzzy and washed out. Her thumb wouldn't be blocking the lens. She knew exactly what the picture would look like, knew her grandmother had been wrong after all.

Maybe happy ever after was bull, but she knew she wanted to take more pictures of moments that *were* happy. Because then they were ever after.

# CHAPTER ONE

On January first, Mac rolled over to smack her alarm clock, and ended up facedown on the floor of her studio.

"Shit. Happy New Year."

She lay, groggy and baffled, until she remembered she'd never made it upstairs into bed—and the alarm was from her computer, set to wake her at noon.

She pushed herself up to stagger to the kitchen and the coffeemaker.

Why did people want to get married on New Year's Eve? Why would they make a formal ritual out of a holiday designed for marathon drinking and probably inappropriate sex? And they just had to drag family and friends into it, not to mention wedding photographers.

Of course, when the reception had finally ended at two A.M., she could've gone to bed like a sane person instead of uploading the shots, reviewing them—spending nearly three more hours on the Hines-Myers wedding photos.

But, boy, she'd gotten some good ones. A few great ones.

Or they were all crap and she'd judged them in a euphoric blur.

No, they were good shots.

She added three spoons of sugar to the black coffee and drank it while standing at the window, looking out at the snow blanketing the gardens and lawns of the Brown Estate.

They'd done a good job on the wedding, she thought. And maybe Bob Hines and Vicky Myers would take a clue from that and do a good job on the marriage.

Either way, the memories of the day wouldn't fade. The moments, big and small, were captured. She'd refine them, finesse them, print them. Bob and Vicky could revisit the day through those images next week or sixty years from next week.

That, she thought, was as potent as sweet, black coffee on a cold winter day.

Opening a cupboard, she pulled out a box of Pop-Tarts and, eating one where she stood, went over her schedule for the day.

Clay-McFearson (Rod and Alison) wedding at six. Which meant the bride and her party would arrive by three, groom and his by four. That gave her until two for the pre-event summit meeting at the main house.

Time enough to shower, dress, go over her notes, check and recheck her equipment. Her last check of the day's weather called for sunny skies, high of thirty-two. She should be able to get some nice preparation shots using natural light and maybe talk Alison—if she was game—into a bridal portrait on the balcony with the snow in the background.

Mother of the bride, Mac remembered—Dorothy (call me Dottie)—was on the pushy and demanding side, but she'd be dealt with. If Mac couldn't handle her personally, God knew Parker would. Parker could and did handle anyone and anything.

Parker's drive and determination had turned Vows into one of the top wedding and event planning companies in the state in a five-year period. It had turned the tragedy of her parents' deaths into hope, and the gorgeous Victorian home and the stunning grounds of the Brown Estate into a thriving and unique business.

And, Mac thought as she swallowed the last of the Pop-Tart, she herself was one of the reasons.

She moved through the studio toward the stairs to her upstairs bed and bath, stopped at one of her favorite photos. The glowing, ecstatic bride with her face lifted, her arms stretched, palms up, caught in a shower of pink rose petals.

Cover of *Today's Bride*, Mac thought. Because I'm just that good.

In her thick socks, flannel pants, and sweatshirt she climbed the stairs to transform herself from tired, pj-clad, Pop-Tart addict into sophisticated wedding photojournalist.

She ignored her unmade bed—why make it when you were just going to mess it up again?—and the bedroom clutter. The hot shower worked with the sugar and caffeine to clear out any remaining cobwebs so she could put her mind seriously to today's job.

She had a bride who was interested in trying the creative, a passive-aggressive MOB who thought she knew best, a groom so dazzling in love he'd do anything to make his bride happy. And both her B and G were seriously photogenic.

The last fact made the job both pleasure and challenge. Just how could she give her clients a photo journey of their day that was spectacular, and uniquely theirs?

Bride's colors, she thought, flipping through her mental files as she washed her short, shaggy crop of red hair. Silver and gold. Elegant, glamorous.

She'd had a look at the flowers and the cake—both getting their finishing touches today—the favors and linens, attendants' wardrobes, headdresses. She had a copy of the playlist from the band with the first dance, mother-son, father-daughter dances highlighted.

So, she thought, for the next several hours, her world would revolve around Rod and Alison.

She chose her suit, her jewelry, her makeup with nearly the same care as she chose her equipment. Loaded, she went out to make the short trek from the pool house that held her studio and little apartment to the main house.

The snow sparkled, crushed diamonds over ermine, and the air was cold and clean as mountain ice. She definitely had to get some outside shots, daylight and evening. Winter wedding, white wedding, snow on the ground, ice glistening on the trees, just dripping from the denuded willows over the pond. And there the fanciful old Victorian with its myriad rooflines, the arched and porthole windows, rising and spreading, soft blue against the hard shell of sky. Its terraces and generous portico heralded the season with their festoons of lights and greenery.

She studied it as she often did as she walked the shoveled paths. She loved the lines of it, the angles of it, with its subtle touches of pale yellow, creamy white picked out in that soft, subtle blue.

It had been as much home to her as her own growing up. Often more so, she admitted, as her own had run on her mother's capricious whims. Parker's parents had been warm, welcoming, loving and—Mac thought now—steady. They'd given her a calm port in the storm of her own childhood.

She'd grieved as much as her friend at their loss nearly seven years before.

Now the Brown Estate was her home. Her business. Her life. And a good one on every level. What could be better than doing something you loved, and doing it with the best friends you'd ever had?

She went in through the mudroom to hang up her outdoor gear, then circled around to peek into Laurel's domain.

Her friend and partner stood on a step stool, meticulously adding silver calla lilies to the five tiers of a wedding cake. Each flower bloomed at the base of a gold acanthus leaf to glimmering, elegant effect.

"That's a winner, McBane."

Laurel's hand was steady as a surgeon's as she added the next lily. Her sunny hair was twisted at the back of her head into a messy knot that somehow suited the angular triangle of her face. As she worked, her eyes, bright as bluebells, held narrowed concentration.

"I'm so glad she went for the lily centerpiece instead of the bride and groom topper. It makes this design. Wait until we get to the ballroom and add it."

Mac pulled out a camera. "It's a good shot for the website. Okay?"

"Sure. Get any sleep?"

"Didn't hit until about five, but I stayed down till noon. You?"

"Down by two thirty. Up at seven to finish the groom's cake, the desserts—and this. I'm so damn glad we have two weeks before the next wedding." She glanced over. "Don't tell Parker I said that."

"She's up, I assume."

"She's been in here twice. She's probably been everywhere twice. I think I heard Emma come in. They may be up in the office by now."

"I'm heading up. Are you coming?"

"Ten minutes. I'll be on time."

"On time is late in Parker's world." Mac grinned. "I'll try to distract her."

"Just tell her some things can't be rushed. And that the MOB's going to get so many compliments on this cake she'll stay off our backs."

"That one could work."

Mac started out, winding through to check the entrance foyer and the massive drawing room where the ceremony itself would take place. Emmaline and her elves had already been at work, she noted, undressing from the last wedding, redressing for the new. Every bride had her own vision, and this one wanted lots of gold and silver ribbon and swag as opposed to the lavender and cream voile of New Year's Eve.

The fire was set in the drawing room and would be lit before the guests began to arrive. White-draped chairs sparkling with silver bows formed row after row. Emma had already dressed the mantel with gold candles in silver holders, and the bride's favorite white calla lilies massed in tall, thin glass vases.

Mac circled the room, considered angles, lighting, composition—and made more notes as she walked out and took the stairs to the third floor.

As she expected, she found Parker in the conference room of their office, surrounded by her laptop, BlackBerry, folders, cell phone, and headset. Her dense brown hair hung in a long tail—sleek and simple. It worked with the suit—a quiet dove gray—that would blend in and complement the bride's colors.

Parker missed no tricks.

She didn't look up but circled a finger in the air as she continued to work on the laptop. Knowing the signal, Mac crossed to the coffee counter and filled mugs for both of them. She sat, laid down her own file, opened her own notebook.

Parker sat back, smiled, and picked up her mug. "It's going to be a good one."

"No doubt."

"Roads are clear, weather's good. The bride's up, had breakfast and a massage. The groom's had a workout and a swim. Caterers are on schedule. All attendants are accounted for." She checked her watch. "Where are Emma and Laurel?"

"Laurel's putting the finishing touches on the cake, which is stupendous. I haven't seen Emma, but she's started dressing the event areas. Pretty. I want some outdoor shots. Before and after."

"Don't keep the bride outside for too long before. We don't want her red-nosed and sniffling."

"You may have to keep the MOB off my back."

"Already noted."

Emma rushed in, a Diet Coke in one hand, a file in the other. "Tink's hungover and a no-show, so I'm one short. Let's keep this brief, okay?" She dropped down at the table. Her curling black hair bounced over the shoulders of her sweatshirt. "The Bride's Suite and the Drawing Room are dressed. Foyer and stairway, nearly finished. The bouquets, corsages, and boutonnieres checked. We've started on the Grand Hall and the Ballroom. I need to get back to that."

"Flower girl?"

"White rose pomander, silver and gold ribbon. I have her halo—roses and baby's breath—ready for the hairdresser. It's adorable. Mac, I need some pictures of the arrangements if you can fit it in. If not, I'll get them."

"I'll take care of it."

"Thanks. The MOB—"

"I'm on it," Parker said.

"I need to—" Emma broke off as Laurel walked in.

"I'm not late," Laurel announced.

"Tink's a no-show," Parker told her. "Emma's short."

"I can fill in. I'll need to set the centerpiece of the cake and arrange the desserts, but I've got time now."

"Let's go over the timetable."

"Wait." Emma lifted her can of Diet Coke. "Toast first. Happy New Year to us, to four amazing, stupendous, and very hot women. Best pals ever."

"Also smart and kick-ass." Laurel raised her bottle of water. "To pals and partners."

"To us. Friendship and brains in four parts," Mac added, "and the sheer coolness of the whole we've made with Vows."

"And to 2009." Parker lifted her coffee mug. "The amazing,

stupendous, hot, smart, kick-ass best pals are going to have their best year ever."

"Damn right." Mac clinked her mug to the rest. "To Wedding Day, then, now, and always."

"Then, now, and always," Parker repeated. "And now. Timetable?"

"I'm on the bride," Mac began, "from her arrival, switch to groom at his. Candids during dressing event, posed as applies. Formal portraits in and out. I'll get the shots of the cake, the arrangements now, do my setup. All family and wedding party shots separate prior to the ceremony. Post-ceremony I should only need forty-five minutes for the family shots, full wedding party, and the bride and groom."

"Floral dressing in bride and groom suites complete by three. Floral dressing in foyer, Parlor, staircase, Grand Hall, and Ballroom by five." Parker glanced at Emma.

"We'll be done."

"Videographer arrives at five thirty. Guest arrivals from five thirty to six. Wedding musicians—string quartet—to begin at five forty. The band will be set up in the Ballroom by six thirty. MOG, attended by son, escorted at five fifty, MOB, escorted by son-in-law, directly after. Groom and groomsmen in place at six." Parker read off the schedule. "FOB, bride, and party in place at six. Descent and procession. Ceremony duration twenty-three minutes, recession, family moments. Guests escorted to Grand Hall at six twenty-five."

"Bar opens," Laurel said, "music, passed food."

"Six twenty-five to seven ten, photographs. Announcement of family, wedding party, and the new Mr. and Mrs. seven fifteen."

"Dinner, toasts," Emma continued. "We've got it, Parks."

"I want to make sure we move to the Ballroom and have the first dance by eight fifteen," Parker continued. "The bride especially wants her grandmother there for the first dance, and after the father-daughter, mother-son dance, for her father and his mother to dance. She's ninety, and may fade early. If we can have the cake cutting at nine thirty, the grandmother should make that, too."

"She's a sweetheart," Mac put in. "I got some nice shots of her and Alison at the rehearsal. I've got it in my notes to get some of them today. Personally, I think she'll stay for the whole deal."

"I hope she does. Cake and desserts served while dancing continues. Bouquet toss at ten fifteen."

"Tossing bouquet is set," Emma added.

"Garter toss, dancing continues. Last dance at ten fifty, bubble blowing, bride and groom depart. Event end, eleven." Parker checked her watch again. "Let's get it done. Emma and Laurel need to change. Everyone remember their headsets."

Parker's phone vibrated, and she glanced at the readout. "MOB. Again. Fourth call this morning."

"Have fun with that," Mac said and escaped.

She scouted room by room, staying out of the way of Emma and her crew as they swarmed over the house with flowers, ribbons, voile. She took shots of Laurel's cake, Emma's arrangements, framed others in her head.

It was a routine she never allowed to become routine. She knew once it became rote, she'd miss shots, opportunities, bog down on fresh angles and ideas. And whenever she felt herself dulling, she thought of a blue butterfly landing on a dandelion.

The air smelled of roses and lilies and rang with voices and footfalls. Light streamed through the tall windows in lovely beams and shafts, and glittered on the gold and silver ribbons.

"Headset, Mac!" Parker rushed down the main staircase. "The bride's arriving."

As Parker hurried down to meet the bride, Mac jogged up. She swung out on the front terrace, ignoring the cold as the white limo sailed down the drive. As it eased to a stop she shifted her angle, set, and waited.

Maid of honor, mother of the bride. "Move, move, just a little," she muttered. Alison stepped out. The bride wore jeans, Uggs, a battered suede jacket and a bright red scarf. Mac zoomed in, changed stops. "Hey! Alison!"

The bride looked up. Surprise turned to amused delight, and to Mac's pleasure, Alison threw up both arms, tossed back her head, and laughed.

And there, Mac thought as she caught the moment, was the beginning of the journey.

Within ten minutes, the Bride's Suite—once Parker's own bedroom—bustled with people and confusion. Two hairdressers plied their tools and talents, curling, straightening, styling, while others wielded paints and pots.

Utterly female, Mac thought as she moved through the room unobtrusively, the scents, the motions, the sounds. The bride remained the focus—no nerves on this one, Mac determined. Alison was confident, beaming, and currently chattering like a magpie.

The MOB, however, was a different story.

"But you have such beautiful hair! Don't you think you should leave it down? At least some of it. Maybe—"

"An updo suits the headdress better. Relax, Mom."

"It's too warm in here. I think it's too warm in here. And Mandy should take a quick nap. She's going to act up, I just know it."

"She'll be fine." Alison glanced toward the flower girl.

"I really think—"

"Ladies!" Parker wheeled in a cart of champagne, with a pretty fruit and cheese tray. "The men are on their way. Alison, your hair's gorgeous. Absolutely regal." She poured a flute, offered it to the bride.

"I really don't think she should drink before the ceremony. She barely ate today, and—"

"Oh, Mrs. McFearson, I'm so glad you're dressed and ready. You look fabulous. If I could just steal you for a few minutes? I'd love for you to take a look at the Drawing Room before the ceremony. We want to make sure it's perfect, don't we? I'll have her back in no time." Parker pushed champagne into the MOB's hand, and steered her out of the room.

Alison said, "Whew!" and laughed.

For the next hour, Mac split herself between the bride's and groom's suites. Between perfume and tulle, cuff links and cummerbunds. She eased back into the bride's domain, circled around the attendants as they dressed and helped one another dress. And found Alison alone, standing in front of her wedding dress.

It was all there, Mac thought as she quietly framed the shot. The wonder, the joy—with just that tiny tug of sorrow. She snapped the image as Alison reached out to brush her fingers over the sparkle of the bodice.

Decisive moment, Mac knew, when everything the woman felt reflected on her face.

Then it passed, and Alison glanced over.

"I didn't expect to feel this way. I'm so happy. I'm so in love with Rod, so ready to marry him. But there's this little clutch right here." She rubbed her fingers just above her heart. "It's not nerves."

"Sadness. Just a touch. One phase of your life ends today. You're allowed to be sad to say good-bye. I know what you need. Wait here."

A moment later, Mac led Alison's grandmother over. And once again stepped back.

Youth and age, she thought. Beginnings and endings, connections and constancy. And, love.

She snapped the embrace, but that wasn't it. She snapped the glitter of tears, and still, no. Then Alison lowered her forehead to her grandmother's, and even as her lips curved, a single tear slid down her cheek while the dress glowed and glittered behind them.

Perfect. The blue butterfly.

She took candids of the ritual while the bride dressed, then the formal portraits with exquisite natural light. As she'd expected, Alison was game to brave the cold on the terrace.

And Mac ignored Parker's voice through her headset as she rushed to the Groom's Suite to repeat the process with Rod.

She passed Parker in the hallway as she strode back to the bride. "I need the groom and party downstairs, Mac. We're running two minutes behind."

"Oh my God!" Mac said in mock horror and ducked into the Bride's Suite.

"Guests are seated," Parker announced in her ear moments later. "Groom and groomsmen taking position. Emma, gather the bridal party."

"On it."

Mac slipped out to take her stand at the bottom of the stairs as Emma organized the bridesmaids.

"Party ready. Cue the music."

"Cuing music," Parker said, "start the procession."

The flower girl would clearly be fine without the nap, Mac decided as the child nearly danced her way down the staircase. She paused like a vet at Laurel's signal, then continued at a dignified pace in her fairy dress across the foyer, into the enormous parlor, and down the aisle formed by the chairs.

The attendants followed, shimmering silver, and at last, the maid of honor in gold.

Mac crouched to aim up as the bride and her father stood at the top of the stairs, holding hands. As the bride's music swelled, he lifted his daughter's hand to his lips, then to his cheek.

Even as she took the shot, Mac's eyes stung.

Where was her own father? she wondered. Jamaica? Switzerland? Cairo?

She pushed the thought and the ache that came with it aside, and did her job.

Using Emma's candlelight, she captured joy and tears. The memories. And stayed invisible and separate.

# CHAPTER TWO

She worked at night because she had a full day of appointments. And because she liked working at night—alone, in her own space, at her own pace. Mornings were for coffee, that first intense, blood-surging hit of it, and days were often for clients, for shoots, for meetings.

Nights, alone in her studio, she could focus entirely on images, how to select, to improve, to enhance. Though she worked almost exclusively digital, she retained the darkroom mind-set when it came to creating the print. She layered, highlighting, shadowing; she removed blemishes or hot spots to create her base for her master print. To this she could refine specific areas, alter density, add contrast. Step-by-step she would shape the print, sharpening or softening to suit the mood, to create an image that expressed that moment in time, until *she* felt what she hoped the client would feel.

Then, as she did most mornings, Mac sat down at her computer to check her thumbnails and to see if her morning self agreed with her night self.

She huddled over them in her flannels and thick socks, her bright red hair a forest of spikes and tufts. And in the utter quiet. At a wedding she was most often surrounded. By people, by chatter, by emotion. She blocked it or used it as she searched for the right angle, the right tone, the right moment.

But here, she was alone with the images, ones she could perfect. She drank her coffee, ate an apple as a concession to the previous morning's Pop-Tart, and studied the hundreds of images she'd captured the day before, the dozens she'd finessed during the night session.

Her morning self congratulated her night self on a job well done. More to do yet, she mused, and when she had the best of the best for the clients to consider, she'd give them one more going-over before scheduling an appointment with the newlyweds to view the images in slide-show format and make their choices.

But that was for another day. In case her memory proved faulty, she checked her calendar before going up to shower and dress for her first appointment.

For a studio shoot, jeans and a sweater would do, but then she'd have to change for the consultation scheduled that afternoon at the main house. Vows policy demanded business attire for client consultations.

Mac pushed through her closet for black pants, a black shirt. She could toss on a jacket after the shoot and meet the dress code. She played with jewelry until she found what suited her mood, slapped on some makeup, and considered the job done.

The studio required more attention than the photographer, in her opinion.

Elizabeth and Charles, she thought as she began the setup. Engagement shot. They'd been firm, she recalled, at the consult. Formal, simple, straightforward.

She wondered why they didn't just get a friend with a

point-and-shoot to take it then. And she recalled now with a quick smirk, that those words had nearly come out of her mouth—before Parker had read her mind and shot her a warning glare.

"Client's king," she reminded herself as she set her backdrop. "They want boring, boring it is."

She hauled in lights, positioned a diffuser—boring could at least be pretty. She brought out her tripod, mostly because she felt the clients would expect equipment. By the time she'd chosen her lenses, checked her lighting, draped a stool, the clients knocked at her door.

"Right on time." She shut the door behind them and blocked a blast of frigid wind. "Brutal out there today. Let me take your coats."

They looked perfect, she thought. Barbie and Ken for the upper-class set. The cool, every hair in place blonde, the handsome, polished, and pressed hero.

Part of her longed to muss them up, just a little, and make them human.

"Can I get you some coffee?" she asked.

"Oh, no, but thank you." Elizabeth granted her a smile. "We'd really like to just get to it. We have a full schedule today." As Mac dealt with their outdoor gear, Elizabeth glanced around the studio. "This used to be the pool house?"

"That's right."

"It's . . . interesting. I suppose I expected something more elaborate. Still." She wandered over to study some of the framed photos on the wall. "Charles's cousin's wedding here in November was wonderful. And she just raves about you and your partners. Isn't that right, Charles?"

"Yes. It's what decided us on your company."

"The wedding planner and I will be working closely together over the next months. Is there anywhere I can freshen up before we start?" Elizabeth asked.

"Absolutely." Mac led the way to the powder room off her studio, and wondered just what there was to freshen.

"So, Charles." Mentally, Mac was loosening the perfectly executed Windsor knot of his tie. "Where are you two off to today?"

"We have a meeting with the wedding planner, and we're taking care of registering. Elizabeth is going on to meet with two of the designers your partner recommended for her gown."

"That's exciting." You look just thrilled, she thought, the way you might for your semiannual dental visit.

"It's a lot of details. I suppose you're used to them."

"Every wedding's the first. Would you mind standing behind the stool here? I can check the lighting and focus while Elizabeth's getting ready."

He moved obediently, stood stiff as a poker.

"Relax," she told him. "This will be easier and quicker than you think, and possibly fun. What kind of music do you like?"

"Music?"

"Yeah, let's have some music." She crossed to her CD player, chose a disk. "Natalie Cole on ballads. Romantic, classic. How's that?"

"Fine. That's fine."

Mac caught him sneaking a peek at his watch as she went back to pretend to adjust her camera. "Have you decided on the honeymoon spot yet?"

"We're leaning toward Paris."

"Do you speak French?"

For the first time he smiled easily. "Not a word."

"Well, there's the adventure," she said as Elizabeth came back looking as precisely perfect as she had when she'd gone in.

The suit was probably Armani, and beautifully tailored. The indigo blue color flattered, and Mac imagined Elizabeth had selected Charles's slate gray to set it off.

"I think we'll start with you sitting, Elizabeth, with Charles behind you. Just a little to the left, Charles. And Elizabeth, if you'd angle toward the windows, just a bit. Lean back toward Charles—relax your body. Charles, put your hand on her left shoulder. Put your hand over his, it'll show off that spectacular engagement ring."

She took a couple of shots just to get them over the initial frozen smiles.

Angle your head.

Weight on the back foot.

Shift your shoulders.

Shy, Mac realized. He was shy, camera shy and just a little people shy. And she was monumentally self-conscious. Terrified of not looking exactly right.

She tried to put them at ease, asking how they met, how they got engaged—though she'd asked the same questions when they'd set up the appointment. And received the same answers now.

She barely cracked the surface.

She could stop now, Mac thought, and give them exactly what they thought they wanted. But it wouldn't be what they needed.

She stepped back from the camera. As she did, their bodies relaxed, and Elizabeth turned her head to smile up and over at Charles. He winked at her.

Okay, okay, Mac thought. Humans in there after all.

"I've got several very nice formal shots. I know that's what you wanted, but I wonder if you'd do something for me?"

"We're really on a schedule," Charles began.

"It'll take less than five minutes. Stand up, Elizabeth. Let me just move the stool." She dragged it away, then took her camera from the tripod. "How about a hug? Not me. Each other."

"I don't—"

"Hugging's legal in Connecticut, even when you're not

engaged. Just a little experiment, and I'll have you out of here in two minutes." She grabbed her light meter, checked, adjusted.

"Put your right cheek on his chest, but cheat it toward me. Turn your face a little toward me," Mac explained. "And look this way. Charles, angle your head down to hers, but tip your chin my way. Take a deep breath, then let it go, just let it go. You're holding on to the person you love, right? Enjoy it. And eyes on me, right on me, and think about what you felt like the first time you kissed."

*There!*

The smiles were quick, spontaneous. Soft on her part, even a little sly, and delighted on his.

"One more, just one more like that." She got three before they stiffened up again. "Done. I'll have several proofs for your approval by—"

"Can't we see some now? It's digital, isn't it?" Elizabeth pressed. "I'd just like a quick idea."

"Sure."

Mac walked to the computer with the camera, set it up to display. "These are raw, but you'll get the gist."

"Yes." Elizabeth frowned at the screen as Mac started the slow slide show. "Yes, they're nice. That's—that one."

Mac stopped on one of the formals. "This?"

"That's what I had in mind. It's very good. We both look good, and I like the angle. This one, I think."

"I'll mark it. Might as well see the rest, to be sure." Mac started the slide show again.

"Yes, they're really very good. Very good. I do think the one I picked is . . ." She trailed off as the shot of them hugging came on screen. "Oh. Well, that's lovely. Really lovely, isn't it?"

"My mother will like the first one you picked." Behind her, Charles rubbed Elizabeth's shoulders.

"She will. Exactly. We'll get it for her, have it framed for her. But . . ." She looked at Mac. "You were right; I was wrong.

This is the one I want, the way I want to be portrayed in our engagement photo. Remind me I said the first part in September, when I try to tell you how to do your job."

"I will. I was wrong, too. I think it's going to be a pleasure to work with you after all."

It took Elizabeth a moment, but she laughed.

She sent them off to Parker, figured Parker now owed her. She was sending off clients who—for the moment, at least—were more open to ideas and direction than they had been.

She settled down to complete packages for clients. One set of proofs, and the other the complete choices, all displayed in albums. For Bride and Groom, for MOB, MOG, the extra photos requested by various members of the families and wedding party.

When they were boxed, she decided she had just enough time for a quick dish of leftover pasta salad before she carted them and herself over to the main house.

She managed a couple of bites, eating over the sink. Frozen fairyland, she thought, staring out the window. Everything still and perfect. She grabbed her glass of Diet Coke, started to drink.

The cardinal smacked right into the window, a bang and blur of red. Diet Coke spewed up at the jerk of her hand to splash all over her shirt.

She watched the idiot bird wing away while her heart vibrated in her throat. Then she looked down at her shirt. "Damn it."

She stripped it off, tossed it on top of her stacked washer/dryer in the kitchen pantry. In bra and black pants, she wiped up the spill on the counter. Irritated, she grabbed the ringing phone. Since the readout indicated Parker's cell, she answered with an aggrieved, "What?"

"Patty Baker's here to pick up her albums."

"Well, she's twenty minutes early. I'll be there, and so will they—on time. Keep her occupied," she added as she moved toward the studio. "And don't bug me." She clicked off, turned.

Then she stared at the man who stood inside her studio.

His eyes popped, he blushed, then with a choked, "Oh God," he spun around. And with a gunshot crack, smacked straight into the doorjamb.

"Jesus! Are you okay?" Mac tossed the phone on a table as she rushed over to where he was currently staggering.

"Yes. Fine. Sorry."

"You're bleeding. Wow, you really hit your head. Maybe you should sit down."

"Maybe." And with that, eyes dazed and slightly unfocused, he sort of slid down the wall to the floor.

Mac crouched, brushed at the dark brown hair that flopped over his forehead and the bleeding scrape that was already growing into an impressive knot. "Okay, it's not cut. You've escaped stitches. It's just really bashed. Boy, it sounded like you hit the door with a hammer. Ice maybe, and then—"

"Excuse me? Um, I'm not sure if you realize . . . I just wonder if you shouldn't . . ."

She saw his gaze aim down, followed it with her own. And noted while she considered triage, that her barely bra-covered breasts were very close to pressing into his face.

"Oops. Forgot. Sit there. Don't move." She leaped up, dashed away.

He wasn't sure he could've moved. Disoriented, bewildered, he sat where he was, back braced against the wall. Even with the cartoon birds circling over his head, he had to admit they'd been very pretty breasts. He couldn't help but notice.

But he wasn't at all sure what to say or do in his current situation. So sitting there, as she'd told him, seemed best all around.

When she came back with a bag of ice, she had a shirt on. It was probably wrong to feel the quick tug of disappointment.

She crouched down again on what he noticed—now that her breasts weren't in view—were very long legs.

"Here, try this." She put the ice in his hand, put his hand on his throbbing forehead. And sat back on her haunches like a catcher behind the plate. Her eyes were the green of a magic sea.

"Who are you?" she asked him.

"What?"

"Hmm. How many fingers do you see?" She held up two.

"Twelve."

And smiled. Dimples creased into her cheeks with the curve of her lips and his heart did a little dance in his chest.

"No, you don't. Let's try this. What are you doing in my studio—or what were you doing here before you concussed yourself over my boobs?"

"Ah. I have an appointment? Or Sherry does. Sherry Maguire?" He thought her smile dimmed a little, and the dimples disappeared.

"Okay, wrong place. You want the main house. I'm Mackensie Elliot, photography end of the business."

"I know. I mean I know who you are. Sherry wasn't very clear, which is usually the case, on where."

"Or when, since your appointment's not until two."

"She said she thought one thirty, which I know means she'll get here at two. I should've gone by Sherry Time, or called to confirm myself. Sorry again."

"It's no problem." She angled her head. His eyes—very nice eyes—were clear again. "How do you know me?"

"Oh. I went to school with Delaney, Delaney Brown, and with Parker. Well, Parker was a couple years behind us. And, you, sort of. For a little while."

She shifted for a closer look at him. Dense, disordered brown hair that needed a style and trim by most standards. Clear, quiet blue eyes surrounded by a forest of lashes. Straight nose, strong mouth in a thinnish face.

She was *good* with faces. Why didn't she place his?

"I knew most of Del's friends, I think."

"Oh, we didn't exactly run in the same circles. But I tutored him once, when we were studying *Henry the Fifth.*"

That clicked. "Carter," she said, pointing at him. "Carter Maguire. You're not marrying your sister, are you?"

"What? No! I'm a stand-in for Nick. She didn't want to do the consult alone, and he got held up. I'm just . . . I don't know what the hell I'm doing here, actually."

"Being a good brother." She patted his knee. "Think you can stand up?"

"Yeah."

She straightened, held out a hand to help him. His heart did another little dance as their hands met. And by the time he'd gained his feet, his head was beating the drum for the rhythm. "Ouch," he said.

"I bet. Want some aspirin?"

"Oh, only enough to beg."

"I'll get it. While I do you can sit down on something that isn't the floor."

When she went back in the kitchen, he started to, but the photographs lining the walls caught his eye. Magazine shots, too, he noted, and had to assume them hers. Beautiful brides, sophisticated brides, sexy brides, laughing brides. Some in color, some in atmospheric black and white—and some with that odd and compelling computer trick of one spot of intense color in a black-and-white shot.

He turned as she came back and had the errant thought that her hair was like that—an intense spot of color.

"Do you take anything else, photographically?"

"Yes." She handed him three pills and a glass of water. "But brides are the focal point and the selling point of a wedding business."

"They're wonderful—creative and individual. But she's the best." He stepped over, gestured to a framed photo of three young girls, and the blue butterfly resting on the head of a dandelion.

"Why?"

"Because it's magic."

She stared at him for what seemed like forever. "That's exactly right. Well, Carter Maguire, I'm going to get my coat, then we'll walk over and take our consult."

She took the bag of melting ice out of his hand. "We'll get you fresh at the main house."

Cute, she thought as she went for a coat and scarf. Very, very cute. Had she noticed he was cute in high school? Maybe he was a late bloomer. But he'd bloomed nicely. Enough that she'd felt a little twinge of regret when she'd thought he was a groom.

But a BOB—Brother of the Bride—that was a different kettle.

If she were interested, that is.

She put on the coat, wound the scarf—then remembered the blast of wind earlier, and pulled a cap over her head. When she went down, Carter was putting his glass of water in the sink like a good boy.

She picked up the enormous cloth bag holding some of the albums, handed it to him. "Here you go. You can carry this. It's heavy."

"Yes. It is."

"I've got this one." She picked up the second, and a smaller one. "I've got a bride waiting for her finished albums, and another due for her proofs. Main house, like the consult."

"I want to apologize for just coming in before. I knocked, but nobody answered. I heard the music, so I just walked in, and then . . ."

"The rest is history."

"Yes. Ah, don't you want to turn the music off?"

"Right. I stopped hearing it." She grabbed the remote, hit Off, tossed the remote down. Before she could open the door, he moved in, opened it for her. "You still live in Greenwich?" she began as her breath sucked in at the shock of cold.

"Well, more again than still. I lived in New Haven awhile."

"Yale."

"Yes, I did some postgraduate work and taught for a couple years."

"At Yale."

"Yes."

She narrowed her eyes at him as they walked the path. "Seriously?"

"Well, yes. People do teach at Yale. It's highly recommended, given the students."

"So you're like a professor."

"I'm like a professor, only now I teach here. At Winterfield Academy."

"You came back to teach high school at your alma mater. That's kind of sweet."

"I missed home. And teaching teenagers is interesting."

She thought it was bound to be more volatile, though that might be interesting. "What do you teach?"

"English Literature, Creative Writing."

"*Henry the Fifth.*"

"There you go. Mrs. Brown had me out here a couple of times when I was working with Del. I was sorry to hear about the accident. She was an incredibly nice woman."

"Best ever. We can go in this way. It's too cold to walk all the way around."

She led him in through the mudroom, into the warmth. "You can stow your gear in here. You're still on the early side. We'll get you some coffee in the meantime." She shed coat, scarf, hat while she spoke, moving quickly. "No event today, so the main kitchen's clear."

She picked up her bags again while he carefully hung his coat, as opposed to the way she'd tossed hers in the direction of the hook. She seemed to vibrate with movement while standing still as he hauled up the large bag again.

"We'll find you a place to—" Mac broke off as Emma walked toward the main kitchen.

"There you are. Parker was about to . . . Carter?"

"Hi, Emmaline, how are you?"

"I'm fine. Good. How did you . . . Sherry. I didn't realize you were coming with Sherry."

"He is and he isn't. He'll explain. Get him some coffee, will you, and some ice for his head? I've got to get these to the bride."

She grabbed the heavy bag from Carter, and was off.

Emma pursed her lips as she studied the scrape, and said, "Ouch. What did you do?"

"I walked into a wall. You can skip the ice, it's doing okay."

"Well, come in, have a seat and some coffee. I was just coming back to do a setup for the consult."

She led the way, gestured to a stool and a long, honey-toned counter. "Are you here to give moral support to the bride and groom?"

"I'm standing in for the groom. He had an emergency."

Emma nodded as she got out a cup and saucer. "You'll have that with doctors. And aren't you the brave brother?"

"I said no, in several different ways. None of them worked. Thanks," he added when she poured the coffee.

"Take comfort. You'll just have to sit there and eat cookies."

He dumped some cream into his coffee. "Can I get that in writing?"

She laughed and began to arrange cookies on a plate. "Trust

me. Added to it, you'll score major good brother points. How're your parents?"

"Good. I saw your mother last week, at the bookstore."

"She loves that job." Emma handed him a cookie. "Mac should be about done with her client. I'm going to take these in and I'll come back for you."

"I guess if I just hid in here, I'd lose the brave brother title."

"You would. I'll be back."

He'd known Emma through Sherry, and their respective parents' friendship, since they'd been children. It was odd, just odd to think of Emma making his sister's bridal bouquet. It was just odd that his little sister would need a bridal bouquet.

It was as disorienting somehow as walking into a stupid wall.

He gave his forehead a little poke, winced. It wasn't so much that it hurt, which it did, but that everyone would ask him what happened. He'd be explaining his own clumsiness repeatedly—and every time he did, he'd get a mental flashback to Mackensie Elliot in a really tiny bra and low-slung black pants.

He ate the cookie and tried to decide if that was a perk or a burden.

Emma came back for him, and for another tray. "You might as well come on out. I'm sure Sherry will be here any minute."

"Because she's already ten minutes late." He took the tray from her. "She's on Sherry Time."

The house was much as he remembered it. The walls were a soft, muted gold now where his memory said they'd been an elegant, understated green. But the wide, ornate trim was as glossy, the space as generous, the furnishings as gleaming.

Art and antiques, flowers in old, exquisite crystal illuminated wealth and class. Yet, as he remembered, it felt not like a mansion, but a home.

It smelled female, sort of floral and citrusy at the same time.

The women sat, forming a cozy conversation area in the large, coffered-ceilinged drawing room where a fire snapped and sizzled in the big hearth, and winter sunlight splashed through the trio of arched windows. He was used to being outnumbered by females, as he was the middle child, with two sisters bookending him.

So he supposed he'd survive the next hour.

Parker popped out of her chair, all smiles and polish, crossing the room, hands extending. "Carter! It's been a while."

She kissed his cheek, kept his hand in hers as she drew him toward the fire. "Do you remember Laurel?"

"Ah . . ."

"We were all kids." Smooth and easy, Parker nudged him into a chair. "Emma mentioned you'd come back to teach at Winterfield. Was it strange, going back as a teacher?"

"At first it was. I kept waiting for somebody to assign homework, then remembered, oh yeah, that's me. Sorry about Sherry. She's on her own clock, and it usually runs behind. I could call—"

The doorbell cut him off, and brought him desperate relief.

"I'll get it." Emma rose, headed out.

"How's the head?" Mac asked, lolling back in her chair with her coffee cup tucked in both hands.

"It's fine. It's nothing."

"What happened?" Parker asked.

"Oh, I just rapped it. I'm always doing things like that."

"Really?" Mac smirked into her coffee.

"I'm sorry! I'm sorry!" Sherry came in like a whirlwind—color, energy, motion, and giggles. "I'm *never* on time. I hate that. Carter, you're the best—" Her happy, flushed face shifted into concern. "What happened to your head?"

"I was mugged. There were three of them, but I fought them off."

"What! Oh my God, you—"

"I hit my head, Sherry. That's all."

"Oh." She dropped down, easy and relaxed, on the arm of his chair. "He's always doing that."

Carter got up, and sort of tugged his sister into the chair, then tried to figure out how to hover discreetly. Emma simply shifted closer to Laurel on the couch, then patted the cushion.

"Have a seat, Carter. Well, Sherry, how excited are you?"

"Off the charts! Nick would've come, but he had an emergency surgery. It's part of the package, marrying a doctor. But I figured Carter could give the male perspective, right? Plus he knows me, and he knows Nick."

She reached over, grabbed Parker's hand, did a little butt wiggle of joy in her chair. "Can you believe this? Remember how we'd play wedding when we were kids? I remember playing that a couple of times out back with you guys. I think I married Laurel."

"And they said it wouldn't last," Laurel responded, teasing the quick, infectious giggle out of Sherry again.

"And here we are. Right here. And I'm getting married."

"Slut threw me over for a doctor." Laurel shook her head, sipped from a glass of ice water with a slice of lemon floating in it.

"He's *amazing.* Wait till you meet him. Oh God! I'm getting married!" She pressed her hands to her cheeks. "And I barely know where to start. I'm so disorganized, and everyone's telling me I should be thinking about this or booking that. I feel like I'm running in circles, and I've only been engaged a couple months."

"That's what we're for," Parker assured her, and picked up a thick notebook. "Why don't we start with you telling us what kind of wedding you want?" Just use three or four words to describe how you see it."

"Um . . ." Sherry sent her brother a pleading look.

"No, jeez, don't look at me. What do I know?"

"You know me. Just say what you *think* I want."

Damn it. "Just eat cookies," he muttered. "Have fun."

*"Yes!"* She shot out her finger at him. "I don't want it to sound like it's not important and solemn and all that, but I want the fun. I want a big, crazy, happy party. I also want Nick to lose the power of speech for five full minutes when he gets the first look at me coming down the aisle. I want to *kill* him—and I want everybody who comes to remember it as the *best* time. I've been to weddings that were really beautiful, but God, I was bored. You know?"

"Exactly. You want to dazzle Nick, then you want a celebration. One that reflects who you are, who he is, and how happy you are together."

Sherry beamed at Parker. "I really do."

"We've got the date down for next October. Have you got a ballpark number on the guest list?"

"We're going to try to top it off at about two hundred."

"Okay." Parker made notes. "Outdoors, you said. The garden wedding."

As Parker discussed some of the potential details with Sherry, Mac observed. *Animated* would be the first word that came to her mind to describe the bride. Bubbly, cheerful, pretty. Streaky blond hair, summer blue eyes, curvy, casual. Some of the photos, the strategy, would depend on the dress, on the colors, but much centered on who was *in* the wedding gown.

She keyed in to some of the details. Six attendants. Bride's colors pink—pale and candy. And when Sherry pulled out a photograph of the dress, Mac gestured for it. Studied it. Smiled.

"I bet it looks amazing on you. It's perfect for you."

"You think? It felt perfect, and I bought it in like two minutes, then—"

"No, sometimes that impulse is right. This is one of those."

The dress boasted a belling acre of sparkly white skirt, an off-the-shoulder bodice and a glittery river of train. "Sexy princess." Since she had Sherry's attention for the moment, she pushed her own agenda. "Will you want an engagement portrait?"

"Ah . . . well, I would, but I just don't like those formal pictures you see so much. You know, he's standing behind her, and they're just smiling at the camera. I don't mean to tell you about your job or anything."

"That's okay. My job's to make you happy. Why don't you tell me what you and Nick like to do." When Sherry gave her a slow, sly grin, Mac laughed and watched Carter flush again.

Pretty cute.

"Besides that."

"We like to eat popcorn and watch really bad movies on DVD. He's trying to teach me to ski, but the Maguires have a major klutz gene. Carter got the lion's share, but I'm right behind him. We like to hang out with friends, that kind of thing. He's a surgical resident, so free time for him's pretty precious. We don't plan a lot of stuff. I guess we're more spontaneous?"

"Got it. If you want, I could come to you. We'd go for casual, relaxed, and at home instead of formal studio."

"Really? I like the idea. Can it be soon?"

Mac dug out her PDA, keyed in her calendar. "I've got a couple of openings this week, a clearer road next. Why don't you check with Nick, give me some dates and times that work for you. We'll juggle it in."

"This is just awesome."

"You'll want to look at sample wedding photos," Mac began.

"I looked at them on the website, like Parker said I should. And the pictures of the flowers, the cakes and stuff. I want it all."

"Why don't we take a look at the different packages," Parker suggested. "To see what might suit you. We can always tailor one of them for you."

"This is where I need Carter. Nick said I should go with whatever I want, but that doesn't *help*."

Damn it again, Carter thought. "Sherry, I don't know anything about this sort of thing. I just—"

"It's scary to decide by myself." She gave him the big-eyed, helpless look that had worked on him since she'd been two. "I don't want to make a mistake."

"You don't have to decide now." Parker kept her tone light and easy. "And even if you do, then change your mind later, it's no problem. You'll have specific consults, with each of us individually. That'll help. And we can just hold the date for now, and you can sign the contract later."

"I'd really like to sign today, just to get that checked off the list. There's so much. Just an opinion, Carter, that's all."

"Why don't you take a look at the options?" Smiling, Parker handed him a binder, opened to the section on packages. "Meanwhile, Sherry, have you decided between a band or a DJ?"

"DJ. We thought it'd be looser, and we could work with him or her, I guess, on the playlist. Do you know anybody good?"

"I do." Out of another folder, Parker pulled a business card. "He's done a lot of events here, and I think he'll suit you. Give him a call. Videographer?"

On the sofa, Carter pulled out his reading glasses, frowned down at the packages.

So serious, Mac thought. And the nerd sex quotient telescoped up with the wire-rim glasses. He actually looked like a guy studying for an exam. Since Parker and Sherry had their heads together, she decided to give him a break.

"Hey, Carter, maybe you can help me get some more coffee." He blinked up at her, blue eyes framed in dull silver wire. "Bring the binder, okay?"

She picked up the pretty coffeepot, strolled to the doorway

to wait for him. He had to skirt around the coffee table and, she noted, barely missed rapping his shin on it.

"Rest of the team can handle it from here," she told him. "Your sister figures since you're big brother, and standing in for the groom, she needs your input. Which, I also figure, she'll kick to the curb if it doesn't jibe with what she wants."

"Okay," he said as they walked back to the kitchen. "Can I just close my eyes and put my finger on the menu here, be done with it?"

"You could. But what you should do is tell her you think Number Three works best."

"Number Three." He laid the binder on the kitchen counter, adjusted his glasses, then read the description. "Why, particularly?"

"Because while it's very inclusive—and I get the sense she wants somebody else to deal with the fine details—it leaves room for upgrading, and gives her a number of options inside the package. You should also tell her to pick the buffet over the plated meal in that package. Because," she said before he could ask, "it's more informal, gives more opportunity for mixing. It suits her. Then, down the road—when you're out of it, she'll meet with Laurel about the cake—flavors, design, size, and all that, and Emma about the flowers. Parker handles the rest, and believe me when I tell you she handles. Right now it's all so big. Once she nails the package, seeing as she's already got the dress, the venue, me, and so on, she'll be able to think about the rest of it."

"Okay." He nodded. "Okay, so I tell her go with Number Three. It covers a lot of the details, has room for upgrading. It has a lot of options included. And she should take the buffet because it's friendlier, and encourages mixing."

"You're good."

"Absorbing facts and text is easy. If she asks me to help her decide on bouquets, I'm bolting."

"I respect that." She handed him the coffeepot. "They don't need me at this point. Take this back, say your piece. And remind her to let me know what dates work for the engagement portrait."

"You're not coming back with me?"

He looked a little panicked. She gave him a quick pat on the cheek. "Bright side. One less woman in the mix. I'll see you around, Carter."

He stood where he was a moment as she walked out, and left him with the coffee and the binder.

# CHAPTER THREE

SKIPPING OUT A LITTLE EARLY GAVE MAC ENOUGH TIME TO answer calls, log in appointments, then add a selection of the latest photos to the website. Since the rest of the afternoon—what was left of it—was free, she decided to spend it doing a last pass of the New Year's Eve wedding shots.

The phone annoyed her, but she reminded herself business was business and picked up. "Mac Photography at Vows."

"Mackensie."

Mac instantly closed her eyes, mimed stabbing herself in the head. *Why* didn't she learn to check the readout, even on the business line? "Mom."

"You haven't answered any of my calls."

"I've been working. I told you I'd be swamped this week. Mom, I've asked you not to call on the business line."

"You answered, didn't you? Which is more than you did the other *three* times I called."

"Sorry." Just roll with it, Mac told herself. Rolling with it might get it over with quicker since there was no point in telling her mother she didn't have time to chat during work hours.

"So, how was your New Year's?" she asked her mother.

There was a single catchy breath that warned Mac a storm was coming.

"I broke up with Martin, which I'd have told you if you'd bothered to answer my calls. It was a horrible night. Horrible, Mac." The catchy breath became thick with tears. "I've been devastated for days."

Martin, Martin . . . She wasn't sure she could conjure a clear picture of the current ex-boyfriend. "I'm sorry to hear that. Holiday breakups are tough, but I guess you could look at it as starting the new year with a fresh slate."

"*How?* You know how I loved Martin! I'm forty-two years old, alone and completely shattered."

Forty-seven, Mac corrected. But what was five years between mother and daughter? At her desk, Mac rubbed her temple. "You broke up with him, right?"

"What difference does it make? It's over. It's over, and I was crazy about him. Now I'm alone again. We had a terrible fight, and he was unreasonable and mean. He called me *selfish*. And overly emotional, and oh, other awful things. What else could I do but break it off? He wasn't the man I thought he was."

"Mmmm. Has Eloisa gone back to school?" she asked, hoping to switch the topic to her half sister.

"Yesterday. She just left me here in this state, when I can barely get out of bed in the morning. I have two daughters. I devoted myself to my girls, and neither of them will make the effort to support me when I'm emotionally shattered."

Since her head was already starting to throb, Mac leaned over to lightly bang it against her desk. "The semester's starting. She has to go back. Maybe Milton—"

*"Martin."*

"Right, maybe he'll apologize, then—"

"It's over. There's no going back. I'd never forgive a man who treated me so shabbily. What I need is to heal, to find myself again. I need some me time, some quiet, a place to detox from the stress of this ugly situation. I've booked myself a week at a spa in Florida. It's just what I need. To get away, out of this awful cold, away from the memories and the pain. I need three thousand dollars."

"Three— Mom, you can't expect me to cough up three grand so you can go get facials in Florida because you're pissed at Marvin."

"Martin, damn it, and it's the least you can do. If I needed medical treatment would you quibble about paying the hospital? I have to go. It's already booked."

"Didn't Grandma send you money last month? An early Christmas—"

"I had expenses. I bought that horrible man a TAG Heuer, a limited edition, for Christmas. How was I to know he'd turn into a monster?"

She began to weep, pitifully.

"You should ask for it back. Or—"

"I would *never* be so tacky. I don't want the damn watch, or him. I want to get away."

"Fine. Go somewhere you can afford, or—"

"I need the spa. Obviously, I'm strapped financially after all the holiday expenses, and I need your help. Your business is doing very well, as you're always happy to tell me. I need three thousand dollars, Mackensie."

"Like you needed another two last summer so you and El could have a week at the beach? And—"

Linda burst into tears again. This time Mac didn't beat her head against the desk, but simply laid it there.

"You won't help me? You won't help your own mother? I suppose if they put me out on the street, you'd just look the other way. Just go on with your own life while mine's destroyed. How can you be so selfish?"

"I'll transfer the money into your account in the morning. Have a good trip," she said, then hung up.

And, rising, she walked to the kitchen, pulled out a bottle of wine.

She needed a drink.

WITH HIS BRAIN NUMB FROM NEARLY TWO HOURS OF TULLE, roses, headdresses, guest lists, and God all—and his system over-hyped on coffee and cookies (damn good cookies), Carter walked back to his car. He'd left it parked closer to Mac's studio than the main house. Because of that geographical choice, he'd been given the assignment of dropping off a package that had been delivered to the main by mistake.

As he carted it under his arm, the first thin flakes of snow began to swirl. He needed to get home, he thought. He had to finish a lesson plan and fine-tune a pop quiz he planned to spring at the end of the week.

He wanted his books, and the quiet. The afternoon of estrogen, sugar, and caffeine had worn him out. Plus his head hurt again.

The snow and the house brought gloom, enough to have the path lights along the walk glow on. Yet, he noted, none glowed in Mackensie's studio.

She could've gone out, he mused, be taking a nap, be walking around half naked again. He considered just propping the package against the front door, but it didn't seem responsible. Added to that, the package served as the perfect excuse to see her again—and reexplore the secret crush he'd had on her when he'd been seventeen.

So he knocked, shifted the package, waited.

She opened the door, fully dressed, which brought both relief and disappointment. In the dim light she stood, a glass of wine in one hand, her other braced on the door.

"Ah, Parker asked if I'd bring this over on my way out. I just—"

"Good, fine. Come on in."

"I was just—"

"Have some wine."

"I'm driving so—" But she was already walking away—that way she did, he noted, that was a kind of gliding, sexy stride.

"I'm having some, as you can plainly see." She got down another glass, poured generously. "You don't want me drinking alone, right?"

"Apparently I'm too late for that."

With a laugh, she pushed the glass into his hand. "So, catch up. I've only had two. No, three. I believe I've had three."

"Uh-huh. Well." Unless he was mistaken, there was anger and upset under the three-glass buzz. Instead of drinking, he reached over to turn on the kitchen light. "Dark in here."

"I guess. You were nice with your sister today. Some families are nice. I observe and so I note. I recall yours being. Didn't know you and Sherry all that well, but I recall. Nice family. Mine sucks."

"Okay."

"Y'know why? Lemme tell you why. You got a sister, right?"

"I do. In fact, I have two. Maybe we should sit down."

"Two, yeah, yeah. Older sister, too. I never met her. So two sibs. Me? I've got one, comprised of two halves. A half sister, a half brother—from each parent—which could be smooshed together into one sib. This is not to count the number of steps I've had throughout. I've lost track there. They come and go, go and come, as my parents marry willy-nilly." She took a glug of wine. "Bet you had a big-ass family Christmas thing, huh?"

"Ah, yes, we—"

"Know what I did?"

Okay, he got it. It wasn't a conversation. He was a sounding board. "No."

"As my father is . . . somewhere. It might be Vail," she considered with a frown, "or possibly Switzerland, with his third wife and their son, he wasn't a factor. However, he did send me a ridiculously expensive bracelet, which did not come from guilt or particularly paternal devotion, of which he has neither. But from the fact that as a trust fund baby he's just careless with money."

She stopped, forehead furrowing, and drank some more. "Where was I?"

"Christmas."

"Right, right. Family Christmas as applies to me. I paid the courtesy call on my mother and Eloisa—that's the half sister—on the twenty-third, because none of us were the least bit interested in spending Christmas together. No goose for us. Exchange gifts, have a drink, wish you the merry, and escape."

She smiled, but there was no humor in it. "We did not sing Christmas carols around the piano. Actually, El escaped quicker than I did, to go out with friends. Can't blame her. My mother'll drive you to drink. See." She held out her glass.

"Yes, I do. Let's take a walk."

"A what? Why?"

"Why not? It's starting to snow." Casually, he took the glass from her hand, set it and his untouched one on the counter. "I like walking in the snow. Hey, there's your coat."

She frowned at him when he retrieved it, then came back to bundle her in it. "I'm not drunk. Yet. Plus, can't a woman have a drunken pity party in her own house if she wants to?"

"Absolutely. Do you have a hat?"

She dug into her coat pocket, dragged out the vivid green cap. "It's not like I sit around every night sucking down the wine or whatever."

"I'm sure you don't." He pulled the cap over her head, then wound her scarf around her neck before buttoning her coat. "That'll do it." He took her arm, led her to the door. And out.

He heard her hiss through her teeth as the cold hit her face, and kept hold on her arm, just in case.

"Warm's better," she mumbled, but when she tried to turn around, he just kept walking.

"I like when it snows at night. Well, it's not night yet, but this looks like it'll go into it. I like watching it out the window, the white against the black."

"We're not watching it out the window. We're in the damn stuff."

He just smiled and kept walking. Plenty of paths, he thought, and all of them carefully cleared before this dusting. "Who shovels all this?"

"This what?"

"Snow, Mackensie."

"We do, or we draft Del or his pal Jack. We pay some teenagers sometimes. Depends. Gotta keep the paths clear. We're a business here, so we have to maintain it. We get the plow guy for the parking areas."

"A lot of work, with a place this size, and a business with this many facets."

"All part of the whole, plus it's home, too, so we . . . Oh, you're changing the subject." Eyes narrowed, she peered up at him from under the cap. "I'm not stupid, just a little buzzed."

"What was the subject?"

"The enormous suckatude of my family. Where was I?"

"I think you left off with Christmas, and your mother driving you to drink."

"That's right, I did. Here's how she drove me to drink this time. She broke up with her latest boyfriend. I use the term *boyfriend* deliberately, as her mind-set is that of a teenager when it comes to men, relationships, marriage. Anyway, drama, drama, and of course now she has to go to a spa to recover from the ordeal and the stress and heartbreak. Which is bullshit, but she *believes* it. And since she can't keep ten dollars in her pocket for more than five minutes, she expects me to front the expense. Three thousand."

"You're supposed to give your mother three thousand dollars because she broke up with her boyfriend and wants to go to the spa?"

"If she needed an operation, would I just let her die?" Trying to express her mother's method of attack, Mac wheeled both arms in the air. "No, no, no, that's not the one she used this time. It was homeless and on the streets this time. She has a collection like that. Maybe she used both. It started to blur. So, yes, I'm supposed to pay for it. Correction, I *am* paying for it because she'll keep hounding and hammering at me until I do, so I'll pay for it. Ergo, the wine, because it disgusts and infuriates me that I always cave."

"It's none of my business, but if you kept saying no, wouldn't she have to stop? If you keep saying yes, why would she?"

"I *know* that." She rapped him in the chest. "Of course, I know that, but she's relentless and I just want her to go away. I keep thinking, why won't she just get married again—make it lucky number four—and move away? Far, far away, like maybe Burma. Effectively disappear like my father. Only pop up occasionally. Maybe she'll meet some guy at this spa, sitting around the pool drinking carrot juice or whatever, fall in love—which is as easy for her as buying shoes. No, easier. Fall in love," Mac continued, "move to Burma, and leave me alone."

She sighed, lifted her face. It didn't feel so cold now, she realized. And the thickening fall of snow was pretty and peaceful. Walking in it, she had to admit, made for a better idea than drinking.

"You're a saver, aren't you?" she asked him.

"Ah, you mean like money or old papers?"

"No, as in rescue. I bet you always open the door for somebody if their hands are full, even if you're in a hurry. And listen to your students' personal problems even if you have something else you need to do." She lowered her face to look into his now. "And take marginally drunk women for walks in the snow."

"It seemed like the thing to do." Less buzz, he noted, looking into those fascinating green eyes. More sadness.

"I bet you're sick of women."

"Do you mean altogether or just at the moment?"

She smiled at him. "I bet you're a really nice guy."

He didn't sigh, but he wanted to. "I've been accused of it." He glanced around, looking for something else to talk about. He should get her back inside, he thought, but he wanted just a little longer with her. In the snowy dark. "So, what kind of birds do you get?" He gestured toward two pretty feeders.

"The kind that fly." She shoved her hands in her pockets. Neither of them had thought of finding her gloves. "I don't know much about birds." Angling her head, she gave him another study. "Are you, like, a bird-watcher?"

"No, not seriously. Just as sort of a hobby." And God, could he get any geekier? Cut your losses, Carter, and go before it's too late. "We'd better go back. The snow's getting heavier."

"Aren't you going to tell me what kind of birds I should be watching for? Emma and I stock the feeders since they're between her place and mine."

"Her place?"

"Yeah, see." She gestured toward the pretty two-story house. "The old guest house, and she uses the greenhouses beyond it. I took the pool house. Laurel and Parker third floor of the main, east and west wings, so it's like having their own place. It's Parker's house, pretty much. But Laurel needs the kitchen, I need studio space, Emma the greenhouses. So this setup made the most sense. We hang out at the big house a lot, but we all have our separate spaces."

"You've been friends a long time."

"Forever."

"That's family, isn't it? The kind without suckatude?"

She gave him a half laugh. "Smart, aren't you? About those birds . . ."

"You'd spot cardinals easily this time of year."

"Okay, everybody knows what a cardinal looks like. It's a cardinal that provided you with a look at my breasts."

"I beg your . . . What?"

"He flew into the kitchen window and I spilled my drink on my shirt. So. Birds. Besides the red ones that fly into windows. I'm thinking of a belly-crested whopado, like that?"

"Unfortunately, the belly-crested whopado is extinct. But you could spot some of the streaked sparrow species in this area, in the winter."

"Streaked sparrow species. Since I managed to repeat that without slurring, I must not be close to drunk anymore."

They walked down the path between the glowing lights and the dark while the snow fell in thick Hollywood flakes. As pretty a night, Mac realized, as you could ask for in January. And she'd have missed it if he hadn't come by, and insisted—in his low-key way—that she take a walk.

"At this point, I feel like I should say I don't make a habit of tossing back multiple glasses of wine before sundown. Usually I'd have channelled the frustration into work or I'd have gone over and dumped on Parker and company. I was too mad for either. And I didn't feel like ice cream, which is also a personal crutch in trying times."

"I figured that out, except for the ice cream. My mother makes soup when she's really upset or seriously mad. Big pots of soup. I've eaten a great deal of soup in my life."

"Nobody really cooks around here but Laurel and Mrs. G."

"Mrs. G. Mrs. Grady? Is she still here? I didn't see her today."

"Still here, still running the place and everybody in it. Thank God for it. She's on her annual winter vacation. She goes to St. Martin's on January first, like clockwork, and stays until April.

As usual, she made a freezer full of casseroles, soups, stews, and so on before she left so none of us would starve in the event of a blizzard or nuclear war."

She stopped by her front door, cocked her head at him again. "It's been a day. You held up, Professor."

"It had some interesting moments. Oh, Sherry's going for Number Three, with buffet."

"Good choice. Thanks for the walk, and the ear."

"I like to walk." He pushed his hands in his pockets since he wasn't sure what to do with them. "I'd better get going because driving in it's a little trickier. And . . . school night."

"School night," she repeated and smiled.

Then she laid her pocket-warmed hands on his cheeks, brushed her lips to his in a light, friendly, close to sisterly kiss.

He blanked. He moved before he thought, acted before he checked. He took her shoulders, pulled her in—pressed her back to the door as he took the simple brush of lips into the long and the dark.

What he'd imagined at seventeen plunged into reality at thirty. The taste of her, the *feel.* That moment of lips and tongue, and the heat rising in the blood. In the quiet of snowfall, that elemental hush, the sound of her breath sighing out broke in his mind like thunder.

A storm gathering.

She didn't nudge him back, push him away, protest his shoving open the door of her friendly gesture into the hot and wild. Her first thought was, who knew? Who knew the nice-guy English professor who walked into walls could *kiss* like this?

Like he planned to drag you off into the nearest cave and rip off your clothes, while you eagerly ripped off his.

Then thinking stopped being an option, and all she could do was try to keep up.

Swept away. She'd never actually believed that one, but this was swept away.

Her hands slid up from his face, forked through his hair. Gripped.

The movement slapped him back. Now he did step away, nearly slipping on the snow that covered the path. She didn't move an inch, but stared out at him from eyes that gleamed in the dark.

God, he thought, God. He'd lost his mind.

"I'm sorry." He fumbled it as arousal and mortification warred inside him. "Sorry. That was—wasn't— Just . . . really sorry."

She continued to stare as he hurried away, his strides made awkward by the fresh fall of snow. She heard, somewhere in the roaring in her head, the beep of his key lock, and watched him climb into his car in the overhead light after he wrenched open the door.

He pulled out before she got her breath and her voice back. As he drove away, she managed a weak, "No problem."

Feeling a lot more buzzed than she had on wine, she let herself into the house. She went to the kitchen, poured his untouched wine down the sink, followed it with what was left in hers. After looking blindly around, she turned, leaned back on the counter.

"Wow," she said.

# CHAPTER FOUR

SOME MORNINGS YOU JUST NEEDED MORE THAN A POP-TART and a hit of coffee, Mac decided. She figured she'd been spared the unhappiness of a hangover—thank you, Carter Maguire—but several fresh inches of snow meant she'd be hauling out the shovel. She wanted real fuel. Knowing where she'd find it, she pulled on her boots, dragged on her coat, and headed out.

And went back inside immediately for her camera.

The light, bold and bright, blasted out of the hard blue sky onto the still white sea. Untouched, untrampled, that sea spread over the ground, washed over it. Drowned it. Shrubs became hunched creatures crossing that frozen sea, and the rocks forming the lagoon of the swimming pool a tumbled barricade.

Her breath drew in, the cold like tiny shards of glass, then expelled in frigid clouds as she framed in the winter palace of a grove.

Landscapes and pictorials rarely gripped her imagination. But this, she thought, this black and white, with so many shades of each, the shadow and light under the almost savage blue sky demanded its moment. So many shapes, so many textures with branches buried and bark laced offered countless possibilities.

And the grand and gorgeous house rose out of the sea, an elegant and graceful island.

She worked her way to it, experimenting with angles, using the light, honing in on the sparkling cotton balls of azaleas that would burst into bloom come spring. A movement caught her eye, and as she turned to follow it she saw the cardinal take its perch on the snow-covered branch of a maple. It sat, a single spot of vivid red, and sang.

Mac crouched, zoomed in rather than risk going closer and losing the shot. Was it the same bird who'd smacked into her kitchen window? she wondered. If so, he certainly seemed undamaged and unruffled as he sat like a single flame on the white-laced branch.

She caught the moment then, taking three shots in rapid succession, slight changes in angles that coated her jeans with snow as she inched left.

Then the bird took wing, swooped over the frozen sea, through the bright light, and was gone.

Emmaline, beautiful Emmaline in her old navy coat, white cap and scarf trudged toward her through the snow. "I wondered how long I'd have to stand there until you finished or the damn bird took off. It's *cold* out here."

"I love winter." Mac swung the camera up again, and with Emma in the crosshairs, depressed the shutter.

"Don't! God, I look awful."

"You look cute. Gotta love the pink Uggs."

"Why did I buy them in pink? What was I thinking?" She shook her head as she joined Mac, and both continued to the house. "I thought you'd already be inside, nagging Laurel to make breakfast. Wasn't it you who called me and said *pancakes* nearly an hour ago?"

"It was, and now we can both nag her into it. I got caught up. It's amazing out here. The light, the tones, the texture. And that damn bird? Bonus round."

"It's twenty degrees, and after pancakes, we're going to be shoveling this snow and freezing our asses off. Why can't it always be summer?"

"We hardly ever get pancakes in the summer. Crepes maybe, but it's not the same."

As she stomped snow off her pink Uggs, Emma slid her baleful gaze toward Mac, then opened the door.

Mac scented coffee instantly. She dumped her gear, set her camera carefully on top of the dryer, then strode in to give Laurel a rib-crushing squeeze. "I knew I could count on you."

"I saw you playing nature girl out the window, and figured you were coming over to whine for pancakes." Hair clipped back, sleeves rolled up, Laurel measured out flour.

"I love you, and not only for your snowy-day pancakes."

"Good, then set the table. Parker's already up, answering e-mail."

"Is she calling for snow removal?" Emma asked. "I've got three consults today."

"For parking. The consensus is there's not enough to call in the troops for the rest. We can handle it."

Emma's face clouded into a pout. "I hate shoveling snow."

"Poor Em," Mac and Laurel said together.

"Bitches."

"I've got a breakfast story." Riding on the impromptu photo session and the near occasion of pancakes, Mac dumped sugar in the coffee she'd poured. "A *sexy* breakfast story."

Emma paused in the act of opening a cabinet for plates. "Spill."

"We're not eating. Anyway, Parker's not down yet."

"I'm going up to drag her down. I want a sexy breakfast

story to keep me warm while I'm shoveling this stupid snow." Emma scurried out of the kitchen.

"Sexy breakfast story." Considering Mac, Laurel picked up her wooden spoon to stir the batter. "Must involve Carter Maguire, unless you got an obscene phone call and consider that sexy."

"Depends who's calling."

"He's fairly adorable. Not your usual type, though."

Mac looked back as she opened the drawer for flatware. "I have a type?"

"You know you do. Athletic, fun-loving, may have creative bent but not a strict requirement, not too intense or serious-minded. Nothing in past history to include cerebral, scholarly, or quietly charming."

It was Mac's turn to pout. "I like smart guys. Maybe I just haven't run into one who hit my hot-o-meter."

"He's also sweet. Not your usual."

"I like sweet," Mac objected. "Taste my coffee!"

With a laugh, Laurel set the batter down to get mixed berries out of the fridge. "Set the table, Elliot."

"I'm doing it." As she did, she evaluated Laurel's list. Maybe it was accurate—to a point. "Everybody's got a type. Parker's got a type. Successful, well-groomed, well-read."

"Bilingual a plus," Laurel added as she washed berries. "Should be able to distinguish between Armani and Hugo Boss at twenty paces."

"Emma's got a type. They must be men."

Laurel's laugh rolled out as Emma came back in. "Parker's heading down. What's the joke?"

"You, sweetie. Griddle's hot," Laurel announced. "Better get moving."

"Good morning, partners." Parker swung in—dark jeans, cashmere sweater, her hair neatly tied back in a tail, makeup subtle. Mac had an errant thought that it would be easy to hate

Parker if she didn't love her. "I just booked three more appointments for the tour and pitch. God! I love the holidays. So many people get engaged during the holidays. And before you know it, it'll be Valentine's Day, and we'll get more hits. Pancakes?"

"Get the syrup," Laurel told her.

"The roads are clear. I don't think we'll have any cancellations on today's schedule. Oh, and the Paulsons sent an e-mail—just back from their honeymoon. I'm going to pull off some quotes for the website."

"No business," Emma interrupted. "Mac has a sexy breakfast story."

"Really?" Eyebrows lifted, Parker set the syrup and butter on the table of the breakfast nook. "Tell all."

"It began, and sexy tales often do, when I spilled Diet Coke on my shirt."

She started the story as Laurel brought a platter of pancakes to the table.

"He *said* he walked into a wall," Emma interrupted. "Poor Carter!" She snorted out a laugh as she cut the first tiny sliver of a single pancake.

"Hard," Mac added. "I mean, the guy rammed it. In a cartoon, he'd have gone through the wall and left a Carter-shaped hole in it. Then he's sitting on the floor and I'm trying to see how bad it is, and my tits are in his face—which he very politely points out."

" 'Excuse me, Miss, your tits appear to be in my face'?"

Mac wagged her fork at Laurel. "Except he didn't say tits, and he kind of stuttered. So I go pull a shirt out of the dryer, get him a bag of ice, and ultimately determine he probably doesn't need the ER."

She continued on while plowing her way through a short stack.

"I'm a little let down," Laurel said. "I expect a sexy breakfast story to have sex, not just your very pretty boobs."

"I'm not done. Part two begins when I'm back home working, and carelessly answer the phone. My mother."

Smile fading, Parker shook her head. "That's not sexy. I've told you to screen, Mac."

"I know, I know, but it was the business line, and I wasn't thinking. Anyway, I did worse. She broke up with her latest, and went on one of her riffs. She's shattered, she's devastated, blah blah blah. The pain and suffering requires a week in a Florida spa and three thousand from me."

"You didn't," Emma murmured. "Tell me you didn't."

Mac shrugged, stabbed another forkful of pancakes. "I wish I could say no."

"Honey, you've got to stop," Laurel told her. "You just have to stop."

"I know." Under the table, Emma rubbed Mac's knee in sympathy. "I know, but I cracked, that's all. After which I opened a fresh bottle of wine and proceeded to drown my sorrow and disgust."

"You should've come back here." Parker reached out, touched Mac's hand. "We were here."

"I know that, too. I was too mad, sad, and full of self-pity and disgust. Then guess who knocked on my door?"

"Oh-oh." Laurel's eyes popped. "Tell me you didn't have drunk, self-pity sex with Carter—but if so, please include all details."

"I invited him in for a drink."

"Oh, boy!" In celebration, Emma ate another sliver of pancake.

"I dumped all over him. My family, suck, suck, suck. The guy comes by to drop off a package and ends up with a half-drunk woman in the middle of a pity party. He listened, which I didn't really understand at the time, being half drunk and on a rant, but he listened to me. Then he took me out for a walk. He just put my coat on me, buttoned it up like I was three, and took me out. Where he listened some more until I'd pretty well run it down. Then he walked me back and—"

"You invite him back in and have sex," Emma prompted.

"Get your own sexy breakfast story. I felt mildly embarrassed, and really grateful, so I give him a little peck. A 'thanks, pal' kind of peck. The next thing I know I'm in the middle of a brain-frying, blood-pumping, jungle-drum-beating kiss. The jerk-you-forward-then-shove-you-back-against-a-solid-surface type."

"Oh." Emma shuddered in pure delight. "I *love* those."

"You love any type of lip-lock," Laurel pointed out.

"Yes, yes, I do. I'd have guessed Carter more for the sexy, slow, and shy type."

"Maybe he is, usually. Because while my head was busy exploding, he stopped, apologized—a couple of times—then slipped and slid his way back to his car. He was gone by the time I regained the power of speech."

Parker nudged her plate away, picked up her coffee. "Well, you have to go get him. Obviously."

"Obviously," Emma concurred, and looked toward Laurel to complete the vote.

"Could be trouble." Laurel shrugged. "He's not her usual type, and he has moves that don't coincide with his general demeanor. I smell complications."

"Because he's a nice, sweet, slightly klutzy guy who kisses like a warrior?" Emma gave Laurel a light kick under the table. "*I* smell romance."

"You smell romance in a traffic jam on ninety-five."

"Maybe. But you know damn well you want to see what happens next. You can't just let a kiss like that hang there," Emma added, turning to Mac.

"Maybe, because as it stands it's a nice sexy breakfast story, and nobody gets hurt. Now, I have to go call the bank and toss away three thousand dollars like it was confetti." She scooted out of the nook. "I'll see you all outside, with shovels."

Parker plucked a raspberry out of the bowl after Mac left. "She's not going to let it hang there. It'll drive her crazy."

"Second contact within forty-eight hours," Laurel agreed, then scowled. "And damn it, she skated out of helping with the dishes."

AT HIS DESK AT THE ACADEMY, CARTER WENT OVER THE DISCUSSION points he planned to introduce in his final period class. Keeping energy and interest up were keys in that last class of the day, when freedom was only fifty short (or endless depending on your point of view) minutes away. The right slants could snag the wandering attention of the clock watcher.

They might learn something.

The problem was he couldn't keep his own attention focused.

Should he call her and apologize again? Maybe he should write her a note. He did better writing things down than saying them. Most of the time.

Should he just let it go? It had been a couple of days. Well, one day and two nights to be anal about it.

He knew he was being anal about it.

He wanted to let it go, just let it go and mark it down on the lengthy list of Carter's Embarrassing Moments. But he couldn't stop thinking about it. About her.

He was right back where he'd been thirteen years before. Suffering from a pathetic crush on Mackensie Elliot.

He'd get over it, Carter reminded himself. He'd gotten over it before. Almost entirely.

He'd just lost his head for a moment, that's all. And it was understandable considering the rest of the experience.

Still, he should probably write her a note of apology.

*Dear Mackensie,*

*I want to offer my sincere apology for my untoward behavior on the evening of January fourth. My actions were inexcusable, and deeply regretted.*

*Yours, Carter*

And could he possibly be any more stiff and stupid?

She'd probably forgotten about it anyway, after having a quick laugh with her friends. Who could blame her?

Let it go, that was the thing to do. Just let it go and get back to leading the class on a discussion of Rosalind as a twenty-first-century woman.

Sexuality. Identity. Guile. Courage. Wit. Loyalty. Love.

How did Rosalind use her dual sexuality in the play to become the woman at its end, rather than the girl she was in the beginning, and the boy she played throughout?

Say "sex," and you drew teenagers' attention, Carter thought.

How did—

He kept scanning notes, and called out an absent, "Come in," at the knock. Ah, evolution, he thought, of identity and courage through disguise and . . .

He glanced up, blinked.

With his mind full of the engaging Rosalind, he stared at Mac.

"Hi, sorry to interrupt."

He lurched to his feet, scattered his papers so some sailed to the floor. "Ah, it's all right. No problem. I was just . . ."

He bent to retrieve papers as she did the same, and knocked his head against hers.

"Sorry, sorry." He stayed down, met her eyes. "Crap."

She smiled, and the dimples came out to play. "Hello, Carter."

"Hello." He took the papers she offered. "I was just going over some launch points for a discussion on Rosalind."

"Rosalind who?"

"Ah, Shakespeare's Rosalind. *As You Like It*?"

"Oh. Is that the one with Emma Thompson?"

"No. That's *Much Ado*. Rosalind, niece of Duke Frederick, is banished from his court, and disguises herself as Ganymede, a young man."

"Her twin brother, right?"

"No, actually that's *Twelfth Night*."

"I get them confused."

"Well, while there are some parallels between *As You Like It* and *Twelfth Night* as far as theme and device, the two plays address markedly divergent . . . Sorry, it doesn't matter."

He laid the papers down, took off his reading glasses. And prepared to face the consequences of his actions. "I want to apologize for—"

"You already did. Do you apologize to every woman you kiss?"

"No, but under the circumstances . . ." Let it *go*, Carter. "Anyway. What can I do for you?"

"I dropped by to give you this. I was going to leave it at the front office, but they told me you had a free period, and were in here. So I thought I'd give it to you in person."

She offered him a package wrapped in brown paper. "You can open it," she said when he only looked flustered. "It's just a token—appreciation for letting me dump on you the other night, and for the hangover you spared me. I thought you might like it."

He opened it carefully, peeling up the tape and flapped ends. And took out the photograph matted in a simple black frame. Against the black and white of snow and winter trees, the cardinal sat like a living flame.

"It's wonderful."

"It's nice." She studied it with him. "One of those lucky breaks. I took it early yesterday morning. It's no belly-crested whopado, but it's our bird, after all."

"Our . . . Oh. Right. And you came in to give it to me." Pleasure flustered him nearly as much as embarrassment. "I thought you'd be angry with me after I . . ."

"Kissed my brains out," she finished. "That would be stupid. Besides, if I'd been pissed, I'd have kicked your ass at the time."

"I suppose that's true. Still, I shouldn't have—"

"I liked it," she interrupted, and rendered him speechless. Turning, she wandered the room. "So, this is your classroom, where it all happens."

"Yes, this is mine." Why, dear God, why couldn't he make his brain and his mouth work together?

"I haven't been back here in years. It all looks so much the same, feels so much the same. Don't people usually say the school seems smaller when they go back as an adult? It actually seems bigger to me. Big and open and bright."

"It's a strong design, the building I mean. Open areas, and . . . But you meant that more metaphorically."

"Maybe I did. I think I had some classes in this room." She walked around the desks to the trio of windows along the south wall. "I think I used to sit here and look out the window instead of paying attention. I loved it here."

"Really? A lot of people don't have fond memories of high school. It's often a war of politics and personalities, set off by the cannon fire of hormones."

Her grin flashed. "You could put that on a T-shirt. No, I didn't like high school all that much. I liked it here, because Parker and Emma were here. I only went here a couple of semesters. One in tenth and one in eleventh, but I liked it better than Jefferson High. Even though Laurel was there, it was so big we didn't get to hang out all that much."

She turned back. "Politics and warfare aside, high school's still a social animal. Since you're back in the classroom, I bet you loved every minute."

"For me, high school was a matter of survival. Nerds are one of the low levels on the social strata, alternately debased, ignored, or reviled by those on others. I could write a paper."

She eyed him curiously. "Did I ever do that?"

"Write a paper? No, you meant the other part. Not noticing is different from ignoring."

"Sometimes it's worse," Mac murmured.

"I wonder if we could go back to the other night, and your 'I liked it' response. Could you be more specific, in case I'm misinterpreting?"

He just made her smile. "I don't think you're misinterpreting. But—"

"Dr. Maguire?"

The girl hesitated in the doorway, radiating freshness and youth in the prim navy uniform of the academy. Mac noted the signs—the rosy flush, the dewy eyes—and thought: serious teacher crush.

"Ah . . . Julie. Yes?"

"You said I could come by this period to talk about my paper."

"Right. I just need a minute to—"

"I'll get out of your way," Mac said. "I'm running behind as it is. Nice to see you again, *Doctor* Maguire."

She strolled out, passing pretty young Julie, and made the turn for the stairs. He caught up with her before she'd made it halfway down.

"Wait."

As she stopped and turned, Carter laid a hand on her arm. "Would not misinterpreting include it being okay for me to call you?"

"You could call me. Or you could meet me for a drink after school."

"Do you know where Coffee Talk is?"

"Vaguely. I can find it."

"Four thirty?"

"I can make five o'clock."

"Five. Great. I'll . . . see you there."

She continued down, glancing back as she reached the base of the staircase. He stood at that halfway point still, hands in the pockets of his khakis, his tweed jacket just a little saggy, and his hair carelessly mussed.

Poor Julie Mac thought and continued on. Poor little Julie, I know exactly how you feel.

"YOU ASKED HER TO COFFEE TALK? WHAT'S WRONG WITH you?"

Carter scowled as he loaded files and books into his briefcase. "What's the matter with Coffee Talk?"

"It's a hangout for staff and students." Bob Tarkinson, math teacher and self-proclaimed expert on affairs of the heart, shook his head sadly. "You want to make it with a woman, you take her out for a drink. A nice bar, Carter. Something with a little sense of atmosphere and intimacy."

"Not every contact with a woman's about making it."

"Just every other one then."

"You're married," Carter pointed out. "With a baby on the way."

"Exactly why I know what I know." Bob rested a hip against Carter's desk, putting his wise expression on his pleasant face. "Do you think I got a woman like Amy to marry me by taking her out for a cup of coffee? Hell, no. You know what turned the tide for me and Amy?"

"Yes, Bob." Because you've told me a thousand times. "You cooked her dinner on your second date, and she fell for you over your chicken cutlets."

Still wise, Bob wagged his finger. "Nobody falls for somebody over a latte, Carter. Trust me."

"She doesn't even know me, not really. So the falling-for portion is irrelevant. And you're making me nervous."

"You were already nervous. Okay, you're stuck with coffee, so see how it goes. If you're still interested, do the follow-up call tomorrow. Next day latest. Dinner."

"I'm not making chicken cutlets."

"You can't cook for shit, Maguire. Besides, this coffee thing isn't officially a first date. Take her out. When you're ready to close the deal, I can give you a recipe. Something simple."

"God." Carter rubbed the space between his eyebrows where tension built. "This is why I avoid dating. It's hell."

"You've avoided dating because Corrine screwed up your self-confidence. It's good you're getting back on the horse, and with somebody outside our sphere." In support, he clapped Carter on the shoulder. "What did you say she does again?"

"She's a photographer. She has a wedding business with three of her friends. They're doing Sherry's wedding. We—Mackensie and I—went to high school together for about five minutes."

"Wait. Wait. Mackensie? The redhead you had a crush on in high school?"

Defeated, Carter rubbed the spot between his eyebrows again. "I should never have told you about that. This is why I rarely drink."

"But, Cart, this is like kismet." Excitement rushed through the words. "It's like return of the nerd. It's the big chance to follow up on a lost opportunity."

"It's coffee," Carter muttered.

Flushed with enthusiasm, Bob jumped up, grabbed a piece of chalk. On the board he drew a circle. "Obvious, the circle.

You're completing one, and completing it just means taking point A and point B—" Within the circle he made two dots, connected them horizontally. "Up to point C." He drew another dot at the apex, then joined it with the other points with two diagonal lines. "See?"

"Yes, I see a triangle inside a circle. I've got to go."

"It's the triangle of fate inside the circle of life!"

Carter hefted his briefcase. "Go home, Bob."

"You can't argue with math, Carter. You'll always lose."

Carter escaped, moving quickly through the largely empty school with his footsteps echoing behind him.

# CHAPTER FIVE

SHE WAS LATE. MAYBE SHE WASN'T COMING AT ALL. ANYTHING could've come up, Carter thought. If he'd had any brain cells working he'd have given her his cell number so she could call and cancel.

Now he just had to sit here, alone.

For how long? he wondered. The fifteen minutes he'd already waited wasn't long enough. A half an hour? An hour? Did waiting alone for an hour make him a pathetic loser?

He thought it probably did.

Stupid, he told himself and pretended to drink more green tea. He'd dated before—plenty. He'd been in a serious, intimate relationship with a woman for nearly a year. For God's sake, he'd lived with her.

Until she'd dumped him and moved in with someone else.

But that was beside the point.

It was *just* coffee. Or, well, tea in his case. And he was working himself up over a casual . . . *encounter*, he decided for lack of a better term, like some silly girl over a prom date.

He went back to pretending to read his book while he pretended to drink his tea. And ordered himself not to watch the door of the coffee shop like a starving cat watches a mouse hole.

He'd forgotten—or had stopped noticing long ago—how noisy the place was. Forgotten how many of his students frequented the cafe. Bob had been right about the bad locale.

Colorful booths and stools were crowded with upperclassmen from the academy and the local high school, along with twentysomethings, with a scatter of teachers.

The lights were too bright, the voices too loud.

"Sorry I'm late. The shoot ran over."

He blinked as Mac slid into the chair across from him. "What?"

"You must've really been into your book." She angled her head to read the title. "Lawrence Block? Shouldn't you be reading Hemingway or Trollope?"

"Popular fiction's a strong and viable force in literature. That's why it's popular. Reading for nothing more than pleasure is . . . another lecture coming on. Sorry."

"Teacher mode suits you."

"I suppose that's a good thing, in the classroom. I didn't realize you were working when you stopped by. We could've made it later."

"Just a couple of client meetings, and a shoot. I have a bride who for some reason wants every moment of her plans photo-documented professionally. Okay with me, as it's money in the bank. I documented her fitting—wedding dress—with her mother in weeping attendance. The weeping added a little more time than I'd scheduled."

She pulled off her cap, finger fluffed her hair as she gazed around the shop. "I haven't stopped in here before. Nice energy." She notched up the smile for the girl who came over to take her order.

"I'm Dee. What can I get you?"

"I think we'll have some fun. How about a tall latte macchiato, double shot, squirt of vanilla."

"Coming up. Another green tea for you, Dr. Maguire?"

"No, I'm good, Dee. Thanks."

"Not a fancy coffee fan?" Mac asked as Dee went to put in the order.

"Just not this late in the day. But it's good here—the coffee. I usually stop in for a cappuccino in the morning before work. They sell the beans, too, so if you like the coffee . . . I have to get this out of the way. I can't think. And not being able to think, my inane conversation's going to put you to sleep despite the double shot."

"Okay." Mac propped her chin on her fist. "Get whatever out of the way."

"I had a crush on you in high school."

Her eyebrows shot up as she straightened. "On me? Seriously?"

"Yes, well, yes, for me. And it's mortifying to bring this up, a dozen years or so after the fact, but it's coloring the current situation. From my side, that is."

"But . . . I barely remember you ever actually speaking to me."

"I didn't. I couldn't. I was painfully shy back then, especially in any kind of social situation. Anything, particularly that involved girls. Girls I was attracted to, that is. And you were so . . ."

"Tall latte mach, double with vanilla." Dee set the oversized cup on the table, added a couple of mini crescents of biscotti on a saucer. "Enjoy!"

"Don't stop now," Mac insisted. "I was so what?"

"Ah, you. The hair, the dimples, the everything."

Mac picked up the biscotti, leaning back to nibble on the end as she studied him. "Carter, I looked like a beanpole with carrots growing out of my head in high school. I have pictures to prove it."

"Not to me. You were bright, vivid, confident." Still are, he thought. Just look at you. "I feel like an idiot telling you this, but I keep tripping over it. I'm clumsy enough without putting up my own stumbling blocks. So, well. There."

"Would the kiss the other night be the result of that old crush?"

"I'd have to say it played a part. It was all so surreal."

She scooted forward again to pick up her coffee. "Neither one of us are who we were in high school."

"God, I hope not. I was a mess back then."

"Who wasn't? You know, Carter, most guys would've used that high-school crush bit as a pickup ploy, or kept it locked away. It interests me, you interest me, because you did neither. Are you always so forthright over coffee dates?"

"I don't know. You're the only one I ever had a crush on."

"Oh boy."

"And that was stupid." Flustered again, he raked his fingers through his hair. "Now I've scared you. That sounded scary and obsessive, like I have an altar somewhere with your pictures over it where I light candles and chant your name. Jesus, that's even scarier. Run now. I won't hold it against you."

She burst out laughing, had to set her coffee back down before she sloshed it over the rim. "I'll stay if you swear you don't have the altar."

"I don't." He swiped his finger in an X over his heart. "If you're staying because you pity me, or because you really like the coffee, it works."

"It is really good coffee." She drank again. "It's not pity, but I'm not sure what it is. You're an interesting man, and you helped me out when I needed it. You give really good kiss. Why not have coffee? Since we are, tell me why someone who was painfully shy went into teaching?"

"I had to get over it. I wanted to teach."

"Always?"

"Practically. I did want to be a superhero previous to that. Possibly one of the X-Men."

"Supermutant teacher. You could've been Educator."

He grinned at her. "Now you've unmasked my secret identity."

"So how did Shy Guy become the mighty Educator?"

"Study, practice. And some practicalities. I panic-sweated my way through the first couple weeks of a public-speaking course I took in college. But it helped. And I worked as a TA for several classes, as a kind of transition. I TA'd one of Delaney's classes our sophomore year. Ah . . ."

He turned his cup in circles. "In case it ever comes up, I did—occasionally—ask him about you. All of you, so you weren't singled out. 'The Quartet' as he called you."

"Still does now and then. He's our lawyer now. The business's."

"I hear he's a good one."

"He is. Del set everything up—the legal stuff. When their parents died, the estate went to Parker and Del. He didn't want to live there. He had his own place by then. Parker couldn't have maintained it as a house, I mean just a house. Just her home. Or even if she could, I don't think she could've stood it, living there alone. The big house, the memories. Not alone."

"No, it would be hard, and lonely. It changes that with all of you there. Living and working together."

"Changed everything for everyone. She had the idea for the business cooking already, had all of us talking about it. Then she went to Del about using the estate for it. He was great about that. His inheritance, too, so he took a hell of a chance on us."

"It looks like he made the right choice. According to my mother and Sherry, Vows is *the* place for weddings in Greenwich."

"We've come a long way. The first year was touch and go, and pretty scary because we'd all put our savings and whatever we could beg, borrow, or steal into it. The start-up costs, licenses, stock, equipment. The expense of turning the pool house into my place, the guest house into Emma's. Jack did the designs for free. Jack Cooke? Do you know him? He and Del met in college."

"Yeah, a little. I remember they were tight."

"The small town that is Yale," Mac commented. "He's an architect. He put a lot of time into the transformation. And saved us God knows how much in fees and false starts. The second year we were barely treading water, with all of us still having to take side jobs to get by. But, by the third, we eased around the first corner. I understand working through the panic sweat to get what you want."

"Why wedding photography? Specifically, I mean, for you. It doesn't feel as if it's only because it fit the bigger picture of the partnership."

"No, not just that. Not even that first, I guess. I like taking photographs of people. The faces, the bodies, the expressions, the dynamics. Before we opened Vows I worked in a photography studio. You know the sort where people come for pictures of their kids, or a publicity shot. It paid the bills, but . . ."

"Didn't satisfy."

"It really didn't. I like taking photographs of people in what I think of as moments. The defining moment? That's the killer, that's the top of the mountain. But there are lots of other moments. Weddings, the ritual of them and how those inside them tilt and angle the ritual to suit them personally—that's a big moment."

Smiling, she lifted her cup with both hands. "Drama, pathos, theater, grief, joy, romance, passion, humor. It's got it all. And I can give them all that through photographs. Show them the journey of the day—and if I'm lucky, that one defining moment that lifts it out of the ordinary into the unique. Which is the really long way of saying I just like my work."

"I get that, and what you mean by the moment. The satisfaction of it. It's like when I can *see* even one student's mind open up and suck in what I've been trying to feed them. It makes the hours when it feels like routine all worth it."

"I probably didn't give my teachers many of those moments. I just wanted to get through it and out where I could do what I wanted. I never saw them as creative entities. More like wardens. I was a crappy student."

"You were smart. Which cycles back to teenage obsession. But I'll just say I noticed you were smart."

"We didn't have any classes together. You were a couple years ahead of me, right? Oh, wait! You were student teacher in one of my English classes, weren't you?"

"Mr. Lowen's fifth period American Literature. Now please forget I said that."

"Not a chance. Now, I'm not running away, but I have to go. I have another shoot. Your sister's engagement portrait, in fact."

"I didn't realize you were getting to that so quickly."

"The doctor has the evening free, so we worked it out. But I need to go, get a sense of their place and the two of them together."

"I'll walk you to your car." He took out bills, tucked the ends under the saucer of his cup.

Before she could shrug into her jacket, he'd taken it to help her into it. He opened the door for her, stepped out with her into the breathless cold.

"I'm a block and a half down," she told him. "You don't have to walk me to my car. It's freezing out here."

"It's fine. I walked from my place anyway."

"You walked?"

"I don't live that far, so I walked."

"Right. You like to walk. Since we are," she said as they walked by cafes, restaurants, "I'll mention something that got bypassed due to the path our conversation took. Dr. Maguire? You got your PhD?"

"Last year, finally."

*"Finally?"*

"Since it was the major focus of my life for about ten years, 'finally' works for me. I started thinking thesis when I was an undergraduate." Which probably made him Mayor Nerd of Nerdville, he supposed. "Are you going to see me again? I know that was a non sequitur but it's buzzing around in my brain. So if the answer's no, I'd rather find out."

She said nothing until they'd reached the car, then studied him as she pulled out her keys. "I bet you have a pen and something to write on. I bet it's pretty handy."

He reached under his coat to the inside of his tweed jacket for a small notebook and pen.

With a nod, Mac took them, flipped to a blank page in the book. "This is my personal line, rather than my business line. Why don't you call me?"

"I can do that. An hour from now's probably too soon, isn't it?"

She laughed, put the notebook and pen back in his hand. "You certainly boost my ego, Carter."

She turned to open her door, but he beat her to it. Touched and amused, she got in, let him close the door behind her. She lowered her window. "Thanks for the coffee."

"You're welcome."

"Get out of the cold, Carter."

When she pulled away from the curb, he watched her car until the taillights disappeared. Then he doubled back toward the coffee shop and walked the frigid three blocks beyond it, to home.

THE BRIEF JANUARY BUSINESS LULL GAVE MAC TOO MUCH TIME on her hands. She knew she could use it to organize her files, to update her various web pages. To clean out the embarrassing mess that was her closet, or to catch up on neglected correspondence. She could use it to read a good book, or fat-ass in front of the TV and gorge on DVDs and popcorn.

But she couldn't settle, and so ended up plopping down on the loveseat in Parker's office.

"Working," Parker said without looking up.

"Contact the media! Parker's working."

Parker continued to tap her keyboard. "After this quick break, we're booked solid for months. Months, Mac. This is going to be our best year. Still, we've got two weeks wide open in August. I'm thinking about a summer's-end package, something that appeals to the smaller wedding. The put-it-together quickly style. We could really push that when we have our open house in March if it doesn't book before."

"Let's all go out."

"Hmm?"

"Let's go out. All four of us. Emma probably has a date, but we'll make her break it and destroy some poor guy none of us know. It'll be fun."

Parker stopped typing, swiveled her chair a few inches. "Go out where?"

"I don't care. The movies, a club. Drinking, dancing, whoring. Hell, let's rent a limo and go to New York and do it right."

"You want to rent a limo, go to New York for drinking, dancing, and whoring."

"Okay, we'll skip the whoring. Let's just get out of here, Park. Spend a night doing fun stuff."

"We have two full consults tomorrow, plus our individual sessions."

"So what?" Mac threw up her hands. "We're young, we're resilient. Let's go to New York and break the hearts and balls of men we've never met before and will never see again."

"I find that idea oddly intriguing. But why? What's up with you?"

Mac pushed off the love seat, stalked around the room. It was such a pretty office. So Perfectly Parker, she thought. Soft, subtle color. Elegance and class polished over almost brutal efficiency.

"I'm thinking about a guy who's thinking about me. And thinking about him thinking about me has me all worked up. I don't actually know if I'm thinking about him because he's thinking about me, or if I'm thinking about him because he's cute and funny and sweet and sexy. He wears tweed, Parker."

She stopped, threw her hands up again. "Grandfathers wear tweed. Old guys in old British movies wear tweed. Why do I find it sexy that he wears tweed? This is a question that haunts me."

"Carter Maguire."

"Yes, yes, Carter Maguire. *Doctor* Carter Maguire—that's the PhD type. He drinks tea and talks about Rosalind."

"Rosalind who?"

"That's what I said!" Vindicated, Mac spun around. "Shakespeare's Rosalind."

"Oh, *As You Like It*."

"Bitch, I should've known you'd know that. You should go out with him."

"Why would I go out with Carter? Besides the fact he's shown no interest in me."

"Because you went to Yale. And I know damn well that doesn't apply, but the fact that I'd say it speaks volumes. I want to go out and get crazy. I *refuse* to sit around waiting for him to call. Do you know the last time I lowered myself to waiting for some guy to call me?"

"Let me see, that would be about never."

"Exactly. I'm not doing this."

"How long have you waited in this case?"

Mac glanced at her watch. "About eighteen hours. He had a crush on me in high school. What kind of man tells you that? Puts the power in your hands that way? Now I have the power and it's scaring me. Let's go to New York."

Parker swiveled back and forth in her chair. "Going to New York to drink and break the hearts of strange men will solve your current dilemma?"

"Yes."

"Well, let's go to New York." Parker plucked up the phone. "Go get Laurel and Emma on board. I'll handle the details."

"Woot!" Mac did a quick dance, rushed over to grab Parker long enough to plant a loud kiss, then raced out of the room.

"Yeah, yeah," Parker muttered as she speed-dialed the limo company. "We'll see if you and your hangover dance and sing in the morning."

In the back of the long black limo, Mac stretched out her legs, highlighted by the short black skirt. She'd kicked off her heels at the start of the two-hour drive to Manhattan. She sipped from her second glass of the champagne Parker had stocked.

"This is so great. I have the best friends ever."

"Yeah, this is a hardship." Laurel lifted her own glass. "Riding in a limo, drinking the bubbly, heading to one of the hottest clubs in New York—thanks to Parker's connections. The sacrifices we make for you, Mackensie."

"Em broke a date."

"I didn't have a date," Emma corrected. "I had a Maybe We'll Do Something Tonight."

"You broke that."

"I did. You so owe me."

"And to Parker, for making it all happen. As always." Mac toasted her friend who sat at the far side of the limo, talking to a client on her cell.

Parker sent her friends a wave of acknowledgment as she continued to pour oil on troubled waters.

"I think we're almost there. Come on, Park, hang it *up*," Mac said in a stage whisper. "We're almost there."

"Breath, makeup, hair," Emma announced as she flipped out a pocket mirror.

Mini Altoids were passed, lipstick freshened. Four pairs of shoes were slipped onto four pairs of feet.

And Parker finally hung up the phone. "God! Naomi Right's maid of honor just found out that her boyfriend—the brother and best man of the groom—has been having an affair with his business partner. MOH is on a rampage, as one might expect, and is refusing to serve unless the cheating bastard is banned from the wedding. Bride is frantic and sides with MOH. Groom is pissed, wants to strangle cheating bastard brother, but feels unable to bar his own brother from his wedding, or replace him as best man. Bride and groom are barely speaking."

"The Right wedding." Laurel narrowed her eyes. "That's soon, isn't it?"

"A week from Saturday. Final guest count is one-ninety-eight. This one's going to be a headache. I've calmed the bride down. Yes, she's right to be upset, yes, she's right to support her friend. But to remember the wedding's about her and her fiance, and what a terrible spot the man she loves is in, through no fault of his own. I'm meeting with them both tomorrow to try to smooth it out."

"Cheating bastard and cheated-on MOH both attend—much less remain in the wedding party—it's going to get ugly."

"Yes." Parker acknowledged Mac's observation with a sigh. "But we'll handle it. It's just a little bit worse, as the business partner's on the invite list—and the cheating bastard's insisting if she's removed, *he* won't attend."

"Well, he's an asshole." Laurel shrugged. "The groom needs to have a serious come-to-Jesus talk with his brother."

"Which is also on my list of suggestions for tomorrow's meeting. But in more diplomatic terms."

"That's tomorrow's business. No business calls during therapeutic drinking, dancing, and heartbreaking."

Parker didn't give her word on Mac's decree, but she did tuck her phone back in her purse. "All right, girls." She flipped her hair back. "Let's go flaunt it."

They slid out of the limo, then streamed past the line of hopefuls outside the club. Parker gave her name at the door. In seconds they were inside the wall of music.

Mac scoped it out. Two levels of booths, tables, and banquettes left room for a central dance floor. On either side, under the rainfall of colored lights, stood stainless steel bars.

Music churned; bodies gyrated. And her mood clicked up a couple of notches.

"I love when a plan comes together."

They hunted up a table first, and Mac considered it an omen of good when they scored a small banquette where they could squeeze in together.

"Observe the species," Mac said. "This is my first rule. Observe the plumage, the rituals before making any attempt to acclimate."

"Screw that, I'm going for drinks. Are we sticking with champagne?" Emma wanted to know.

"Get a bottle," Parker decided.

Laurel rolled her eyes as Emma wiggled out and started toward the nearest bar. "You know she'll get hit on a dozen times before she orders anything, and feel obliged to have actual conversations with the guys who drool on her. We'll all die of thirst before she gets back. Parker, you should go, and put on your invisible cloak of Back Off until we're set up here."

"Give her a few minutes first. How's the fear factor, Mac?"

"Diminishing. I can't even imagine the undeniably cute Dr. Maguire in a place like this, can you? At a poetry reading, sure, but not here."

"Now, see, that's assumption and conclusion based on profession. Like saying because I'm a baker, I must resemble the Pillsbury Doughboy."

"Yes, yes, it is, but it helps my cause. I don't want to get involved with him."

"Because he has a PhD?"

"Yes, and great eyes, a really soft blue that go all sexy when he's wearing his glasses. And there's the unexpected superior kisser factor, which could blind me to the basic fact that we're not suited. Plus any relationship with him outside the most casual of friendships would be a *serious* relationship. What would I do about that? *And* he helped me on with my coat, twice."

"Dear God!" Parker widened her eyes in shock. "You have to nip this in the bud, quickly, finally. I understand it all now. Any man who would do that is . . . Words fail."

"Oh, shut up. I want to dance. Laurel's going to dance with me while Parker swirls on her Back-Off cloak and rescues our champagne—and rescues Emma from her own magnetism."

"Apparently it's time to acclimate," Laurel said when Mac pulled her up and toward the dance floor.

SHE DANCED, WITH HER FRIENDS, WITH MEN WHO ASKED, OR whom she asked. She drank more champagne. In the silver and red ladies room, she rubbed her sore feet while Emma joined the army of women at the mirrors.

"How many numbers have you collected so far?"

Emma carefully applied fresh lip gloss. "I haven't counted."

"Approximate?"

"About ten, I guess."

"And how will you tell them apart later?"

"It's a gift." She glanced over. "You've got one on the line, I noticed. The guy in the gray shirt. He's got some moves on the floor."

"Mitch. Smooth on the floor, great smile. Doesn't strike me as an asshole."

"There you go."

"I should get the tingles for Mitch," Mac considered. "But I'm not getting them. Maybe I've been detingled. That would be seriously unfair."

"Maybe you're not getting them for him because you've got them for Carter."

"You get the tingles for more than one guy at a time."

"Yes, yes, I do. But I'm me and you're you. I figure men are there to make me tingle, and if I can do the same for them, everybody's happy. You're much more serious about such matters."

"I'm not serious. That's a mean thing to say. I'm going out there and dancing with Mitch again, open to tingles. You'll eat those words, Emmaline. With chocolate sauce."

It didn't work. It *should* have worked, Mac thought as she settled at the bar with Mitch after another dance. The man was great-looking, funny, built, had an interesting job as a travel journalist but didn't bore her senseless with countless stories about his adventures.

He didn't get pissy or pushy when she turned down his suggestion they go somewhere more quiet. In the end they exchanged business numbers, and parted ways.

"Forget men." At two A.M. Mac crawled back into the limo, and sprawled. "I came to have fun with my best pals in the land, and said mission was accomplished. God, do we have any water in here?"

Laurel passed her a bottle, then groaned. "My feet. My feet are screaming like voices of the damned."

"I had the best time." Emma slid onto the limo's side bench and pillowed her head on her hands. "We should do this once a month."

Parker yawned, but tapped her purse. "I have two new contacts for vendors, *and* a potential client."

And so, Mac thought as the limo streamed north, we each define ourselves. She toed off her now very painful shoes, shut her eyes, and slept the rest of the way home.

# CHAPTER SIX

In the morning the sun was just a little stronger than it needed to be, in Mac's estimation. But otherwise, all was well.

See, she told herself. Young and resilient.

In her pajamas she ate a mini Hostess coffee cake with her coffee and watched the birds swoop and dive at the feeder. Ms. Cardinal enjoyed breakfast this morning, too, she noted. Along with her brightly plumed mate, and some unidentified neighbors.

She'd need her zoom lens to get a closer look and identify them. Probably some sort of book or guide, too, as the visual wouldn't tell her anything unless it was a robin or a blue jay.

Catching herself, she stepped away from the window. What the hell did she care? They were just birds. She wasn't going to sideline into nature photography or birdography.

Annoyed with herself, she crossed into her studio to check her appointment book and her messages. She had an afternoon appointment with a former Vows bride, now an expectant mother for pregnancy portraits. That, Mac thought, would be fun. And a nice stroke for the ego that her wedding photos had been so well received, the mom-to-be wanted this follow-up.

It gave her the rest of the morning to complete some work already ordered, to take the meeting at the main house, and to review the client's wedding portrait for ideas on baby-in-waiting.

An hour or so toggled in, either side of the studio shoot for website work, she determined, and that was a good day.

Shifting, she pressed Play on her answering machine, business line. She followed up when necessary, congratulated herself on being a good girl, then checked her personal line.

Three messages in, she got the tingle.

"Damn it," she said under her breath as Carter's voice hit her straight in the belly.

"Ah, hi. It's Carter. I wonder if you might want to go out to dinner, or maybe the movies. Maybe you like plays better than movies. I should've looked up what might be available before I called. I didn't think of it. Or we could just have coffee again if you want to do that. Or . . . I'm not articulate on these things. I can't use a tape recorder either. And why would you care? If you're at all interested in any of the above, please feel free to call me. Thanks. Um. Good-bye."

"Damn you, Carter Maguire, for your insanely cute quotient. You should be annoying. Why aren't I annoyed? Oh God, I'm going to call you back. I know I'm going to call you back. I'm in such trouble."

Calculating, she decided the odds were strong in her favor that he'd already left for work. She preferred the idea of talking to his answering machine in turn.

When his clicked on she relaxed. Unlike Carter, she *was* articulate on answering machines. "Carter, Mac. I might like to go out to dinner, or the movies, possibly a play. I have no objection to coffee. How about Friday, as it's not a school night? Pick the activity and let me know.

"Tag, you're it."

See, it doesn't have to be serious, she reminded herself. I can set the tone. Just having some fun with a perfectly nice guy.

Satisfied, she decided to indulge by working the first hour of her day in her pjs. Nicely on schedule, she dressed and took the consult at the main house, breezed back to her own with time to spare before her shoot.

Her message light blinked at her.

"Uh, it's Carter again. Is this annoying? I hope it's not annoying. I happened to check my messages at home on my lunch break. Actually, I made a point to check them in case you called me back. Which you did. I'm afraid I have a faculty dinner to attend Friday. I'd invite you but if you accepted and attended, you'd never go out with me again. I'd rather not risk it. If another night would do, even—ha ha—a school night, I'd like very much to take you out. If you'd like that, maybe we could do dinner and a movie. Is that too much? It's probably too much. I'm confusing myself. I'd like to add, though it may not seem possible, I have asked women out before.

"I guess this makes you it."

She grinned, as she'd grinned throughout the message. "Okay, Carter, try this one on." She punched Call Back, waited for the beep. "Hi, Professor, guess who this is? I appreciate being shielded from the faculty dinner. Showing both good sense and chivalry has earned you points. How about Saturday night? Why don't we start with dinner and see where it goes? You can pick me up at seven.

"And, yes, this makes you it again to confirm."

In the best of moods, Mac switched on some music, dropped down at her computer. She sang along as she reviewed her upcoming client's wedding shots. As possibilities and angles ran through her mind, she made notes. She clicked back through her files to see what equipment, what lighting, what techniques she'd used on the bridal portraits.

Considering the client's olive complexion, the dark hair, the deep brown, exotic eyes, Mac chose an ivory drop. And remembering the client as just a little shy, just a bit demure, Mac decided to save what she thought could be the money shot until after she'd warmed mom-to-be up a little.

But she could prepare for it. She grabbed the phone, hitting the button for Emma as she opened the door to what she considered her prop room. "Hey, I need a bag of red rose petals. I've got a client coming any minute or I'd come down and steal them myself. Can you run them up here? And maybe, just in case, a couple of long-stemmed reds? They can be silk. Thanks. Bye."

Juiced, she checked the bright pink tackle box she used for professional makeup, then switched the music to a New-Agey CD she thought suited the shoot. She was adjusting the backlight when Emma came in.

"You didn't say what color red roses. It does matter, you know."

"Not so much for this. And I can always manipulate them in Photoshop. Besides . . ." She walked over to take the ones Emma held. "Perfect."

"The rose petals are real, so—"

"I'll charge them off. Listen, since you're here, can you stand in? You've got close to the same coloring, and you're about the same height. Here." She pushed the roses back at Emma. "Go over there, give me a three-quarter body angle, facing the window, head turned to the camera."

"What's this for?"

"Pregnancy shoot."

"Oh, for Rosa." Emma assumed the position. "Laurel did the cake for her shower last week. Don't you love the follow-up clients? How we get to see these important scenes in their life."

"Yeah, I do. Light's good, I think. For the standard shots anyway."

"What are you doing with the petals?"

"They're for later, for the real shot—after I convince Rosa to get pretty much naked."

"Rosa?" Emma gave an eye-rolling laugh. "Good luck with that."

"You know her, right? I mean before she was a client. The wedding gig came through you. Your third cousin once removed or something?"

"My mother's uncle's cousin-by-marriage's granddaughter. I think. But yeah, I know her. I know everyone, and everyone knows me."

Could be a stroke of luck, Mac calculated. "Can you stick around for a while? You could help put her at ease."

"I can give you a little time," Emma decided after a check of her watch, "mostly because I'm dying to see how you try to get her undressed."

"Don't say anything about it," Mac said quickly when she heard the knock on the door. "I need to guide her toward it."

Mac's first thought on opening the door was *Wow! Look at the shape.* And her mind shot off in various directions on how to exploit it, showcase it, intensify it as she drew Rosa inside.

Having Emma there served as a plus; nobody put people at ease quicker than Emmaline.

"Oh, Rosa, look at you!" All warmth, all welcome, Emma lifted her hands. "You're gorgeous!"

With a quick laugh, Rosa shook her head while Mac took her coat. "I'm enormous."

"Gorgeously. Oh, I bet you can't wait. Let's sit down for just a minute. Have you picked out names?"

"We keep thinking we have, then change our minds." With a little whoosh of breath, her hand on the mountain of her belly, Rosa eased into a chair. "Today it's Catherine Grace for a girl, Lucas Anthony for a boy."

"Wonderful."

"You don't know the sex?" Mac asked.

"We talked ourselves out of it."

"I love a surprise, don't you? And it's exciting to have Mac photograph you now."

"My sister nagged me into it. I guess, at some point, I'll appreciate looking back and seeing myself looking like I swallowed a hot air balloon."

"You're beautiful," Mac said simply. "I'm going to show you. Why don't you stand up here so I can take some test shots? Do you want anything first? Water? Tea?"

Rosa pulled a bottle of water out of her purse. "I drink like a camel, pee like an elephant."

"Bathroom's right over there, any time you need it. And any time you just want a break, say so."

"Okay." Rosa levered herself out of the chair. "Is my hair all right? This outfit? Everything?"

She'd pulled her dark hair back in a tail—very tidy. Mac intended to fix that. She'd chosen simple black pants and a bright blue sweater that skinned over the mountain. They would, Mac thought, start there.

"You're fine. Just test shots. See the tape on the floor there? Stand right on the X."

"I can't even see my feet." But Rosa moved to the mark, stood stiffly while Mac checked her light meter.

"Turn to the side, head toward me. Chin up a little, not that much. Yes, put your hands on the baby." She glanced toward Emma.

Picking up the signal, Emma got up to wander behind Mac. "Have you set up the nursery?"

Emma kept Rosa talking, made her laugh and Mac took the first Polaroid. She rubbed it on her thigh to speed the developing, then, opening it, walked to Rosa. "See? You're beautiful."

Rosa took the print, stared. "I may be enormous, but I sure look happy. It's really pretty, Mac."

"We're going to do even better. Let's try a few in that same pose."

Warming up now, Mac noted as she chatted Rosa up along with Emma. She tossed in quick directions. Tilt your head to the right, shift your shoulders. Halfway through she handed Rosa one of Emma's long-stems, tried shots with the flower as a prop.

She got a full roll of what she considered very nice, very ordinary pregnant woman shots.

"Let's try something else. A different angle, a different top."

"Oh, I didn't bring another top."

"I've got something."

Rosa patted her mound. "You couldn't possibly have anything that would fit me."

"It's not about fit. Trust me." Mac pulled a plain white man's shirt out of the prop room. "We're going to leave it unbuttoned."

"But—"

"The contrast of the sharp lines of the shirt against the round curve of your belly. Trust me. And if you don't like the look, no harm."

"Oh, that'll be fun." Emma poured out enthusiasm. "Baby bumps are so cute."

"I'm at thirty-eight weeks. The bump is Mount Everest."

"It's a beautiful shape," Mac told her. "And you have great skin. The tone, the texture."

"It's just us girls," Emma reminded her. "I'd love to see how it looks. The lighting's so pretty, so flattering."

"Well, maybe. But I'm just going to look fat." Reluctantly, Rosa pulled off the sweater.

"I want one!" Emma exclaimed, and stroked a hand lightly over the baby. "Sorry. But it's just . . . magnetic. It's us, you know? We're the only ones who can do it."

"Celebrating the female." Mac slipped the shirt on Rosa,

fussed with the lines, turned up the cuffs a couple of times. "Let's let your hair down. Contrast again, and it's more womanly. I'm going to add a little more gloss to your lips, okay? So they read a little deeper."

Flustered now, Mac thought as she worked. But that was all right. She could use that. "More a three-quarter angle for this, shoulder more forward. Good! Maybe cup your hands under your belly. Very pretty. I just need to adjust the light."

"Are you sure I don't look stupid? Sloppy? I feel like a cow who's gone way past milking time."

"Rosa." Emma sighed. "You look sexy."

Mac captured the surprise, the pleasure—and finally, the pride. "Big smile, okay. Straight at me. I mean, jeez, look what you did! That's good. Okay? Need a break?"

"No, I'm fine. I just feel a little silly, I guess."

"You don't look silly, trust me. Emma, dress the sleeve a little, right side. See where it's—perfect," she said when Emma stepped over and adjusted. "Now, Rosa, turn a little more toward me. Little more. There. Hands on the sides of your belly. Good."

She could see it coming together as she shot. See the moment, the magic. Nearly there, she thought. "I want you to look down, but lift your eyes—just your eyes to me. Look at the secret you have, the power. Think, for just a minute, how that secret got in there. Pow! Rosa, you're *fabulous*."

"I wish I'd worn a nicer bra."

With that door cracked open, Mac lowered her camera. "Take it off."

"Mackensie!" Rosa released a horrified giggle.

"We're going to try a figure study. You're going to love it." Voice brisk, Mac gestured. "Sit down, relax, rest a minute. I need to set up."

"What does she mean, figure study? Is that naked?"

"I guess we'll find out." Emma took Rosa's arm. "Come on

and sit. We might as well see what she's up to. Mac!" Emma called when the phone rang. "Should I get that?"

*"No!"* Mac rushed out, carrying a low stool. "It might be . . . I've got this game going on." She set her stool on the mark, began to drape it with another ivory sheet as Carter's voice came on.

"I imagine you can guess who this is. Saturday, starting with dinner and then, well . . . hmm. Seven o'clock. So that's good. That's great. I, ah, don't know if there's anything you particularly like to eat—or really hate, for that matter. You'd have mentioned if you were a vegan, right? I think you'd have brought that up. And I'm overthinking this again. So, I guess this concludes our game of tag. I'll see you Saturday. Unless you need to call me about . . . I'm shutting up now. Bye."

"He sounds so cute." Rosa turned back to where Mac refined the drape of the sheet.

"Yes, he does."

"A first date?"

"Technically the second. Or possibly, unofficially, a third. It's very unclear. Rosa, there's another sheet in the bathroom. I want you to go in, take your clothes off. You can wrap yourself in the sheet if you're shy. But from what I hear labor and delivery dispenses with all modesty. So, this should be a breeze."

"I can't do a nude, Mac. It's just not . . . What would I *do* with it?"

"You can decide that after I'm done, but I promise it's not going to be embarrassing or suggestive. It's just the next step in the theme. It's about what you are, Rosa, what's inside you."

"I just don't know if I can—"

"It's about the journey you're on, and the knowledge of it. It's the life, and the light in you. And the love."

"Oh." Rosa's eyes went damp as she crossed her hands over her belly. "I guess I could, at least, try it. You'll delete the pictures if I'm not comfortable with them?"

"Absolutely."

"Well, all right. I have to pee anyway."

"Take your time."

Emma waited until Rosa went inside the bathroom and shut the door. "You are good, Elliot. You are damn good."

"Yes, yes, I am."

"And a Saturday night date."

"Apparently. Am I out of my mind, Emma, for starting this up?"

"It's already started up, honey. And I'd say you'd be out of your mind not to see where it ends up. I wish I could stay and see the rest of the shoot, but I have to get back."

"I'll show you the prints."

"Not only good, but confident. Rosa! I have to get back to work. I'll be in touch."

The bathroom door opened a crack. "Do you have to? I wish you could stay just a little longer."

"I wish I could, too. But you're in good hands with Mac. If I don't see you before, have a happy, beautiful, healthy, miraculous baby."

Emma grabbed her coat on the fly, then mouthed "good luck" to Mac as she dashed out.

AT JUST AFTER FIVE, MAC LET HERSELF INTO THE MAIN HOUSE. She wanted real food, the kind Mrs. G stashed in the freezer. She carted her laptop into the kitchen, and found Parker sitting at the counter, staring into a glass of wine.

"Hey. Early for you to be sitting down, and/or drinking wine."

"I just finished with Naomi and Brent. I so earned this wine."

"Did you fix it?"

"Of course I fixed it, but it wasn't a snap. The bride and groom are now united in their love, commitment, and determination to have *their* wedding. Slut Business Partner is out. Groom will have a serious chat with Cheating Bastard Best Man, and remind him the wedding isn't about him and this woman, but if he feels unable to stand as best man if SBP is excluded, that's his choice. Bride will have a talk with MOH, supportive, understanding, but again firm on just whose wedding it is, and though her anger with Cheating Bastard knows no bounds, he remains her husband's brother. Plus, she will add the incentive of a hot guy who will now attend the wedding as MOH's date—and make the CBBM look like the idiot he is."

Parker stopped, took a breath. "I earned this wine," she repeated.

"Who's the hot guy?"

"I bribed Jack." Parker lifted her glass and drank. "It's costing me a case of Pinot Noir but it's worth it."

"He is hot," Mac agreed. "Well done, master."

"I'm exhausted. How did your shoot go?"

"Funny you should ask. How about I show you?" She opened her laptop, and while it booted up, began to explore the freezer. "What are you having for dinner?"

"I don't know. It's only five."

"I'm hungry. I missed lunch. Chicken pot pie. Mmmmm, chicken pot pie." She pulled out the casserole. "Let's have that."

"Fine. I want a long, hot bath first. I want to eat in my pajamas."

"That sounds so good. Why didn't I think of that? Okay, check these out."

Working the computer, Mac brought up the photos of the first pose.

"God, she's really big!" Parker laughed, leaned in. "And looks so happy and staggered by it. Sweet. They're nice, Mac."

"Yeah, they're nice." She scrolled to the second pose.

"Okay, these are great. Sexy, female, powerful, fun. I love

them. This one, especially, where she's got her head down and her eyes on the camera? Just a hint of witchy. The lighting really adds to it."

"I'm going to finesse that even more. We did one more setup."

Once again, Mac scrolled down, then eased back.

Parker straightened in her chair. "My God, Mac, these are amazing. They're . . . She looks like a Roman goddess."

She studied each shot as the slide show projected them. The white drapery spread from the waist, under that turgid belly, and pooling like a river scattered with deep red rose petals. And the woman, her hair tumbled over her shoulders with an arm crossed over her breasts, a hand at the peak of that pregnant mound.

And the eyes, straight at the camera.

"I love the curves, the folds, the lines. The light—the way it brings out her eyes. The knowledge and power in them. Did you show her any?"

"All. She was so nervous about them I had to show her the lot, so she'd be sure I'd delete any she didn't like."

"What did she think?"

"She cried. In a good way. Must be a hormone thing. Tears just started rolling down her cheeks and scared the shit out of me. Then she said the best thing." Mac paused, letting the memory glow inside her. "She said she was never going to think of herself as big and clumsy because she was magnificent."

"Oh."

"I know. I got teary myself. She wanted to order right then and there. I had to put her off until I tweak a little, and I want her to wait until she's not so emotional before she picks."

"It's rewarding, isn't it, to make someone so happy, to bring that into their life by what you do? Here we are, tired and hungry, but we did damn good work today."

"In that case, how about lending me a pair of pajamas?"

"Why don't you put that in the oven on low, and we'll both get some pajamas."

"Deal. I feel like a chick flick. Do you feel like a chick flick? Dinner and a movie?"

"Sounds really good actually."

"Speaking of dinner and a movie, I'm doing at least the first with Carter Saturday night."

"I knew it." Parker wagged a finger.

"I'm going to keep it low-key. Sex will, potentially, be involved at some point. But low-key."

"Establishing limitations to the relationship prior to embarking thereon. Wise."

"Subtle underlayments of sarcasm can't hide from me." Mac shut the oven door, leaned back against it. "Yesterday was just an anomaly, a spurt of panic brought on by the lack of interesting dateage in my life recently."

"I'm sure you're right." Parker got up, draped her arm around Mac's shoulders as they walked out of the kitchen. "Interesting dateage is in short supply around here, unless you're Emma."

"You don't make time to date."

"I know. It's a conundrum. What kind of movie? Weepy or happy-ever-after?"

"Gotta go with the HEA, especially with chicken pot pie."

"Good call. Why don't we see if the others want in?"

They started the climb to the third floor. "Hey, Parks, what're you going to do when you're really old and can't trudge up all these stairs?"

"I guess I'll put in an elevator. I'm not giving this place up. Ever."

"The house or the business?"

"Either."

Before they could start up the last flight, the cell phone hooked to Parker's waistband jingled.

"Crap."

"Go on up," Parker told her. "Grab the pjs. I'll deal with this and be right behind you." She flipped the phone open after a quick glance at the readout. "Hi, Shannon! Are you ready for next week?" Laughing, Parker turned toward her office. "I know. It's a thousand things. Don't worry. We're on top of every one."

Brides, Mac thought as she finished the climb. Most of them were so worried about the minutiae. If she ever got married—highly unlikely—she'd focus on the big picture.

And leave the details to Parker.

She stepped into Parker's room where the duvet on the luscious four-poster was fluffed under its straw-colored cover, and the flowers were fresh and perky in their vase. No clothes strewn, no shoes kicked in corners.

No dust, no fuss, Mac thought as she opened the drawer of the bureau where she found—as she knew she would—four pairs of pajamas neatly folded.

"I'm tidy," Mac muttered. "I'm just not so anal about it."

She took a pair into the guest bedroom, tossed them on the bed. A long, hot bath sounded too good to miss. She ran one, tossed some bath salts in. As she slid down in the hot, fragrant water, she considered their options for girl movies with happy endings.

Movies, she thought—certainly about love and romance—*should* have happy endings. Because life, too often, didn't. Love faded, or flipped over into loathing. Or settled somewhere in between into a kind of grinding detachment.

It could snap like a dry twig, with one careless step. Then you needed a week at a spa, Mac thought sourly. That someone else paid for.

She knew how Parker felt about the house, and the business. But to Mac's mind, nothing lasted forever.

Except friendship, if you were really lucky—and there, she was Lady Luck herself.

But homes, love affairs? Different deals. And she wasn't looking for forever there. Right now was plenty.

A Saturday night date. A guy who interested and attracted her across the table. Yeah, that was just enough. A week from Saturday? Well, you just couldn't tell, could you?

That's what photographs were for—everything changes, so you can preserve what was. Before tomorrow took it all away.

She sank down to her chin in the water just as Laurel stepped in. "What're you doing? Hot water out at your place?"

"No, I'm seizing the moment, also chicken pot pie and chick flick. Want in? And I don't mean the tub."

"Maybe. I just finished—for the fifth time—redesigning the Holly-Deburke wedding cake. I could use chicken pot pie."

"It's warming in the oven. Emma needs a call, in case."

"Fine. I'll go do that and leave you to your seizing."

Mac closed her eyes and sighed. Yeah, friendship. That was the one thing a woman could always count on.

IN THE MORNING, STILL WEARING PARKER'S PAJAMAS, MAC LET herself into her studio. She'd woken just after dawn, curled up like a shrimp on the sofa of the sitting room, and tucked in with a cashmere throw.

Two helpings of Mrs. G's chicken pot pie made the idea of breakfast somewhat revolting. But coffee . . .

Still, before she set up her morning hit, she wandered—casually—to her answering machine.

No messages.

Instant disappointment made her feel foolish. She hadn't sat around waiting for him to call—again. She'd enjoyed her evening. Besides, it had been her turn to call, if she'd wanted to extend the little game.

And besides, she was being stupid.

She wasn't going to think about Carter Maguire and his sexy

glasses or frumpy tweed jacket—and his amazing lips. She had coffee to brew, work to do, life to lead.

"SATURDAY NIGHT DATE? OKAY, THIS IS MAJOR."

Why, Carter asked himself, *why* had he opened his mouth? What had made him think mentioning it would simply be a little conversation over coffee in the teachers' lounge before classes began?

"Well, I should go over the quiz I'm—"

"Major," Bob repeated, drilling a finger into the coffee counter to mark his point. "You need to take her flowers. Not roses. Roses are too important, too symbolic. A more casual flower, or those mixed deals."

"I don't know. Maybe." Something else to worry about now.

"Nothing big or flashy. She's going to want to put them in a vase, and that gives you time to go in, talk, break that ice. So make sure you make the reservations accordingly. What time are they?"

"I haven't made them yet."

"You need to get on that." With a wise nod, Bob sipped his coffee with low-fat creamer. "Where are you taking her?"

"I'm not entirely sure."

"You need a place just a click over middle range. Don't want to go all-out first time, but you don't want to run on the cheap either. You want atmosphere, but not stuffy. A nice established place."

"Bob, you're going to give me an ulcer."

"This is all ammunition, Cart. All ammo. You want to be able to order a nice bottle of wine. Oh, and after dinner, if she says how she doesn't want dessert, you suggest she pick one and you'll split it. Women *love* that. Sharing dessert's sexy. Do *not* go on and on about your job over dinner. Certain death. Get her to talk about hers, and what she likes to do. Then—"

"Should I be writing this down?"

"It wouldn't hurt. If dinner goes to say ten, or over, you should have a second venue picked out. Music's best. A place you can go listen to music. If it winds up earlier, you should have a movie picked out. This is assuming she isn't sending you the 'let's go back to my place' signals. In that case—"

"Don't go there, Bob. Let's just not go there." He thought, *Literally, saved by the bell*, when it rang. "I've got to get to my first period class."

"We'll talk later. I'll try to write some of this down for you."

"Great." Carter made his escape, joined the flock of students and teachers in the corridor.

He thought he might not make it to Saturday. At least not sanely.

# CHAPTER SEVEN

He bought flowers. It annoyed him because he'd intended to take her flowers in the first place. But Bob's tutorial changed the simple gesture into a complex and essential symbolic act so fraught with pitfalls, he'd decided to skip the step.

One of her best friends was a florist, wasn't she? Mackensie could carpet her studio with flowers if she wanted to.

Then he worried that by not bringing the damn flowers he'd be committing some unwritten but universally known dating faux pas. In the end, he'd doubled back—he'd left plenty of time for the drive from his place to Mackensie's. There might've been traffic, a five-car collision. Many casualties.

He rushed into the supermarket, and had stood studying, debating, questioning the flowers on display until sweat beaded on his forehead.

Bob, he assumed, would have something cutting to say about the choice of supermarket flowers. But he'd left it too late for a florist, and he could hardly rush over to Emma's and throw himself on her mercy.

He wished he'd just left it at coffee. They'd had a nice conversation, a pleasant time. You go your way now, I'll go mine, and that's that. All this was just too complicated, too intense. But he could hardly call her now, make up some excuse, even if he could successfully lie his way through it. And the chances of that were slim to none.

People dated all the time, didn't they? They rarely died due to the activity. He grabbed what seemed to be a colorful, casual arrangement, and stalked over to the express line.

They were colorful, he thought with some resentment. They smelled nice. A couple of those big gerbera daisies were mixed in, and they struck him as a friendly flower. None of the dreaded roses, he mused, which, according to the Law of Bob, meant he'd basically be asking Mackensie to marry him and bear his children.

So, they should be safe.

Maybe they were too safe.

The kind-eyed cashier gave him a quick smile. "Aren't those pretty! A surprise for your wife?"

"No. No. I don't have a wife."

"Oh, for your girl then."

"Not exactly." He fumbled out his wallet as she rang them up. "Just a . . . Could I just ask you if you think these are appropriate for a date? I mean to give to the woman I'm taking out to dinner."

"Sure they are. Most everybody likes flowers, don't they? Especially us girls. She's going to think you're real sweet, and thoughtful, too."

"But not too . . ." Stop while you're ahead, Carter told himself.

She took the money, made the change. "Here you go now." She slid the bouquet into a clear plastic bag. "You have a real good time tonight."

"Thank you." More relaxed, Carter walked back to his car.

If you couldn't trust the checker in the express line at the supermarket, who could you trust?

He checked his watch, calculated that barring fatal collisions he was still on schedule. Though he felt foolish, he pulled the list the helpful Bob had printed out from his pocket, and carefully crossed off Buy Flowers (not roses).

Following, there were several suggestions for greetings or initial conversation points such as *You look beautiful, Great dress, I saw these (flowers) and thought of you.*

Carter stuffed the list back in his pocket before any of them imprinted on his brain. But not before he'd noted Bob's decree to tune the car radio to classic lite or smooth jazz, on low volume.

He might end up killing Bob, Carter mused.

He drove the next few miles while obsessing about background music before snapping off the radio. The hell with it. He turned into the long, winding drive of the estate.

"What if she's not wearing a dress," he muttered, as despite all efforts Bob's list popped back into his mind. And unfortunately, his own question had the image of Mac in black pants and white bra crowding Bob out.

"I don't mean that. For God's sake. I mean, she might be wearing something *other* than a dress. What do I say then: Nice pants? Outfit, outfit, great outfit. You know it's called an outfit. Dear God, shut up."

He rounded the main house and followed the narrowing drive to Mac's.

The lights were on, up and down, so the entire place glowed. Through the generous windows of the first floor he could see her studio, the light stands, a dark blue curtain held up with big, silver clips. In front of the curtain stood a small table and two chairs. Wineglasses glinted on the table.

Did that mean she wanted to have drinks first? He hadn't allowed time for drinks. Should he move the reservation? He got out of the car, started down her walk. Went back to the car to get the flowers he'd left on the passenger seat.

He wished the evening was over. He really did. With a sick feeling in his gut he had to force his hand up to knock. He wanted it to be tomorrow morning, a quiet Sunday morning. He'd grade papers, read, take a walk. Get back to his comfortable routine.

Then she opened the door.

He didn't know what she was wearing. All he saw was her face. It had always been her face—that smooth milk skin framed by bright, bold hair. Those witch green eyes and the unexpected charm of dimples.

He didn't want the evening to be over, he realized. He just wanted it to begin.

"Hello, Carter."

"Hello, Mackensie." None of Bob's listed suggestions occurred to him. He offered the flowers. "For you."

"I was hoping they were. Come on in." She closed the door behind him. "They're so pretty. I love gerbera daisies. They're happy. I want to put these in water. Do you want a drink?"

"Ah . . ." He glanced over at the table. "If you'd planned to."

"That? No, that's a setup from a shoot I had this afternoon." She walked toward the kitchen, giving him a little come-ahead gesture. "Engagement shoot. They're wine buffs. Actually, she writes for a wine-buff mag, and he's a restaurant critic. So I got the idea of doing it as a bistro deal." She got out a vase as she talked, and began to unwrap the flowers.

"It's great the way you're able to tailor a photograph like that to the people in it. Sherry loved what you did with hers."

"That was easy. A couple of people madly in love snuggling on the couch."

"It's only easy if you've got the instincts to know Sherry and Nick wouldn't sit in a sophisticated bistro drinking wine, or sit on the floor surrounded by books—and a very big cat.

"The Mason-Collari engagement. That ran today, didn't it? Do you always check on the wedding and engagement section of the paper?"

"Only since I met you again."

"Aren't you the smooth one?"

As no one had ever applied that adjective to him, he couldn't think of anything to say.

She set the vase in the center of her kitchen counter. "Those will perk me up in the morning, even before coffee."

"The cashier at the market said you'd like them. I had a small crisis; she got me through it."

Amusement made the dimples flicker in her cheeks. "You can always count on the cashier at the market."

"That's what I thought."

She walked out, and over to the couch to pick up the coat draped over the arm. "I'm ready if you are."

"Sure." He crossed to her to take the coat. As he helped her into it, she glanced back over her shoulder. "Every time you do this I wish I had longer hair, so you'd have to pull it out of the collar."

"I like your hair short. It shows off your neck. You have a very nice neck."

She turned, stared at him. "We're going out to dinner."

"Yes. I made reservations. Seven thirty at—"

"No, no, I mean we're going out to dinner, so this is not to be interpreted as let's stay in. But I think I really need to get this out of the way, so I can enjoy the meal without thinking about it."

She rose on her toes, linked her hands behind his head. And laid her mouth, soft and inviting, on his. The jolt of pleasure shot straight through him. He had to fight the urge to grab her as he had before, to release even a portion of that pent-up lust. He ran his hands up her body, regrettably shielded by the coat, then down it again until the jolt mellowed to a shimmer.

She drew back, and a pretty flush warmed that milk porcelain skin. "You have a real talent for that, Professor."

"I spent a lot of time thinking about kissing you back—way back. I've recently revisited that thinking. That might be why."

"Or, you're just a natural. We'd better go, or I'm going to talk myself out of dinner."

"I don't expect you to—"

"I might."

Because he was, again, momentarily stunned, she beat him to the door, and opened it herself.

She filled the car. It's how he thought of it. Her scent, her voice, her laugh. The simple reality of her. As strange as it was, his nerves calmed.

"Do you always drive the exact speed limit?" she asked.

"It's irritating, isn't it?" He glanced her way, and when he saw her eyes laughing at him, he had to grin. "If I go over by more than a couple miles an hour, I feel like a criminal. Corrine used to . . ."

"Corrine?" she said when he trailed off.

"Just someone I annoyed with my driving." And everything else, apparently.

"An old girlfriend."

"Nothing, really." Why hadn't he turned on the radio?

"See, now it's a mystery, and I'm more curious. I'll tell you about one of my exes first—to prime the pump." She turned her face to him until he could feel those green eyes laughing again. "How about the fledgling rock star, the one who resembled Jon Bon Jovi through the filter of infatuation. In looks, not talent. His name was Greg, but he liked to be called Rock. He actually did."

"Rock what?"

"Ah, *just* Rock. Like Prince, or Madonna. Anyway, at twenty, he seemed incredibly hot and cool, and in my sexual delirium I spent a lot of time, talent, and money taking head shots of him and his band, group shots, shots for their self-produced CD. I drove their van, played groupie and roadie. For over two months. Until I caught him sucking face with his bass player. A guy named Dirk."

"Oh. Well, that's very sad."

"I heard the amusement in that."

"Not if you were really hurt."

"I was *crushed*. For at least five minutes. Then I was pissed for weeks. I'd been his beard, the bastard. My satisfaction comes from the fact that he now sells kitchen appliances in Stamford. Not major appliances either. I mean like blenders and toaster ovens."

"I like a good toaster oven."

She laughed as he turned into a parking lot. "The Willows—nice choice, Carter. The food's always good here. Laurel worked here as pastry chef before we started Vows, and for a while after when we were getting off the ground."

"I didn't know that. I haven't been here for a couple months, but the last time I came with—"

"Corrine."

"No." He smiled a little. "With a couple of friends who set me up with a blind date. Very strange evening, but the food was, as you said, good."

He got out of the car, started to walk around to open her door. But she climbed out before he got there. When she held out a hand to him, casually, his heart took a quick, extra, thump.

"Why strange?"

"She had a voice like a violin might have made if you neglected to rosin the bow. It's an unfair observation, but pretty accurate. Plus she'd recently gone on a no-carb, no-fat, no-salt diet. She ate an undressed salad, one leaf, one sprig, one carrot curl at a time. It was disconcerting."

"I eat like a horse."

"That's hard to believe."

"You watch."

Just as they reached the door, it opened. The man who stepped out wore an open coat, no hat, gloves, or scarf. The wind immediately kicked the dark hair around his ridiculously handsome face. One glance at Mac had his well-cut lips curving, and his sea-at-midnight eyes lighting.

"Hey, Macadamia." He hoisted her up by the elbows, smacked a kiss to her lips. "Of all the gin joints in all the . . . Carter?" He dumped Mac back on her feet, shot out a friendly hand. "How the hell are you?"

"I'm fine, Del. How are you?"

"Good. It's been too long. What're you two doing here?"

"We thought, since we're told they have food here, we'd eat."

Del grinned at Mac. "That's a plan. So you're having dinner. Together. I didn't realize you were an item."

"We're not," they said together. Then Carter cleared his throat.

"We're having dinner."

"Yeah, that's been established. I had a quick business meeting over a drink, and I'm meeting some friends across town. Or I'd come in and have one with you, and cross-examine the witnesses. But, gotta go. Later."

Mac watched Delaney Brown jog toward the parking lot. "Who was that guy?" she asked, and made Carter laugh.

As she slid in, Mac wondered if Carter had requested a corner booth, or if they'd just gotten lucky. It added just a hint of intimacy to play against the upscale casual tone of the restaurant. She turned down the offer of a cocktail in favor of wine with dinner, then ignoring her menu, turned to Carter.

"So, the salad-eating squeaky violin. No follow-up?"

"I don't think either party was interested in one."

"Do you go on many blind dates?"

"That was my first and last. You?"

"Never. Too scary. Plus, the four of us made a pact, years ago, never to try to fix each other up. It's worked out for the best. So, are you interested in sharing a bottle of wine, Dr. Maguire?"

He slid the wine list toward her. "You pick."

"That's brave of you." She opened it, scanned. "I'm not a wine buff, I just take pictures of them, but they do have this Shiraz I like."

Even as she spoke, their server stepped to the table with a bottle of Shiraz.

"That's excellent service," Mac commented.

"Mr. Maguire? Mr. Brown phoned and would like you to have this with his compliments. Or, if it doesn't suit, whatever bottle you'd like."

"Those Brown kids." Mac shook her head. "They never miss. I'd love a glass, thanks. Okay?" she said to Carter.

"Sure. That was awfully nice of him."

It was, Mac thought, as well as a subtle little wink. First chance he got, she knew, Del would be teasing her brainless.

SHE DIDN'T EAT LIKE A HORSE IN CARTER'S ESTIMATION, BUT she didn't pick her way through a lonely salad for ninety minutes either. He liked the way she gestured with her wineglass or with her fork as she talked. And the way she stabbed a bite of his sea bass from his plate to try it without asking if he minded.

He wouldn't have, but not asking was . . . friendlier.

"Here, take a hunk of this steak." She cut off a portion.

"No, I'm fine."

"Do you eat red meat?"

"Yes."

"Just try it. It's like we've got the surf and turf thing going."

"All right. Do you want some of this rice?"

"No. I can never figure out why anyone would. Anyway, back to the topic at hand. You actually had your English Lit class watch *Clueless* to evaluate the updating of Austen's *Emma*."

"It demonstrates that literature—and storytelling—isn't stagnant, that the themes, dynamics, even social mores of *Emma* translate to the contemporary."

"I wished I'd had teachers like you. Did you like it? *Clueless*?"

"Yes. It's clever."

"I love movies. We had a double-feature last night, but I OD'd on the pot pie and fell asleep during *Music and Lyrics*. Hugh Grant." She gestured with her wineglass again. "*Sense and Sensibility*. Did you see it?"

"I did. I thought it was a lovely and respectful adaptation. Did you read it?"

"No. I know, terrible. I did read *Pride and Prejudice*. Loved it. I keep meaning to read it again now that I'd have Colin Firth as Mr. Darcy in my brain, so even better. What's your favorite book-to-movie deal?"

"Personal favorite? *Mockingbird*."

"Oh, Gregory Peck. I read the book," she added. "It's great, but oh, Gregory Peck. Atticus Finch. The perfect father. That scene at the very end, where she's—what's her name?"

"Scout."

"Yeah, where she's narrating and you see him through the window, sitting beside his son's bed. It kills me. It's so beautiful. When I watched it as a kid, I used to imagine Atticus was my father. Or Gregory Peck—either one would do. He'd be there, when you woke up in the morning. I guess I've never gotten over that. Pitiful."

"I don't think so. I don't know what it's like, growing up without a father. You don't see yours often?"

"No, hardly ever. When I do—every few years—he's enormously charming, very affectionate. I end up getting sucked in, then bruised when he goes off and ignores me immediately after. He's an in-the-moment sort of person. If you're not in that moment with him, you don't exist."

"It hurts you."

"Yes, it does. Over and over. And that's too depressing a topic for this really nice dinner. Give me one more. Another adaptation you like."

He wanted to stroke her hair, to put an arm around her. But that wasn't the comfort she wanted. He circled through his brain. "*Stand by Me*."

She frowned, obviously trying to place it. "I don't know that one. Who wrote it? Steinbeck? Fitzgerald? Yeats?"

"Stephen King. It's based on his novella *The Body*."

"Seriously? You read King? He scares the crap out of me, but I can't resist it. Wait! That's the one with the kids, the boys hiking to look for somebody, some dead guy, who maybe got hit by a train? I'm remembering this. Kiefer Sutherland plays a complete asshole hood. He was great."

"It's about friendship and loyalty. Coming of age, standing together."

"You're right," she said, studying his face. "It is. I bet you're a really amazing teacher."

"Some days."

She nudged her plate aside, then leaned back with her wine. "What do you do when you're not teaching, reading, or watching movies based on novels or novellas?"

"That's a lot right there."

"Golf, rock climbing, stamp collecting?"

He smiled, shook his head. "No."

"International intrigue, watercolors, duck hunting?"

"I had to give up the international intrigue due to travel fatigue. I'm pretty boring."

"No, you're not. And believe me I keep expecting you to be."

"Ah . . . thank you?"

She leaned forward to poke a finger in his arm, leaned back again. "All right, Carter, now that you've indulged in—good God—nearly three-quarters of a single glass of wine—"

"I'm driving."

"At the speed limit," she agreed. "It's time to tell me about Corrine."

"Oh, well, there's really nothing to tell."

She saw it, just a flicker of it in his eyes. "She hurt you. I'm sorry. I'm insensitive and pushy."

"No, you're not. And I keep expecting you to be."

She smiled. "Look how cute you are in your smarty-pants. Now why don't you order dessert, so I can pretend to be self-righteous and not—then eat half of yours?"

They lingered. She'd forgotten what it was like to have a meal with a man she could have long, twisty conversation with. One who listened, who paid attention—whether or not he was thinking about the possible bonus round at the end of the evening.

He made her think, she realized. And entertained her. And damn it, the man was charming, in such a low-key, unstudied way.

Plus, when he'd put his glasses on to read the menu, it just set her juices on simmer.

"Do you want to go somewhere else?" he asked her when they walked back to the car. "It's probably too late for a movie. A club?"

"I clubbed out with the pals the other night." Another time though, she thought. It occurred to her she might've been very wrong in assuming Carter Maguire wouldn't fit in the club scene. "I should get back. I've put in a few long ones this week, and I have work to catch up on tomorrow."

He opened her door. "Are you going to see me again?"

It gave her a little jump in the belly that he'd ask, and just that way. Giving her the power, she thought. Terrifying. "I'm thinking about it."

"Okay."

When he'd joined her, started the car, she angled toward him. "Top five reasons you want to see me again."

"Do they have to be in order of priority?"

Damn it, *damn* it, she really liked him. "No. Just quick, top of your head answers."

"Okay. I like the way you talk. I like the way you look. I want to know more about you. I want to sleep with you. And when I'm with you, I feel."

"Feel what?"

"Just feel."

"Those are good answers," she said after a moment. "Really good answers."

"Are you going to give me your five?"

"I'm still working on them. But in the interest of full disclosure, you should know I'm good on a date, but tend to grade lower on relationships."

"I don't see that. How can you when you've had lifelong relationships with your three friends? Layers of relationships with them."

"I don't have sex with them."

"That's an interesting disclaimer, but intimacy's only a part of relationships that go beyond friendship. It doesn't define them."

"Come on, Carter, sex is a whopper. Not to mention the work and effort that goes into maintaining a relationship that includes it. But just to focus on sex for a minute."

"I'm not sure that's smart when I'm driving."

"What if we hit that level, and it's a bust? What then?"

"Well, I'd first apply the basic rule. Most things improve with practice. I'd be willing to practice quite a bit."

"Cute. But if it isn't a bust, that's when things start getting complicated."

He glanced at her. "Do you always borrow trouble?"

"Yes, in this area, I do. I haven't stayed friendly with any of my exes. I don't mean it's all 'I hate his guts and wish he'd die a lingering death, or at least be doomed to selling toaster ovens for all eternity.' But after it's done, we just stop connecting. And I *like* you."

He drove for a while in silence. "Let me sum up. You like me, and feel if we have sex and it's not good, we won't like each other. If it *is* good, we'll complicate things and end up not liking each other."

"It sounds stupid when you say it."

"Food for thought."

She muffled a snort of laughter. "You're a smart-ass, Carter. You're subtle and sneaky about it, but you're a smart-ass. I like that, too."

"I like that you're not particularly subtle about it. So I guess this relationship is doomed."

She slid him a damning glance, but her lips twitched. When he parked in front of her studio, he smiled at her. "You keep my mind engaged, Mackensie. When I'm with you, and when I'm not."

He got out of the car, walked her to the door. "If I called you tomorrow, would that be pushy?"

"No." She kept her eyes on his as she reached in her bag for her keys. "I'm thinking about asking you in."

"But—"

"Hey. I'm supposed to be the one who says *but*."

"And you're free to expand on that. But it's not a good idea. Yet. Because when, if," he corrected, "we go to bed, it shouldn't be to prove a point or answer a question. I think it just has to be because we want each other."

"You're a rational man, Carter. I think you'd better kiss me good night."

He leaned in, and he framed her face with his hands. Long

fingers, she thought, cool against her skin. Eyes soft in color, intense in expression holding hers. A moment, another, so that her heart already raced before his lips brushed hers.

Gentle, easy, so that her racing heart sighed.

As her skin, her blood warmed, he drew her closer and deepened, deepened the kiss, a whisper at a time until everything blurred.

She went pliant, and the long, low sigh she made was surrender. He wanted to touch her, to feel those lovely breasts in his hands, to stroke his fingers down the length of her back, to know the thrill of having her legs locked around him.

He wanted more than a rational man could.

He stepped back, contenting himself with a brush of his thumb over her bottom lip.

"This could be a mistake," she said. Letting herself in, quickly, she leaned back against the door. And she wondered if the mistake was not asking him in, or knowing that she would before much longer.

# CHAPTER EIGHT

MAC PUT IN A SOLID FOUR HOURS WITH THUMBNAILS, Photoshop, prints. The work kept her focused and level. There could be no mind-wandering journeys about sexy English teachers when she had clients expecting—and deserving—her best.

She concentrated on balancing color, brightening or dulling the saturation to translate the mood, the emotion.

She sharpened a candid of the bride and groom, both laughing as they charged down the aisle, hands locked together, and blurred the background, everything but the two of them.

Just the two of them, she thought, wildly happy in those first seconds of marriage. Everything around them soft-focus and dreamlike, and their faces, their movement, their unity vivid.

It would come rushing back, she thought, other voices, movement, demands, connections. But in this instant, in this image, they were all.

Pleased, she added noise, just a hint of grain before she tried a soft proof to test her paper. Once she'd printed it, she studied it, searching for flaws.

She added it, as she sometimes did, to the order placed. A little gift for the new couple. Shifting work stations, she unboxed the combination album her clients had chosen, and began to assemble the pages with images that told the story of the day.

She repeated the process for the smaller albums and photos chosen by parents.

Back at the computer, she generated the custom thank-you cards using the portrait the client had selected. She boxed them in units of twenty-five, tied each with a thin white ribbon before taking a break.

She still had to mat and frame a dozen portraits for the couple's personal gallery and what they'd chosen as gifts.

But she'd get it done, today, Mac thought as she stood and stretched. She was on a roll, and she'd contact her client in the morning to arrange pickup or delivery.

She bent over at the waist, letting her arms hang loosely, and called out at the knock on her door. "It's open."

"You've still got no ass."

Mac turned her head for an upside-down view of Delaney. "I had a feeling."

"Stopped by to drop off some paperwork, catch up with Parker before I headed over to Jack's to watch the game." He peeled off his coat, tossed it toward the couch. "So, how was the wine?"

"Good, thanks, Mr. Cutie."

"You and Carter Maguire, huh?" At home, he strolled into her kitchen. She heard the fridge open, then his aggrieved voice. "Mac, you have *no* ass. Why do you only have Diet Coke in here?"

"So people like you don't suck down all my supply."

She straightened as he came back, popping the top on a can. "Beggars, choosers. Word is you and Carter hooked up because his sister's a client."

"We ran into each other again because of that."

"And you flashed him your tits, first chance."

She lifted her eyebrows. "Those would not be Parker's words, which is your source. If you're going to be such a girl about this, why don't we sit down and braid each other's hair while we gossip."

"You don't have enough hair." He took a slug of the soft drink, grimaced a little. "Blah. Anyway, back to topic. A man's got to be curious, and mildly suspicious about other guys and his honorary little sister."

She went in for her own Coke. "We went out to dinner. According to my data, people have been doing that for several years."

"Date two, according to my unimpeachable source. Not including the flashing." He wiggled his eyebrows at her when she came back in.

"There was no flashing, only the momentary lack of shirt. Pervert Boy."

"I'm known by many names. And your evasions make me wonder if this is serious business."

"I'm not evading, and what's your problem with Carter?"

"I don't have a problem with Carter, other than you're you and he's a man. I like him." With a shrug, he sat on the arm of her sofa. "Always did. I haven't run into him since he moved back, until last night. I heard he'd been hooked up with Corrine Melton—she worked for a client of Jack's—and he, that would be Jack, found her a pain in the ass."

"What do you know about her?"

"Aha, so we are serious."

"Shut up. Tell me."

"Impossible to do both at once."

"Come on, Del."

"I know nothing, except she irritated Jack and apparently came on to him. While she was still hooked up with Carter. Which I'm now assuming she's not."

"What does she look like? Is she pretty?"

"Jesus, Mac, now you are being a girl. I have no idea. Ask Jack."

Scowling, she pointed to the door. "If you have no juice, take your drink and go. I'm working."

He grinned at her, that potent flash of Brown grin. "But I'm having such a good time."

"No juice from you, you get none from me."

The phone rang. She checked the readout, didn't recognize the name or number. "Mac Photography at Vows."

"Mackensie! Hello from beautiful, sunny Florida."

"Mom." She immediately held a finger at her temple and flicked her thumb like a trigger.

Del tossed his coat back on the couch. Friends didn't leave friends in a twist. And if Linda was on the phone, Mac would end up twisted.

"I'm having the *best* time. I feel like a new woman!"

"Whose phone is this?"

"Oh, it's Ari's. I left mine in my room, and we're sitting out by the pool. Or I am. He just went to see what's taking so long with our drinks. The sweetie. It's glorious here! I have a treatment soon, but just had to talk to you first, so Ari lent me his phone. He's *such* a gentleman."

Jesus, Mac thought, she'd actually predicted this. "I'm glad you're having a good time."

"It's been amazing for me. For my health and well-being, my mental, emotional, and spiritual well-being. I need another week."

Mac closed her eyes. "I can't help you."

"Of course you can! Sweetie, I have to finish this. If I don't I'll come back and slide right down again. It'll all have been wasted, as if you'd thrown your money away. I just need you to clear another thousand. Well, two to be absolutely safe. I need to complete myself."

"I don't have any more to spare." She thought of the work she'd done, more than four hours of work on a Sunday.

"You can charge it," Linda said with a trill that went sharp around the edges. "It's not like you have to run down here with cash, for God's sake. Just call the office here with your credit card information, and they'll do the rest. Simple as that. I've already told them you'd be calling, so—"

"You can't keep doing this to me." Her voice wanted to break. "You can't keep expecting me to pay and pay and pay. I—"

Mac jolted when Del grabbed the phone out of her hand. "Don't," she began, and he cut her off with a look.

"Linda? Hi, this is Delaney Brown. Sorry, Mackensie's been called away from the phone."

"We haven't finished—"

"Yes, you have, Linda. You've finished. Whatever you're pushing her for this time, she said no. Now she's busy."

"You have no right to talk to me this way. You think because you're a *Brown*, because you have *money* you can push yourself between me and my own child?"

"No, I think I can do that because I'm Mac's friend. You have a real good day."

He hung up and turned to where Mac stood, misery shining in her eyes. "Don't cry," he ordered.

She shook her head, went straight into his arms to press her face to his shoulder. "Goddamn it, goddamn it, why do I let her do this to me?"

"Because if you had the choice, you'd be a good and loving daughter. She doesn't give you the choice. It's on her, Mac. Money again?"

"Yes, again."

He rubbed her back. "You did the right thing. You said no. Keep saying that. Now I want you to promise me you're not going to answer the phone if—when—she calls back. If you don't give me your word, I'm dragging you out of here, forcing you to watch the game at Jack's."

"I promise. I wouldn't have answered, but I didn't recognize the number. She used somebody named Ari's phone and called the business line. She knows how to get to me."

"Screen your calls, at least for a while, unless you're sure who it is. Okay?"

"Yeah, okay. Thanks, Del. Thanks."

"I love you, baby."

"I know." She stepped back, smiled at him. "I love you, too. Go watch football. Don't tell Parker. If I need to, I will."

"All right." He picked up his coat again. "If you need me—"

"I'll call. That's another promise."

She couldn't go back to work, not yet, not until she cleared her head and could focus again. And the pity party she felt coming on, with balloons and streamers, wouldn't clear anything.

Take a walk, she thought. It had worked before, with Carter. She'd see if it worked on her own.

It wasn't evening, and it wasn't snowing, but the air was clear and cold. Everyone else tucked inside, she thought. Tucked in, but close. If she wanted or needed company, she could find it.

Not now, she thought again, not yet. Remembering the bird feeders, she hiked through the snow to fill them from the lidded can. Running low, she realized as she scooped out feed. Something for the grocery list.

Ten pounds of bird feed. A quart of milk. A new spine.

Too bad she couldn't buy the last on the list at the local market. She'd just have to grow one when it came to Linda Elliot Meyers Barrington.

After locking the lid back down, she walked to the pond, stepped under one of the willows. There, she brushed off the snow on the bench under the fan of whippy branches and sat for a while. The grounds remained coated in white, but the sun had stripped the branches so trees speared up, winter bones, toward a sky the color of old, faded denim.

She could see the rose arbor, white as the snow, with the canes twined and twisted, and sharp with thorns. And beyond, the pergola, massed with dormant wisteria.

She supposed it looked peaceful, color and life sleeping through the winter. But at the moment, at that moment, lonely was the only word that came to mind.

She rose to go back to the house. She'd do better with work. If she made mistakes, she'd do it over and over until she passed through this mood.

She'd turn on music, loud, so she didn't have to hear her own thoughts.

Even as she opened the door she heard the weeping, and her mother's sobbing voice. "I don't know how you can be so cold, so unfeeling. I need your *help.* Just a few more days, Mackensie. Just—"

And, thank God, her machine cut the call off.

Mac closed the door, took off her coat. Work? Who was she kidding?

She curled on the couch, dragged the throw over her. She'd sleep it off, she promised herself. Sleep off the misery.

When the phone rang again, she tucked into a defensive ball. "Oh God, oh God, leave me alone, please leave me alone. Give me some peace."

"Ah, hello. It's Carter. You must be working, or you needed to go out. Or, ha, you're just not in the mood to talk."

"Can't talk," she murmured from the couch. "Can't. You talk. You just talk to me."

She closed her eyes and let his voice soothe her.

IN HIS TOWNHOUSE, CARTER HUNG UP THE PHONE. THE THREE-legged orange cat he called Triad leaped into his lap. He sat, scratching the cat absently between the ears and wishing he'd been able to talk to Mac. Even just for a minute. If he had, he wouldn't be sitting here, thinking about her, instead of doing his Sunday chores.

He had laundry to deal with, tomorrow's lesson plans to review. More papers to grade, and the story outlines from his Creative Writing class to read and approve. He hadn't finished his paper on "Shakespeare's Women: The Duality." Or given enough attention to the short story he had in the works.

Then he was expected for Sunday dinner at his parents'.

He was mooning over her, and realizing it didn't seem to make a damn bit of difference.

"Laundry first," he told the cat, and poured Triad onto the chair as he himself vacated it. He put the first load in the washer in the claustrophobic little laundry room off his kitchen. He started to make himself a cup of tea, then scowled.

"I can have coffee if I want. There's no law that says I can't have a damn cup of coffee in the afternoon." He brewed it with a kind of defiance that made him feel foolish even though no one was there to see it. While his clothes washed, he took the coffee back upstairs to the smaller of the two bedrooms, outfitted as his office.

He began grading the papers, and sighed over the C minus he was forced to give one of his brightest—and laziest—students. He felt a conference coming on. No point in putting it off, he decided, and wrote *See me after class* under the grade.

When the timer he'd set signaled, he went back down to put the wet clothes in the dryer, load a second batch in the washer.

Back at his desk, he evaluated outlines. He made comments, suggestions, corrections. Using his red pencil he added words of praise and advice. He loved this kind of work—seeing how his students used their minds, organized thoughts, created their worlds.

He finished the work, and the laundry, and still had more than an hour to kill before he needed to leave for dinner.

Casually he began to search for recipes on the Internet.

It didn't mean he'd ask her over for dinner. It was just an in case sort of thing. If he lost his mind and actually followed Bob's advice, it would be good to have a plan.

An outline, so to speak.

Nothing too fancy or complicated, he thought, as *that* would be a disaster. But not too basic or ordinary. If you were going to cook for a woman, shouldn't you make more of an effort than tossing something in the microwave?

He printed out a few possibilities, and made notes on potential menus. And wines. She liked wine. He didn't know anything about wine, but he could learn. He put everything in a file.

He'd probably ask her to the movies anyway. The standard movie date, followed by pizza. Casual, no pressure or expectations. That was what he'd most likely do, he thought as he walked out of the office into his bedroom to change into a fresh shirt.

Still, it wouldn't hurt to pick up some candles, maybe some flowers. He glanced around the room, and imagined her there. In candlelight. Imagined lowering her to the bed, feeling her move under him. Watching her face, the light shimmering over it, as he touched her. Tasted her.

"Oh boy."

After a calming breath, Carter stared down at the cat who stared up at him. "She's right. Sex is a whopper."

THE HOUSE ON CHESTNUT LANE WITH ITS BIG YARD AND OLD trees had been one of the reasons Carter had given up his position at Yale. He'd missed it—the blue shutters and white clapboard, the sturdy porch and tall dormers—and the people who lived inside it.

He couldn't say he came to the house any more often now than when he'd lived and worked in New Haven. But he found contentment knowing he could drop by if the mood struck. He stepped in, turned out of the foyer to glance into the big parlor where Chauncy, the family cocker spaniel, curled on the sofa.

He wasn't allowed on the furniture, and knew it, so his sheepish expression and hopefully thumping tail were pleas for silence.

"I didn't see a thing," Carter whispered, and continued on toward the great room, and the noise. He smelled his mother's Yankee pot roast, heard his younger sister's laugh, followed by multiple male shouts and curses.

The game, he concluded, was on.

He stopped at the entryway to study the tableau. His mother, raw-boned, sturdy as New England bedrock, stirred something on the stove while Sherry leaned on the counter beside her talking a mile a minute and gesturing with a glass of wine. His older sister, Diane, stood with her hands fisted on her hips, watching through the wall of windows. He could see her two kids bundled to the eyeballs, riding a couple of colorful sled disks down the slope of the backyard.

His father, his brother-in-law, and Nick continued to shout at the action on the TV on the other side of the breakfast counter. Since football either gave him a headache or put him to sleep, Carter chose the girls' side of the room and came up on his mother from behind to lean down and kiss the top of her head.

"Thought you'd forgotten about us." Pam Maguire offered her son a tasting spoon of the split-pea soup simmering on the range.

"I had a couple of things to finish up. It's good," he said when he'd obediently tasted the soup.

"The kids asked about you. They assumed you'd be here in time to sled with them."

There was the faintest hint of censure in Diane's tone. Knowing she was happiest if she had something or someone to complain about, he walked over to kiss her cheek. "Nice to see you."

"Have some wine, Carter." Behind Diane's back, Sherry gave him a quick eye-roll. "We can't eat until the game's over anyway. Plenty of time."

"We don't put off family dinner for sports at our house," Diane said.

Which, Carter thought, probably explained why his brother-in-law took advantage of the more lax Maguire rules.

His mother just hummed over her soup as, to a man, the football enthusiasts leaped from chair and sofa to cheer.

Touchdown.

"Why don't you have a nice glass of wine, too, Di?" Pam tapped her spoon, adjusted the flame under the pot. "Those kids are fine out there. We haven't had an avalanche in more than ten years now. Michael! Your son's here."

Mike Maguire held up a finger, pumping his other hand as the kicker set for the extra point. "And it's *good*!" He sent Carter a grin over his shoulder, his pale Irish skin flushed with joy and framed by his neat silver beard. "Giants are up by five!"

Sherry handed Carter a glass. "Since everything's under control in here, and in there," she added, nodding toward the stands, "why don't you sit down and tell us all about you and Mackensie Elliot."

"Mackensie Elliot? The photographer? *Really?*" Pam said, drawing out the word.

"I think I'll catch the end of the game."

"Not a chance." Sherry maneuvered him back against the counter. "I heard from someone who heard from someone who saw the two of you getting cozy at Coffee Talk."

"We had coffee. And talked. It's the Coffee Talk way."

"*Then* I heard from someone who heard from someone that you were even cozier at the Willows last night. What gives?"

Sherry was always hearing from someone who'd heard from someone, Carter thought wearily. His sister was like a human radio receiver. "We went out a couple of times."

"You're dating Mackensie Elliot?" Pam asked.

"Apparently."

"The same Mackensie Elliot you mooned over for months back in high school."

"How do you know I . . ." Stupid, Carter thought. His mother knew everything. "We just had dinner. It's not national news."

"It is around here," Pam corrected. "You could've invited her here tonight. You know there's always plenty."

"We're not . . . it's not . . . We're not at the point of family gatherings. We had dinner. It's one date."

"Two with the coffee," Sherry corrected. "Are you seeing her again?"

"Probably. Maybe." He felt his shoulders hunch as he shoved his hands in his pockets. "I don't know."

"I hear good things about her, and she does very good work. Otherwise, she wouldn't be doing Sherry's wedding."

"Isn't she Linda Elliot's daughter? Or it's Barrington now."

"I haven't met her mother. It was dinner."

The news pulled Diane away from the window. "Linda Barrington, sure. Her daughter's close friends with the Browns, and Emmaline Grant, and that other one. They run that wedding business together."

"I guess that's the one then," Carter acknowledged.

"Linda Barrington." Diane's jaw tightened as she compressed her lips in an expression Carter knew reflected disapproval. "That's the woman who had an affair with Stu Gibbons, and broke up his marriage."

"She can hardly be held responsible for her mother's behavior." Pam opened the oven to check her roast. "And Stu broke up his own marriage."

"Well, I heard that she pushed Stu to leave Maureen, and when he wouldn't she told Maureen about the affair herself. Maureen skinned Stu in the divorce—and who could blame her—and after that *she* wasn't so interested anymore."

"Are we talking about Mackensie or her mother?" Pam wondered.

Diane shrugged. "I'm just saying what I know. People say she's always on the hunt for the next husband, especially if he's someone else's."

"I'm not dating Mackensie's mother." Carter's tone was quiet enough, cool enough, to light a fire in Diane's eyes.

"Who said you were? But you know what they say about apples and trees. You might want to be careful, that's all, so you don't have another Corrine Melton on your hands."

"Di, why do you have to be such a bitch?" Sherry demanded.

"I'll just keep my mouth shut."

"Good plan."

Pam cast her eyes at the ceiling as her oldest daughter stalked back to the windows. "She's been in a mood since she got here."

"She's been in a mood since she was born," Sherry muttered.

"That's enough. She's a pretty girl, as I recall. Mackensie Elliot. And as I said, I've heard good things about her. Her mother's a difficult woman, no question. As I recall, her father's charming and absent. It takes a lot of spine and stomach to make yourself into something when no one gives you a foundation."

Carter leaned down, kissed his mother's cheek. "Not everyone's as lucky as we are."

"Damn right. Diane, call those kids in so they can get cleaned up. That's the two-minute warning."

When dinner conversation jumped from a rehash of the game, to his niece's school play, veered into wedding talk and skipped over to his nephew's desperate desire for a puppy, Carter relaxed.

His relationship with Mac—if there was one—had apparently been taken off the table.

Nick cleared, a gesture that had endeared him to Pam since his first family dinner. Mike sat back, looked down the long length of table in the formal dining room. "I have an announcement."

"Are you going to get me a puppy, Grandpa?"

Mike leaned down to his grandson, whispered, "Let me work on your mom a little more." He eased back again. "Your mother and I have an anniversary coming up next month. You're still my valentine," he added and winked at her.

"I thought you might like a small party at the club," Diane began. "Just family, and close friends."

"That's a nice thought, Diane, but my bride and I will be celebrating thirty-six years of marital bliss in sunny Spain. That is, if she agrees to go with me."

"Michael!"

"I know we had to put off the trip we'd planned a couple of years ago when I took over as chief of surgery. I've cleared two weeks in February, written them in stone. How about it, sugar? Let's go eat paella."

"Give me five minutes to pack, and I'm there." Pam shot out of her chair, raced over, and dropped into Mike's lap.

"You're all excused," he said, waving at his children.

There it was, Carter thought, there was another reason he'd come home.

The constancy.

# CHAPTER NINE

A CRAPPY MOOD DIDN'T SERVE AS AN EXCUSE FOR MISSING A Monday morning breakfast meeting. So Mac took it with her, like a snarling dog on a leash, to the conference room at the main house. Laurel and Parker sat nibbling on cranberry muffins in what had once been the Browns' library.

The books remained, a kind of frame to the space. The fire crackled cheerfully in the hearth. The old gleaming library table held the setup for coffee, and she knew the engraved console hid a supply of bottled water.

Her friends sat at the round inlaid table in the center of the room. Bright and beautiful, she thought, both of them. Every damn hair in place at eight-freaking-A.M. Just looking at them made her feel sloppy and gawky and somehow *less* in the torn jeans she'd dragged on.

"And when I called him on it?" Laurel lifted her cup of what Mac knew would be perfectly prepared cappuccino. "He said, 'I never leave the house without my toothbrush.'" She let out a snort of derision, then smiled at Mackensie. "You've just missed my retelling of The Demise of Martin Boggs. Why the hell did I go out with someone named Martin Boggs anyway? I hope your date was better than mine."

"It was fine."

"Mmm, that good, huh?"

"I said it was fine." Mac dumped her laptop on the conference table and stalked over to the coffee bar. "Can we get started on this? I have a lot to deal with today."

"Somebody got up on the cranky side of the bed."

Mac flipped up her middle finger.

"Right back at you, pal."

"Girls, girls." Parker let out a long, windy sigh. "Do I have to separate you? Have a muffin, Mac."

"I don't want a goddamn muffin. What I want is to get on with this meeting that's a total waste of time anyway."

"We have three events this weekend, Mac," Parker reminded her.

"Which have all been outlined, organized, scheduled, discussed, blueprinted, and microscoped down to the last overblown detail. We know what we're doing. We don't have to talk it to death."

"Drink some coffee," Parker suggested, but her tone had cooled. "It sounds like you need it."

"I don't need coffee, or a stupid muffin." Mac spun back around. "Let me just sum all this up. People will come. Two of them will get married—most likely. Something will go wrong and be fixed. Someone will get drunk and be dealt with. Food will be eaten, music will be played. People will leave and we'll get paid. The two who most likely get married will most likely divorce within five years. But that's not our problem. Meeting over."

"In that case, there's the door." Laurel gestured. "Why don't you use it?"

Mac slammed her coffee back on the counter. "Good idea."

"Just a minute. Just a damn minute!" Parker's voice snapped out, spoiling Mac's furious exit. "This is business. *Our* business. If you don't like the way it's run, we'll schedule a meeting so you can air your grievances. But your bitch-fit isn't on this morning's agenda."

"Right, I forgot we live and die by agenda. If it's not on the Holy Spreadsheet or keyed into the Magic BlackBerry it isn't Parker-worthy. Clients are allowed to believe they're human beings with actual brains and emotions, while you herd them down your preordained path. Everybody falls in line for Parker, or God help them."

Parker got to her feet, slowly. "If you have a problem with the way I'm managing the business, we'll discuss it. But I have a group coming in about fifty minutes for a tour. I have an hour free today at two, so we can take this up then. In the meantime, I think Laurel had an excellent idea. There's the door."

Flushed from the cold, Emma rushed in. "I wouldn't be late, but I dropped a whole—" She stared when Mac shoved by her, and kept going. "What's wrong with Mac? What happened?"

"Mac had her bitch on." Temper smoldering in her eyes, Laurel picked up her coffee. "We didn't want to play."

"Well, did you ask her why?"

"She was too busy slapping us around for that."

"Oh, for God's sake. I'm going after her."

"Don't." Temper iced in her eyes, Parker shook her head. "Just don't. She'll only put her foot up your ass for your trouble. I've got potential clients coming this morning, and we have current ones who need attention. We'll work around her for now."

"Parker, when one of us has a problem, we all have a problem. Not just in the business."

"I know that, Emma." Parker pressed her fingers to her temple. "Even if she'd listen right now, which she wouldn't, we don't have time."

"Besides if we all went 'splody every time one of us had a lousy date, this room would be full of our bloody body parts."

"Mac and Carter?" Emma shook her head at Laurel. "I don't see how that could be it. My mother talked to his last night and called me after to try to pump me. As far as I know, everything went fine when they went out."

"What else?" Laurel demanded. "What makes a woman bitchier than a man? And okay, maybe occasionally each other. But . . ." She trailed off, closed her eyes. "Her mother. God, we're idiots. Nothing crawls up Mac's butt like her mother."

"I thought her mother was in Florida."

"Do you think distance is any deterrent to the force that is Linda Elliot?" Laurel asked Parker. "Maybe that's it. That's probably it, or part of it. But it's still no reason to rip at us the way she did."

"We'll deal with it. We will. But we've got three events lined up, and we need to go over the details."

Emma opened her mouth again, then swallowed the words when she saw Parker flip a Tums off the roll she took out of her pocket. No point, she thought, in having two friends upset. "Actually, I wanted to talk to you about the urns for Friday."

"Great." Parker sat back down. "Let's get started."

SHE KNEW WHEN SHE'D ACTED THE BITCH. SHE DIDN'T NEED A diagram, or to be offered muffins like she was a two-year-old who needed a cookie. *And* she didn't need her friends showing her the door. She knew exactly where it was.

She knew how to do her job. She was *doing* her job right this minute, wasn't she? Mac cut the first mat for the photos she hadn't had the heart or the energy to mount the night before. In a few hours, she'd have a completed custom package and a very satisfied client. Because she knew what the hell she was doing without explaining every damn step of the process to her business partners.

Did she need to know why Emmaline selected eucalyptus over asparagus fern as filler in an arrangement?

No, she did not.

Did she need to know Laurel's secret ingredient for buttercream frosting?

Right back with the no.

Did she need to discuss Parker's latest entry in her CrackBerry?

Dear God, no.

So why the hell did anyone care what filter she planned to use or which camera bodies she'd decided to strap on?

They did theirs, she did hers, and everybody was happy.

She pulled her weight. She put in the time, the effort, the hours the same as the rest. She . . .

She cut the damn mat wrong.

Disgusted, Mac tossed the ruined board across the room. She grabbed another, checked and rechecked her measurements. But when she lifted her mat knife, her hand shook.

With considerable care, she set it down, then took two steps back.

Yes, she knew when she'd acted the bitch, she thought. And she knew when she had to get a grip on herself. As in right now. She knew, too, she admitted with a sigh, when she owed two of the people she loved most in the world an apology.

Even if they had been snotty—and they damn well had—she'd been snotty first.

She checked the time and sighed. She couldn't do it now. Couldn't get this weight off, not when Parker was currently escorting clients through the house.

*We're full service. We can tailor every detail to reflect your needs, and your vision of the day. Here's our crazy bitch of a photographer who'll be documenting that day for you in pictures.*

Wouldn't that be perfect?

She stepped into the powder room to splash cold water on her face. They were her friends, she reminded herself. They had to forgive her. That was the rule.

Steadier, she went back into her studio.

She let her machine take her calls and gave her current task all her concentration. When she'd finished she decided the client would never know the package had been created by a bitch in the throes of a massive attack of self-pity. Once everything was loaded in her car, Mac drove to the main house.

True, they had to forgive her, but first she had to ask. That was another rule.

Out of habit, she went in the back. When she stepped into the kitchen, she saw Laurel working at the prep counter. With a hand steady and precise as a surgeon's, she monogrammed heart-shaped chocolate.

Knowing better than to interrupt, Mac held her silence.

"I can hear you breathing," Laurel said after a moment. "Go away."

"I just came in to eat some crow. I'll be quick."

"Make that very. I've got another five hundred of these to finish."

"I'm sorry. I'm sorry for acting that way, for saying those things. Things I didn't mean in the first place. I'm sorry for walking out on the meeting."

"Okay." Laurel laid down her brush and turned. "Now, the question would be why."

Mac started to speak, found her throat snapped shut. The sudden barrier had her eyes filling. She could only shake her head as tears spilled over.

"Okay, okay." Laurel crossed over, folded Mac into a hug. "It's going to be all right. Come on. Sit down."

"You have five hundred chocolate hearts to monogram."

"It's probably more like four hundred and ninety-five at this point."

"Oh, God, Laurel, I'm so stupid!"

"Yeah, you are."

Quickly, efficiently, Laurel had Mac sitting at the counter with a box of tissues and a small plate of as yet unadorned chocolate hearts.

"I can't take your candy."

"It tastes a lot better than crow, and I've got plenty."

Sniffling, Mac took one. "You make the best."

"Godiva should tremble in its boots. What happened, honey? Was it your mother? Light went on," she added when Mac didn't speak. "Right after you did the outraged stalk."

"Why can't I suck it up, Laurel?"

"Because she knows every button to push when it comes to you. And no matter how much you suck up, she's got more."

It was, Mac had to admit, the heart of the target. "It's never going to change."

"She's never going to change."

"Meaning that's on me." Mac took another bite of chocolate. "I know it. I do. I said no. I said no, and I meant no, and I would've kept saying it even if Del hadn't taken the phone and hung up on her."

In the act of getting down a glass, Laurel glanced back. "Del was there?"

"Yeah, he came by to tease me about Carter—which is a whole other area of what the hell am I doing—and she called from Florida wanting another couple thousand so she could stay another week and finish her recovery."

"I'll give Del credit for hanging up on her, but he should've come back here to tell us."

"I asked him not to."

"So what?" Laurel demanded. "If he had any sense, he'd

have done what you needed not what you asked. Then you wouldn't have wallowed all night and woken up the bitch."

She set a glass of ice water beside the chocolate. "Drink that. You're probably dehydrated. How many times did she call after Del left you alone?"

"It's not his fault. Twice. I didn't answer." Mac heaved a sigh. "I'm really sorry I took it out on you."

"What are friends for?"

"Let's hope Parker sees it that way. Can I take these up, to sort of sweeten the deal?"

Laurel chose two white chocolate hearts from her supply. "She's no match for the white chocolate, and you might need the edge. Me, you just pissed off. Easy to get over it. You hurt her feelings."

"Oh, God."

"I figure it's better you know that going in. She's pissed, too, but it's the hurt feelings you'll need to get down to."

"Okay. Thanks."

Knowing Parker, and she did, Mac went directly to the conference room. The *incident* had occurred there, so Parker-logic dictated its follow-up would take place in the same venue.

As she'd expected, Parker sat at the table working with her Crack—her BlackBerry. The fire had calmed to a cozy simmer, and the coffee had been replaced with the bottle of water Parker was rarely without. Her laptop sat open and beside it rested a tidy stack of files and printouts.

Parker was never anything but *prepared*.

As Mac came in, Parker set the BlackBerry aside. Her face was cool and blank. Her business-to-attend-to face, Mac knew.

"Don't say anything. Please. I come bearing chocolate and every possible variety of apology. You can have as many of them as you want—the chocolate and the apologies. My behavior was ass-hatty in the extreme. Everything I said was from the box of stupid I brought in with me. Since I can't take it back, you have to forgive me. You don't have a choice."

She set the plate down. "There's white chocolate."

"So I see." Silently, Parker studied her friend's face. Even if she hadn't known Mac nearly all of her life, she'd have seen the signs of a recent crying jag.

"You're just going to come in here and say you're sorry after I did all this work so we could fight it out and I could make you crawl?"

"Yes."

Considering, Parker picked up a white chocolate heart. "I assume you've already been through this with Laurel."

"Yes. Hence the chocolate. I blubbered all over her. I got most of it out, but if you don't eat that so I know we're okay, I'm going to start up again. It's like a symbol. Men shake hands after they beat each other up. We eat chocolate."

With her eyes on Mac, Parker bit into the heart.

"Thanks, Parker." Mac dropped into a chair. "I feel like such an idiot."

"That helps. Let's just clear the air. If you've got a problem with how I'm managing Vows, we have to be able to discuss it, one-on-one or as a group."

"I don't. Parks, how could I? How could any of us? Sure the repetition gets old sometimes, but we all know the reason for it. Just like we all know that you hammering out and handling a zillion details frees the rest of us up to focus on our specific parts of the whole. I can do what I do—and the same for Em and Laurel—because you think about everything else. Including thinking about everything the rest of us do so we can all kick wedding ass."

"I didn't bring it up so you could stroke my ego." Parker took another bite of chocolate. "But do go on."

And we're back, Mac thought with a laugh. "It's a fact. You're anal, obsessive, and a little bit scary with the memory you have for minutiae. And it's a fact that's a big part of the reason we kick that ass. I don't want to do what you do, Parks. None of us do. And because I opened the box of stupid and put my ass hat on, I hit you where I knew it would hurt most."

Mac glanced at the files. "You put reports together, didn't you? Documentation, cost analyses and other really mean stuff."

"I was prepared to squash you like a bug."

Mac nodded, chose a dark chocolate heart. "Eating candy's better."

"It really is."

"So . . . how did the tour go?"

"They brought their mothers, and an aunt. And a toddler."

"A toddler?"

"The aunt's granddaughter. She was cute—and really, really fast on her feet. They toured Felfoot Manor yesterday, and the Swan Resort last week."

"Hitting the big ones. How'd we measure up?"

"They want a Saturday in April of next year. An entire Saturday."

"We got it? On a tour and a pitch? A double booking?"

"No booty dance yet." Parker lifted her water bottle and sipped. "MOB—the one with the gorgeous Prada bag on her arm with the checkbook inside it—wants to meet with all of us. Full consult before commitment. She's got ideas."

"Oh-oh."

"No, she's got *ideas*, the sort that would make this a major event. The kind of event that generates serious attention. Father of the bride is Wyatt Seaman, of Seaman Furniture."

"The 'We make your house your home' Seaman Furniture?"

"The same, and his wife has deemed us potentially worthy. Not capital *W* worthy, yet. But we're going to give her the presentation to end all presentations."

Challenge lit Parker's face, fired in her eyes. "After which, she'll be taking her checkbook out of that gorgeous Prada bag and giving us a deposit that'll have our hearts singing hallelujahs."

"Then we dance."

"Then we dance."

"When's the presentation?"

"A week from today. You'll need new packages. We want it very fresh. They took a look at Emma's space, and she did a quick pitch. Since you were wearing the ass hat, I steered them clear of the studio."

"Very wise."

"But we had your samples here, so we could give her the feel. Next Monday, we'll want to highlight every shot you've had in a magazine. And . . . you know exactly what to do."

"And I'll do it."

Parker pushed over a file. "Here's a rundown of who we'll be dealing with. I did some Googling. And here's bullet points and the latest schedules for the three upcomings."

"I'll cram."

"Do that." Parker passed Mac a bottle of water. "Now tell me what happened."

"Just Lindaitis, again. Fever's broke, and I'm fine."

"She couldn't have wanted money. You just . . ." Parker trailed off as she read Mac's expression. *"Already?"*

"I said no—repeatedly. Then Del hung up on her."

"That's my brother." The pride came through. "I'm glad he was there when she called. Still, Del could probably do more than hang up on her. Something legal. It may be time for that, Mac."

Mac brooded into the fire. "Could you do that, if it was your mother?"

"I don't know. But I think I probably could. I'm meaner than you."

"I'm pretty mean."

"I'm mean, Laurel's hard-assed, Emma's a pushover. And you fall between Laurel and Em. We run the gamut," Parker said, closing her hand over Mac's. "It's why we work so well as a team. Why did you tell Del not to tell me?"

"How do you know I told him not to tell you?"

"Because otherwise he would have."

Mac blew out a breath. "I didn't want to suck you guys into the Linda vortex. Then I sulked and brooded, woke up Bitch Queen, and ended up sucking you in anyway."

"Next time avoid the middle part and remember we're always willing to get sucked in."

"Got it. Now before I go back to earning a living and being a productive member of the team, I have a question. Would you sleep with Carter Maguire?"

"Well, he hasn't asked me. Will he be buying me dinner first?"

"I'm serious."

"So am I. He can't expect me to hop into bed with him without even springing for a meal. But if we were talking about you," she said, gesturing with the water, "I'd have to ask if you find him attractive, sexually."

"You can't just sleep with every guy you find sexually attractive. Even if dinner's included."

"True, we'd never get anything else done. Obviously you like him, and you're thinking about him, spending time with him—and considering having sex with him."

"I've had sex before."

Parker gave up and ate the other white chocolate heart. "I've heard that."

"I don't know why I'm so hung up on this one issue when it comes to Carter. I should deal with it. I should just have sex with him, get it done, and move on."

"You're a romantic fool, Mackensie. Stars always blinding your eyes."

"It's what I get for being in the wedding business."

IT WASN'T OUT OF HER WAY, EXACTLY, TO DRIVE BY THE ACADemy en route to the next client. In any case she had a little time to kill before her appointment. In any *any* case, she hadn't returned Carter's call, which was rude, so what was the harm in doing a quick drop by?

He'd be in class, she supposed. She'd take a quick peek—check *that* out, then leave him a note at the front office. She'd think of something amusing and breezy, thereby putting the ball they kept batting around back in his court.

Had it been this quiet in the corridors back in the days she'd gone here? Had the air been this echoey, shooting her footsteps off like gunfire?

The stairs she climbed were the same she'd climbed a dozen years before. A lifetime before. So long before she couldn't quite picture herself as she'd been, only a vague image, like a print that had been softened to a blur.

It seemed she walked with a ghost of herself, one full of potential and possibility.

One who was fearless.

Where had that girl gone?

Mac walked to the classroom door, peeked in the porthole window. The pensive mood vanished.

He wore the tweed jacket again, with a shirt, tie, and V-necked sweater under it. Thank God he wasn't wearing his glasses or she'd have been a gooey puddle of lust on the floor.

He leaned back against his desk, a half smile on his face and his attention centered on a student who—if the expression on her face and her gestures were any indication—spoke passionately.

She watched him nod, speak, then shift his attention—all of it—to another student.

He's in love, she realized. In love with the moment, and all the moments that made up what happened in that room. He was so completely there. Did they know it? she wondered. Did those kids understand they had all of him?

Did they know, could they know—the young and fearless—what a miraculous thing it was to have all of anyone?

She jolted when the bell rang, pressed a hand to her heart when it thumped in surprise. Chairs scraped, bodies sprang into motion. Mac barely skipped out of the way before the door slammed open.

"Read act three for tomorrow, and be prepared to discuss. That goes for you, too, Grant."

"Aw, come on, Dr. Maguire."

She stayed out of the way of the stampede, but managed to angle herself to see three students stop at his desk. He didn't rush them away, then—God help her—he put his glasses on to check a paper one of them handed him.

Mackensie, she thought as her hormones twanged, you are toast.

"You made some good points today, Marcie. Let's see if we can expand on them tomorrow when we discuss the third act. I'll be . . ."

Mac watched him glance over as she moved into the doorway. Watched him blink, then take off his glasses to bring her into focus. "I'll be interested in your take."

"Thanks, Dr. Maguire. See you tomorrow."

As the classroom emptied, as the corridors filled with noise, Carter set his glasses down. "Mackensie."

"I was in the neighborhood, and it occurred to me I didn't return your call," she said, walking to his desk.

"This is better."

"Certainly more interesting for me. You're all professorial looking."

He glanced down as she gave the knot of his tie a little wiggle. "Oh. Monday morning faculty meeting."

"You, too? Hope yours went better than mine."

"Sorry?"

"Nothing. Water over the bridge."

"Under, generally. Well, barring flood."

"Right. I enjoyed seeing you in your natural habitat."

"Would you like to go for coffee? That was the last class of the day. We could—"

"Hey, Carter, I was going to grab a . . ." A short man with horn-rims and a fat shoulder-bag briefcase wandered in. He stopped, gave Mac a baffled look. "Oh, sorry. Didn't mean to interrupt."

"Um, Mackensie Elliot, one of my colleagues, Bob Tarkinson."

"Nice to meet you," Mac said as Bob's eyes went wide behind the lenses. "Do you teach English?"

"English? No, no, I'm in the Math Department."

"I liked math. Geometry especially. I like figuring the angles."

"Mackensie's a photographer," Carter explained, then remembered Bob already knew that. And maybe just a little too much more.

"Right. Photography, angles. Good. Soooo, you and Carter are—"

"Talking about having coffee," Carter said quickly. "I'll see you tomorrow, Bob."

"Well, I could . . . Oh, right, right." With only the first half ton of bricks landing on him, Bob clued in. "Tomorrow. Nice meeting you, Mackensie."

"Bye, Bob." Mac turned back to Carter.

Bob took the opportunity to shoot Carter a wide grin and two enthusiastic thumbs-up on his way out.

"So, ah, coffee."

"I'd like that, but I'm on my way to a client. When I'm done I have to go home and do my homework. I'm cramming for a test."

"Oh. What?"

"Big job, major client. Super-duper presentation required. We've got a week to put something together that clinches it. But if you're done for the day, maybe you could walk me out to my car."

"Of course."

She waited while he got his coat. "I almost wish I had some books for you to carry. It would circle around to the nostalgia I get when I come in here. Although I don't recall ever having a guy carry my books."

"You never asked me."

"Oh, if we knew then what we know now. You looked good in there, Dr. Maguire. And I don't mean in your professor suit. Teaching looks good on you."

"Oh. Well. Really I was just leading a discussion. Letting them do the work. That was more along the lines of conducting."

"Carter, say thank you."

"Thank you."

They stepped outside, down the entrance steps to turn for the walk to visitors' parking. "Never too cold to hang out when you're a teenager," Mac observed.

Kids milled the lawn, sat on the stone steps, loitered in the parking lot.

"I had my first serious kiss right over there." She gestured toward the side of the building. "John C. Prowder laid one on me right after a pep rally. I had to round up Parker and Emma between fifth and sixth periods and recount the entire event in the girls' room."

"I saw you kiss him one afternoon, standing on the steps. My heart shattered."

"If we knew then. I'll just have to make it up to you." She turned into him, wound her arms around his neck, pressed her lips to his. She kissed him in the shadow of the academy, with all the ghosts stirring in its corridors, all the old dreams shifting.

"Way to go, Dr. Maguire," someone called out, with a few hoots of approval following.

Her face full of fun, she gave his tie another tug. "Now I've ruined your reputation."

"Or seriously improved it." He cleared his throat when they reached her car. "I suppose you'll be busy all week with the proposal."

"Busy, yes," she agreed when he opened the door for her. "But I'll come up for air."

"I could make you dinner, maybe Thursday, if you could come up for air then."

"You cook?"

"I'm not entirely sure. It's a gamble."

"I'm not opposed to gambling, especially when food's involved. Seven? Your place?"

"That would be perfect. I'll give you my address."

"I can find you." She got in the car. "I'll bring dessert," she said, then went breathless with laughter at his expression. "That wasn't a metaphor for sex, Carter. I meant actual dessert. I'll hit Laurel up for something."

"Understood. But I do love a good metaphor."

She drove away shaking her head. Points for the professor. Now she had until Thursday to decide if she'd settle for a piece of Laurel's Italian cream cake, or add on the metaphor.

# CHAPTER TEN

CARTER CHECKED THE TABLE IN WHAT PASSED FOR HIS DINING room for a third time. He rarely used it as he tended to eat at the kitchen counter or at his desk. In fact, this was the first time he'd put a tablecloth on it.

He thought it hit the right tone between fussy and casual. White plates on a dark blue cloth, and the yellow stripes in the napkins brightened it up. He thought. He hoped.

He took the trio of votive candles off the table, they were too studied. Then put them back. It looked unfinished without them.

After dragging his hand through his hair, ordering himself to stop obsessing, he turned his back on the table to go into the kitchen.

That was the real worry, after all.

The menu passed muster. He'd run it by the Domestic Science instructor, adjusted for her suggestions, and added her recipe for the honey vinaigrette for the field greens salad.

She'd given him a list—what had to be done and when, how much time to allow, and helpful suggestions for presentation.

Presentation, apparently, was as important as the food. Which was why he now owned a tablecloth and cheerful napkins.

He'd had his dry run. Everything was set, everything looked . . . fine.

He had nearly an hour to drive himself completely crazy. In that spirit, he eased open the drawer holding Bob's list. The list Carter promised himself he would ignore.

"Music. Damn it. I'd have thought of it," he muttered to Bob's spirit. "I would have."

He hurried to the living room to tear through his collection of CDs. The cat uncurled itself from a chair and walked its lopsided way to join him.

"It's not going to be Barry White, I don't care what Bob says about slam dunk. No offense to Mr. White, but we're not going to be a cliché. Right?"

Triad bumped his head against Carter's knee.

While he obsessed over CDs, the door opened and Sherry burst in.

"Hi! Can I leave this here?"

"Yes. Why? What is it?"

"It's a Valentine's Day present for Nick. It's a doctor's bag. I had it engraved, and just picked it up. He's going to love it! I know if I take it home I won't be able to resist giving it to him now. So you have to hide it from him. And me." She sniffed the air. "Are you cooking?"

"Yes. God, is something burning?"

He was up like a shot.

"No, it smells good. Really good." Since he was already running toward the kitchen she went after him. "And not like the grilled cheese sandwiches you usually . . . Wow, Carter, look! You have food in the oven. Oh, the table's so pretty. Candles and wineglasses and . . . You're cooking dinner for a woman." She drilled her finger into his belly the way she had ever since they'd been kids. "Mackensie Elliot!"

"Stop." He could literally feel the fresh nerves sprouting in his stomach. "I'm begging you. I'm already a lunatic."

"I think it's wonderful. So sweet. Nick made me dinner when we were first going out. It was a disaster." She sighed, dreamily. "I just loved it."

"You loved the disaster?"

"He tried so hard. Too hard, because he's actually good in the kitchen. He screwed everything up because he was so worried about impressing me. Oh." She sighed again, with a hand to her heart. "It was so sweet."

"I didn't know I was supposed to screw everything up. Why isn't there a handbook for this sort of thing?"

"No, no, you're not supposed to. It just worked for him because, well, because." She pulled open the fridge to snoop. "You're marinating chicken. Carter, you're *marinating.* It must be love."

"Go away. Get out."

"Is that what you're wearing?"

His voice took on a dangerous bite. "I'm a man on the edge, Sherry."

"Just change your shirt. Put on the blue one, the one Mom got you. It looks really good on you."

"If I promise to change my shirt, will you leave?"

"Yes."

"Before you leave will you pick out some music? Because I can't take any more pressure."

"Got you covered. Go up, change your shirt." Grabbing his hand, she pulled him out of the kitchen. "I'll pick the mood music and be gone before you get down. Take the present up, will you? Don't tell me where you hide it in case I try to sneak over and get it before V-Day."

"Done."

"Carter?" she added when he started upstairs. "Light the candles about ten minutes before she's due."

"Okay."

"And have a nice time."

"Thanks. Be sure to go away now."

He changed the shirt, dawdling over it to give Sherry enough time to finish up and go. He hid the gift-wrapped box in his office closet.

When he went down, he found a sticky note on his CD player. *Hit Play five minutes before she's due. XXOO*

"It's like a war campaign," Carter muttered, and crumpled up the note as he walked into the kitchen to start the chicken.

He minced, he crushed, he sautéed, measured, timed—and only burned himself once. When the chicken simmered fragrantly, he lit the candles on the table, the ones on the skinny sideboard. He set out the little bowls of olives and cashews. When he hit the five-minute mark, he switched on the stereo. Alanis Morissette.

Nice choice.

At seven, she knocked.

"I'm Parker-trained," Mac told him when he opened the door. "So I'm obsessively prompt. I hope that's okay."

"It's absolutely okay. Let me take your coat. Oh, and . . ."

"Dessert," she said, handing him the glossy Vows bakery box. "Italian cream cake, a personal favorite. Nice house, Carter. Very you," she added wandering into the living room with its wall of books. "Oh, you have a cat."

"I didn't think to ask if you were allergic."

"I'm not. Hello, pal." She started to crouch, then stopped, angling her head. "You have a cat with three legs."

"Triad. He was hit by a car."

"Oh, poor baby!" Instantly, she was down on the floor, stroking and scratching the delighted cat. "It had to be awful for both of you. Thank God you were home."

"No, actually I was driving home from school. They—the car in front of me hit him, and just kept going. I don't understand how anybody could do that. When I pulled over, I thought he'd be dead, but he was lying there, in shock, I guess. The vet couldn't save the leg, but he does okay."

Mac continued to stroke the cat down his length as she stared at Carter. "I bet he does."

"Would you like a glass of wine?"

"I would." She gave Triad a last scratch, then rose. "And I'd like to check out what smells so good."

"I thought that was you."

"Besides me," she said while he hung her coat tidily in his hall closet.

"Come on back." He took her hand to lead her to the kitchen. "You look nice. I should've said that right away."

"Only if you're working off bullet points."

As he felt himself wince, he was grateful her attention focused on the kitchen instead of his face.

"It really does smell good. What've you got going here, Carter?" She walked to the stove to sniff at the skillet.

"Well, let's see. There's a field green salad, rosemary chicken in a white wine reduction, roasted red-skinned potatoes, and asparagus."

Her jaw dropped. "You're kidding me."

"You don't like asparagus? I can—"

"No, that's not what I mean. You made all this?" She lifted the lid of the skillet.

"You're not really supposed to take that off until . . . Well, okay." He shrugged as she sniffed again, then replaced the lid.

"This is trouble, Carter."

"Why? Is it the chicken?"

"You *went* to all this trouble. I figured you'd toss a couple steaks under the broiler, or dump a jar of Ragú in a pot and call it your own. But this is cooking. Considerable time and trouble. I'm wowed. And look at the pretty table you made."

She wandered into the dining room to walk around it. "You're just a man of levels, aren't you?"

"Why didn't I think of the Ragú?" He picked up the bottle of wine he'd opened. "I got white because of the chicken, but I didn't know what kind you liked. This is supposed to be good."

"Supposed?"

"I don't know a lot about wine. I looked it up."

She took the glass he offered, sampled, watching him all the while. "Your research paid off."

"Mackensie." He leaned down, brushed his lips lightly over hers. "There. I feel better."

"Than?"

"Probably every man within a twenty-mile radius because they can't kiss you in the kitchen."

"You're dazzling me, Carter."

"That was part of the plan. I just have to put a few things together. You should sit down."

"I could help."

"I have a system—I hope. If you're in the system, it changes the, well, system. I did a draft Tuesday night, so I think I have it down."

"A draft?"

He asked himself why he'd babbled that one out as he adjusted the heat under the skillet. "Ah, well, I wasn't sure how it might turn out, and there's the whole getting everything done at the right time. So, I did a draft of the meal."

"You had a dinner rehearsal?"

"More or less. Bob's wife had her book club meeting, so he came by. I cooked. We ate. So, you should be safe. How did your studying go?"

"My studying?"

"For the presentation on Monday."

"I am so ready. Which is good because starting tomorrow we're booked back-to-back. We had a roundup this morning, two rehearsals this afternoon. The second of which was full of pitfalls as the maid of honor and best man, who are recent exes since his affair with his business partner came to light, aren't speaking."

"How do you handle that?"

"Like you would a handful of sweating dynamite. The wedding biz isn't for sissies."

"I can see that."

"And come Monday, we'll be putting on a show for Mrs. Seaman Furniture that'll make her stand up and cheer."

"Seaman Furniture's the potential client?"

"Technically Seaman Furniture's daughter, but the mother's paying the freight."

"We'll be eating on a table and sitting in chairs I bought there. I'd say that counts as good luck."

They sat in the lucky chairs at the lucky table with candlelight and wine and music. She was, Mac realized, being thoroughly and unashamedly romanced.

And she liked it.

"You know, Carter, this is so good I've stopped feeling guilty about the fact you've eaten this exact meal twice this week."

"You could consider it upscale leftovers. Leftovers are a major part of the menu around here, usually." He glanced over at the cat who sat beside his chair, staring up with unblinking yellow eyes.

"I guess your pal's waiting for his."

"He's not used to seeing me eat at the table. It's usually counter food, so I guess he's confused. Do you want me to put him out?"

"No. I like cats. In fact, I've been married to cats several times."

"I didn't know that. I take it things didn't work out."

"That depends on your point of view. I have very fond memories of those marriages, however fleeting. When we were kids, the four of us used to play Wedding Day. A lot." She laughed over her wine. "I guess we began as we meant to go on, even if we didn't know it. We had costumes and props, each took different roles. We married each other, pets, Del if Parker could blackmail him into it."

"The photograph in your studio. With the butterfly."

"The camera was a gift from my father that was probably age inappropriate. My grandmother used the gift to bitch about him. Again. A hot summer day when I wanted to go swimming instead of playing the game. Parker placating my mood by declaring me official wedding photographer instead of the MOH."

"Sorry?"

"MOH. Maid of honor. I didn't want to put on the dress, so Parker deemed me official wedding photographer."

"Portentous."

"I guess so. Add the serendipitous flight of that butterfly and elements coalesced into a personal epiphany. I realized not only that I could preserve a memory, a moment, an image, but I wanted to."

She ate another bite of chicken. "I bet you made Sherry play Classroom."

"Maybe. Now and then. She could be bribed with stickers."

"Who can't? I don't know if it makes us lucky or boring that we knew what we wanted to do when we were still so young."

"Actually, I thought I'd impart my wisdom in the halls of the rarified air of Yale while I wrote the great American novel."

"Really? Why haven't you? Or didn't you?"

"I realized I like playing Classroom."

Yes, she thought, he did. She'd seen that for herself. "Did you write the book?"

"Oh, I've got a novel in progress like any self-respecting English professor. And it'll likely be in progress for the considerable part of ever."

"What's it about?"

"It's about two hundred pages so far."

"No." She poked his shoulder. "What's the story?"

"It's about great love, loss, sacrifice, betrayal, and courage. You know, the usual. I've been thinking it needs a three-legged cat, possibly a potted palm."

"Who's the main character?"

"You can't possibly want to hear about this."

"I wouldn't ask if I didn't. Who is he, what does he do?"

"The protagonist is—and you'll be shocked to hear this—a teacher." He smiled as he topped off her wine. He could always drive her home. "He's betrayed, by a woman, of course."

"Of course."

"His life is shattered, along with his career, his soul. Damaged, he has to start again, has to find the courage to fix what's broken in him. To learn to trust again, to love again. It really needs the potted palm."

"Why did she betray him?"

"Because he loved her but didn't see her. She ruined him so he would. I think."

"So the three-legged cat could be a metaphor for his wounded soul, and his determination to live with the scars."

"That's good. You'd get an A."

"Now, for the important question." She leaned toward him. "Is there sex, violence, and adult language?"

"There is."

"Sold. You need to finish it. Isn't there that publish-or-perish business in your world?"

"It doesn't have to be a book. I've got articles, papers, short stories published to keep that wolf from the door."

"Short stories? Seriously?"

"Just small press. The sort of thing that doesn't move out of academia. You should publish your photography. An art book."

"I play around with it sometimes. I guess it's like the novel. When it's not what you actually do, it gets shuffled back. Parker's idea is for us to put together coffee table books. Wedding flowers, wedding cakes, wedding photography. The best of our best kind of thing."

"It's a good idea."

"Parker rarely has any other kind. It's a matter of carving out the time to put it all together in a way that could be pitched to whoever publishes that kind of thing. Meanwhile we've got three events in three days, with our Saturday job a very thorny rose. You should come."

"To . . . to someone's wedding. I couldn't. I wasn't invited."

"You'll be staff," Mac decided on the spot. "God knows we could use another man with a brain in his head for this one. I use a photographer's assistant for some events—when I have to. For the most part I like not to. But I was going to for this one due to holding all that sweating dynamite. The couple of people I usually tap aren't available. You're hired."

"I don't know anything about photography."

"I do. You'll hand me what I ask for, do stand-ins, and play pack mule when necessary. Do you have a dark suit? That isn't tweed?"

"I—yes, but—"

She gave him a slow, seductive smile. "There'll be cake."

"Oh, in that case."

"Jack's pinch-hitting as escort for the MOH, due to CBBM."

"Excuse me?"

"Maid of Honor, Cheating Bastard Best Man. And Del's helping out because Jack's making him. You know them. You know us." She ate another bite of potato. "And you'll have cake."

None of which turned the tide for him. But the idea of being with her instead of just thinking about being with her did. "All right, if you're sure."

"Three o'clock Saturday. It'll be great."

"And I'll see you in your natural habitat this time."

"Yes, you will. Speaking of cake, I don't have room for dessert yet. I'll work off this amazing meal by doing the dishes."

"No, I don't want you to bother."

"You made dinner, twice. I'll clean it up while you have brandy and a cigar."

"I don't have any brandy, or a cigar."

She patted his shoulder as she rose. "An English professor ought to recognize a metaphor when he hears one. Have another glass of wine since you're not driving."

She poured it for him herself before stacking the plates. "I actually like doing dishes. It's the only household chore I do like."

She ran hot water in the sink, found the detergent in the under-cabinet and squirted it in for the pots and pans. He liked sitting there, watching her perform the basic, mundane chore. And he hoped she wasn't saying anything important because his mind was blurring.

It had nothing to do with the wine, and everything to do with imagining her being there, tidying up the kitchen next week, next month. Next year. Imagining her sitting with him to share a meal.

Too far, too fast, he knew it. But couldn't help it. Infatuation had taken a quick, hard turn on him so he was rushing down the steep road into love.

"Where are your dish towels?"

"What? Sorry?"

"Dish towels," she said and opened a drawer at random.

"No, not there. Other side. I'll get it."

He rose, opened the right drawer and got out a towel. "Why don't I dry the pans?" he began. When he turned, his stomach sank down to his toes.

She stood, head cocked, reading Bob's list.

"You have a list."

"No. Yes. It's not mine. I mean to say, yes, it's mine, but I didn't write it. Make it. God."

With a thoughtful expression, she continued to read. "It's very detailed."

"Bob. You met him. He's a lunatic—I don't believe I mentioned that in the introduction."

"It has bullet points."

"I know. I know. I'm sorry. He's determined to play Cyrano. I mean—"

She looked over the paper, into his eyes. "I get the Cyrano reference, Carter."

"Oh, of course. He got married a couple years ago, has a baby on the way."

"Congratulations to Bob."

"He has this idea stuck in his head about helping me, ah, in this area. He brought it over Tuesday. I told you he came over for dinner Tuesday, didn't I?"

"For the draft."

"Yes, exactly, for the draft. I should've thrown it away after he left, but I tossed it in the drawer. Just . . ."

"In case? Like backup."

"Yes. Yes, and I have no defense. I don't blame you for being upset."

She shifted her attention from the list to Carter. "Do I look upset?"

"Ah . . . No, now that you mention it. You don't. Which is good. Which is a relief. Would you say you're . . . amused?"

"That would be one level," she replied. "According to the List of Bob, we're pretty much on schedule."

"I didn't go by that. My word on it." He held up a hand, palm out as if taking an oath. "I have my own list. A mental list. Which I suddenly realize is equally stupid."

"How are we doing on yours?"

She smiled, but he couldn't quite read the meaning. There

could be subtext. "Good. We're fine. Maybe we could have cake."

She shook a finger at him when he reached for the printout. "I see here we were merely to stack the dishes—unless, I note here in parentheses, you sense I'd feel that was sloppy. Bob believes—and we know Bob—that doing the dishes together, if necessary, could be employed as foreplay."

Mortified, he closed his eyes. "Just kill me. Please."

"Sorry, but that's not on the list. The list says that after making sure you have the appropriate music on—Barry White is his considered suggestion—you dance with me. Kitchen or living room each are acceptable as venues. Slow dance, which proceeds into the seduction portion of the evening. He advises that you should be able to tell, at this point, whether I'm amenable to taking it upstairs."

"Would you like me to kill him? I've thought about it."

"I don't hear Barry White."

"I don't think I have any . . . Even if I did, I wouldn't have—Did I mention Bob's a lunatic?"

"Here's something I wonder, Carter." Watching him, she set the list on the counter. "I wonder why you're not dancing with me." She stepped to him, lifted her arms to wind them around his neck.

"Oh."

"We wouldn't want to disappoint Bob."

"He is an awfully good friend." He rested his cheek on the top of her head as everything settled back into place. "I'm not a very good dancer. My feet are too big. If I step on yours just—"

She tipped her face up to his. "Shut up and kiss me, Carter."

"I can do that."

Swaying, he covered her mouth with his. Soft and quiet, to fit the moment. He circled, cautiously, while her fingers slid into his hair, and her sigh filled his mind with mists.

She turned her head to skim her lips along his jaw. "Carter?"

"Mmm?"

"If you're paying attention you should sense that I'm amenable." She kept her eyes open and on his when their lips met again. "Why don't you take me upstairs?"

She stepped back, held out her hand. "If you want me."

He took her hand, brought it to his lips. "It feels as if I've spent my whole life wanting you."

He drew her out of the kitchen. At the base of the steps he had to stop, had to kiss her again. He wondered if the wine, the needs, the images swam in her head as they did his.

He led her up, his pulse thumping with every step.

"I thought about flowers and candles, in case," he said as they walked into his bedroom. "Then I thought—and I'm not normally superstitious—that would be the way to jinx it. And I wanted you here, too much, to risk it. I wanted you in my bed."

"Having you say that to me is better than candles and flowers, believe me." Like the house, she thought, the room suited him. Simple lines, quiet colors, ordered space.

"I wanted to be here. I wanted to be in your bed."

Walking toward it, she saw the photograph of the cardinal on the facing wall. Touched, she turned to look at him, and wanted him more than she'd imagined she could.

She reached up to undo the buttons of her shirt.

"Don't. Please. I want to undress you. If you don't mind."

She dropped her hands. "No. I don't mind."

He reached over, turned the lamp beside the bed on low. "And I want to see you while I do."

He stroked a hand down her cheek, ran both hands down her body as he drew her against him.

Then his mouth took hers.

# CHAPTER ELEVEN

HAD SHE BEEN KISSED LIKE THIS BEFORE? SO THAT THE MEETING of lips, of tongues vibrated through her entire body? Had she ever been seduced so completely, as much by words as by that single, dazzling kiss?

How had the tables turned on her? She'd thought to seduce *him*, to tease him upstairs, and into bed. She'd thought to keep it light and easy, as the evening had been—for the simple and basic purpose of releasing the ball of lust that gathered inside her when she was around him.

It should be simple, basic.

But it wasn't.

He touched his lips to her cheeks, her brow, then those quiet blue eyes watched her as he unbuttoned her shirt. He barely touched her, and still the breath backed up in her lungs. He barely touched her, and still the control passed from her hands to his.

Standing in that quiet light, his eyes on hers, she didn't care.

With the shirt open, he trailed a fingertip along her collarbone, then down over the swell of her breasts. Just a whisper, barely a graze. But it set her skin to humming.

"Are you cold?" he asked when she trembled.

"No."

And he smiled. "Then . . ." Slowly he nudged the shirt off her shoulders, let it slide to the floor. "Pretty," he murmured, skimming his thumbs over the lacy cups of her bra.

Her breath released, hitched, caught again. "Carter, you make me weak."

"I love your eyes. Magic seas." He traced his fingers down her torso, up again, down, leaving little paths of shimmering sensation in their wake. "I've wanted to watch them when I touch you. Like this."

Patient, steady, he explored. Swells and dips, curves and angles. While her body quivered in response, he flipped open the button at her waistband, eased down the zipper.

Once again he ran his hands down the sides of her body, inch by inch. Her pants slipped down her hips, her legs.

"Here." He took her hand. "Step out."

She obeyed like a woman in a trance, and felt her pulse scramble as he ran his gaze down her as he had his hands. Slowly. His lips curved. "I like your boots."

She looked down, saw the thin-heeled ankle boots she now wore with only her bra and panties. "It's a look."

Smiling, he hooked his fingertip in the waist of the panties. She managed an "Oh, God" as he tugged to bring her body to his again.

This time, his mouth met hers like a fever, a flashpoint of heat. Even as she melted in it, he turned her, drawing her back against him. His teeth nibbled at the curve of her throat as her head fell back.

He let his free hand roam, over smooth skin, angles and

curves, while he undid his own shirt. When they were skin to skin, her arm hooked around his neck, and her body began to move sinuously against him.

Not too fast, he reminded himself. He wanted to savor every moment, every touch, every breath. He had Mackensie in his arms.

Her heart hammered under his hand, and he thought that alone a miracle. She was with him, she felt him, wanted him. And tonight, at last, the dreams of the boy, the longings of the man would both be eclipsed by the reality of the woman.

He toed off his shoes, indulging himself with the taste and texture of the back of her neck. He caught the strap of her bra in his teeth, nudging it aside so he could free the lovely, lovely curve of her shoulders.

She arched back against him, shuddered.

Pleasure, he thought, so much here to give and to take. He wanted to please her, to saturate her with sensation, and to watch her rise and ride. While his own needs hammered inside him, he unhooked her bra as his hand all but floated over the narrow vee of her panties. He traced her inner thigh, teased, just barely teased a fingertip under the lace.

"Carter." Her hand pressed down on his, urging him on. But he retreated, and once again turned her to face him.

"Sorry. I'm not finished."

Those magic eyes were full of storms now, the porcelain skin flushed with passion. For him, he thought. Another miracle. She reached for him, and her mouth took his in a desperate kiss.

Wait, he thought, as his blood pounded. Wait, there's more.

He nudged her onto the bed, eased down with her.

"The boots," she began.

"I like them." And he lowered his head to take her breast.

Her body shuddered and shone, it ached and sighed. Her mind simply emptied of all else but him and what he brought to her.

Slow hands, skilled lips swamped her body with sensations, layer after gossamer layer until they lay so thick she couldn't find air through them.

"I can't. I can't."

"It's all right." He slid a finger down, gliding over her, into her.

The veils ripped away with a blast of release.

As her body quaked through it, he ran his lips down and used his mouth to destroy her. She rose and fell. So fast, so fast. So much, as sensation poured over sensation until all blurred into shadow and light and mad movement. A sea of feeling swamped her, with a storm rolling through, pitching her toward desperation until she broke over the next swell.

When at last he slipped inside her, they moaned together.

She bowed up, nearly snapping his thinning leash of control. He stared into her eyes, gone dark, gone glassy while he drove them both mad with long, slow strokes. He felt her climb, watched her climb, steeped himself in her.

"Mackensie," he said, just "Mackensie," as he let himself fall into her eyes, into her body, and drown.

SHE FELT DRUNK AND DRUGGED. EVEN HER TOES FELT HEAVY, Mac thought. Air went in and out of her lungs again, and that was good. She was pretty sure she'd stopped breathing a number of times while Carter had . . .

Annihilated her, she decided.

Even now, when he was splayed over her like a man suffering from blunt force trauma, and their heartbeats knocked together like a couple of manic tennis balls, he touched his lips gently to the side of her throat.

"Okay?" he asked.

*Okay?* Was he out of his mind? You were okay when you slipped on the ice and caught yourself before you fell and broke an ankle. You were okay when you sank into a nice warm bath after a tough day.

You were not *okay* when your system had been turned inside out and right side in again.

"Yeah." What could she say? "You?"

"Mmm. Mackensie's naked in bed with me. I'm really okay."

"I'm still wearing my boots."

"Yeah. Even better. Sorry, I must be heavy." He rolled off to tuck her up against him.

"Carter, you're nearly as skinny as I am. You're not heavy."

"I know—about the skinny part, I mean. Nothing seems to change it. Cor—somebody talked me into working with a personal trainer once. But who has time for all that? Buff isn't in my DNA."

"You have an appealingly lanky body. Don't let anyone tell you different. Besides, you use it like a stevedore."

"I've been saving up." He grinned, studied her face. "You're so beautiful."

"I'm not. I know this because I'm a professional. I have an interesting face, and can play up its assets. I have a skinny build as well, which is reasonably toned from—well, thinking about working out as much as actually. It's like a coat hanger. Clothes look pretty good on it. Otherwise it's just wire."

"You're beautiful. Don't let anyone tell you different . . . ly. Sorry, can't help it. It's differently."

She laughed and snuggled in. "Yes, Professor. And aren't we both being post-coital—ly—complimentary."

"You've always been beautiful. You have red hair and sea-witch eyes. And dimples." He thought if he had another fifteen minutes or so, he could lap her up like ice cream and watch her rise again.

She tipped up her head to smile at him. His eyes were closed, his face utterly relaxed. He'd look like that when he slept, she thought. If she woke up before him, she'd see him just like this.

Lazily, she traced her finger under his jaw. "And what's this intriguing little scar here?"

"From a fencing mishap."

"You fence—like Captain Jack Sparrow?"

"If only. I bet you have a thing for Johnny Depp."

"I am alive. I am female. Next question."

"He transcends generations. It's interesting. Grown women find him compelling, sexually, as do the teenage girls I teach."

"I saw him first. But I'm actually finding another man compelling, sexually, at the moment. Fencing mishap," she prompted as he grinned.

"Oh, that. I was running from a couple of kids who wanted to entertain themselves by pounding on me. I had to climb a fence, and in my usually nimble and graceful way, which unfortunately doesn't resemble pirates or the actors who play them, managed to slip. Gashed myself on the wire."

"Ouch. When was this?"

"Just last week."

Chuckling, she rolled on top of him. "Brutal little midgets."

"They were. I was ten, but they were brutal little midgets."

"Did you get away?"

"That time."

He tugged the short ends of her hair to bring her down for a kiss. Sighing with it, she nestled her head in the curve of his shoulder.

It felt so good, she thought, cuddled up like this. Skin to skin, with the twin beats of hearts quieting, and every square inch of her body perfectly tended by a man she found ridiculously appealing on every possible level.

She could stay like this, exactly like this, for hours. Days. All sleepy and warm and tangled up with the delicious Carter Maguire. And in the morning, they could . . .

Her eyes flashed open. What was she thinking? What was she *doing*? The morning? Hours and days? The quick kick of panic had her jolting upright.

"What's wrong?"

"What? Oh, nothing. Nothing. What could be wrong?"

He sat up with her, all kinds of rumpled and sexy until her heart and hormones threatened rampage.

She had to get out. Get out now. Back to reality. Back to sanity before she did something stupid like fall in love.

"I just . . . God, look at the time! I have to go."

"Go? But—"

"This was great. Everything . . . really great." Jesus, Jesus, she was wearing nothing but boots. "I really lost track of the time. It's late."

Obviously baffled, he looked at the clock. "Not especially. Don't—"

"School night," she said, trying desperately to keep it light while she hunted for her underwear and panic galloped inside her like wild mustangs.

Where was her bra, where was her bra?

The hell with the bra.

"I've got a million things left to do. I have to get started really early tomorrow."

"I'll set the alarm. I'm up by six anyway. Stay, Mackensie."

"I really wish I could. Really." How many times could she say *really* in five minutes? She was about to beat the standing record. "But, well, duty calls. No, don't get up."

Please, please don't get up, she thought as he got out of bed.

"Stay," he said, and touched her cheek as she dragged on her shirt. "I want to sleep with you."

"We checked that one off the list, big-time." She added a big, bright smile.

"Sleep."

"Oh, that's really sweet, Carter. I'd love that—another time.

Three events, presentation. Busy, busy." She gave him a quick kiss. "Gotta run. Thanks for everything. I'll call you."

And fled.

OH, SHE WAS A TERRIBLE PERSON. A CRAZY PERSON, MAC thought as she drove home. She was probably going to hell, too. She deserved it. But she'd done the right thing, the only thing. For herself, and for Carter.

Absolutely for Carter, she told herself.

Going to hell? Ridiculous. She should get a medal—they should erect a damn statue for her, for doing the right thing.

She'd done the right thing, and that was all there was to it. Now everything would be fine. Everything would be okay.

Perfect, in fact.

She saw the lights on in the main house and thought: Thank God. Parker and Laurel would agree with her. They'd support her actions. That's what she needed, she decided as she squealed to a stop in front of the house. Just a little affirmation from friends so her stomach would untwist.

She rushed into the house, tore up the stairs, shouting for Parker.

"We're all up here." Parker came into the hallway. "God, what's the matter? Was there an accident?"

"No, it was all on purpose. Or maybe not. There was a list."

"Okay. You're obviously not hurt. We're in my parlor, just going over some last details since we were all up."

"Emma, too?"

"Yeah."

"Good, good, that's even better."

She dashed by Parker and into the parlor where Laurel and Emma sat with cookies, tea, and files.

"Hey. We figured you for the walk of shame in the morning."

Laurel tossed down a pencil. "We were thinking of setting up a video camera."

"How was dinner?" Emma asked her.

"I left. I just left." Eyes a little wild, Mac dragged off her coat. "You'd have done the same."

"That good, huh?" Laurel picked up the plate. "So, have a cookie."

"No, no. He had a rehearsal on Tuesday. Can you imagine that? And tonight this wonderful meal with candles and wine reductions."

"Wine reductions." With a little hum, Parker took a seat. "Thank God you got out alive. We should call the police."

"Okay, wait, you're not seeing the whole picture." Trying to steady herself, Mac took a few careful breaths. It didn't seem to help. "He went to so much trouble, and it was, well, lovely. And fun. Bob made a list."

"Who the hell is Bob?" Laurel demanded.

"Doesn't matter, but Carter was so embarrassed. It's so cute. The tips of his ears blush."

"Aww," Emma said.

"I *know*. What can you do? I'm all stirred up. I had to go to bed with him."

"I know when a guy's ears blush, I start tearing my clothes off." Since Mac didn't appear to want one, Laurel helped herself to another cookie. "So you had sex."

"We didn't have sex. We had the most amazing, world-bending, melt-your-brain-cells sex in the history of the planet."

"Now it's getting interesting." Crossing her legs, Parker settled in. "Would that be tender, soft-focus, angels-weeping sex, or jungle-drums, swinging-from-the-chandelier sex?"

"It was . . . No one's ever made me feel that way, or felt that way about me." She sat on the arm of Parker's chair, staring into the fire as she tried to find the words. "It's like knowing you're the focus, the only thing he sees. Nothing else but you. And it's tender and hot, it's terrifying and amazing. There's this person who doesn't see anyone but you. When he touches you, there's no one but him."

There were three humming sighs, and a moment of reverent silence.

"Why aren't you snuggled up in bed with him?" Emma asked.

"Well, Jesus!" Mac's head snapped around so she could stare at Emma. "Haven't you been listening?"

"Listening, imagining, envying."

"I had to leave. I wanted to stay so I had to leave." Gesturing wildly, Mac pushed back to her feet. "I wanted to stay curled up there with him. I wanted to *live* in that damn bed, so I had to get out."

"You panicked," Parker prompted.

"Of course I panicked. Who wouldn't? He's all sweet and sleepy and satisfied, and with that little fencing scar."

"Carter fences?" Emma demanded.

"No, never mind. Off topic. I'm telling you, it was like I was hypnotized, or drugged. I had to get out of there. And . . . oh, God, I acted like a guy." As it replayed in her head, Mac covered her face with her hands. "The kind of guy who rolls off you after, gets up and says, 'That was great, babe. Got an early day tomorrow. I'll call you.'"

"Oh, Mac, you didn't."

Mac jabbed a finger at Emma. "I *had* to. It was self-preservation. And Carter-preservation, too. I was supposed to *de*-lust after we had sex. Not go all gooey. It's too much for me, that's all. He's too much for me. He's sweet and funny, he's smart and genuinely kind. He's sexy and he's got those glasses. He's got the ear-blush thing happening. He loves teaching. I watched him lead a class, and it's . . . It gets everything stuck right here." She rubbed a hand between her breasts. "All this feeling and need clogged up."

She picked up the nearest cup of tea and downed it. "He pays attention. He listens, and he *thinks* about what I say. He makes me think."

"Clearly he must be stopped." Laurel shook her head. "Mac, honey? You're in love with him."

"That's just not an option. Why do you think I left the way I did? It's like being sucked into quicksand. Only really soft, warm, pretty quicksand. I'm not built for this. I don't believe in this kind of thing. It doesn't last. It's the moment, or the series of moments until it goes south, or it erodes, fades. God, how many weddings have we done that are the second time around? Hell, we've done a few where for at least one of the parties involved, it was the third go. Who needs that? I know what it's like when it falls apart. It can't be worth it."

"Let's whittle this down," Laurel suggested. "You're afraid to be in love with a man you've just described as the Mary Poppins of men. Practically perfect in every way," she explained when she got blank looks all around. "You panicked and ran after you had what appears to be sex as a religious experience, with this guy you respect and admire and have the hots for, because your mother's a big ho."

"Laurel!"

"No." Mac shook her head at Emma. "That's fair. My mother is a big ho. But she doesn't see herself that way, which is part of my point. She sees herself as eternally searching for love. It's more about money, status, and security, but she'd swear it was all about love. My father strolled away from her, for which I can't blame him, and from me—for which I damn well can—because it just wasn't worth the effort."

"They're not you, Mac," Parker said quietly.

"No. I know. And maybe it's cynical to believe they're not so much the exception as par. But that's how it strikes me. And I like the way my life's working out, I'm comfortable with the direction of it."

A little calmer, she sat again. "Carter's a serious man. Under it all he's a serious man with a traditional mind-set. He's got a major crush on me, that's what it is. A crush that's been flickering in there for *years*. If I let this escalate, he's going to start thinking about hiring us for the event. He's going to end up asking Parker where he should buy the ring. I can't do that to him. I was right to leave. It's better to cut it off now than to—"

"Risk being happy with someone who's crazy about you?" Emma suggested.

"Okay, when you put it like that . . . yes. From where I'm standing that's about right."

"Can I have him?"

Mac glared at Laurel. "That's not funny."

"No, it's really not."

"You know what it's about right from where you're standing?" Emma studied Mac with her big, dark eyes. "Because nobody's ever been crazy about you before, not in a way that matters, that's solid and real. And you've never felt it for anyone. That's what I know because I'm in the same place—I'd say all of us are. The difference is, with me, I'm always hoping it'll happen."

"Hence, the serial dating."

"Knock it off, Laurel," Parker told her.

"You're right. I'm sorry. I'm being a smart-ass because I'm jealous. Right down to my bones. Nobody's ever seen only me."

"But he's seeing me through the filter of an old crush."

"I don't know him as well as you, in the biblical sense or otherwise, but he strikes me as smarter than that."

"Love and smart don't go hand in hand."

"No, they don't." Laurel lifted her arms toward Mac. "And here stands living proof of that. You're stupid in love with the guy."

"You're not helping. Parker?"

"You're afraid you'll crush him. That because he is, at the core, a nice guy, you'll walk all over him on the way to breaking his heart and leaving him shattered."

"That's a little dramatic, but yes. Basically."

"And you're determined to believe yourself incapable of sustaining a mature, committed relationship. Of not only seeing yourself as not worthy of love, but doubting you've got the backbone and balls to work at maintaining it."

"That's a little harsh, but—"

"I think you underestimate him, and yourself." She rose, walked to the mantel for a photograph framed in silver. "Remember this?"

Mac took the photo of Parker's parents, caught in a laughing hug, their eyes full of delight, of life, of each other. "Of course, I do."

"You took that, just a few months before they died. Of all the pictures I have of them, this is my favorite. You know why?"

It made Mac's eyes sting to look at it. It always did.

"You can see how much they loved each other," Parker continued. "How happy they made each other. They fought, and they argued, and I imagine there were times they each got thoroughly sick of each other. But they loved anyway. For half their lives, they made it work. You captured that in this picture. Because you saw that. You recognized that."

"They were exceptional."

"So are you. I don't waste my time on friends who aren't exceptional." She took the photo, set it back on the mantel. "Take a breath, Mac. Love's scary, and sometimes it's transient.

But it's worth the risks and the nerves. It's even worth the pain."

SHE WASN'T SURE. HOW COULD ANYONE BE SURE? BUT MAC knew the single thing she could do, had to do, was put it all aside for work. Her partners, her business, their clients depended on her doing her part. So she had to settle down and respect priorities.

A good night's sleep, she determined, an early start. And a complete and professional focus on her clients' needs.

She spent a restless night arguing with herself, then thought—bitterly—that she hadn't lost a night's sleep over a man since she'd been sixteen.

She brewed coffee so strong it all but stood up and howled. But it smothered fatigue under a buzz of caffeine. Because the box of Pop-Tarts seemed to indicate she had the appetite and the emotional stability of a six-year-old, she prepared what she thought of as an adult breakfast of yogurt, fresh fruit, and a muffin she'd stolen from Laurel's stash.

Dishes dutifully washed, she reviewed her notes for the day's event, checked her equipment. A relatively small event, she mused as she selected what she needed. A single attendant serving as MOH. The client wanted intimacy, simplicity.

The bride, she knew, had opted to wear a tea length gown in blue, and a very smart hat in lieu of veil and headdress. She'd carry a trio of white gardenias, the stems wrapped in satin ribbon.

Good choices all, in Mac's opinion, as this was a second marriage for both.

See?

"Don't get started on that," she muttered.

FOB would walk the bride down the aisle, but they were

skipping the "giving away" part. Because, hello, already did that once before.

With her gear, the event schedule, and her notes in place, she checked the time. Plenty of it left to do a quick check on e-mail.

She toggled over, scanned and homed in instantly on an unopened from *MaguireC101.* She pushed away from her work station, paced around the studio.

She stalked back to the kitchen for another cup of brutal coffee.

She didn't have to open the e-mail now. In fact she shouldn't open it now. She had to keep her mind on work, didn't she? That was the responsible thing to do. The grown-up thing, like yogurt and fresh fruit.

It couldn't be urgent. He'd have called if there was anything important to tell her. Or to discuss.

Like, why did you blow me off after I got you off?

Not that he'd ever say anything so crude.

The thing to do was go upstairs, shower, dress, then go over to the main house for the review and setup. She didn't have time for any personal . . .

"Oh, please, who are you kidding?"

She walked back to the computer, clicked open Carter's e-mail.

*Mackensie,*

*I got this address from your business card. I hope it's all right to contact you this way. Knowing how busy you'd be today, I didn't want to call and disturb you.*

*I wanted to say, first, how much I enjoyed last night. Every minute with you. My house seems brighter and fuller today because you've been in it.*

"Oh God. Carter."

*Also, on behalf of Bob, his wife, and their unborn child, I should express my relief that I won't be required to murder him. He owes you.*

*Lastly, in case you've been looking for it, I found one of your gloves on the floor of the closet. It must've fallen out when you got your coat. Initially, I thought to ask if I might keep it as a token, such as women in medieval times bestowed on their knights. However, on reflection that seemed a little scary, even for me.*

*I'll get it back to you.*

*Meanwhile, I hope your event today goes well. Best wishes to the happy couple.*

*Carter*

"Oh, man."

Thinking Carter Maguire was like a drug in her system, she read the entire e-mail through again. Then, feeling foolish, she printed it out. She took it upstairs, tucked it away in a drawer.

# CHAPTER TWELVE

BY SATURDAY MORNING, MAC FELT SHE'D FOUND HER BALANCE again. Friday's event had not only gone off without a hitch, but Vows had secured another client. The parents of the groom booked the works for their wedding anniversary the following November.

Added to it, she'd dealt with a cheerful, nerve-free bride who'd photographed like a dream.

The buzz had kept Mac working with the prints until well past midnight.

And she'd only read Carter's e-mail twice more before dropping dreamlessly into bed.

It was all about focus, she reminded herself. About knowing yourself, your strengths, your weaknesses, your goals. She just had to turn it down a few notches with Carter, make it clear where both of them stood—and the boundaries outside that. Then they could enjoy each other and nobody would get hurt.

She'd overreacted; she could see that now. A little space, a little distance, a little time, and everything balanced out. The manic weekend and today's minefield of a wedding were the perfect antidote. In a few days, maybe a week, they'd have a talk. He was a reasonable man. He'd understand it didn't make sense for this *thing* between them to get out of hand.

He'd been hurt before in a relationship, she was certain, by the mysterious Corrine. Surely he didn't want to repeat the experience. In fact, she decided he probably felt exactly the way she did, and he'd be grateful she'd brought it all to the surface.

Friendly, rational, straightforward. Those were the tickets.

And, on the professional front, she and her partners would be vigilant so today's minefield would be negotiated. With no casualties.

She chose a pearl gray suit with just a hint of sheen, and low heels dressy enough to suit the formal affair and comfortable enough to respect the feet she'd be standing on most of the day.

As she packed her tools for the day, she ran through her notes and impressions. The dress was a showpiece, she remembered, glittery strapless bodice and miles and miles of skirt. She remembered, too, the bride was a workout fanatic, and beautifully toned. And the couple, college sweethearts, were of a traditional bent.

Armed and armored, she arrived at the main house.

"Red alert!"

Mac gaped at Emma as her friend flew down the stairs. "Already?"

"You didn't answer your phone, or your cell."

"I just left the studio. I haven't turned on the cell yet. What?"

"MOH got wind that the CBBM plans to bring SBP to the reception. His idea of a compromise, which he did not bother to discuss with either the B or G. The B and G, upon hearing this, are threatening violence against the CBBM, which he'd richly deserve if rumor is fact. Parker's trying to put out the fire."

"Shit. Just shit." Mac had no problem deciphering the code.

Cheating Bastard Best Man, Slut Business Partner. And if the fire could be put out, Parker would do it.

But it didn't bode well.

"What's our assignment?"

"All the subs have to be alerted. Parker got a picture of the SBP from a newspaper article. She's making copies. Every sub needs one. If the SBP is spotted, she has to be stopped, barred, tackled to the ground." As if to prove she meant it, Emma slapped her fist into her palm. "Whatever works until Parker can deal with her."

"I hope it's the tackling. It would make a good shot for our outtakes file."

"Laurel's contacting Jack so he can get here early and charm the MOH out of whatever plans of retaliation she might be brewing. I've got to round up my people, brief them, then start hauling over the flowers. Laurel's still got to fuss with the cake. It's her Silk and Lace."

"I know. It's in my notes."

"That one weighs a ton, and gets the beadwork and tiara topper at reception. She'll need a couple of people to help her carry it in, which means less on patrol for the SBP.

"Pre-event briefing's ditched," Emma added once she'd sucked in a breath, "so we're minute by minute. You need to help set up in the Grand Hall. Somebody'll beep you when we have a sighting on the bride."

"Okay, I'm on it. Let me set up what I can in the Bride's Suite first. Stay strong."

"I am ready to kick me some ass."

Upstairs, Mac set up in the Bride's Suite, then strapped on her bag with one camera body and a selection of lenses. She'd add on the second body once the bride arrived. Before going down, she headed up, to check on Parker's progress.

She found her friend opening a fresh roll of Tums.

"It's bad?"

"No, no, it's currently under control. But I am pissed. I just got off the phone, at the bride's request, with the CBBM. Who started off informing me that nobody, including his brother, was going to tell him who he could date. Fucking selfish child."

"You said fucking. You are pissed."

"Then, then, he reams *me* for interfering in his personal life. I have to take it, because better me than either the B or G, but I want to hurt him. I managed to calm him down, appeal to the minute sliver of decency and consideration in him. He'll do his duty, and intends to leave immediately following his—sure to be heartfelt—toast to the new couple."

"Do you believe him?"

Parker's eyes slitted. "Not for a minute. He's primed to make a scene. He'll need to be watched like a hawk because he's going to parade that woman into the reception if we don't stop him. Which we won't be telling anyone in the wedding party."

Huffing out a breath, Parker handed Mac a stack of printouts with the photograph of an attractive blonde. Under the photo it read:

ROXANNE POULSEN

NO ADMITTANCE

"Pass these out to subs. I'll give Laurel a stack for the caterers."

"I'm on it. You know, Parks, sometimes I just love this job beyond reason. Oddly, this is one of those times."

"Right there with you." Parker crunched down on the antacid. "We probably need therapy."

MAC DELIVERED WHAT SHE THOUGHT OF AS THE MUG SHOTS TO Emma and her crew, then passed the rest to the small hive working in the Grand Hall. She helped dress the tables—lavender cloths over blue—adding setups while Emma delivered centerpieces. In widemouthed glass bowls white star lilies floated above a bed of shimmering stones.

"Nice," Mac decreed.

Emma set little vases holding the heads of fat roses and white candles around the center bowl, scattered petals and tiny red hearts, blue stars. "Nicer. Only nineteen more to go. Let's get the favors set up," she called out. "Let's finish the . . . Oh, hello, Carter."

"What?" Mac spun around.

In a dark gray suit, Carter stood in the middle of the pre-event chaos. He looked, Mac thought, like an island of baffled calm in a sea of motion and color.

"Ah, somebody named Lois said I should just come back. There's a lot going on. I'm probably in the way."

"No, you're not," Emma assured him. "But be careful, anybody capable of moving, lifting, or hauling may be put to use at any time."

"I'm happy to help if I can."

"The magic words. We have a hundred and ninety-eight favors, bubble bottles, and candy nets to set out. Mac, why don't you get our newest slave started? I have to check on the Parlor."

"Sure." How could she have forgotten she'd asked him to come? And what was she supposed to do about this flutter in her belly that just wouldn't stop when she looked at him? "Nice suit."

"It's not tweed. You look beautiful and professional at the same time."

"Staff needs to blend. I'm sorry, I'm distracted. We're on red alert. The CBBM may try to sneak the SBP into the reception."

"Wait a minute." His brow furrowed. "I think I've got it. The best man and the business partner. The one he had an affair with. He's going to bring her? That's rude."

"At bare minimum. Violence may ensue. So." She opened

her camera bag, took out the mug shot. "This is the target. See it, report it. Okay?"

"All right." He studied the photo, smiled a little, then folded it to tuck it in his inside pocket. "Is there something else? It feels . . . You seem upset."

"Upset? No. No. Just distracted. I said that already, didn't I? The bride's upset, and that could affect the portraits, so . . ."

Deal with it, she ordered herself. Just explain the way things are.

"Actually, Carter." She took his arm to lead him to a relatively quiet corner in a room that buzzed like a hive of hornets. "I did want to say I've been thinking we should discuss— Damn it." She tipped up the walkie hooked to her pocket. "That's my cue. Bride's on the property. I have to go. I guess you'd better come with me."

"Do you need me to get any of your equipment?" he asked as he adjusted to her hurried pace.

"No, I have what I need for this. Everything else is up in the Bride's Suite. She'll go there. But I need shots of her arrival. Just make sure you stay out of the shot."

"Hey, Carter," Parker said as she fell into quick step with them. She flicked the faintest questioning glance at Mac, then switched to full-business mode. "The bride's a solid nine point five on the emotion scale. Constant reassurance, support."

"Got it."

"We need her upstairs, busy, and focused on herself ASAP. I've already put champagne up there, but let's not let her pull a Karen."

"Won't be a problem."

"MOH and two of the BAs are with her, as well as the MOB. MOB is a rock. If I'm not available and the bride or the MOH go on, get the MOB."

"Is Jack on his way?"

"ETA fifteen minutes. I'll send him straight up."

"Who's Karen?" Carter wondered.

"Former bride, arrived half drunk, finished the job before we got a handle on it. Puked over the terrace shortly before the ceremony."

"Oh."

Outside, the women stepped to the side of the porch where the rails were already dressed in Italian lights and tulle.

"Where are your coats?" Carter asked. "I'll get them for you?"

"No need." Mac took out her camera. "Adrenaline works."

As the white limo cruised down the drive, Emma and Laurel came out.

"I wanted all four of us," Parker explained. "Solid wall of 'we're here to make your day perfect.' Happy faces, everyone."

The limo stopped. Mac framed a shot of the bride turning to exit the open door with what could only be called a brave and wobbling smile on her face.

Mac thought: Crap.

"Your day," Parker said from the steps. "Guaranteed."

The smile brightened, just enough. Mac got the shot before the bride's face crumbled. She sprang out of the car, arms outstretched, and said, "Oh, Parker!"

"Hey!" Mac's voice stopped the bride in midstride. "Are you going to let that bitch give you puffy red eyes in your portraits? Give me one, give me a beaut. One that'll make her cry like a baby when she sees it."

It might've been rage, but the bride's face went radiant. "I'm getting married!"

"Damn right."

"One of both of us." The bride grabbed the hand of her maid of honor, grinned fiercely at her friend. "Together. Solidarity."

"Now we're talking."

She captured the movement, the energy, as garment bags and totes were unloaded, as women milled together. And undoubtedly, she thought, caught the tension as well.

"Parker, what will I do if—"

"Not a thing," Parker assured the bride. "We're completely on top of it. All you have to do is be beautiful, be happy, and we'll handle the rest. Let's go up. There's a bottle of champagne waiting."

Giving Carter the come-ahead signal, Mac skirted around Parker and the bridal party. "We get a glass of champagne in her, and in the MOH. Celebrate their friendship," Mac said as she bounded up the stairs. "It's about the journey, and in this case, that relationship is part of the whole. We'll play on that, so instead of keeping a little distance between them as I initially figured, we document the unity. The bride prep as female bond as much as mating ritual."

"Okay." He turned into the room behind Mac. "It's a lovely space." He scanned lace, flowers, candles, swags of silk. "Ah, very female."

"Well, duh." Mac pulled out the second camera body, strapped it on.

"Should I be in here? It doesn't seem quite . . . proper."

"I may be able to use you. But for now, you're stationed at the door. Nobody gets in without the password."

"What's the password?"

"Make one up."

He took up his station as Parker swept the bride past him. A brunette stopped, gave him a once-over that made his stomach twitch.

"Jack?"

"Ah, no. I'm Carter."

"Oh. Too bad." She gave him a hard, sharp smile. "Stick around, Carter. You may come in handy."

The door closed with a snap. Through the panel he could

hear female voices, then the happy pop of a cork leaving the bottle. The laughter that followed had to be a good sign.

Moments later a small troop of men and women carting totes and cases started toward him.

"Excuse me," he began, and the door swung open behind him.

"It's okay, Carter. They're hair and face." Parker gestured them in. "Let Jack through when he gets here."

The door shut again, and the noise level rose behind it.

He wondered if this was typical, if Mac and the rest of them repeated this pattern several times a week. Emotion, immediacy, red alerts, strange codes, headsets, walkie-talkies. It was like a continuous battle.

Or a long-running Broadway show.

Either way, he decided he'd be exhausted at the end of every day.

Mac opened the door, stuck a glass of champagne in his hand. "Here you go." And closed the door again.

He stared down at the glass, wondered if he was allowed to drink on duty. Amused at himself, he shrugged, took a sip.

He glanced over at the man who turned at the top of the steps and started his way.

"Hey, Carter, how's it going?"

Jack wore a dark suit with subtle chalk stripes. His dark blond hair curled casually around his face. Eyes, smoky gray and friendly, sparked under brows arched in question. "You in the wedding?"

"No. I'm helping out."

"Me, too." He dipped his hands in his pockets, relaxed. Jack Cooke always appeared relaxed to Carter. "So, I've got a date in there. Did you happen to get a look at her? Megan. Meg to her pals."

"Oh, the maid of honor. Yes, she's in there."

"Well?" Jack waited a beat. "Give me a gauge. Parker gave

me the 'she's beautiful' routine, but Parker had an agenda. I'm in either way, but I might as well get an objective opinion."

"Very attractive. Brunette."

"Mood?"

"A little scary, actually. They're doing something with hair in there now."

"Great." Jack blew out a breath. "What we do for friendship and a case of good wine. Well, into the breach." He knocked. "Foreign chromosome," he called out.

Parker opened the door. "Perfect timing," she said and yanked him in.

Carter leaned against the wall beside the door, sipped champagne, and pondered human rituals.

The next time the door opened, Mac pulled him in.

Women sat under protective cloaks while hairdressers plied their trade with implements that always made Carter vaguely uneasy. If hair was straight, here was a strange tool to curl it. If hair was curly, another tool would straighten it.

*Why* was the question.

But he kept it to himself and held a light meter when he was told to, a length of white lace over a window, a lens. He didn't mind, even when Jack deserted the field and he was left the lone male among the female army.

He'd never seen Mac work before, and that alone was both education and pleasure. Confident, intent, he thought, with efficiency and fluidity in her movements. She changed angles, cameras, lenses, circling and winding through the women, speaking rarely to those she photographed.

She let them be, he realized. How they were and who they were.

She tapped her headset. "Groom's heading in. We're on the move."

Solidarity wasn't the theme here, Carter noted, as the best

man didn't arrive with his brother. Mac did her work, in the cold, with her breath wisping vapors.

"Groom's coming up," she said into headset. "CBBM among the missing. Got it." She turned to Carter. "We've set a lookout for the asshole. I'm going to go set for the formal gown portraits. Why don't you find Jack and Del, relax awhile?"

"All right." He looked around the Parlor at the rows of white draped chairs, the floods of flowers, the groupings of candles. "It's quite a transformation. Like magic."

"Yeah, and magic takes sweat. I'll find you."

He didn't doubt that, but wasn't sure where he should go to be found.

He wandered through the flowers and tulle, the tiny sparkling lights and into the Grand Hall. There, with some relief, he found Jack and Del, sitting at the bar.

"Want a beer?" Del called out.

"No. Thanks. I'm just getting out of the way."

"Best place for all of us," Jack agreed. "You hit the nail with Megan." Jack lifted his bottle of Bass. "There are worse ways to spend a Saturday than comforting a pretty brunette. Canape?"

Carter perused the small tray of food. "Maybe."

"Del seduced a sampling out of the caterer."

"There are worse ways to spend a Saturday," Del agreed. "So, Carter, now that we're all here, what's going on with you and my girl?"

"Your—what?"

"You've got your eye on my Macadamia. You got anything else on her?"

"Del's territorial. Have a shrimp ball."

So was he, Carter realized. "When did she become yours—from your point of view?"

"Since she was about two. Throttle back, Carter. The question's brotherly."

"Then you'd better ask her."

"Discreet." Del nodded. "That's a good quality. Hurt her, and I'll mess you up."

"Protectiveness. That's a good quality," Carter returned.

"Then we're square. And also busted," he declared when Emma came in.

"Didn't I tell you this area is off limits?" In her blue suit, her mass of hair pinned back, she clipped around the tables. "Where did you get that food?"

"Del did it." Jack threw his friend into the fire without hesitation.

"I'm not having beer bottles and crumbs in here. Get out, and take that with you. Go outside or up to the family wing. I expect this sort of thing from these two," Emma added. "But I'm surprised at you, Carter."

"I just . . . I didn't have a beer. Or anything."

She only gave him a steely look and pointed to the door.

"We were going to clean it up." Jack skulked out with the others, and turned to watch Emma check the table arrangements.

Carter bumped into him in the doorway. "Sorry."

"No problem." Jack glanced over as Del's walkie beeped.

"I'm hooked up," Del explained. "The asshole just got here. He's alone. I guess that means we don't get to go out and intimidate him, maybe smack him around. Too bad."

IT SEEMED TO GO WELL, CARTER DECIDED. IF HE HADN'T SEEN so much of the behind-the-scenes, he might have believed it just unfolded. The flowers, the music, the radiant bride bathed in candlelight. He stood in the back with Del and Jack watching two people promise to love.

But he couldn't keep his eyes off Mac.

She moved so smoothly, so silently. Not like a shadow, he thought. She was too bright for shadows. Still it seemed she barely stirred the air so all around her attention centered on the two people in front of the crackling fire.

"Got it bad, don't you?" Del murmured.

"Yes, I do."

As the newly married couple turned to start the recession, Mac dashed back, nudged Carter to the left. When they passed by into the foyer, she lowered her camera briefly. "I can use you for the group shots. Just stay behind me."

Guests were escorted through another door. Mac made use of the staircase, the foyer, the now empty parlor.

She worked quickly, Carter observed. She didn't seem to hurry, but she clicked along, posing various groups and couples—and smoothly avoiding any pose that put the feuding maid of honor and best man together.

The minute she was finished, Parker took over.

"Parker's going to line them up for the introductions. We'll go around this way."

"Let me carry the bag for you."

"No, I'm used to it." She led him around, through doorways, through the kitchen bustling with catering, and out into the Grand Hall. "I'll get some shots as they come in. B and G have the sweetheart table there. It's a plated meal, numbered tables. Once everyone's down, it's just a matter of keeping an eye out for an op. How are you holding up?"

"Fine. You're doing all the work."

"We're still on red alert. We need to keep an eye on the CBBM. If he leaves the hall, one of us has to go after him, make sure he's just going to pee or catch a smoke. When we're done in here and move up to the Ballroom for the dancing, that's when it's going to get crazy. Less structured, and harder to keep a bead on him."

SHE WAS RIGHT. HE STUCK WITH HER WHEN HE COULD ONCE the party began in earnest. Guests took advantage of the band and danced, or gathered in groups to chat. Some wandered in, some wandered out. Since he knew what to look for, he noted various staff members by the exits. It was oddly exciting.

"I think we might be clear." Laurel joined them. "I'm bringing the cake out after this next set, and he hasn't made a move. No sign of the target either. The B and G don't look worried about it."

"Couldn't look happier," Mac agreed. "Another ninety and we're clear."

"I'm going to check the dessert table."

"Wait till you get a load of it," Mac told Carter. "The cake. It's amazing."

"Carter? Carter!" A pretty blonde in a red dress dashed over to grab his arms and beam up at him. "I thought that was you. How *are* you?"

"I'm fine. Ah . . ."

"Steph. Stephanie Gorden. Corrine's friend. How quickly they forget." She laughed and tipped up to her toes to kiss his cheek. "I didn't realize you were friends of Naomi and Brent."

"Actually, I'm—"

"Brent's my cousin. What a beautiful wedding. This place is just fabulous. Really, imagine having an actual *ballroom* in your own house. Of course I suppose the Browns lease it out for events so they can maintain it. I'm going to have to find Greg—you remember my husband, Greg, don't you? He'll be so surprised to see you. What's it been? It's been a year at least. We haven't seen you since you and Corrine—"

She broke off, gave him a sympathetic look. "I'm sorry that didn't work out. We thought you were perfect for each other."

"Uh, well. No. This is Mackensie Elliot. The wedding photographer."

"Hello, how are you? You must be exhausted! I've seen you running around, snapping pictures. Naomi must be making it easy for you. She's such a beautiful bride."

"It's been . . . a snap."

"I've gotten some really nice pictures myself. Those digital cameras practically work themselves, don't they?"

"Hardly need me at all. You'll have to excuse me. I have to go pretend to work."

When Carter caught up with her, Mac was taking candids on the dance floor.

"I'm sorry. I don't think she meant to be insulting, but she's an idiot and can't help it."

"No problem." She switched cameras, handed him the other. "Fresh memory card. Remember how to do it?"

"Yes."

"They're decorating the limo. I want to go get a few shots out there before they bring in the cake." She started out with Carter in her wake. "So a year ago—the breakup?"

"The . . . right. More or less. We were together almost that long, and lived together for about eight months. Maybe it was nine. Then she decided she wanted to live with someone else. So she did."

Mac paused. "She hurt you."

"Not as much as she should've been able to, given the situation. Which means we weren't perfect for each other. Far from it."

"If you lived with her you must've been in love with her."

"No. I wanted to be in love with her. It's not the same thing at all. Mackensie," he began as they moved outside.

"Shit, damn, fuck!"

"Excuse me?"

"SBP. Red alert!" she said into her headset. "SBP sighted south side of main entrance. CBBM's with her. Come on, Carter, we've got to head them off until reinforcements get here."

# CHAPTER THIRTEEN

He wasn't sure what he intended to do, and was less sure of what she intended to do. But when Mac cut across the snowy lawn, Carter instinctively picked her up.

"What? What?"

"You're only wearing shoes."

"So are you! Put me down! I can't project a stern and forbidding demeanor when you're carrying me. Down, down, or they'll get by us."

The minute he set her down, she was off. In a kind of lope, Carter thought. A long-legged gazelle leaping through the snow. He wasn't graceful, he knew. But he was fast when he had to be.

He passed her. Carter figured his ungainly slide on the path, thanks to his now ruined and snow-slicked shoes, cut back on the impact of the barrier, but he blocked the forward motion of the furious best man and his current amore.

"I'm sorry. Mr. and Mrs. Lester have expressly ordered that Ms. Poulsen not be admitted to this event."

"She's with me, and we're going in."

Not just furious, Carter noted, but a little bit drunk. "Again, I'm sorry, but we have to respect the wishes of the bride and groom."

Just slightly out of breath, Mac reached them. "You were told, specifically and repeatedly, that your friend here isn't allowed."

"Donny." Roxanne tugged on Donny's sleeve. "You said it was all right."

A combination of anger and embarrassment heated Donny's face. "It's all right because I say it is. It's my brother's wedding, and I can bring whoever I want to bring. Meg's bent, and that's too bad. But she doesn't run my life. Out of my way." He jabbed a finger at Mac and Carter. "You're just the hired help."

"She's not going in," Mac said. Too many trips to the bar, Mac calculated, so his ego, his pride, his resentment all swam in a pool of alcohol.

Where the hell was the backup?

"You just said it yourself, it's your brother's wedding. If she's more important to you than his happiness today, then you can turn around and go with her. This is private property, and she's not welcome at this time."

"Donny." Roxanne tugged at his arm again. "There's no point—"

"I said you're with me." He whirled back to Mac. "Who the hell do you think you are? You don't tell me about my brother. Now move!" Temper ripe in his eyes, he planted a hand on Mac's shoulder and shoved.

Like a flash, Carter stood between them. "Don't touch her again. Now, you're drunk, and you're obviously stupid so I'll factor that in. You need to cool off and calm down, because you really don't want to do this."

"You're right. I want to do this."

He smashed his fist into Carter's face. Carter's head snapped back, but he didn't give ground. Roxanne squealed, Mac cursed. Before she could leap forward, Carter pushed her back behind him.

"She's not going in. You're not going back in. All you've proven is that you're too selfish to think of anyone but yourself. You've embarrassed Ms. Poulsen, and that's a shame. But you're not going to get the opportunity to embarrass your brother and his wife today. Now you can leave on your own, or I can help you with that."

"Why don't we all help him with that?" Del said as he and Jack flanked Carter.

"I don't think there's any need for that." Parker clipped down the path, then muscled her way through. She stood, an ice queen in Armani, and stared down the best man. "Is there, Donny?"

"We've got better things to do. Come on, Roxie. This place is a dump anyway."

"I'll make sure they leave." Del shook his head in disgust. "Go on back in. How's the face, Carter?"

"It's not the first time I've had a fist smash into it." He wiggled his jaw experimentally. "It always hurts though."

"Ice pack." Parker watched the CBBM and SBP's departure with cold eyes. "Emma."

"Come with me, Carter."

"It's all right. Really."

"Ice pack." Parker's tone brooked no nonsense. "I'll signal the all-clear, and let's get back inside. Nobody hears about this."

"Did you see what he did?" Mac murmured.

"He who?" Del asked.

"Carter. He just . . . Every time I think I have him figured out, he shifts on me. It's confusing."

Somebody else had it bad, Del noted as Mac hurried down the path to finish her job.

IT TOOK NEARLY TWO HOURS BEFORE MAC COULD FINISH AND track Carter down in Laurel's kitchen. He sat alone in the breakfast nook, reading. As she came in, he glanced up, took off his glasses. "All clear?"

"More or less. I'm sorry it took so long. Carter, you should've gone home. It's after midnight. I should've gotten word back to you. Oh, your poor face." She winced at the bruise on his jaw.

"It's not so bad. But we decided I should stay here. If I'd come back out, I might've had to explain how I came by this." He touched his fingers gingerly to the bruise. "I'm terrible at lying, so this was simpler. Plus, as promised, there was cake."

She slid in across from him. "What are you reading?"

"Oh, Parker had a copy of a John Irving novel I hadn't read yet. I've been tended, entertained, and fed. Your partners made sure of it. And both Jack and Del each came back for a while. I've been fine."

"You didn't even wobble."

"Sorry?"

"When that stupid bastard belted you. You barely reacted."

"He was half drunk so there wasn't that much behind it. He shouldn't have put his hands on you."

"You never even raised your voice. You shut him down—I could see it happen in his face, even before the troops arrived. And you never touched him or raised your voice."

"Teacher training, I suppose. And a wide and varied experience with bullies. Did the newlyweds get off all right?"

"Yes. They don't know what happened. They'll find out, I imagine, but they had their day—and that was the point. You were a big part of that."

"Well, it was an experience. All it cost me was a sore jaw and a pair of shoes."

"And you're still here."

"I was waiting for you."

She stared at him, then just gave in to the shimmer inside her heart. "I guess you'd better come home with me, Carter."

He smiled. "I guess I'd better."

MISTAKES HAPPENED, RIGHT? MAC REMINDED HERSELF AS SHE opened the door of her studio. If this was a mistake, she'd fix it. Later. When she could think more clearly. But at the moment, it was after midnight, and there was Carter in his three-piece suit and ruined shoes.

"I'm not as tidy as you."

"*Tidy*'s such a fussy word, don't you think?" He gave her an easy smile. "The sort that makes you think of your great-aunt Margaret and her tea cozies."

"I don't have a great-aunt Margaret."

"If you did, she'd probably be a tidy sort with a tea cozy. I prefer the word *organized*."

Mac tossed her coat over the arm of her couch. Unlike Carter, she didn't have a coat closet. "I'm organized then, when it comes to my work, my business."

"I could see that today. It seemed you knew exactly what to do, where to be, what to look for before it was there." He laid his coat over hers. "That's creative instinct married to organization."

"And I use them both for the work. Outside of that, I'm a messy woman."

"Everyone's messy, Mackensie. Some people just shove the disorder into a closet or a drawer—at least when company's coming—but it's still there."

"And some people have more drawers and closets than others.

But since it's been a long day, let's step back from the edge of the philosophical cliff, and just say I'm telling you this as my bedroom isn't at its best."

"Are you looking for a grade?"

"As long as there's a very generous curve. Come on up, Dr. Maguire."

"This used to be the pool house," he said as she led the way.

"The Browns did a lot of entertaining, so they redesigned it as a kind of spare guest house. Then when we opened the business, we redesigned again for the studio. But up here, it's all personal space."

A master suite sprawled over the second story, layed out, Carter saw, to accommodate a sitting area where he imagined she might read, nap, watch TV.

Color dominated, with the muted, misty gold of the walls serving as a backdrop for strong blues, greens, reds. Like a jewel box, he thought, with everything cluttered in, tangled, and gleaming. Clothes draped over the arms of chairs. Bright sweaters, soft shirts. Throws and pillows tumbled over the bed, the couch, like bold stones and rivers.

A wildly ornate mirror hung over a painted chest that served as a dresser. The top held jumbled and fascinating pieces of her. Earrings, magazines, bottles, and pots. Photographs served as art, portraits of those close to her. Posed and candid, pensive and joyful. With them scattered over the walls, she'd never be alone here.

"There's so much of you here."

"I try to shovel some of it out every couple of weeks."

"No, I mean it reflects. Downstairs reflects your professional side, and this, the personal."

"Which circles back to my point about being a messy woman." She opened a drawer, pushed in a discarded sweater. "With a lot of drawers."

"So much color and energy in here." It was how he saw her. Color and energy. "How do you sleep?"

"With the lights off."

She stepped to him, laid her finger on his bruised jaw. "Still hurt?"

"Actually . . . yes." Now, alone in her jewel-box room, he did what he'd wanted to do all day. He kissed her. "There you are," he murmured when her lips warmed to his. "Right there."

She let herself lean into him, let herself sigh as she rested her head on his shoulder. Yes, she'd think later. When he wasn't holding her, when her mind wasn't fuzzed with fatigue and longing.

"Let's get you into bed." He kissed the top of her head. "Where are your pajamas?"

It took her a minute to process the question, then she leaned back to stare at him. "My *pajamas*?"

"You're so tired." He stroked a finger down her cheek. "Look how pale you are."

"Yeah, and me with my ruddy complexion. Carter, I'm confused here. I thought you were staying."

"I am. You've been on your feet all day, and waged war for part of it. You're tired."

He unbuttoned her suit jacket in the practical way that reminded her of the way he'd once buttoned her coat.

"What do you sleep in? Oh, maybe you don't." His eyes came back to hers. "Sleep in anything, I mean."

"I . . ." She shook her head, but none of the thoughts inside it fell into place. "You don't want to go to bed with me?"

"I am going to bed with you. To sleep with you because you need sleep."

"But—"

He kissed her, soft and slow. "I can wait. Now, pajamas? I hope you say yes because otherwise one of us isn't going to get much sleep."

"You're a strange and confusing man, Carter." She turned, opened a drawer to pull out flannel pants and a faded T-shirt. "This is what I call pajamas."

"Good."

"I don't have any in stock that'll fit you."

"I don't actually wear . . . Oh. Ha."

He'd change his mind when they were in bed, she thought as they undressed. But he got points for good intentions. Yes, she was tired, her feet ached and her brain felt dull, but that didn't mean she couldn't find energy for sex.

Especially really good sex.

When he slid into bed beside her, she curled into him, trailing her hand over his chest, lifting her mouth to his. She would arouse and seduce, and then—

"Did I tell you about the lecture I'm planning on methodological and theoretical analysis of the novel, with a specific emphasis on home—both literal and metaphorical—as motif?"

"Ah . . . uh-uh."

He smiled in the dark, gently, rhythmically rubbing her back. "It's for seniors in my advanced classes." In a quiet monotone designed to bore the dead, he began to explain his approach. And he explained it as tediously as possible. He gauged it would take five minutes, tops, to put her to sleep.

She went out in two.

Satisfied, he rested his cheek on top of her head, closed his eyes, and let himself drift off with her.

SHE AWOKE WITH THE WINTER SUN SLANTED OVER HER FACE. She awoke warm.

Sometime in the night he'd spooned her, and now she lay snugged back up against him, wrapped close. Cozy, she thought, rested and relaxed.

He'd wanted her to sleep, so she'd slept. Wasn't it funny how he managed to get his way without demanding, without pushing?

Sneaky.

Well, he wasn't the only one.

His arm wrapped around her waist. She took his hand, pressed it to her breast. *Touch me.* She pressed back against him, sliding her leg between his. *Feel me.*

She smiled when his hand moved under hers, when it cupped her. And when his lips pressed to the nape of her neck. *Taste me.*

She turned so they were face-to-face, so her eyes could look into the soft blue of his. "I feel . . . refreshed," she murmured. And still looking into his eyes, let her hand glide down his chest, over his belly until she found him. "Hey, you, too."

"It often happens that certain parts of me wake up before others."

"Is that so?" She shifted, rolling him to his back to straddle him. "I think I'm going to have to take advantage of that."

"If you must." In a lazy morning caress, he ran his hands down her torso, over her hips. "You even look beautiful when you wake up."

"I have bed hair, but the part of you that wakes up first doesn't notice." She crossed her arms, gripped the hem of her T-shirt. Pulled it up, off, tossed it. "Now that part doesn't know if I even have hair."

"It's like the sun set on fire."

"You've got a way, Carter." She leaned down, caught his bottom lip with her teeth. "Now, I'm going to have my way."

"Okay." As she leaned back, he sat up. "But do you mind if I . . ." And closed his mouth on her breast.

"No." Her belly clutched in response. "I don't mind a bit. God, you're good at this."

"Anything worth doing."

Soft, firm, warm, smooth. She was all those things. He could feast on her, break his fast with the enticing, alluring flavors of her. She pressed him closer, urging him to take more while her hips rocked him into heat.

She bowed over him, back from him, wriggling out of the flannel pants. She pushed him back, rose up, her body lean and pale, dappled by the thin light that eked through the windows. She took him in, surrounding.

She arched, trapped in her own web of pleasure, and moved to the beat of her own blood. Slow and thick and deep, gliding silk to silk, steel to velvet. In that morning hush, there were only sighs, a tremble of breath, a whispered name.

And the beat quickened while pleasure tipped toward ache. She watched him watch her, watched what she was fill his eyes as that ache spread, swelled. The beat pounded—urgent now, faster now. She rode him, rode them both until the ache peaked, tore, and shattered.

When she went limp, he drew her down and held her close as he had in the night.

Floating, she thought, it was like floating down a long, quiet river where the water was warm and clear. And even if you sank, he'd be there, to hold on to you.

Why couldn't she have this, just enjoy this, without creating obstacles, digging up problems, worrying about mistakes, about tomorrows? Why let the maybes, the ifs, the probablies spoil something so lovely?

"I'd like to stay right here," she said quietly. "Just like this. All day."

"Okay."

Her lips curved. "Are you ever lazy? Do the serious sloth?"

"Being with you isn't lazy. We could consider it an experiment. How long can we stay in this bed, without food or drink or outside activities? How many times can we make love on a Sunday?"

"I wish I could find out, but I have to work. We have another event today."

"What time?"

"Mmm, three o'clock, which means I have to be over there by one. And I have to upload the shots from yesterday."

"You need me out of the way."

"No, I was thinking shower and coffee for two. I might even scramble some eggs instead of offering you my usual Pop-Tart."

"I like Pop-Tarts."

"I bet you eat the grown-up breakfast."

"I rely heavily on Toaster Strudels."

She lifted her head. "Those are great. If I can provide hot water, coffee, Pop-Tarts with a side of eggs, would you consider hanging out for today's event?"

"I would—if a toothbrush and a razor get tossed in. I don't suppose you have a spare pair of shoes."

"I have many shoes, but I assume you're talking about manly ones."

"That would be best. High heels make my toes cramp."

"Funny guy. Actually, we may be able to help you out. Parker keeps a supply of dress shoes for events. Standard black dress for men, black heels for women."

"That's . . . efficient."

"It's compulsive, but we've actually dipped into them several times. What size?"

"Fourteen."

This time her head shot up. "Fourteen?"

"I'm afraid so."

"That's like aircraft carrier size." She tossed off the covers to study his feet. "You have battleship feet."

"Which is why I trip over them so much. I don't think Parker's compulsive enough to carry fourteens."

"No, not even Parker. Sorry, but I can provide the toothbrush and razor."

"Then it's a deal."

"I think we should start with the shower. We need to get hot and wet and all kinds of slippery." She glanced down at him and grinned. "Hey, look who's awake again!" Laughing, she rolled out of bed, raced for the shower.

BY THE TIME MAC WRAPPED HERSELF IN A TOWEL, SHE'D DEcided Carter was as creative vertically as he was horizontally. Wonderfully loose, she dug out a spare toothbrush, a disposable razor, and a travel-sized can of shaving cream.

"There you go." She turned as he rapped his elbow getting out of the shower. "I have a question. How come you're not clumsy when you're having sex?"

"I guess I pay better attention." Frowning, he rubbed his elbow. "Plus you distracted me in your towel."

"Since you're going to shave, I'm going down to start the coffee. That way I won't distract you into cutting your face to ribbons."

She gave his face a pat, ended up yanked against him and thoroughly distracted. When she managed to wiggle away, she tossed him her towel. "You take it since it's a problem."

She grabbed her robe off the back of the door, and sauntered out naked.

When she disappeared, Carter picked up the razor, studied it dubiously before eyeing the nasty sunset of bruising on his jaw. "Okay, let's see if we can do this without any facial scarring."

Downstairs, Mac hummed as she measured out beans. She didn't really need coffee to jump-start her day, she thought. Carter had taken care of that. He took care, she thought with a sigh, so she felt tended and appreciated, challenged and excited.

When was the last time she had a man bring out all those things in her? Let's see . . . Absolutely never. And above all those things? She felt happy.

She opened the fridge, counted four eggs. That ought to do it. She got out a bowl, a whisk, a skillet. She wanted to fix him breakfast, she realized—such as it was. Wanted to put a little meal together for him. To tend, she supposed, as he tended.

It must be—

Her thoughts scattered as she heard the door open. "Em? If you've come to mooch coffee, you'd better be carrying one of my mugs you've walked off with."

She turned, expecting to see her friend, and watched her mother walk into the kitchen.

"Mom." Mac's face went numb. "What are you doing here?"

"Dropping by to see my daughter." Beaming smiles, Linda tossed open her arms as she rushed across the kitchen to grab Mac in a hard hug. "Oh, you're so thin! You should've been a model instead of the one taking pictures. Coffee, wonderful. Have you got any skim milk?"

"No. Mom, I'm sorry, this isn't a good time."

"Oh, why do you want to hurt my feelings?" On Linda, a pout was both pretty and effective—and she knew it. Her baby blue eyes radiated hurt, her soft, pink mouth projected defenselessness—with the slightest of quivers.

"I don't mean to. It's just . . . we have an event today and—"

"You *always* have an event." Linda waved it off. "You can spare five minutes for your mother." As she spoke, Linda tossed her coat over a stool. "I came all the way over here to thank you for the spa. And to apologize." Those blue eyes took on a sheen of emotion and unshed tears. "I shouldn't have been so cranky with you, and after you were so sweet to me. I'm so sorry."

She meant it, Mac knew. For as long as it lasted.

Rather than acknowledge sentiments that would be fleeting, Mac got out a mug. Give her coffee, get her gone, she thought. "Great outfit. You're awfully suited up for a drop-by."

"Oh, this?" Linda did a runway turn in the sharp red suit that set off her curves and burned against her fall of blond hair. "It's fabulous, isn't it?" She threw back her head and laughed, until Mac had to smile.

"It is. Especially on you."

"What do you think, the pearls are good with it, aren't they? Not too matron lady?"

"Nothing could look matronly on you." Mac offered the mug.

"Oh, honey, don't you have a decent cup and saucer?"

"No. Where are you taking the outfit?"

"I'm having brunch in the city, at Elmo. With Ari."

"Who?"

"Ari. I met him at the spa. I told you. He lives in the city. He owns olive groves and vineyards—and, well, I'm not sure exactly, but it doesn't matter. His son runs most of the businesses now. He's a widower."

"Ah."

"He may be the one." Forgoing the coffee, Linda pressed a hand to her heart. "Oh, Mac, we had such a meeting of the minds and spirits, such an instant connection. It must've been fate that sent me to the spa at the same time he was there."

My three thousand sent you to the spa, Mac thought.

"He's very handsome, in a distinguished kind of way. He travels *everywhere*. He has a second home on Corfu, a pied-à-terre in London, and a summer home in the Hamptons. I'd barely gotten in the door from the spa when he called to ask me to brunch today."

"Have a good time. You should get started, it's a long drive into the city."

"It really is, and my car made a funny noise yesterday. I need to borrow yours."

"I can't lend you my car. I need it."

"Well, you'll have mine."

With the funny noise, Mac thought. "Your two-seater convertible won't work for me. I have client meetings tomorrow, and an outside shoot, which means equipment. I need my own car."

"I'll have it back tonight. God, Mackensie."

"That's what you said the last time I let you borrow it, and I didn't see it or you for three days."

"That was a spontaneous long weekend. Your trouble is you never do anything spontaneous. Everything has to be scheduled and regimented. Do you want me to have a breakdown on the side of the road? Or an accident? Can't you think of anyone but yourself?"

"Excuse me." Carter stood at the bottom of the stairs. "Sorry to interrupt. Hello, you must be Mackensie's mother."

# CHAPTER FOURTEEN

THEY COULDN'T HAVE LOOKED MORE DISSIMILAR TO CARTER'S eyes, the petite, curvy blonde in the tailored red suit and the willow-stem redhead in a plaid robe.

Still, both of them froze, and both shot him stares of mingled horror and embarrassment. Then even that connection shattered as Mac's eyes shifted to misery, and Linda's to sly calculation.

"Well, well. Mackensie didn't mention she had company. And such handsome company, too. Mackensie, where are your manners? You'd think she'd been raised in a barn. I'm Linda Barrington, Mackensie's mother." She stayed where she was, but held out a hand. "And I'm delighted to meet you."

"Carter Maguire." He crossed to her, took her hand. When he would have shaken it, she sandwiched his between hers.

"Good morning, Carter. Where did Mac happen to find you?"

"I like to think I found her."

"Aren't you the charmer?" With a light laugh, she tossed her hair. "Are you from Greenwich, Carter?"

"Yes. My family's here."

"Maguire, Maguire. I wonder if I know them. Mackensie, for heaven's sake, get the man some coffee. Sit down, Carter." She patted the seat of a stool in invitation. "And tell me everything."

"I wish there was time, but Mackensie and I have to get ready for an event."

"Oh? Are you a photographer, too?"

"No, just helping out."

She let her gaze sweep over him, quick and flirtatious. "You certainly look helpful. At least keep me company while I have my coffee and Mac goes up to dress. Mac, go up and put yourself together. You look like a ragamuffin."

"I was just thinking how pretty you look," Carter said to Mac. "So Sunday morning."

Linda let out a light laugh. "I said you were a charmer. I can always spot them. Watch your step, Mackensie. Someone might steal this one. Now, Carter, sit right down here and tell me all about yourself. I insist."

"Take the car." Mac grabbed her keys out of the basket on the counter. "Take the car and go."

"Really, Mackensie, there's no need to be rude." But Linda took the keys.

"You want the car, you've got the keys. Offer holds for exactly thirty seconds."

Chin lifted, Linda picked up her coat. "I apologize for my daughter's behavior, Carter."

"No need. No need at all."

"Better hope this one's tolerant, or you'll end up alone. Again." With a last glance at Mac, Linda sailed out.

"Well. That was bracing. I wish you hadn't given her the keys," he began and started toward her.

Mac threw up a hand to stop him. "Don't. Please don't. I'm sorry you got caught in the middle of that, but please don't."

"Please don't what?"

"Anything." She lifted her hand a little higher as she took a step back. "I don't know what I was thinking. God knows what I was thinking. I told myself it was a mistake. I knew I should stop it, just stop it before it got this complicated. But I got caught up. It's my fault."

"I take it you're not talking about your mother anymore."

"I'm sorry. I'm sorry, Carter. This? This you and me thing? It can't go anywhere. It can't go where you want it to. It's not you, it's—"

"Don't." He cut her off. "Don't make it a cliché. You're better than that. We're better than that."

"It *is* me." Because her voice wanted to break, she sharpened it. "I'm not equipped for this. I'm not the long-haul girl. I'm the one who panics and runs out of your house because it got a little too comfortable."

"Ah. That explains that."

"That's *me*. Do you get it? I'm not what you're looking for."

"You can tell me what you want, Mackensie, but not what I want."

"Of course I can. You're . . . infatuated enough to imagine we've got a future. To want one. You're traditional to your bones, Carter, and it won't take long for you to want a solid commitment, marriage, family, the house, and the three-legged cat. It's how you're wired, and I'm telling you the wires got crossed with me."

She tossed the whisk she'd yet to use in the sink. "You don't even know me. This has been a flirtation, a sexual buzz, a reflection of something old. A crush that intrigued you and flattered me, and we've let it go too far too fast. We're rushing along here to nowhere because the road's been smooth. But there are potholes and bumps. God, we haven't even had a fight, so how can we think—"

"That's all right," he interrupted. "We're about to. I'm not sure who you think less of at this moment, yourself or me. Do I want commitment, marriage, family, the house, and the damn cat—which I already have, thanks. I do, eventually. That doesn't make me an idiot."

"I didn't say—"

"Potholes and bumps? Welcome to the world. Every road has them. They're there to be navigated, avoided, driven over or through to the other side. Your problem is you keep driving straight into the pothole that is your mother, and letting that wreck the rest of the trip. She's not to blame for your poor navigation skills. You are."

"I know very well . . . Wait a minute. Poor navigation skills?" The first hints of temper flushed her cheeks. "I know where I'm going, and how to get there. I just took a detour. Stop talking in metaphors."

He cocked his brow. "I believe you took that one and ran with it. Detour my ass. We have something together. It may be something neither of us anticipated, but it's real."

"I have feelings for you, Carter. Of course I do. Obviously I do. And that's why I'm telling you we need to step back. We need to reevaluate."

"Why do you let her run your life?"

"What? I don't."

"She's a selfish, self-involved woman who strips you emotionally because you allow it. You give in, give her what she wants rather than standing up to her."

"That's ridiculous and unfair!" The anger in her tone contrasted with the calm in his, and made her feel foolish. "I lent her the damn car to get her out of here. And that doesn't have anything to do with this."

"Then I'd say you need to reevaluate that apparently unhealthy relationship."

"That's my business."

"Yes, it is."

She took a breath, then another. "I don't want to fight with you. I can't fight with you right now even if I wanted to. I have to work and prep for the event, and . . . God."

"Understood. I'll get out of your way."

"Carter, I don't want us to be mad at each other." She dragged a hand through her hair as he picked up his coat. "I don't want to hurt you. I don't want you to feel like you, like all of this doesn't mean anything to me."

"That's a lot of don'ts, Mackensie." Studying her, he put on his coat. "You might turn that coin and take a look at what you do want." He walked to the door. "And a correction? I'm not infatuated with you. I'm in love with you. That's something we'll both have to deal with."

He went out, closed the door quietly.

SHE GOT THROUGH IT. WHATEVER WENT ON IN HER HEART, IN her gut, couldn't be allowed in her head during an event. Crop it out, she ordered herself, because the day wasn't about her any more than the day before had been about the idiot brother of the groom.

"Are you going to tell me what's wrong?" Emma asked her as they circled the dance floor.

"No. It doesn't belong here."

"I saw your mother's car outside your studio. I didn't see yours."

"Not now, Em."

"This is winding down. I'll talk to you after."

"I don't want to talk. I don't have time for cookies and soul-searching. I'm working."

As if, Emma thought, and hunted down Parker. "Something's wrong with Mac."

"Yes, I know." Parker stood by the long entry table supervising the transfer of gifts to the limo outside. "We'll deal with it after."

"She's going to try to evade." Like Parker, Emma kept an easy smile on her face. "I'm worried because she's not mad. Usually dealing with her mother makes her mad. It can bring her down, but the mad's there."

"Nothing to do until we can do it. Last dance is coming up," Parker calculated after a glance at her watch. "She'll want to take the departure shots outside. If she's in serious brood mode, she'll go home directly from there. So, we'll head her off, gauge the ground."

If she'd been using her head, Mac would have known they were laying for her. But the sheer relief of having it over, of knowing she'd done her job and done it well blocked out the rest.

She lowered her camera as the limo glided down the drive.

"Quick meeting when we're clear," Parker announced.

"Listen, I'm behind at the studio. I'll copy your notes."

"It won't take long. We need to make sure everything's as it should be for the presentation tomorrow. Good evening. Drive safely." Parker smiled at a group of departing guests. "I think that's about the last of them. Let's do the sweep. Take the second floor, will you?"

Annoyed, Mac stomped upstairs. She wanted to go home, damn it. She wanted to be alone, to work. And she wanted to work until her eyes blurred. Then she wanted to go to bed and sleep off this misery.

But no, everything had to be in place first. It was Parker-law.

The subs had set the bride's and groom's suites to rights again, but she checked the bathrooms, just in case. They'd once found a wedding guest curled up asleep in the clawfoot tub in the bride's space—the morning *after* an event.

While she finished the security check, she considered ducking out one of the side doors to avoid the meeting. But that would just piss the rest of them off, and they'd come after her.

She didn't want another confrontation, another emotional

scene. Over my quota already, she thought. So she'd be a good girl, do the postevent roundup, get through the briefing for tomorrow's proposal.

Better anyway, she decided. Less time to think. Thinking was far down the list of activities she wanted to pursue.

It didn't surprise her to see Laurel setting up tea and finger sandwiches. Vows meetings traditionally included food and beverage of some sort.

"Nice event," Laurel said casually. "Nobody punched anybody in the face. No booting in the shrubbery, and as far as we know, no one used any of the facilities for inappropriate sex."

"Sunday events tend to be tame." Emma slipped out of her shoes and stretched.

"You forget the Greenburg-Fogelman wedding."

"Oh, yeah. That had all of the above, and more."

Unable to sit, to settle, Mac wandered to the window. "It's starting to snow. At least it waited until we were clear."

"Which we are," Parker said as she came in. "Cleaning crew's starting on the Ballroom. Mrs. Seaman may want another look around tomorrow, so we need to shine. Laurel, menu?"

"An assortment of mini pastries, coffee, tea, fresh orange juice. To be followed during my presentation—which is the final—with the cake tasting. We'll also have an assortment of chocolate with the B and G's names or monogram in gold. I've used various styles. I've got both photographs and sketches of cakes—wedding and groom's as well as some suggestions should they want to do guest cakes—the same with options for the dessert bar. I have gift boxes of the chocolate to give to the bride and her mother, and a couple extra in case someone else comes along. I'm covered."

"Okay. Emma?"

"The bride likes tulips, and indicated she wanted them as her signature flower for the event. I'm going garden wedding, since it's an April affair. I'll have masses of tulips—clear glass vases, varying shapes and sizes in here. And roses, of course. I'm putting together arrangements—spring colors, scents. Plus boutonnieres. White tulip with a little sprig of lavender to set it off. I've done three silk bouquets, designed specifically for her. And I'll have one that pushes on her tulips. Because that's the one I think she'll go with. If she goes, that is."

She paused to rub her left foot while she worked down her list. "I've also done a few varieties for attendants—spring colors again as she hasn't settled on her colors. I've got photos in addition to the samples I made. She's already seen my space and a lot of my samples and displays, but I've changed some up and tailored them to her.

"Laurel helped me sketch out a couple ideas for the pergola area. I had this idea for dogwoods. Young dogwood trees in white urns as a backdrop. We can string them with lights. I want to suggest tussie-mussies instead of corsages for the mothers. I've made a few up to show her. I'll pack arrangements for each of them to take home."

"We've got plenty of photos of all the spaces dressed for spring weddings." Parker glanced toward Mac.

"I've culled out what I feel are the best examples for this client. And ones that I've taken on details. As we already discussed, April's iffy weather and they'll want tents."

"Silk tents."

Mac nodded at Parker. "I've read your proposal. And seen Laurel's sketches. We don't have photographs of that specific layout, but we have a few that are close. I've put together a really strong portfolio of portraits—engagement and wedding, and a separate one with photographs we've had in magazines. They skimmed over the albums when they came through—and you indicated Mom's eyes lit up at the idea of doing an art book. I'm bringing a sample of one. I'm going to take a portrait of the mother and daughter here, during the presentation. I'll go print it out, frame it, box it, and give it to Mom."

"That's great." Parker grinned. "That's excellent. For my part I have three scenarios, different styles, that take them from the rehearsal all the way through to departure. I've gone back and forth, but I've decided to lead off with the one I think is the best."

"The twenty-first-century fairy princess one," Emma said. "My favorite."

"We've already put about a hundred hours into this among the four of us," Laurel pointed out. "Every digit I have is crossed."

Emma gave a decisive nod. "I have a good feeling about this."

"You have a good feeling about pretty much everything. If that's it, I have a mountain of work."

"Almost," Parker said as Mac started to rise. "What hurts, Mac?"

"My feet mostly."

"You might as well spill." Laurel chose a finger sandwich. "It's three against one."

"It's nothing. And I don't see why we have to gush every time one of us has a mood."

"We're girls," Emma reminded her. "Your mother has your car."

"Yes, my mother has my car. She ambushed me this morning. I'm irritated. I'll be irritated when she decides to bring it back, certainly out of gas, probably with a dent in the fender. End of story."

"I know when you're irritated." Parker tucked up her legs. "That's not what you were today."

"It's what I am now."

"Because that's the least of it. Carter was there when she ambushed you, wasn't he?"

"She came on to him, the way she does with anything that has a penis. Can you imagine how embarrassing that was?"

"Was he upset?" Emma asked.

"About her?" She pushed up to walk back to the window. "I

don't know, I'm not sure. I was too busy being mortified to notice. So I gave her the keys to get her out."

"I won't ask what she wanted your car for." Laurel poured out a cup of tea. "What difference does it make? What I'm wondering is why you're upset with Carter."

"I'm not. I'm upset with myself. For letting it happen, for letting it get this far, and not *thinking*, not staying anywhere close to Planet Reality."

"You're not talking about Scary Linda now," Laurel concluded.

"Oh, Mac." Emma's eyes darkened in sympathy. "You had a fight with Carter."

"No. Yes. No." Frustrated, Mac spun around. "You can't have a fight with someone like him. People in a fight yell, or storm around. They say things they regret later. That's why they call them fights. All he can do is be reasonable."

"Damn the man," Laurel stated and earned a vicious glare.

"You try it. You try to make someone like Carter understand you've taken the wrong direction and have everything you say bounce off the wall of calm logic."

"You broke up with him." From the tone, Emma's sympathy took a sharp turn toward Carter.

"I don't know what I did. Besides, how can you break up with someone when you haven't said you're together? Officially. It's me, it's my fault, and he won't even listen to that. I know I let it go too far. I got caught up, swept up. Something. And when my mother walked in this morning, it was a solid slap back to reality."

"You're going to let her push your buttons on this?" Parker demanded.

"No. It's not like that." Mac spoke fiercely because part of her worried it was like that. Exactly like that. "I don't want to hurt him. That's what it comes down to. He thinks he's in love with me."

"Thinks?" Laurel repeated. "Can't *be*?"

"He's romanticized it. Me. Everything."

"This would be the same man who can only be reasonable. The calm wall of logic." Lips pursed, Parker tilted her head. "But about you he's stuck in fantasy?"

"He can have layers," Mac argued, suddenly feeling tired and defeated.

"I think the question on the table should be not how Carter feels or doesn't feel about you, but how you feel or don't about him. Are you in love with him, Mac?"

Mac stared at Parker. "I care about him. That's the point."

"I call evasion," Laurel said. "It's a question that can be answered yes or no."

"I don't know! I don't know what to do with all these feelings crammed inside me. He walks into my life, smacks his head into the wall, and I'm the one who's dizzy. You said he wasn't my type, right off the bat you said that. And you were right."

"Actually, I think that's one of the rare times I've been wrong. But you have to decide that for yourself. What'll piss me off, Mac, what'll disappoint is if you use Linda as your yardstick when it comes to love. Because she doesn't even rate a measure."

"I need some time, that's all. I need time to find my balance, my rhythm. I can't seem to find either when I'm around him."

"Then take it," Parker advised. "Be sure."

"I will. I have to be."

"One thing. If he loves you, I'm on his side."

KATHRYN SEAMAN ARRIVED WITH HER DAUGHTER JESSICA AT exactly ten Monday morning. It was the sort of punctuality, Mac knew, that would warm Parker's efficient heart. But she found it just a little scary.

Overwork, nerves, and emotional turmoil roiled an uneasy mix in her belly as she sat with her partners and potential clients in the parlor. Emma's flood of tulips brought spring into the room even as the crackling fire in the hearth warmed it. Parker had set up her grandmother's gorgeous Meissen tea and coffee sets, the Waterford crystal, and Georgian silver, all the perfect complement to Laurel's glossy pastries.

If she'd needed a picture of lush, sophisticated, and female, this would've been it.

After the ritual small talk about the weather, Parker eased right in. "We're so excited you're considering Vows for your big day. We understand how important it is that you feel comfortable and confident in every detail that goes into creating a wedding that reflects who you are, and what you and Josh mean to each other. We want you to enjoy that day, and all the days leading up to it, knowing *you* are our focus. We want what you want, a perfect and beautiful day full of memories to last the rest of your life.

"With that goal in mind, we've put together a few ideas. Before I show you the first proposal, do you have any questions?"

"Yes." Kate Seaman opened the notebook on her lap. As her daughter laughed and rolled her eyes, she began peppering Parker with questions.

Parker's answers were invariably yes. They provided that, would handle that, had a source for or a sample of that. When questions veered off into landscape, Emma took over.

"In addition to the wedding flowers, we'll use annuals and pots in the flower beds and gardens, and those plantings will be specifically selected to enhance the arrangements Jessica ultimately selects. I realize it's early in the season, but I can promise you spring on your wedding day."

"If they'd wait till May."

"Mom." Jessica patted her mother's hand. "We met in April, and we're determined to be sentimental. It seems like a long time, plenty for all the planning. But already there are a million details."

"That's what we're here for," Parker told her.

"Right now, it's the engagement party at the club, and the Save the Date announcements."

"We can handle that for you."

Jessica stopped, pursed her lips. "Really?"

"Absolutely. All we need is your list. We have several sources for cards. One of the more personal styles is to create a card from your engagement photo, or a photo of you and Josh you particularly like."

"I love that idea. Don't you, Mom?"

And I'm up, Mac thought. "The engagement photo itself might help you decide if you like that style, or want to go more traditional. Setting the date, your venue, finding that perfect dress, and the engagement photo are all early details that, once done, free your mind and your time for the rest. And also, they set the tone for your wedding."

"You have samples of photos you've taken."

"Yes." Rising Mac picked up the portfolio of engagement shots, offered it to Kate. "I feel the engagement portrait is as important as a wedding portrait. It illustrates the promise made, the intent, the joy and anticipation. What brought these people together? Why have they exchanged this first promise? Tailoring that portrait, which announces to friends, to family, to everyone that Jessica and Josh found each other is my job."

"In your studio?" Kate asked.

"Yes, or at whatever venue suits the couple."

"At the club," Kate decreed. "At the engagement party. Jessie has a stunning gown. She and Josh look wonderful together in black tie. And Jessie will be wearing my mother's rubies."

As her eyes misted, Kate reached over, took her daughter's hand.

"It's a lovely idea, and I'd be happy to set that up. But I did have another idea for this portrait. You and Josh met while riding, and that's a passion you both share. I'd like to take a portrait of you on horseback."

"On horseback?" Kate frowned. "It isn't a snapshot. I don't want Jessica in jodhpurs and a riding hat for her engagement portrait. I want her to sparkle."

"I was thinking more a soft gleam. Romantic, a little fanciful. You have a chestnut gelding. Trooper."

"How did you know that?"

"It's our job to know about our clients. But not in a creepy way," Mac added and made Jessica laugh.

"I see you and Josh on Trooper, riding double. Josh in a tux, the tie loose, the first few studs undone, and you behind him, in a gorgeous, flowing gown—and your grandmother's rubies," she added. "Your arms around his waist, your hair down, caught in the wind. The background just a blur of color and shape."

"Oh my God." Jessica just breathed it. "I love that. I really love it. Mom."

"It sounds . . . beautiful. Magical."

"And I think you'll find the idea flows right into what we've put together as the theme for the wedding. Parker."

Rising, Parker stepped to the easel that was set up. "We have photos that will show you overviews and details of what we've done in the past, what we can do, but as your wedding will be unique, we're using sketches of our vision for your day."

She removed the cover from the first sketch. "Fairyland," she said, and Mac imagined each of her partners felt the same quick thrill she did when the bride gasped.

"I THINK WE GOT IT. DON'T YOU THINK WE GOT IT? GOD, I'M exhausted." Emma sprawled out on the sofa. "And a little sick. I ate too much candy to calm my nerves. Don't you think we got it?"

"If we didn't, I'm taking up a collection to order a hit on Kathryn Seaman." Laurel propped her feet on the stack of albums on the coffee table. "That woman is tough."

"She loves her daughter," Parker commented.

"Yeah, that came through, but God, we practically bled wedding perfection here, and couldn't get her to commit."

"She's going to. Otherwise we won't need the collection. I'll kill her myself." Rubbing her neck, Parker paced. "She needs to think it over, discuss it with her husband, just as Jessica has to talk it over with Josh and get his take. That's reasonable. That's normal."

"Kate drives the train," Mac pointed out. "I think she just wants to torture us. She was completely sold on the royal palace wedding cake."

Laurel gnawed her lip. "You think?"

"I was watching her, I started watching her like a cat watches a mouse—or maybe I was the mouse and she was the cat. But I was watching her. Her eyes gleamed over that cake. I could hear her thinking, 'Nobody's getting that palace of a cake but my baby girl.' We hit every note. Both of them got dreamy over Emma's dogwoods and fairy lights. And the tulip cascade bouquet? Jessie wants it for her own. Then Mom casually mentions her husband's two left feet, and Parker reaches into her magic collection of business cards and pulls out a personal dance instructor."

"That was a good one," Emma agreed. "Anyway, Mom wants what Baby wants, and Baby wants us. I can feel it." She let out a sigh, pushed herself up. "I've got to go pot up fifty-five narcissus for a wedding shower. Everybody take some tulips."

"I'm going to go see if my car's back. I have an outside shoot and a bunch of errands." Mac looked at Parker. "If she didn't show, can I borrow your car?"

SOME PEOPLE, PARKER THOUGHT, WOULD SAY SHE WAS INTERfering, that this was none of her business. Some people, she thought, didn't know her.

She fixed problems. And if she didn't at least try to fix one for her oldest friend, then what was the point in being a fixer in the first place?

She walked into Coffee Talk determined to do her best, for everyone.

The Sunday night crowd set up a low hum of conversation. She could hear the whoosh of the frother, the buzz of the grinder as she glanced around. She spotted Carter at a two-top, and putting on a smile walked over to join him.

"Hi, Carter, thanks for meeting me."

"Sure. You had an event today."

"This afternoon. It went very well." No point in wasting time, she thought. "Mac was unhappy and upset, but she put that aside for the clients."

"I'm sorry I upset her."

"And she you. But," Parker continued before he could speak, "her mother's at the root of it. I imagine all three of us know that, even if we react to it differently."

"She was embarrassed. Mackensie. She didn't need to be. Not for me."

"Her mother will always embarrass her." Parker glanced at the waitress who stopped at the table. "Some jasmine tea, thanks."

"Coming right up. Dr. Maguire?"

"That's fine. Two of those."

"Carter, I want to give you a little background, so you understand the why of it all. What you and Mac do about it, that's up to you."

As she spoke, Parker pulled off her gloves, loosened her coat. "I don't know how much she's told you, and she'd be royally pissed at me for expanding on whatever she has, but here it is. Her parents divorced when she was four. Her father—and she adored him—walked away from her as easily as he did Linda. He's a careless man. Not calculating like Linda, just careless. He grew up privileged, and with a nice fat trust fund. That may seem hypocritical coming from me, but—"

"No, it doesn't. You and Del, your parents, you always contributed. That's the word for it."

"Thank you. Geoffrey Elliot just goes where he likes, does as he pleases, and prefers to avoid any sort of upheaval. Linda shoves, pushes, wheedles her way through life. She got a very nice settlement from Mac's father, and blew through the bulk of it."

She smiled. "Children hear things, even when they're not supposed to know what they mean."

"There had to be child support."

"Yes. Mac was housed and fed and clothed very well. So, of course, was her mother. They both remarried before Mac was seven. Linda divorced again within two years."

She paused as their tea was served. "After that, there were a lot of men, a lot of love affairs, and a lot of drama. Linda feeds on drama. Geoffrey divorced again, and married again. He has a son with his third wife, and they spend most of their time in Europe. Linda has a daughter by her second husband."

"Yes, Mac told me she had two half siblings."

"They rarely see each other. Eloisa spent, and spends, a lot of time with her father, who obviously loves her very much."

"That must've been hard. To see her sister have that, while she didn't."

"Yeah. And because it was, for the most part, only Mac at home, Linda expected, demanded, used. It's her way. She married again. Every time she married, they moved to another house, another neighborhood. Another school for Mac. Linda pulled Mac out of the academy when she divorced her third husband. Then put her back in, briefly, a couple of years later because, it turned out, she was involved with a man—a married one—on the board of directors."

"No stability, ever. Nothing she could count on," Carter murmured.

Parker sighed. "All of her life, Mac's had her mother weeping on her shoulder over some slight, some broken heart, some trouble. Linda was raised to believe herself the center of the universe, and she did her best to raise Mac to believe it, too. She's a strong woman, our Mac. Smart, self-reliant, brilliant at what she does. But this vulnerable spot is like an aching wound. Linda continually yanks the scab off. She grew up with callousness, and fears being callous."

"She doesn't trust us, because nothing in her life has ever given her the foundation to trust."

"You do listen. That was one of the first things she told me about you. I'm going to give you an advantage, Carter, another thing she wouldn't thank me for. I'm giving it to you because I love her."

"I could use one."

Parker reached out to lay her hand over his on the table. "I've never seen her the way she is with you, not with anyone else. I've never seen her care, so much. Because of that, what she has with you, what she's finding with you, scares her."

"I've figured some of that, at least the scared part. As someone who loves her, what would you advise me to do?"

"I was hoping you'd ask," Parker said with a smile. "Give her a little space, a little time—but not too much. And don't give up on her. The only constants in her life have been me and my family, Emma and Laurel. She needs you."

"I can't give up on her," Carter said simply. "I've been waiting for her most of my life."

# CHAPTER FIFTEEN

NEITHER THE CAR NOR HER MOTHER SHOWED ON MONDAY. ON Tuesday, when her patience ran thin, Mac's calls to her mother's house and cell went directly to voice mail.

By Wednesday, she actively entertained the thought of reporting her car stolen. But then she'd just have to bail her mother out of jail.

So she went over to the main house to mooch breakfast.

"Parker's on an emergency house call. Saturday's bride woke up with a zit or something. Emma's waiting on an early delivery, so it's just you and me."

"Does that mean there won't be pancakes?"

"I don't have time for pancakes—and God, I wish Mrs. G would shake off the island sand and get home. I've got to make foliage and flowers. Have a muffin."

"Did Parker have any idea when she'd get back?"

Laurel glanced up, stopped rolling out her flower paste. "Your car's not back?"

"Both it and Linda are MIA. I've left a dozen messages. Her

ears are going to bleed and fall off when she gets them. I threatened to report it stolen."

"Do it. There's the phone."

"I'll probably be arrested for sheer stupidity for giving her the keys. I'm going to go by her place. I have another shoot, and I need to pick up some custom paper that wasn't ready Monday. And I think I want some shoes."

"Haven't heard from Carter?"

"Why do you say that?"

"Because you're going to buy shoes, which is comfort food for you. Have you called him?"

"To say what? I'm sorry? I already said that. I was wrong? I was, I know I was wrong, but it doesn't change what I feel."

"Which is?"

"Confused, afraid, stupid. Double all of that because I miss seeing him," she admitted. "I miss talking to him. So I think it's better if I don't see him or talk to him."

"Your logic doesn't resemble the logic of humans."

"He probably doesn't want to see or talk to me anyway."

"Coward."

"Maybe. I'm a coward without a car." She waited in silence while Laurel rolled out her paste. "You could lend me yours."

"I could. But that would be enabling, which is what you continue to do with Linda. I love you too much to do that."

"It's not enabling. It's business. I could cram my equipment into her ridiculous little toy, but funny, she left the car and not the keys. It's not the client's fault I caved or she's so self-centered she hasn't brought it back."

"No, it's not." With care, Laurel used a template and began cutting out the first flowers.

"I'm so pissed off. I admit the pissed off portion helps balance out the sheer misery of the Carter situation, but at this point I'd rather be miserable about him and have my wheels. Why does she *do* this? And don't say because I let her. I swear, and I'll swear it in blood, I had no intention of lending her the damn car. I never would've put myself in this position again if it hadn't been for those exact circumstances."

"I'd like to believe that, but here you are, Mac, paying the price as usual. While as usual she pays nothing. No consequences for Linda. She'll bring your car back when she's damn good and ready. You'll confront her, bitch, complain. She'll pull out all her usual crap. Then she'll forget the whole thing because she'll have gotten and done what she wanted, and topped it off by being the center of your world while you bitch and complain."

"What am I supposed to do? Beat her to death with my tripod?"

"I'll help you hide the body."

"You would." Mac sighed. "You're a true friend. I'm not a coward or a pushover about most things."

"No, you're not. Anything but. I guess that's why it irritates me down to the marrow when you are. When she causes you to be both. Make her pay for once, Mackensie. I bet once you do, the next time will come easier."

"How? Believe me when I say I want to. I can't actually call the cops. I gave her the damn keys. And maybe I think—know," she corrected, "it was passive-aggressive bullshit that she didn't leave me hers, it still . . ."

"I like that look. That is not the look of cowardly pushover. What?"

"She left her car."

"Oh, oh, we're going to smash the toy. I'll get my coat and Del's old baseball bat."

"No. God, you're a violent soul."

"I like smashing. It's therapeutic."

"We're not going to beat up the car. It's an innocent bystander in this. But I am going to have it towed."

"That's not bad, but having it towed to her house just means she doesn't have to bother to come get it."

"Not to her house." Mac's eyes narrowed as she thought it through. "Remember a few months ago, that guy rear-ended Del's new car. It had to be towed. The guy, the mechanic guy who took care of all that. He's got the tow truck, the garage, the lot. Damn it, what's the name? Where is Parker with her magic business cards?"

"Call Del. He'll remember. And let me just say this is why we're friends. When you get your teeth into it, Mac, you're beautiful."

"So lend me your car."

"Make the calls, and it's yours."

SHE FELT RIGHTEOUS. SHE FELT STRONG. BY THE TIME SHE'D completed her shoot, run her errands, stopped off to buy more twenty-gauge wire for Laurel, she decided she deserved new shoes. Maybe, considering the trauma and triumph of the last few weeks, she deserved new earrings, too.

Earrings for Linda, she decided. Shoes for Carter. Celebration and commiseration.

Maybe she'd go by his place on the way home. While she was feeling strong and righteous. They were two smart people who cared about each other. Surely they could find a compromise, some middle ground, some solution.

She didn't want to lose him, she thought. She didn't want to go through her life Carter-less.

She wandered through the mall until she hit the Holy Grail. The shoe department at Nordstrom.

Maybe she needed new boots, too. You could never really have too many boots. New shoes *and* new boots would give her that firm sense of self-reliance she needed to go to Carter's. She could pick up a bottle of wine, like a peace offering. And they'd talk, and he'd look at her that way he looked at her. And . . . that would be pulling a Linda, she decided, as she had Laurel's car.

But she could still go by, still take the wine. She could ask him to dinner at her place. It could be a kind of joke, an icebreaker. Hey, I brought you this wine. Why don't you come over for dinner later tonight and bring this with you? Of course then she'd have to stop off and buy something to fix. Or she could just raid Mrs. G's supply.

No, no, she thought as she picked up a pair of electric blue ankle boots that sang her name. She had to *cook*. Had to show him he mattered enough for her to make the effort. He mattered. It all mattered.

Which was why she was so screwed up over it in the first place.

"It's . . . Meredith, isn't it?"

Mac turned, glanced at a vaguely familiar blonde. "No, sorry."

"But aren't you the wedding photographer?"

"Yes. It's Mackensie."

"Of course! Sorry. I'm Stephanie Gorden. I met you at my cousin's wedding last Saturday."

"Oh, right. How are you?"

"Surrounded by shoes. I'm great. What fabulous boots! Corrine and I are playing hooky this afternoon. Corrine! Come over and meet Mackensie."

Oh God, Mac thought. How could fate hand her fabulous boots and a kick in the ass at the same time?

"Corrine, this is Mackensie. She's a wedding photographer, and a *very* good friend of Carter's."

"Oh?"

And Corrine was perfect, Mac thought. So make that a kick in the ass along with a slap in the face. She glided over in exquisite red peep-toe pumps with her glossy dark hair spilling in romantic curls to her shoulders. Eyes, deep and sultry, scanned Mac as her soft, shapely lips curved in a cool smile.

"Hello."

"Hi. Great shoes."

"Yes. I think they're going to be mine."

Even her voice was perfect, Mac thought bitterly. Low and just a little throaty.

"So, you know Carter Maguire."

"Yes. We went to high school together. For a while."

"Really?" Absently, Corrine picked up a pair of kitten-heel slides. "He never mentioned you. We were involved for quite some time."

"Corrine and Carter," Stephanie said cheerfully. "It was practically one word. It's so funny running into you like this. I was just telling Corrine I'd heard Carter was seeing someone, and that I'd seen you together at Brent's wedding."

"Funny."

"And how is Carter?" Corrine asked, as she set the slides back down. "Still buried in his books?"

"He seems to have time to come up for air."

"Haven't been seeing him very long, have you?"

"Long enough, thanks."

"You two should compare notes." Stephanie gave Corrine a friendly hip bump. "Corrine could give you a lot of pointers where Carter's concerned, Mackensie."

"Wouldn't that be fun? But, I like the discovery. Carter's a fascinating and exciting man, entirely too much of one for notes. Excuse me. I see a pair of slingbacks with my name on them."

As Mac aimed for the other side of the department, Stephanie arched her eyebrows. "Exciting? Carter? He must've evolved since you dumped him, Cor. I have to say, he did look on the hot side when I saw him Saturday. Maybe you should've hung on there a bit longer."

"Who says I can't have him back if I want him?" She looked down at the pumps. "In fact, I may take my new shoes on a little visit."

Stephanie snickered. "You're a bad girl."

"What I am, is bored." She frowned over at Mac. She thought *she* should be the one to have those boots. They'd certainly look better on her than some skinny, orange-headed tight ass. "Besides, why should she have Carter? I saw him first."

"I thought Carter bored you."

"That was before." On a long sigh, Corrine sat, scanned the small mountain of shoes she was considering. "The trouble with you, Steph, is you're married. You've forgotten the thrill of the hunt, the competition. The score."

She slipped off the pumps, slipped on a pair of spikeheeled sandals in metallic pink. "Men are like shoes. You're supposed to try them on, wear them awhile—as long as they look good on you. Then toss them in the closet and shop for more."

She stood, angled to study the results in the mirror. "And every now and then, you pluck something out of the closet, try them on again and see how they look."

She glanced over, scowled when she saw Mac trying on the blue boots. "The one thing you don't do is let somebody else go rooting around in your closet."

ROUTINE, CARTER THOUGHT, HAD ITS PURPOSE. IT GOT THINGS done, offered a certain comfort and kept hands and mind occupied. He hung up his coat, went to his home office to lay his evening's work on the desk. He checked his messages.

There was a pang when Mac's voice failed to breeze into the room, but that was routine, too.

Parker had advised a little time and space. He'd give Mac more time. Another day or two.

He could wait. He was good at waiting. And more than anything, he realized, he wanted her to come to him.

He went downstairs to feed the cat and make himself some tea. At the counter, he drank the tea while he went through the day's mail.

And he wondered if his life could be any more ordinary, any more staid. Would he find himself in this same loop—read rut—in another year? God, in another decade?

He'd been comfortable enough before Mackensie had reentered his life.

"It's not as if I'd planned to be alone forever," he said to the cat. "But there was plenty of time, wasn't there? Time to enjoy a certain routine, time to enjoy my home, my work, the freedom that comes from being single. I'm barely thirty, for God's sake.

"And I'm talking to a cat, which is not how I want to spend my evenings for the rest of my life. No offense. But no one wants to merely settle. To be with someone because being alone's the only other option. Love's not some amorphous concept created for books and poetry and not attainable. It's real and vital, and it's *necessary.* Damn it. It changes things. Everything. I can't be what I was before I loved her. It's ridiculous for anyone to expect that."

Having finished his meal, the cat sat, gave Carter a long stare, then began to wash.

"Well, she's not as reasonable as you. I'll tell you something else while we're on the subject. I'm good for her. I'm exactly what she needs. I understand her. All right, no, I don't. I take that back. But I know her, which is a different thing altogether. And I know I can make her happy once she gets over being too pigheaded to admit it."

He decided then and there she had another twenty-four hours. If she didn't come to him within that time frame, he'd just have to take control of the situation. He'd need a plan of some sort, an outline of what needed to be said and done. He rose to get a pad and pencil.

"Oh, for God's sake. The hell with plans and outlines. We'll just deal with it." Annoyed, he slammed the drawer on his finger. Typical, he thought, sucking at the ache. He decided to console himself with a grilled cheese sandwich.

If she'd come to her senses, they'd be together right now, maybe fixing an actual meal. Something they could talk over. He wanted to know if she'd gotten the big job. Wanted to celebrate with her. To share it with her.

He wanted to tell her about the funny short story one of his students had turned in—and about the excuses another had given him for not completing an assignment.

He had to admit the temporary amnesia gambit had been inventive.

He wanted to share all that with her. The big things, the little ones, all the bits and pieces that made up their lives. He just had to show her she wanted it, too. No, not only wanted it, he remembered. He had to show her she could have it.

He put the sandwich in the skillet, opened a cupboard for a plate. When the knock sounded at his front door, he barely missed rapping his head on the corner of the open cupboard.

He thought: Mackensie, and hurried out of the kitchen.

The image of her was already in his mind when he opened the door, so it took him several awkward seconds to process Corrine.

"Carter." She came in laughing, did a graceful turn to end with her arms around him. She tipped her head back, eyes sparkling dark, and pressed her lips to his.

"Surprise," she said, on a little purr.

"Ah, yes. It certainly is. Corrine." He disentangled himself. "You're . . . looking well."

"Oh, I'm a wreck. I must've driven around the block three times before I worked up the nerve to stop. Don't break my heart, Carter, and say you're not happy to see me."

"No. I mean . . . I certainly wasn't expecting to."

"Aren't you going to ask me in?"

"You are in."

"Always so literal. Are you going to close the door, or make me grovel in the cold?"

"Sorry." He shut the door. "You caught me off guard. What do you want, Corrine?"

"More than I deserve." She took off her coat, offered it to him along with a plea in her eyes. "Hear me out, won't you?"

Trapped between manners and puzzlement, he hung up her coat. "I thought I already did."

"I was stupid, and so careless with you. You have every right to toss me out on my ass." She wandered into the living room. "When I look back at what I did, what I said . . . Carter, I'm so ashamed. You were so good to me, so good for me. You made me better than I was. I've been thinking about you. Thinking about you a lot."

"What about—" He had to dig for the name. "James?"

She rolled those sultry eyes. "My mistake. My punishment for hurting you. It didn't take me long to realize he was just a reckless adventure. He was a boy compared to you, Carter. Please say you forgive me."

"It's old business, Corrine."

"I want to make it up to you, if you'll let me. Give me a chance to show you." She walked back to him, trailed her fingers over his cheek. "You remember how it was with us, how good it was. We could have that again. Carter." She wound around him. "You could have me again. You just have to take me."

"I think we should—"

"Let's be sensible later." She pressed in as he tried to ease her back. "I want you. I want you so much. I can't think about anything else."

"Wait. Stop. This isn't going to—"

"All right. You're the boss." With that sparkling smile in place, she tossed her hair. "We'll talk first, all you want. Why don't you pour me a glass of wine and we'll . . . Is something burning?"

"I don't— Oh, hell."

He raced to the kitchen, and Corrine's smile went sharp. This would take more time and effort, she realized. But she didn't mind the challenge. Actually, she thought, the fact that Carter hadn't come to heel as she'd expected only made him more exciting. And it would make seducing him all the more satisfying.

After all, the one place he hadn't bored her was in bed.

She softened her smile as she heard him coming back.

"Sorry, I was cooking something. Corrine, I appreciate the apology and the . . . offer, but— Sorry," he repeated at the knock on the front door.

"It's all right. I'll wait."

With a shake of his head, Carter walked out to open the door. His brain, already on overload, hit the red zone when he saw Mac.

"Hi. Peace offering." She held out a bottle of wine. "I handled things badly, and I'm hoping you'll give me a chance to do better. If you're up for that, I thought maybe you could come over for dinner tonight. Maybe bring a bottle of wine. Hey, that's a nice label you've got there."

"You—I—Mackensie."

"Who is it, Carter?"

Not good, was all Carter could think. This could not be good, as Corrine strolled out. He saw shock rush over Mac's face.

"This isn't—"

"Oh, wine, how nice." Corrine took the bottle from Carter's numb hand. "Carter was just about to pour me a glass."

"Actually, I . . . Mackensie Elliot, this is Corrine Melton."

"Yes, I know. Well, enjoy the wine."

"No. Don't." He all but leaped out the door to grab her arm. "Wait. Just wait. Come inside."

She shook his hand off. "Are you joking? Grab me again," she warned, "you'll have more than a bruise on your jaw."

She stalked off to a car he realized wasn't hers as Corrine called out from the doorway.

"Carter! Sweetie, come inside before you catch cold!"

Routine, he thought? Had he actually been worried about falling into the rut of routine?

MAC STORMED INTO THE HOUSE. "WHERE THE HELL IS everybody?" she shouted.

"We're back in the kitchen! We've been trying your cell," Emma called out. "Get back here."

"You would not believe the day I had. First I run into Carter's sexy ex in the shoe department at Nordstrom, which nearly spoiled my petty pleasure in having my mother's car towed. Why didn't anyone bother to tell me she was gorgeous?" Mac complained and tossed her coat on a stool.

"And as if that wasn't bad enough with all sexy and sultry in these fabulous red peep-toes and her Catwoman with a whip voice, I spent sixty bucks on a bottle of wine as a peace offering to Carter, and another eighty at the market buying all this *crap* to fix a makeup dinner for him and what do I find when I go by his place? What do I find? I'll tell you what I find. *Her.* Her in a black cashmere sweater cut down to here, with just enough pink lace under it to say, *dive in, honey.* And he stands there, *introducing* us, all flustered and befuddled.

"Now she's drinking my goddamn wine."

Parker held up both hands. "Wait a minute. Carter was with Corrine—his ex?"

"Didn't I just say that? Isn't that what I said? And she's 'Oh, sweetie, come in before you catch cold.' Except in sexy voice. And he was cooking something. I could smell it. It smelled like burnt toast, but still. We have one little disagreement and he's making her burnt toast and pouring her my wine?"

"I can't see Carter jumping back there." Emma shook her head. "No possible way."

"She was there, wasn't she, with her pink lace cleavage?"

"If so, you should've kicked his ass, then hers, then taken your wine." Laurel moved over to give Mac a back rub. "But I tend to lean with Emma. Let us travel back to the shoe department at Nordstrom. First, did you buy any?"

"Shoe department, Nordstrom. What do you think?"

"You can show us later. How did you know it was Carter's ex? Or did she know you?"

"She had that what's-her-name with her. Cousin of the groom from Saturday's event. She recognized me. And they're both giving me the once-over, which I resent. I seriously resent, and the what's-her-name is giggling, and 'You two should compare notes.' Asinine bitch."

"And doesn't it strike you as strange and coincidental," Parker said, "that the evening of the same day you just happen to find her at Carter's? Does no one else smell plot?"

Laurel and Emma raised their hands.

"Oh, Jesus Christ." Disgusted, Mac lowered to a stool. "She *played* me. I was too stunned and mad and, okay, jealous, to see it. But, what, she didn't know I was going over there. So—"

"I think that was just icing. I know her a little, remember," Emma reminded Mac. "She's always had the 'I want what you want, but more I want yours.' She probably went over just to see if she could take him away from you, and then—"

"I give her a bottle of wine." Mac dropped her head in her hands. "I'm an idiot."

"No, you're not. You're just not mean and calculating, like she is. And neither is Carter," Parker said. "He wasn't with her, Mac. She was just there."

"You're right. You're absolutely right. And I walked away, left her the field. But he introduced us."

"Mishandled, I'll grant you." Parker nodded. "What do you want to do?"

"I don't know. It's too much. Emotionally exhausting. I guess I'll eat ice cream and sulk."

"You could eat caviar and celebrate."

Mac frowned at Parker. "Celebrate what? The idiocy that is relationships?"

"No, the triumph of Vows signing a contract for the Seaman wedding. We got the job."

"Yay. No, sorry, give me just a minute to change gears." She scrubbed her hands over her face, tried to shove down the sick anger and find the triumph. "We actually got it?"

"We got it, and we've got Cristal and beluga to prove it. We've been waiting for you so we could pop this cork."

"What a strange day." Mac pressed her fingers to her eyes. "What a hell of a strange day. And you know what? This is a really good way to end it. Open that big boy, Parker."

"Once it pops, this is officially a no-sulking zone."

"Already done." She pushed to her feet. "I feel a happy dance coming on. Pop it!"

At the celebrational sound Mac let out a cheer.

"To us." Parker lifted her glass. "Best friends ever, and damn smart women."

They clinked, they drank. And Mac thought she could get through anything, anything that came, as long as she had them.

# CHAPTER SIXTEEN

Bob stared at Carter across the table in Coffee Talk, his eyes glazed, his jaw slack. "Holy shit."

"She didn't answer the phone. After I finally got Corrine out of the house, I called. Her house—both lines—her cell. She wouldn't answer. I thought about just going over, but if she didn't answer the phone . . . She thought I'd— She shouldn't have thought that, but given the situation at the time, I can't blame her. Not really." He brooded into his green tea. "I need to explain. Obviously I need to explain. But I'm out of my depth here. I don't know where to start."

"You have two women after you. Two. Man, Carter, you're a dog. You're the big dog."

"For God's sake, Bob, you're completely missing the point."

"Not me, pal." The slack jaw had morphed into a grin of pure admiration. "The point is two hot chicks got it for you. Plus, I heard you had a thing going with Parker Brown. A trio of hot."

"I— *What?* Who . . . No. Where did that come from?"

"You were cozy right here at the Talk the other night. At the Talk, people talk."

"God, when did this turn into a soap opera? We had coffee, and talked about Mackensie. We're friends. Just. Only. Hardly even that really."

"That's good." Bob issued his wise nod. "Because I was going to tell you that, man, you *never* date girlfriends. It's not only not cool, but it's lethal. They'll rip you up, then go shopping together."

"That's good to know, Bob." Carter watched the sarcasm float harmlessly over Bob's head. "But I'm not dating Parker. And since when can't a man and a woman have coffee—tea—together in a public place without . . . Never mind." As he felt a headache coming on, Carter let it go. "It just doesn't matter."

"Right. Back on topic. Two hot chicks squaring off over the Cartman. I bet if the redhead had come in, you'd have had a chick fight. Chicks fighting over you, Carter." Bob's eyes went bright with fantasy. "You're the big, bad dog."

"I don't want to be the dog." There was a reason he'd kept the incident to himself through the workday. But what madness had overtaken him to make him believe he could get reasonable advice out of Bob anywhere, anytime? "Try to stay with me on this, Bob."

"I'm trying, but I keep getting flashes of the girl fight. You know, with the rolling around on the floor and ripping each other's clothes." Bob lifted his skinny cinnamon latte. "It's pretty vivid."

"There was no fight."

"There could have been. Okay, so you don't want to try juggling the two of them. Me, I think you've got the skills for it, but I'm sensing you want me to help you figure out which one to pick."

"No. No. No." Carter dropped his head in his hands. "They're not ties, Bob. This is not a comparison study. I'm in love with Mackensie."

"Seriously? Well, hey, you never said you had the Big L for

her. I thought you just had a thing." Rubbing his chin, Bob sat back. "This is a different equation. How pissed off was she?"

"Take a guess, then double it."

Bob nodded wisely. "Beyond the taking her flowers and apologizing. You've got to get your foot in the door first, that's the thing. Something like this, when you're the innocent party . . . You are an innocent party, right?"

"Bob."

"Okay. You're going to have to let her kick your ass first, that's my advice." Considering, Bob sipped his latte. "Then you've got to tell her how you're innocent. Then you've got to beg. You're going to want to top it off with something that sparkles in a case like this."

"Jewelry? A bribe?"

"You don't look at it like a bribe. It's an *apology.* It doesn't matter that you didn't do anything, Carter. It never does. You want this to go away, get things back, get her back and have sex with her again in this decade, you spring for something shiny. It's coming up on Valentine's Day anyway."

"That's shallow and manipulative."

"Damn right."

Carter laughed. "I'll keep the something shiny as a backup plan. But I think you're right about the rest. Especially letting her kick my ass first. It looked bad. It looked very bad."

"Did you take the brunette for a tumble?"

"No. God."

"Then you're a righteous man. Remember that. You're a righteous man, Carter. But you're also the big, bad dog. I'm proud to know you."

IN HER STUDIO, MAC FINISHED A SET OF PROOFS. SHE BOXED them for the client, along with a price sheet, her business card, and a list of options.

She glanced at the phone and congratulated herself for having the spine *not* to return Carter's calls. Maybe Corrine had been playing games. Probably she'd been playing games. But he'd still been on the field.

It would take more than a couple of apologetic phone calls to make up for that. Besides, if he hadn't done anything, what was he apologizing for?

Didn't matter, she reminded herself.

She was going to reward herself for a productive day with a bubble bath, a glass of wine, and an evening of popcorn and TV. An action movie, she decided. Where lots of things blew up, and there was absolutely not the slightest whiff of romance.

She set her completed work in a Vows shopping bag for delivery, then whirled around as she heard her door open.

Linda, in full, spitting rage, stormed in. "How dare you? How dare you have my car towed to some second-rate garage? Do you know they expected me to pay two hundred dollars to release it? You'd better write me a check right this minute."

Okay, Mac thought, there's the bell for this round. And for once, I'm ready. "Not on your life. Give me my keys."

"I'll give you your keys when you give me my two hundred dollars."

Mac stepped forward, grabbed her mother's purse, and emptied the contents on the floor. Linda's utter shock gave Mac time to crouch down, shove through the debris, and pocket her keys.

"How—"

"Dare I?" Mac said coolly. "I dare because you borrowed my car on Sunday, because you didn't return it, or my calls, for five days. I dare because I'm finished being used and abused. Believe me when I say I'm finished. I'm done. This stops now."

"It *snowed*. You could hardly expect me to risk driving home from New York in a snowstorm. I could have had an accident. I could have—"

"Called," Mac interrupted. "But leaving that aside, there was no storm; there was a dusting. Less than a quarter of an inch. That was Sunday."

"Ari wouldn't hear of me driving home. He invited me to stay over, so I did." She shrugged it off. "We spent a few days together. We went shopping, to the theater. Why shouldn't I have a life?"

"You're welcome to one. Have it somewhere else."

"Oh, don't be such a baby, Mackensie. I left you my car."

"You left me a car I couldn't use, even if you'd bothered to also include the goddamn keys."

"An oversight. You pushed me out the door so fast that day, it's no wonder I didn't remember. Don't swear at me." She burst into tears, lovely drops spilling copiously out of shattered blue eyes. "How can you treat me this way? How can you begrudge me a chance for happiness?"

It won't work, Mac told herself even as her stomach cramped. Not this time. "You know I used to ask myself those questions, reversing the you and me. I've never been able to find the answer."

"I'm sorry. I'm sorry. I'm in *love.* You don't know what it's like to feel this way about someone. How it takes over everything else so it's only the two of you. It was just a car, Mackensie."

"It was just *my* car."

"Look what you did to mine!" Even with tears still gleaming on her cheeks, the outrage came through. "You had it towed to that—that grease pit. And that horrible man is holding it hostage."

"So pay the ransom," Mac suggested.

"I don't know how you can be this mean to me. It's because you never let yourself feel. You take pictures of feelings, you don't have them. Now you're punishing me because I do."

"Okay." Mac crouched again, scooped, shoved, pushed the

scattered contents on the floor back into her mother's bag. "I have no feelings. I'm a horrible daughter. And in that vein, I want you to leave. I want you to go."

"I need the money for my car."

"You're not getting it from me."

"But . . . you have to—"

"No." She shoved the bag into Linda's hand. "That's the thing, Mom. I don't have to. And I'm not going to. Your problem, you fix it."

Linda's lip trembled, her chin quivered. Not manipulation, Mac thought, not entirely. She felt what she felt, after all. And believed herself the victim.

"How am I going to get home?"

Mac picked up the phone. "I'll call you a cab."

"You're not my daughter."

"You know, the sad thing for both of us is I am."

"I'll wait outside. In the cold. I'm not going to stand in the same room with you for another minute."

"They'll pick you up in front of the main house." Mac turned away, shut her eyes as she heard the door slam. "Yes, I need a cab at the Brown Estate. As quickly as possible."

With her stomach in ugly knots, Mac walked over and locked her door. She'd need to add aspirin to that post-workday relaxation plan, she thought. A whole bottle ought to just about do it. Maybe she'd take the aspirin and lie down in a dark room, try to sleep off the feelings she apparently didn't have.

She took the aspirin first, washed it down with a full glass of icy water to try to soothe the rawness in her throat. Then she simply sat down on the kitchen floor.

That was far enough.

She'd sit there until her knees stopped shaking, until her head stopped throbbing. Until the urge to burst into wild tears passed.

When the phone rang, she reached up, managed to grab it

from the counter. She read the ID, answered Parker. "I'm all right."

"I'm here."

"I know. Thanks. But I'm all right. I called her a cab. It'll be here in another couple minutes. Don't let her in."

"All right. I'm here," she repeated. "Whatever you need."

"Parker? She's never going to change, so I have to. I didn't know it would be so painful. I thought it would feel good, good and satisfying. Maybe with a little triumphant thrown in. But it doesn't. It feels awful."

"You wouldn't be you if it didn't hurt. You did the right thing, if that helps. The right thing for you. And Linda will bounce. You know she will."

"I want to be mad." Weary and weepy, Mac pressed her face into her updrawn knees. "It's so much easier when I'm mad at her. Why does this break my heart?"

"She's your mother. Nothing changes that. You're miserable when you let her use you, too."

"This is worse. But you've got a point."

"The cab's here. She's going."

"Okay." Mac closed her eyes again. "I'm all right. I'll talk to you tomorrow."

"Call if you need me before."

"I will. Thanks."

SHE COULDN'T WORK UP THE ENTHUSIASM FOR BUBBLES AND candles and wine, but took the hot bath. She put on her oldest flannel pants, a soft comfort. She no longer wanted sleep and thought drudgery might be an answer. She'd clean her bedroom, organize her closet, her dresser, scrub the bathroom for good measure.

It was way past time for household chores and it would keep her busy for hours. Possibly days. Best of all, it was a cleansing, she decided, a symbolic act to go along with her stand with Linda.

Out with the old, in with the new. And everything fresh and ordered when the task was done. Her new life order.

She opened her closet, puffed out her cheeks, expelled a balloon of air. The only way to approach it, she decided, was the way they did it on the improvement shows on TV. Haul it out, sort, toss.

Maybe she could just burn everything and start over. Burning bridges seemed to be her current theme anyway. Squaring her shoulders, she grabbed an armload, tossed it on the bed. By the third load she asked herself why she needed so many clothes. It was a sickness, that's what it was. No one person needed fifteen white shirts.

Fifty percent, she decided. That would be her goal. To purge out fifty percent of her wardrobe. And she'd buy those nice padded hangers. Color coordinated. And the clear, stackable shoe boxes. Like Parker.

When the contents of her closet lay heaped on her bed, on her sofa, she stood a little wild-eyed. Shouldn't she have bought the hangers, the boxes first? And one of those closet organizer kits. Drawer dividers. Now all she had was a big, terrible mess and no place to sleep.

"Why, why in God's name can I run a business, *be* a business, and not be able to cope with my own life? This is your life, Mackensie Elliot. Big heaps of stuff you don't know what to do with."

She would fix it. Change it. Deal with it. God, she'd kicked her own mother out of the house, surely she could deal with clothes and shoes and handbags. She'd cut down on the clutter in her life, in her head. Minimalize, she decided.

She'd go Zen.

Her home, her life, her damn closet would be a place of peace and tranquility. In clear plastic shoe boxes.

Starting now. Today was a new day, a new start, and a new, tougher, smarter, more formidable Mackensie Elliot. She went downstairs for a box of Hefty bags with a gleam in her eye.

The knock on the door struck her with such profound relief she actually shuddered. Parker, she thought. Thank God. What she needed now were the superpowers of Organizer Girl.

Eyes crazed, hair sticking up in spikes, she wrenched open the door. "Parker—oh. Oh. Of course. Perfect."

"You wouldn't answer your phone. I know you're upset," Carter continued. "If you'd just let me come in, just for a few minutes, to explain."

"Sure." She threw up her hands. "Why not. It just caps it off. Let's have a drink."

"I don't want a drink."

"Right. Driving." She waved her hands in the air as she stomped toward the kitchen. "I'm not driving." She slapped a bottle of wine on the counter, got out a corkscrew. "What? No date tonight?"

"Mackensie."

Somehow, she thought as she attacked the cork, he managed to make her name an apology, and a mild scold. The guy had skills.

"I know how it might have looked. Probably looked. How it looked." He stepped to the other side of the counter. "But it wasn't. Corrine . . . Let me do that," he said as she struggled with the cork.

She simply shot a finger at him.

"She just dropped by. Came over."

"Let me tell you something." She braced the bottle between her knees, raging as she yanked on the corkscrew. "Just because we had a fight, just because I felt I needed to set some reasonable boundaries, doesn't mean you get to entertain your mysterious, sexy ex five minutes later."

"I wasn't. She isn't. Damn it," he growled, and reached down to grab the bottle from her just as she managed to release the cork.

Her fist caught him square on the chin. The force knocked him back a full step.

"Feel better now?"

"I didn't mean . . . Your face got in the way." Setting the wine on the counter, she pressed her hand to her mouth to muffle the sudden laughter she feared might reach toward hysteria. "Oh God, it just gets more ridiculous."

"Can we sit down?"

She shook her head, walked to the window. "I don't sit down when I'm worked up. I don't have calm, reasonable discussions."

"So you think the second part is news to me? You left. You just ran off without giving me the chance to explain the situation."

"Here's one level. You're a free agent. We didn't agree, or even discuss, exclusivity."

"I assumed it was understood. We're sleeping together. Whatever the boundaries you may want, I'm with you. Only you. I expect the same. If that makes me traditional and priggish, it can't be helped."

She turned back to him. "Priggish. Not a term you hear every day. And it doesn't, Carter. It doesn't make you priggish. It makes you decent. I'm trying to tell you that, on one level, I had absolutely no right to be upset. But that level is mostly bullshit. The other level is we had a disagreement, and when I came over to try to work it out with you, you were with her."

"I wasn't with her. She was there."

"She was there. You were pouring her wine. You gave her my wine."

"I didn't give her your wine."

"Well, that's something."

"I didn't give her any wine. There was no wine involved. I told her she had to go. I made her cry." Remembering, he rubbed the back of his neck. "I sent her away in tears, and you wouldn't answer your phone. If you'd only waited, if you'd come in, given me a chance—"

"You made polite introductions."

He stopped, frowned at her. "I . . . yes."

"I nearly beat you to death with the damn bottle of wine for that. Oh, hello, Mac, this is the woman I lived with for nearly a damn year who I'm so careful to tell you as little as possible about. And she's standing there with her cleavage and perfect hair purring to you about pouring her a nice glass of the wine the idiot brought over."

"I—"

"Not to mention the fact that we'd already met just a couple hours before in the shoe department at Nordstrom."

"Who? What? When?"

"Your mutual friend what's-her-name already made the introductions while she and your ex were in *my* shoe department during *my* shoe therapy session."

Even the thought of it had Mac hitting the red zone. "And her with her damn red peep-toe pumps and single sarcastically lifted eyebrow as she checks *me* out. And smirks." She jabbed a finger at him. "*Smirks* with her perfectly sculpted lips. But I let it go, screw her and her attitude. I was going to buy my fabulous blue boots, and the adorable silver slingbacks, a really good bottle of wine to take to your place—after I stopped by the MAC counter for a new eyeliner, and got buffed up a little because I wanted to look good when I went to see you. Especially after I got a load of her. Then there was this great DKNY jacket, and cashmere was on sale. Which is why I'm going Zen. Well, that's partially because of the tow truck and emotional turmoil, but that's the root of it."

Shell-shocked, Carter let out a long breath. "I've changed my mind. Could I have a glass of wine?"

"And I don't know how you could think for one minute that

I'd stick around," she continued as she reached for a wineglass. "What? You expect me to go head-to-head with her. Have a slugfest?"

"No, that was Bob."

"If you'd had possession of the single brain men seem to pass around among them, you'd have introduced me to her—as the woman you're involved with. Not like I was just some delivery girl."

"You're absolutely right. I mishandled it. My only excuse is I was completely out of my depth. Everything was confused and inexplicable, and I'd burned the grilled cheese sandwich."

"You made her a *sandwich*?"

"No. No. I made myself a sandwich. Or I was making one when she came over, and I forgot I had the pan on the stove because she . . ." As it occurred to him mentioning what happened between Corrine's arrival and the burned sandwich wasn't a particularly good idea, he took a long drink of wine. "Interrupted. In any case, do I understand you ran into Corrine and Stephanie Gorden while you were shopping?"

"That's what I said."

"Somewhere in there," he mumbled. "I see. That certainly explains . . ." Boggy ground again, he realized. "Can I just say, bottom line, I didn't want her there. I wanted you. I want you. I'm in love with you."

"Don't pull out the love area when I'm having a crisis. Do you want to make me more crazed?"

"Is that actually possible? But no, I really don't."

"She had on seduction wear."

"I'm sorry? What?"

"Don't think I don't know why she 'dropped by.' She takes a look at me and thinks, *pfft*, as if I can't outgun that one, puts on the seduction wear and comes over. She came on to you, don't deny it."

His shoulders wanted to hunch. He had to make a genuine

and physical effort to straighten them. "I was making a sandwich. Doesn't that count for anything? I was making a sandwich and thinking about you. How could I possibly expect or prepare for her to come over and kiss me?"

"She *kissed* you?"

"Oh God. I should've bought the shiny thing. She just—it all caught me off guard."

"And you got a really big stick to defend yourself from her unwelcome advances?"

"I didn't— Are you jealous? Seriously jealous over this?"

She folded her arms. "Apparently. And don't take that as a compliment."

"Sorry, I can't seem to help it." He smiled. "She means nothing to me. I thought of you the whole time."

"Very funny." She picked up his wine, took a sip. "She's beautiful."

"Yes, she is."

She seared him with a glance. "Do you know nothing? Do you need Bob's list to tell you you're supposed to say something like she's nothing compared to you?"

"She's not. She never was."

"Please. Bee-stung lipped, sloe-eyed D cup." She took another sip, pushed the wine back to him. "I know it's shallow for me to hate her for her looks, but I don't have much else. And they're a lot. I get she caught you off guard. But the fact is, Carter, she blindsided me. Both times. All I know is you had a serious, live-together relationship with this woman, and she broke it off. You didn't, she did. You loved her, and she hurt you."

"I didn't love her. And the hurt? I suppose it's relative to the circumstances. I realize I've made this more complicated, and more important, because I've avoided talking about it. It's not my finest hour. I met her at a party at the Gordens. The mutual friends. I hadn't been back long, just a few months. We started seeing each other, casually at first. Then, ah, more seriously."

"You started sleeping together. I'm on to your semantics, Professor."

"Hmmm. She thought I'd eventually go back to Yale, and couldn't understand why I wanted to teach here, to be here. But that was a small, subtle thing initially. Living together just, well, it just sort of happened."

"How does that just sort of happen?"

"She was moving to a new place. A bigger apartment. Something fell through there, I can't remember the details. Exactly. But she'd already given notice where she lived, and had to move out. I had all that room, and it was only going to be for a few weeks, maybe a month. Until she found another place. And somehow . . ."

"She never found another place."

"I let it happen. It was nice, having someone there to have dinner with, or go out to dinner with. We went out to dinner quite a bit now that I think about it. I liked the company, having someone to come home to. The regular sex. And apparently I do need Cyrano."

"Everyone likes regular sex."

"I thought about asking her to marry me. Then I realized I was thinking about it because it was expected. Everyone just assumed . . . Then I felt guilty because I didn't want to ask her to marry me. I was living with her, sleeping with her, paying the bills, doing—"

Like a traffic cop, Mac threw up her hand. "You paid her bills?"

He shrugged. "Initially she was trying to save for her own place, then . . . It got to be a habit. What I mean to say is we were living together very much like a married couple, and I didn't love her. I wanted to. She must have felt it, and I could see she wasn't completely happy. She went out more. Why should she be stuck at home when I was buried in books and papers?

She realized I wasn't going to be what she wanted, or give her what she wanted, so she found someone else."

He stared at the wineglass on the counter. "I might not have loved her, but it's painful, and it's humiliating to be cast off for someone else. To be cheated on. She had an affair, to which I was oblivious. Which I wouldn't have been, admittedly, if I'd been paying more attention to her. She left me for him, and while it was hurtful, and embarrassing, it was also a relief."

Mac took a moment to absorb. "Let me just sum all that up, take it down to its basic formula. Because it's one I know very well. She maneuvered you into providing her with housing—for which she paid nothing."

"I could hardly ask her for rent."

"She shared none of the household expenses, and in fact sweet-talked you into fronting her for her expenses. You probably lent her cash from time to time. You'll never see that again. You bought her things—clothes, jewelry. If you balked, she used tears or sex to smooth that out and get what she was after."

"Well, I suppose, but—"

"Let me finish it out. When she got tired of it, or saw something shinier, she lied, cheated, betrayed, then laid it all out as your fault for not caring enough. Would that be about right?"

"Yes, but it doesn't factor in—"

Mac held up her hand again. "She's Linda. She's . . . Corrinda. She's the same model as my mother, just a younger version. I've lived my entire life in that cycle, except for the sex. And I know it's easier to see the cycle from outside it. You and me, Carter, we're a couple of patsies. Worse, we let them convince us we're at fault for their selfish, demeaning behavior. If I'd known all this I wouldn't have . . . yes, I would. I'd have reacted exactly the same way because it's knee-jerk. It's the Linda factor."

"That doesn't erase the fact that I helped create the situation, and let it continue when I didn't love her."

"I love my mother. God knows why, but I do. Under the seething resentment, the frustration and rage, I love her. And I know that under the selfish, abusive whininess, she—in her strange Linda way—loves me. Or, at least, I like to think so. But we'll never have a healthy relationship. We'll never have what I want. It's not my fault. Corrinda—as she will now and forever be to me—wasn't yours."

"I wish I hadn't let it hurt you, what happened. I wish I'd handled it better."

"Next time we run into her, you can introduce me properly as the woman you're involved with."

"Are we?" Those quiet blue eyes looked into hers. "Involved?"

"Is that going to be enough? Can you understand I'm trying to deal with the fact my emotional closet is cluttered, disorganized, and messy? That I don't know how long it might take me to sort it out?"

"I'm in love with you. That doesn't mean I want you to be with me, stay with me because you think it's expected. I want to be here when you sort it out, while you sort it out. I want to know it's truth when you tell me you love me."

"If I do, if I'm able to say that to you, it'll be the first time I've ever said it to a man. And it'll be the truth."

"I know." He took her hand, kissed it. "I can wait."

"This has been the strangest week." She brought their joined hands to her cheek. It felt right, she realized. It felt right to have him there with her. "I think we should go upstairs and finish making up."

# CHAPTER SEVENTEEN

SHE KISSED HIM ON THE STAIRS AND FELT THE LONG DAY SETTLE into place. "No wonder we're attracted to each other." She snuggled in briefly before taking his hand to continue up. "We both carry the patsy gene. It's probably like a pheromone."

"Speak for yourself. I prefer thinking of it as being considerate by nature and thinking the best of others."

"Yeah. Patsy." She laughed up at him, then jerked to a halt when she saw stupefied shock rush over his face. "What? What's the— Oh God. Oh my God."

She stood, as he was, staring at the tornado debris of her room. "I forgot. I . . . forgot to tell you I'm actually an international spy, a double agent. And my arch nemesis broke in earlier to search for the secret code. There was a terrible battle."

"I'd like to believe that."

"It's Zen."

"Your arch nemesis?"

"No. No, the ultimate goal. Look, just go downstairs until I stuff all this back. It won't take that long."

"It's a small department store," Carter said with some wonder. "It's a boutique."

"Yes, for the temporarily insane." She hauled up an armful of clothes. "Really, give me ten minutes. It's not as bad as it looks."

"I applaud your optimism. Mackensie, I'm sorry what happened upset you this much."

"How did you—"

"I have two sisters and a mother. I recognize the signs of an angry cleaning spree."

"Oh." She dumped the armload back on the sofa. "I forgot you have knowledge of the basic framework."

"I'll help you put everything back. Somewhere. Since I was part of the problem."

"No. Yes. I mean, yes, you were part of the problem. Like the tip of the iceberg. But under the surface was the really massive . . . rest of the iceberg," she decided. "Like *Titanic*'s. You know from my mother's mortifying visit up to Corrinda—"

"You're really going to keep calling her that?"

"Yes. Anyway, you know that part of it, but what set this off, the last twitch of the finger on the trigger circles back to Linda."

She walked to the bed this time, took an armload. "She didn't bring my car back. And, because she didn't want to bring my car back, as that would have entailed bringing herself back when she was having a good time in New York, she didn't answer her phone."

She turned after hanging up the load and turned to find him behind her with another. "Thanks. She also neglected to leave me the keys to hers, so I couldn't have used it if I'd wanted to. By yesterday morning I was ready to do murder, but then I had a pep talk from Laurel—who takes no crap from anyone. I so admire that in her. After that, I had my mother's car towed to this garage, this mechanic's place."

"That was brilliant. Appropriate consequences for inappropriate behavior."

"That sounds so Dr. Maguire. Appropriate maybe, but it's mean, too, especially since the guy knows Del and agreed to charge Linda for the towing and the storage."

"I take it, since your car's out front, she finally brought it back. She'd have been furious about hers being towed."

"And then some. It was ugly. Very ugly, during which I learned even when you stand your ground, do what's right, it hurts. A fist in the face, you could say," she added with a small smile for him. "And skipping over the details, I ended by calling her a cab and locking her out of the house."

"Good. She'll think twice before pulling something like that again."

"There's that optimism. It's so shiny. She never thinks twice, Carter. It's going to take a lot more of the same before we're done. It's on me to do it. To keep doing it, and to keep taking that fist in the face without giving ground."

"But you will."

"I have to. Anyway, I decided to work off the upset by cleaning up my mess. I made a bigger one first, but with the goal of decluttering and restructuring. Which became symbolic for tossing out old habits and mind-sets. So . . ."

She broke off as she turned with another armload and caught sight of herself in the mirror. "Oh Jesus, Jesus, I look like I escaped from the institution for the terminally sloppy and unkempt. Couldn't you have told me my hair looked like a couple of cats fought in it?"

"I like your hair."

She raked her fingers through it. "You know, this is just one more world of irritating. I looked really good the night I came by your place. Those MAC girls know their stuff. Plus I sprang for La Perla, and I was wearing it. My credit card had a minor stroke, but now that we landed the Seaman job, it'll recover nicely. Still, I—"

"You got the job?" He picked her off her feet, gave her a quick spin. "That's—damn it."

"Almost the reaction I might've expected."

"I bought a bottle of champagne to celebrate with you when you got the job. I didn't bring it with me."

"You bought champagne to celebrate with me." She could all but feel her pupils take the shape of hearts as she stared at him. "You're the sweetest man."

"We'll celebrate tomorrow."

"Event tomorrow night."

"First chance then. Congratulations. This is major."

"Majorly major, to be redundant about it. Event of the year, and it's going to test all our skills, push us to develop new ones."

"You must . . . What's La Perla?"

Her smile spread slowly. "Ah, so two sisters and a mother haven't taught you everything about the female. You still have a few things to learn, Professor. Go downstairs."

"I don't want to go downstairs." He lowered his head to nibble at her lips. "I've missed you. Missed your face. Missed touching you. Look how we cleaned a spot off the bed. It looks just big enough."

"Downstairs." She pressed a finger at his chest, pushed him back. "I'll tell you when to come back up. You'll thank me."

"Why don't I just thank you now and—"

"Out."

She gave him a shove.

He paced the studio, studied her photographs, poked at bridal magazines. He wondered what the term was for what was running around inside him, this intense joy and ragged impatience. Mackensie was upstairs, and that was wonderful. Mackensie was upstairs, and he wasn't. That was making him crazy.

He wandered to the door to make sure it was locked, wondering if he should take up the wine. He didn't want any, but she—

"Why don't you come on up?"

Thank God, he thought, and left the wine where it was.

He saw from the shadows and flickering light that she'd lit candles. The faintest scent drifted through the air, alluringly. He should have brought the wine, he realized.

Then, when he stepped into the bedroom, his heart stopped.

In the shifting shadows, the golden light, in the drifting scent she lay on the bed, turned toward him, her head propped on her elbow. She'd done something to her hair, something sleek, and darkened her lips and eyes to exotic. And on her long, lovely body were wisps and whirls of tiny black lace.

"This," she said, sweeping her free hand along her side, "is La Perla."

"Oh. Thank you."

She crooked a finger. "Why don't you come over here and take a closer look."

He walked to her. "You take my breath away."

He sat, ran his hand over her side, cruising the curves. "You were wearing this the other night?"

"Mmm-hmmm."

"If I'd known, you'd never have made it to the car."

"Really? Why don't you demonstrate what you'd have done, had you but known."

He leaned down, touched his lips to hers for one shimmering moment. Then devoured. Instant need, wild and wicked urgency lashed him, whipping for speed. He swallowed her muffled gasp and demanded more.

Arousal, longing, love rampaged inside him, snarling into a desperate greed for her mouth under his, her body under his. The taste of her, just the first taste, sparked the fire in the blood.

While his mouth conquered, his hands plundered.

Her body exploded under his, arching, writhing as she dragged at his shirt. She pulled it up, nails scraping flesh in her rush, and over his head to heave it away. She rolled with him, her breath sobbing as they wrapped together, as they sought each other. Sought darker, deeper pleasure that slicked the skin, racked the heart.

Touch, taste, possess.

To be wanted like this, needed like this—to want and need in return—seemed impossible to her. It was like being burned alive, feeling every inch, to be aware of every inch of her body while it blazed. While he consumed.

He rolled her over on her back, jerked her hips up. And drove himself into her. She couldn't find the breath to scream.

Stunned, staggered, helpless, she flailed for purchase, and her hands clutched the tangled sheets as she might a lifeline. His clamped over them, wrenched her arms over her head. He plunged into her, again, again. A hard, primal beat that propelled them both to the edge, and over.

When he collapsed on her, their hands remained clasped. While the candlelight flickered over the damp tangle of them, he turned his head. And gave her a kiss of exquisite tenderness.

She lay as she was, steeped in a kind of wonder.

"I was rough," he murmured. "Did I—"

"You know what?" she interrupted, smiling in the flickering dark. "I'm going back to Nordstrom. I'm going to buy out their entire stock of La Perla. Whatever they've got in my size will be mine. I'm never wearing anything else."

"While you're out, maybe you could pick up some vitamins. A whole lot of vitamins. And minerals."

She laughed, rolling to her side as he rolled to his, so they were nose to nose. "You have such quiet eyes. No one would ever know you're an animal in bed."

"You have this body that makes me want it. Are you cold?"

"Not now, possibly never again. Can you stay?"

"Yes."

"Good. I owe you some scrambled eggs."

EMMALINE STOOD WITH HER HANDS ON HER HIPS IN THE MIDdle of the disaster now known as Mac's bedroom. "I had no idea, no idea that you and Carter were such sex monkeys."

"We are. But I have to cop to doing this all by myself."

"Which begs the question: Why?"

"I'm organizing."

"In this world, organizing generally means putting things in place."

"Which will come. Do you want this purse? I never use this purse."

Emma stepped around and through the hillocks of clothes and accessories to take the brown flap bag. "This color looks like dried poop. Maybe you don't use it because it's ugly."

"It really is I don't know what I was thinking that day. Toss it in discard. That pile," she added, gesturing.

Moving over, Emma dropped the bag. "You're getting rid of these shoes."

Mac glanced over as Emma examined one of the pair of sky-high lime green pumps. "They kill my feet. I get blisters every time I wear them."

"They're really great shoes."

"I know, but I never wear them because of the blister element." Mac shook her head at the gleam in Emma's eyes. "They won't fit you."

"I know. It's just not fair that Laurel and Parker wear the same size, and you and I are the odd men out. It's injustice." With the shoe still in hand, she turned a little circle. "How do you and Carter have sex in here?"

"We manage. Mostly I've been going over to his place just

lately, but that's really because when he sees this he wants to help. You can't have a man involved in closet and dresser organizing. He started counting my shoes."

"They never understand the shoes."

"Speaking of which, put those back in the keep pile—over there. They're too fabulous to toss. I'll wear them when I'm going to sit down a lot."

"Much better idea."

"See, this he would never get. And he'd get that thoughtful furrow between his eyebrows."

"So, other than thoughtful furrows, you two are doing good?"

"We're doing great. Close to perfect. I don't know why I got all twisted up and crazed about it. What about this shirt? It's a lot like this shirt. I should get rid of one of them, but which?"

Emma studied the two black camp shirts. "They're black. There's no limit on black shirts. They're wardrobe basics."

"See. That's why I asked you to come by."

"You really need Parker in here, Mac. You said you started this on Thursday. Last Thursday."

"Parker can't come in here. She'd take one look, and her nervous system would implode. She'd be in a coma for months. I wouldn't do that to her. And I ordered stuff. Shoe boxes, hangers, and this thing with all these hooks on it for hanging bags or belts. I think. I looked at closet organizers, but I found them confusing. Plus I'm tossing twenty-five percent. It was going to be fifty, but that was before I came to my senses."

"But you've been at it for nearly a week."

"I haven't had that much time for it, between work and Carter, and my strange reluctance to come up here at all. But I'm going to stick with it tonight."

"You're not seeing Carter?"

"Parent-teacher deal at the academy. Besides, we don't see each other every night."

"Right. Only on the ones that end with Y. You look happy. He makes you happy."

"He does. There was this little thing."

"Oh-oh."

"No, just a little thing. He said I might want to keep some things there. Some of my things."

"Such as a change of clothes, a toothbrush. Mac."

"I know. I *know.* It's logical, and it's considerate. But I felt myself wanting to get twisted up and crazed. I didn't, but I wanted to. And, I mean, look at my things. There are so many of them. If I start mixing them with his, how will I know where they are? And what if I leave something over there, then I need it here?"

"You do know you're looking at this, trying to find the flaws, the barriers, the drop chutes. You know that, right?"

"Knowing I'm looking for them doesn't mean they aren't there. I'm just getting used to being with him—an official couple—and now he's offering me closet space. I'm trying to deal with my own closet."

"And doing a remarkable job of it."

She studied the piles. "It's a work in progress."

"So are you. So's your relationship with Carter. People and relationships never stop being a work in progress."

"I know you're right. It's just . . . I want to get everything in place." She blew out a breath as she scanned the piles. "I want to get my life organized and feel in control. Get some clarity. I want to know what I'm doing with that, the way I do with the work."

"Do you love him?"

"How do people know that? I keep asking myself, and the answer keeps coming back yes. Yes, I do. But people fall in and out of love all the time. The falling-in part's scary and exciting, but the falling-out is horrible. It's all going really well right now, so I'd like to keep it that way."

"Do you know how much I wish I was in love with a man who loved me?"

"I don't think you'd be picking out your bridal bouquet."

"You're really wrong. If I had what you have right now? I wouldn't be standing in the middle of chaos trying to organize my life. I'd be looking forward to making a life. If you—"

She broke off as she heard the door downstairs slam.

"Hey, Mac? You here?"

"What's Jack doing here?" Emma wanted to know.

"Oh, I forgot. Upstairs!" she called out. "He was coming by to talk to Parker, so I told her to ask him to stop over. Confused by closet organizers, I figured why not consult an architect?"

"You want an architect—a man—*Jack*—to organize your closet?"

"No, to give me a vision of what to use to organize it."

Emma gave Mac a dubious look. "You've now entered Parker territory."

"Maybe, but have you seen her closet? It's like a layout in a magazine. It's like what the Queen of England probably has. Without all the odd hats. Jack! Just the man I wanted to see."

He stood in the doorway, tall, clad in jeans, work shirt, and boots—and very male. "I don't want to come in there. You're not supposed to touch anything at a crime scene."

"The only crime here is that." She pointed at her closet. "An empty closet with one stupid bar and shelf. You have to help me."

"I told you we needed to design the closet when we altered the space."

"I was in a hurry back then. Now I'm not. I know I need at least two bars, right—a lower one. And more shelves. Maybe some drawers."

He glanced around. "You're going to need a bigger boat."

"I'm purging. Don't start with me."

He walked in, hooked his thumbs in his belt loops. "Roomy."

"Yes, which is part of the problem. All that room, I've felt obliged to fill it. You can make it better."

"Sure I can make it better. A kit from Home Depot would make it better."

"I've looked at them. I want something more . . . More."

"Ought to line it in cedar while we're at it. You've got enough room for some built-ins here. Run a short rod on the side, maybe some box shelves there. I don't know. I'll think about it. I know a guy who could knock it out for you."

She beamed a smile at him. "See, I knew you'd know what to do with it."

"Hauling all this stuff back in's on you."

"Goes without saying. While you're here—"

"You'd like me to design your broom closet?"

"No, but thanks. Male point of view."

"I've got that on me."

"What does it mean when you tell a woman she should leave some of her things at your place?"

"How did I get the concussion?"

"Typical," Emma muttered.

"Hey, she asked."

"It's a woman you're involved with exclusively. Intimately," Mac explained.

"And now she wants to leave her strange female products in the bathroom. Then she needs a drawer. Before you know it she's buying throw pillows for the bed, and your beer has to make room in the refrigerator for her diet drinks and low-fat yogurt. Then, wham, you're going antiquing instead of watching the game on Sunday afternoon."

"And that's all it is?" Emma demanded. "Sure, she can roll around in the bed, tear up the sheets, but hell no, she can't leave a toothbrush in *your* bathroom. Or have a few inches of a drawer. That's too pushy, that's too much. Why not just leave the money on the dresser and call it what it is?"

"Whoa. That's not what I—"

"Why should she be comfortable, why should she expect you

to make any room in your life for her needs? God forbid she should infringe on your precious time, your sacred space. Pathetic," she said. "Both of you." And stormed out.

Jack stared at the empty doorway. "What was that? Why is she so pissed off at me?"

"It's me. It started with me."

"Next time warn me so I can dodge the ricochets. Is she . . . seeing someone who's giving her trouble?"

"No. She's not seeing anyone special. I am, and she's frustrated because she thinks I don't appreciate it—him—enough. She's wrong. I do. But she's right in that my thought process takes the same downward spiral you just outlined. And actually, she's right. It is pathetic."

"It's not a downward spiral, necessarily. Maybe you want the yogurt or the antiquing. It depends."

"On what?"

"Who's leaving their stuff in your drawer. Got any beer?"

"Yeah."

"Let's go have a beer. I'll sketch something out. If you like it, I'll have the guy I know come over and measure, knock it out."

"That's worth a beer."

"So, you and Carter Maguire."

"Me and Carter Maguire," she said as they started down. "Is it weird?"

"Why would it be?"

"I don't know. Maybe since we sort of knew each other in high school when I was going through my artistic free spirit phase and he was a nerd. And he was tutoring Del when I had my obligatory crush on Del."

"You had a crush on Del?"

"Obligatory five-minute one," she repeated as she got out the beer. "In fact, I think it only lasted three. Emma made the five."

"Emma had . . . hmm."

"And my attention sort of skimmed over him. Carter, I mean.

The oh, there's that guy, the smart one. Then fast-forward to now, and it's like *oh*, there's that guy! Funny."

"It looks good on you."

"Feels good, most of the time." She handed him the beer, tapped hers to it. "When it's not scary. I've never been in love before. In lust, in serious like, but love's a whole new level of good and scary. He's got a school thing tonight, which is another strange and funny thing. Me, falling for a teacher. The PhD. I'm the only one of us who didn't go to college. Photography courses, business courses, but not the dorms and campus and the whole shot. And I'm wrapped up in a guy who grades term papers, gives homework, leads discussions on Shakespeare.

"You'd make more sense, come to think of it."

"Me?" Jack blinked at her. "I would?"

"No need to wear the panic face. I'm just saying you'd be a more logical choice. We both think in images, in concepts. We need to visualize to create. We both run our own businesses, work with clients. We have divorced parents and half sibs, though your parents are really nice. We have a close circle of mutual friends, are commitment phobic. And we like the occasional beer.

"Plus," she realized, "our names rhyme."

"You're right. Let's go have sex."

She laughed. "Missed that boat."

"I guess we did."

Amused at both of them, she tipped up her beer. "You never made the move."

"If I'd made the move, Del would've beaten me to death with a shovel. Nobody messes with his girls."

"He does know we've all had sex."

"He prefers to pretend otherwise, but none of you have had sex with me. To my misfortune. That's key."

"I guess you're right about that. Besides, while logically we may seem suited, we'd end up fighting over drawer space and hating each other. Carter makes room. He's got the innate ability to open up and accept."

"Got the starry eyes on you," Jack commented. "So how does it work? Who takes the wedding photographer's pictures when she walks down the aisle?"

"Aisle?" She choked on her beer. "I never said anything about aisle. I'm not—we're not. What makes you think we're thinking about getting married? Where'd that come from?"

"Oh, I don't know." He swiveled on his stool, gestured at the walls lined with wedding photos. "Being surrounded maybe, added to the starry eyes."

"That's business. Those are business. Just because I think about weddings doesn't mean I'm thinking about a wedding."

"Okay, no need to go to Crazytown."

"I'm not. I'm just—" She sucked in a breath. Marching to her desk, she came back with a large pad and a pencil. "Sketch. Earn the beer."

SHE SPENT THE REST OF THE EVENING STICKING WITH THE PLAN. As the hills and piles became more manageable, her stress level decreased, and a sense of accomplishment rose. She'd have her living space back, and better than ever in no time, she thought. She'd feel more in control then.

It was nice to have the evening alone, to deal with her own business, to have her own space. She could do that and miss Carter at the same time. In fact, doing that meant she was handling the relationship.

Love him, love being with him, but be perfectly content to spend time on her own. Unlike—

When the phone rang, she checked the readout.

Linda.

Mac closed her eyes, reminded herself she couldn't avoid

speaking to her mother forever. Avoiding calls was childish. Confront and stand your ground, she told herself.

"Yes, Mom."

"Mackensie, you have to come! Please, please, come right away."

Alarm ripped straight through annoyance, and had Mac's heartbeat jagged with fear. "What is it? What's wrong?"

"Hurry. Oh, you have to come. I don't know what to do."

"Are you hurt? Have you—"

"Yes. Yes, I'm hurt. Please help me. I need you. Please help me."

"Call nine-one-one. I'm on my way."

She flew out of the house, grabbing a coat on the fly. Dozens of images, each worse than the last rushed through her mind. A suicide attempt, an accident, a break-in.

Icy, treacherous roads, she thought as she risked life and limb and punched the speed through the nasty fall of freezing rain. A careless driver in the best of circumstances, Linda could've wrecked that toy car of hers, and—

No, no, she'd called from home, not the cell. She was home.

Mac fought to keep control of the wheel, gripped it with hands that wanted to shake, as she rounded a curve too fast for safety.

She fishtailed to the curb in front of her mother's dollhouse Cape Cod, ran up the slippery walk to the door. She found it unlocked. The thought of break-in shoved through the door with her.

Had she been raped? Beaten?

She leaped over a shattered vase of roses, into the living room where Linda lay curled on the floor, weeping.

"Mom! Mom, I'm here." She dropped to the floor beside Linda, frantically checking for injuries. "Where are you hurt? What did he do? Did you call the police, an ambulance?"

"Oh! I want to die!" Linda turned her ravaged, tear-streaked face into Mac's shoulder. "I can't bear it."

"No, don't say that. It's not your fault. I'll call for help, and we'll—"

"Don't leave me!"

"I won't. I won't." Rocking, she stroked her mother's hair. "It's going to be all right, I promise."

"How can it be? He's gone. He left me here."

"Did you get a good look at him? Was it someone you knew?"

"I thought I knew him. I trusted him with my *heart.* And now he's gone."

"Who?" Rage boiled inside her burning off the fear. "Who did this to you?"

"Ari. Of course, Ari. I thought I meant something to him. He said I'd brought the light back to his life. He said all these things to me, then he does this. How could he do this to me? How could he be so cruel?"

"It's all right. It's going to be all right. He'll pay for it."

"He said it was an emergency. There wasn't *time.* It had to be tonight. What difference could a few days make? How could I have known my passport had expired?"

"What?" Mac jerked back. "What are you saying? What exactly did he do?"

"He's gone to Paris. To Paris, Mac. He left without me. He called from his plane. He said he had to go tonight. Some business that couldn't wait the way he'd promised he would so I could get the passport straightened out. Business." Fury burned through the flood of tears. "Lies. It's another woman, I know it. Some French whore. He promised me, and now he's gone!"

Mac got slowly to her feet as Linda wept into her hands. "You called me, this time of night, let me think you were hurt."

"I am hurt! Look at me."

"I am looking at you. I see a spoiled, angry child having a tantrum because she didn't get her way."

"I *love* him."

"You don't know the meaning. God, I nearly killed myself getting here."

"I needed you. I need someone. You'll never understand what that's like."

"I hope not. There's water and glass all over your floor. You're going to want to clean that up."

"You're not leaving? You're not leaving me alone like this."

"Yes, I am. And next time, I won't come. For God's sake, Linda, grow up."

She kicked broken glass out of her way, and walked out.

# CHAPTER EIGHTEEN

MAC GATHERED HER EQUIPMENT FOR THE REHEARSAL, CHECKED her notes while Carter sat at the counter grading papers. From upstairs the sound of a nail gun whooshed and boomed.

"You can't possibly concentrate with all that noise."

"I teach teenagers." Carter red-penciled some comments in the margin. "I can concentrate during thermonuclear war when necessary."

Curious, she peeked over his shoulder as he marked the grade. "Got a B, not bad."

"And real progress for this student. He's opening up. Are you ready to go?"

"I have a little time yet. Sorry I forgot to tell you I had to work tonight."

"You've already said that. It's fine."

"Valentine's Day wedding, always the big of big deals. Parker and I have to be there, every step of tonight's rehearsal. And tomorrow." She leaned in to kiss him. "People in my business tend to work on Valentine's Day."

"Understood."

"I'll send you a schmaltzy, sloppy e-card. And I got you something. Major step for me, as it's my first Valentine's Day gift."

She went to her desk, took a slim package out of the drawer. "I'll give it to you now in case this thing runs longer than we plan, and you decide to go."

"I'll wait. You got me a present." He took off his glasses, set them aside. "That's the second gift you've given me. The cardinal," he reminded her.

"That was more of a token. This is a gift. Open it."

He untied the ribbon, opened the lid. "*As You Like It.*"

"It caught my eye because it's all battered and worn. It looks like it's been read a couple of million times."

"It does, and it's perfect." He cupped her cheek to draw her to him. "Thank you. Would you like yours?"

"Let me answer that with: duh."

He reached into his briefcase and took out a small box wrapped in white paper with a glossy red ribbon. The size and shape of it had Mac's heart dropping to her stomach then bouncing up to her throat.

"Carter."

"You're my valentine. Open it."

That heart thudded like a fist as she unwrapped the box. She held her breath, lifted the lid. And let it out again at the sparkle of earrings.

Two tiny diamond hearts dangled from the stud of a third in a delicate, elegant trio. "My God, Carter, they're gorgeous. They're . . . wow."

"I can't take full credit. Sherry helped me pick them out."

"They're amazing. I love them. I—" The words tangled on her tongue. Unable to say them, she threw her arms around him instead. "Thank you. I am definitely your valentine. Oh, I have to try them on."

She spun away to take the simple hoops out of her ears and replace them. She dashed to the mirror across from her workstation. "Oh, wow, sparkly!" Tipping her head from side to side, she watched them glint.

"Putting them on right away means you like them."

"I'd be crazy not to. How do they look?"

"A little dim compared to your eyes, but they'll do."

"Carter, you leave me speechless. I never know what—wait." Inspired, she ran over for a tripod. "I'm going to be late, but fabulous earrings for Valentine's Day trump punctuality. Even Parker would give me a bye on this."

"What are you doing?"

"It'll take two minutes. Just stay right there," she told him as she dug her camera out of her bag.

"You want to take my picture?" Watching her set up, he shifted on the stool. "I always feel so stiff in pictures."

"I'll fix that. Remember, I'm a professional." She smiled over the camera as she fixed it to the tripod. "You look really cute."

"Now you're just making me self-conscious."

She set the angle, framed it in. "Light's good, I think. We'll try it." Palming the remote, she walked to him. "Now, happy Valentine's Day." She linked her arms around his neck, laid her lips on his.

She let herself sink in, let him draw her a little closer.

She captured the moment, and when she eased back, looked in his eyes, captured another.

"Now," she murmured, turning so her cheek rested against his. "Smile." She pressed the remote, then again as backup. "There." She turned to him again, bumped noses. "That wasn't so bad."

"Maybe we should try that again." He cupped the back of her neck with his hand. "I think I blinked."

"I've got to go," she said with a laugh. Pulling away, she went over, checked her shots before taking the camera off the tripod.

"Aren't you going to let me see?"

"Not until I'm finished fussing with them. Then you can consider the print the second part of your present."

"I was hoping I'd get that when you finished work."

"Why, Dr. Maguire." She repacked her camera. "All right, we'll call it a three-parter."

He rose to help her on with her coat. Mac hefted her equipment bag. "Now you have to wait."

"I'm good at it," he said and opened the door for her.

Apparently he was, she thought, and set off for the main house at a lope.

"I DON'T KNOW HOW TO GET OUT OF IT, BUT THERE HAS TO BE A way."

"Mac." Parker held the champagne flute up to the light to check for spots before setting it on the table in the Bride's Suite. "It's just dinner."

"It is not. You know it's not just. It's meet-the-parents dinner. *Family* dinner."

"You've been seeing Carter for about two months now. It's time."

"Where is that written down?" Mac demanded. "I want to see where that's written down in a rule book." She flopped the napkins down in a way that had Parker sighing, then arranging them properly. "You know what it means when a man takes you home to meet his mother."

"Yes, I do. It means he wants two women who are an important part of his life to get to know each other. He wants to show both of them off."

"I don't want to be shown off. I'm not a poodle. Why can't we just keep things the way they are? Him and me."

"It's called a relationship. Look it up."

Laurel came in on the tail end with a plate of fruit and cheese. "If you're going to be such an ass about it, Mac, why didn't you just say no?"

"Hello, diamond earrings." Mac lifted both hands, pointed her fingers at the dangling hearts. "I was blinded by the sparkle. Plus, he was sneaky, and he asked oh-so casually after I said we had an early event today and we should do something together after. He trapped me into it."

"Ass," Laurel said.

"I know. Do you think I don't know that? Knowing it, even knowing the ass is rooted in mother phobia doesn't make it less real."

"No, it doesn't," Parker agreed. "You could have said the same to him."

"It's important to him. I could see it through the oh-so casual. He deserves someone who'd go to family dinner and meet his mother. I wish it was later, or that it had happened last week and was over—but they were in Spain last week, apparently. Not that it matters because if it had been last week, I'd wish it was the week before."

"We know her too well," Laurel decided. "Because I know both of us followed that."

"Every time I think I have a handle on this, and one on myself, something new crops up. And you know they're all going to be checking me out, talking about me."

"Personally, I think it's good to get it done in one big splash." Laurel stepped back, studied the table. "Dive in all at once into the big family pool. Easier and quicker than going in inch by inch."

"That's actually a good point," Mac said after a moment.

"You're good with people," Parker pointed out. "Getting them to talk about themselves, figuring them out. Do that."

"Also a good point. And bright side, maybe this nice, intimate wedding will turn into an all-night drunken brawl."

"The FOB looked like a troublemaker," Laurel commented.

Cheered, Mac draped her arms over her friends' shoulders. "I'll just think positive thoughts. I guess we should go down and help Emma finish. It's almost showtime."

THERE WAS NO DRUNKEN BRAWL, AND NO ESCAPE. MAC COULD be grateful she'd insisted on meeting Carter at his parents' home, so she had the drive alone, a little time to calm down.

Diving into the pool, she reminded herself. And she was a strong swimmer. Generally. She followed the directions Carter had given her, complete with landmarks, into the pretty, settled neighborhood.

Exactly what she'd expected, she realized. Solid New England home, on the upper-middle-class side of things. Patches of melting snow over generous lawns, old trees full of character, tidy hedges, neat fences.

Dignified, but not stuffy. Well-to-do but not showy.

God, what was she doing here?

Swallowing hard, she pulled into the left of the double drive, parked behind Carter's Volvo. A lot of cars, she thought. An awful lot of cars beside the sturdy, two-story house with its comfortable sitting porch.

She started to flip down the vanity mirror, check her makeup. But what if someone was looking out, she thought. Then she'd look vain and prissy. God, Mac, get over yourself.

She got out, walked around to get the basket of flowers. She'd second-guessed that simple gesture a half dozen times. Leftover wedding flowers as a hostess gift. Was it tacky?

The vote had been for sweet and thoughtful, but . . .

Too late now.

She climbed to the porch, wished fleetingly she'd checked her makeup after all, and knocked.

It took only seconds—she wasn't prepared—but she felt a trickle of relief when she saw Sherry's familiar face.

"Hi! Oh, wow, look at those! Mom's going to flip. Welcome to Maguire madness." She bustled Mac right in. "Wii," she continued, gesturing toward the shouts. "The game? We got it for Dad for Christmas. Nick and Sam—my brother-in-law—are taking on the kids in baseball. Here, let me hold that while you get out of your coat. Most everybody's back in the great room. Oh, you're wearing the earrings! Aren't they fabulous? Here, let me take your coat."

Sherry pushed the basket back at Mac, took the coat. And realizing she'd yet to have to say a word, Mac smiled.

"Mom's fussing with dinner. She's nervous. Are you? When I first met Nick's family, I was so nervous I hid in the bathroom for ten minutes. It never occurred to me Georgia—that's Nick's mom—it never occurred to me *she'd* be nervous, too. Later, she told me she'd changed her outfit three times before I got there. It made me feel better. So, Mom's nervous. Feel better."

"Thanks. I do."

As Sherry whisked her in, Mac had an impression of people, of movement inside a bright, open space, of Carter laughing with a handsome man with white hair and a trim beard. Of the good aromas of home cooking.

A moment, was all Mac could think. Easy family moment. She'd never once had one of her own, but she recognized it.

"Hey, everybody, Mac's here."

Then the movement stopped—freeze-frame, Mac thought—as the attention shifted to focus on her.

Carter moved first, pushing off the counter where he'd been

leaning to come to her. "You made it." He kissed her lightly over the fragrant white lilies and Bianca roses. Since her hands gripped the basket, he brushed a hand over her shoulder as he turned. "Mom, this is Mackensie."

The woman who walked over from the stove had a strong face, clear eyes. Her smile was polite, with a hint of warmth. And, Mac thought, a hint of reservation. "It's nice to meet you, at last."

"Thank you for having me, Mrs. Maguire." She offered the basket. "These are from today's event. Emma—you know Emma—does the flowers. We thought you might like them."

"They're stunning." Pam leaned in to sniff. "And delicious. Thank you. Sherry, put these on the coffee table, will you? We'll all enjoy them. How about a glass of wine?"

"I'd love one."

"Diane, pour Mac some wine."

"My sister Diane," Carter said.

"Hello. Cabernet or Pinot? We're having chicken."

"Ah, Pinot, thanks."

"My father, Michael Maguire. Dad."

"Welcome." He gave Mac's hand a strong shake. "Irish, are you?"

"Ah, some of me."

"My grandmother had hair like yours. Bright as a sunset. You're a photographer."

"Yes. Thanks," she said when Diane handed her a glass of wine. "My partners and I run a wedding business. Well, you know that, as we're doing Sherry's wedding."

He shot out a teasing grin. "As father of the bride, I just get handed the bills."

"Oh, Dad."

He winked at Mac as Sherry rolled her eyes at him.

"We send a flask along with the final invoice."

His laugh was full and rich. "I like your girl, Carter."

"So do I."

By the time they sat down to the meal, Mac had a good sense of who was who. Mike Maguire liked a laugh, adored and was adored by his family. While he might have been the doctor, it was his wife who had her finger on every pulse. She'd have said they worked as a team, and it appeared to be a strong one. But when nitty met gritty, Pam ran the show.

Sherry was the baby, a bundle of energy and fun, secure, loving, and in love. Her fiance behaved like and was treated like a son. She imagined his obvious delight in Sherry earned him major points.

Diane, the oldest, leaned toward the bossy side. Motherhood suited her, and the kids beamed bright, but she came off vaguely dissatisfied. Not young and starting her life as Sherry was, not content and secure in her position like her mother. Her husband was easygoing, a joker with his kids. Mac sensed his unruffled nature often irritated his wife.

She understood dynamics and personalities, how they formed and re-formed images. Here was tradition for them, conversation over a Sunday family dinner, bits and pieces of their lives passed around like the mashed potatoes.

She was the X factor. The outside element that—at least for the moment—altered the image.

"Weekends must be your busiest time," Pam commented.

"Generally. We do a lot of weekday evening events."

"A lot of work during the week, too," Carter pointed out. "All the planning. It's not just showing up with a camera. Then there's after the event. I've seen a couple of the packages, the albums Mackensie's done. They're works of art."

"Everything's digital now." Diane shrugged, poked at her chicken.

"Primarily. I still work with film now and then. This is a wonderful meal, Mrs. Maguire. You must love to cook."

"I like the production and drama of big meals. And it's

Pam. I also like the idea of four women, four friends, forming and running a business together. Running your own company takes a lot of stamina, a lot of dedication, along with the creativity."

"But it's such a happy business," Sherry put in. "It's like an endless celebration. Flowers and beautiful dresses, music, champagne."

"Weddings keep getting more elaborate. All that time, that stress, that expense, for one day." Diane lifted a shoulder even as her mouth turned down in a frown. "People more worried about who sits where or what color ribbon to use than what marriage means. And the people getting married are so tired and stressed from all of that the day's just a blur anyway."

"You had your day, Di." A little fire burned in Sherry's eyes. "I'm having mine."

"And all I'm saying is that by the time I got to the altar I was so worn out I can barely remember saying I do."

"You said it." Her husband smiled at her. "And looked beautiful when you did."

"Be that as it may—"

"You're absolutely right," Mac cut in. "It can be exhausting. And what should be the most vivid and important day of your life to that point can become anticlimactic, even tedious. That's what we're there to prevent. Believe me, if you'd had my partners when you were planning your wedding, the day wouldn't have been a blur."

"I don't mean to be critical, really, of what you do. I'm just saying that if the people involved didn't feel obliged to put on such a production, well, they wouldn't need companies like yours to handle everything."

"Probably true," Mac said easily. "Still, a bride's going to stress and worry, even obsess, but she can leave the details to us. As many as she feels comfortable with. She—sorry, Nick," she added with a smile. "She's the focus of the day, and for us, she's the focus for months leading up to that day. It's what we do."

"I'm sure you're very good. In fact, everything I've heard about you and your company indicates you are. I just think simple is better."

"It's all a matter of taste and individuality, isn't it?" Pam reached for the basket of dinner rolls. "More bread?"

"And I don't want simple. I want fun."

"We've got it." Mac sent Sherry a quick grin. "But simple can be better, depending on that taste and individuality. Even simple takes an eye for detail. We did a small, simple wedding today. Late morning ceremony. The bride's sister was her only attendant. She carried a small, hand-tied bouquet and wore flowers in her hair instead of a veil. We had a champagne brunch after and a jazz trio for dancing. It was lovely. She looked radiant. And I'd estimate Vows put about a hundred and fifty hours in, to make sure it was perfect for her. I'm pretty sure she'll remember every moment of it."

WHEN THE EVENING WAS DONE, AND THEY WENT TO CARTER'S, he waited until they were inside and hugged her. "Thanks. I imagine it's nerve-wracking to meet a horde like that—and to get the third degree."

"Let me just say: Whew. Do you think I passed the audition?"

"Definitely."

She bent down to pet the cat who came to greet them. "You have a very nice family. I figured you would. You love each other. It shows."

"We do. Should I apologize for Diane? She likes to pull off the silver lining to find the clouds inside."

"No. I get her, because I often do the same. I just internalize it more. I liked them, even her. They're all so normal. It gives me family envy."

"You can share mine. And I wish I could say that without putting that look in your eyes."

"So do I. It's my fatal flaw, not yours."

"That's bullshit."

Her jaw dropped. He rarely swore. "It's—"

"You don't have any fatal flaw. What you have is an ingrained habit of looking at marriage, for yourself, from one angle only. And from that angle all you see is failure."

"That may be true, it's probably true. But I've shifted that angle more for you, with you, than I have with anyone. I don't know if I'm capable of more."

"I'm not going to push you, but I won't lie and say I haven't thought about it. That I haven't thought about making a life with you. It's difficult to look inside myself and know, without a single reservation, that's what I want. And to look at you, and know it's not what you think you can have."

"I don't want to hurt you. I don't know if you can understand I'm more afraid of that than being hurt myself."

"I don't need your protection." He reached out, tapped the dangle of diamonds she wore. "You thought when I gave you these there might be an engagement ring in that box. You looked stricken."

"Carter—"

"What would you have said, I wonder, if there had been? I'm not asking. We'll call it a rhetorical question. I'll make you a promise right here and now, which may put your mind at ease. There won't be a ring or a question until you ask for them."

"You're too good for me."

"I'm forced to repeat myself. That's bullshit."

"It's not. And I actually think quite a bit of myself. What I should be, Carter, is on my knees asking you if you'd have me. And I can't get it out. It's stuck. It's stuck right here." She pressed her fist to her chest. "And every time it starts to loosen, just a little, something slams it back down. You're so much better than I deserve."

"Don't do that to me." He took her by the shoulders. "Don't put me somewhere I don't want to be."

"I don't know what I'd have said if there'd been a ring in that box. And that scares me. I don't know, and I can't see if whatever I'd have said would've been the right thing or the wrong thing for both of us. I have to see. I know the angle's wrong. More, the lens is defective, and I *know* it."

She stepped back from him. "I want to change it, and that's a first."

"That's a start. I'll settle for that, for now."

"You shouldn't settle for anything. That's my point."

"Don't tell me what to do, or who to love. You're the one. You're going to be the one tomorrow, and fifty years from tomorrow."

"I've never been the one. Not for anybody."

He closed the distance between them. "You'll get used to it." He tipped her face up to his, kissed her.

"Why? Why am I the one?"

"Because my life opened up, and it flooded with color when you walked back into it."

She wrapped her arms tight around him, pressed her face to his shoulder as emotion swamped her. "If you asked, I couldn't say no."

"That's not good enough, for either of us. When I ask, you need to want to say yes."

# CHAPTER NINETEEN

MAC HEARD THE THUMP, THE HISS OF BREATH, AND OPENED one eye. Snuggled in bed, she watched Carter hobble over to get his shoes.

"What time is it?"

"Early. Go back to sleep. I managed to get up, shower, and nearly get dressed before I ran into something and woke you up."

"It's all right. I should get up, get an early start anyway." Her eyes drooped closed again.

Carrying his shoes—and limping only a little—he walked over to kiss the top of her head. She made a murmuring sound of pleasure, and dropped back into sleep.

By the time she surfaced, the sun was beaming in.

Not such an early start after all, she mused as she rolled out of bed. Still, one of the perks of running your own business—and having no morning appointments—was sleeping in a little. She started for the bathroom, then shook her head and went back to make the bed.

It was the new Mac, she reminded herself. The tidy and

organized in all areas of her personal and professional lives Mackensie Elliot. The Mac with the new, fabulously designed closet where everything had its place—and was in it.

She fluffed the pillows, smoothed the sheets, spread the duvet neatly. See, she told herself as she did every morning, it only took two minutes. With a nod of satisfaction, she surveyed her room.

No clothes tossed anywhere, no shoes kicked under a chair, no jewelry carelessly scattered on the dresser. This was the room of a grown-up, a woman of taste—and a woman in control.

She showered, then reminded herself to hang up the towel. In the bedroom she gave herself the pleasure of opening her closet and just standing there, looking at it.

"That's what I'm talking about."

Her clothes hung in precise lines, according to function and color. Every pair of her impressive collection of shoes nestled inside its clear protective box, in stacks of type. Evening shoes, daywear, sandals, boots—pumps, peeps, spikes, wedges.

Things of beauty.

Handbags, again by function and color, sat easily accessed in generous cubbies. Inside the glossy white drawers of the built-ins lived scarves—once doomed to tangled knots or jumbled piles, neatly folded, as did her dressier sweaters, her hosiery.

It made getting dressed an absolute stress-free pleasure. No more hunting, no more cursing, no more wondering where the hell she'd put that blue shirt with the French cuffs then having to settle for another blue shirt when she couldn't find it.

Because the blue shirt with the French cuffs was right there, where it belonged.

She pulled on a white tank, a navy V-neck with jeans, suitable wardrobe for the morning's work, and the early afternoon shoot. Satisfied and smug, she strolled out.

Strode back in to stuff her pajamas in the hamper.

She walked downstairs just as Emma came in the front door.

"I'm out of coffee. Help me."

"Sure. I was just about to . . . Oh, Carter must've made some before he left."

"I don't want to hate you for having someone who'll make coffee while you sleep, but I need caffeine for my altruistic side to wake up." Emma poured herself a mug, all but inhaled the first sip. "Life. It's good again."

Mac poured her own and drank in agreement. "Wanna see my closet?"

"I've seen it three times now. Yes, it's the queen of all the closets in all the land."

"Well, Parker's is the queen."

"Parker's is the goddess of closets. You take queen. Saturday's bride called," Emma continued. "She thinks she wants to change the flower girl flowers from rose petals in a basket to a blush pink pomander."

"I thought she changed from the pomander to the basket."

"Yes. And from crescent bouquet to cascade and back again." Emma closed her big brown eyes, circled her neck. "I'll be glad when this one's over."

"She's the kind who makes Carter's sister right."

"Sherry?"

"No, his older sister who says weddings are too stressful, too elaborate, and basically too big a deal. It's just one day."

"It's *the* day. Plus, you know, our livelihood."

"Agreed. But Saturday's bride is going to be a handful right up to the walk down the aisle. She called me yesterday, and faxed a shot she'd found in a magazine. Which she wants me to duplicate on Saturday. Hey, no problem. Except for the fact her dress is completely different, as is her body type, her headdress, her hair. Oh, and we don't happen to have the stone archway from an ancient Irish castle for her to pose in. At least not right handy."

"It's just nerves. The nerves of a control freak. I need another hit, then I've got to get to work." Emma topped off the mug. "I'll bring it back."

"That's what you always say."

"I'll bring the entire collection back," Emma promised and scooted out.

Alone, Mac turned to open a cupboard. Some sugar and preservatives, she thought, along with her coffee. When she opened the cupboard, she found a shiny red apple in front of the box of Pop-Tarts. The note propped on it read: *Eat me, too!*

She snorted out a laugh as she took the apple, and laid the note on the counter. Sweet boy, she thought, taking a bite. Funny boy. What could she do for him short of marrying him at this stage?

She destroyed him with La Perla, she'd cooked an actual meal. She— "The photograph!"

She dashed to her workstation to boot up her computer. She hadn't forgotten about phase three of the gift. She just hadn't been able to decide which shot, and how to present it.

"Should be working, should be working," she mumbled. "But it'll only take a minute."

It took her more than forty, but she selected the shot—one of the post-kiss, cheek-to-cheek images. He looked so relaxed and happy, and she . . . right there with him, she mused as she studied the final result. Tweaked, cropped, printed, and framed. To do it right she boxed it, tied it with a red ribbon, and tucked a sprig of silk lily of the valley in the bow.

Delighted, she printed out another of the shots for herself, selected a frame. She put the finished photo in a drawer. She wouldn't set it out until he had his.

She turned music on, clicked the volume down to background. She worked, happy with the world in general, until the timer she'd set beeped telling her it was time to set up for her studio shoot.

Engagement portrait. She a doctor, he a musician. Mac had

some ideas for them, and had asked him to bring his guitar. Medium gray background, bride and groom sitting on the floor and—

She turned, a fat floor pillow in her hands as her door burst open. Her mother all but exploded into the room, wrapped in a new jacket of sheared silver mink.

"Mackensie! Look!" She did a twirl, ending in a hipshot runway pose.

"You can't be here now," Mac said flatly. "I have clients coming."

"I'm a client. I'm here for a consult. I came here first, but we have to get the rest of the team. Oh, Mac!" Linda rushed forward, all scissoring legs, gorgeous shoes, sumptuous fur. "I'm getting married!"

Caught in her mother's perfumed embrace, Mac just closed her eyes. "Congratulations. Again."

"Oh, don't be that way." Linda eased back, pouted for half a second, then did another laughing spin. "Be happy. Be happy for me. I'm so happy! Look what Ari brought me back from Paris."

"Yes, it's a beautiful jacket."

"It really is." Tipping her head down, Linda rubbed her chin against the fur. "But that's not all!" She flung out her hand, wiggled her fingers. On the third rode an enormous square-cut diamond set in platinum.

Hell of a rock, Mac thought. Biggest so far. "It's impressive."

"The darling. He was miserable without me. He called me night and day from Paris." She hugged herself, then did another spin. "Of course, I wouldn't speak to him for the first three days. It was so mean of him to go without me. Naturally I refused to see him when he first got back."

"Naturally," Mac agreed.

"He begged me to come to New York. He sent a limo and a

driver for me—and the car was *full* of white roses. And a bottle of Dom. But first, he sent dozens of roses, every day. Every day! I had to give in and go to him. Oh, it was so romantic."

Closing her eyes, Linda crossed her arms over her chest. "Like a dream or a movie. We had dinner alone, at home. He had it catered with all my favorites, and more champagne, candlelight, more roses. He told me he couldn't live without me, then he gave me this. Have you ever seen anything like it?"

Mac watched her mother admire the ring. "I hope you'll be very happy together. I do. And I'm glad you're happy now. But I have a shoot."

"Oh." With a wave of her hand, Linda dismissed it. "Reschedule, for heaven's sake. This is major. Your mother's getting married."

"For the fourth time, Mom."

"For the last time. To the right man. And I want you to do the wedding, of course. I need your very best for this. Ari said not to consider the cost. I want something fabulous and romantic and elegant. Sophisticated and lavish. I'm thinking pale pink gown. Valentino, I think, he suits me. Or I might look for something vintage, something old Hollywood. And a wonderful hat rather than a veil."

Eyes sparkling, she fluffed a hand through her hair. "Some sleek updo, and I'll have Ari buy me some amazing earrings to set it all off. Pink diamonds, I think. Then masses and masses of white and pink roses. I'll speak to Emmaline there. We'll need the invitations to go out right away. I'm sure Parker can take care of it. And the cake. I want massive. The Taj Mahal of wedding cakes, so Laurel will have to outdo herself. And—"

"When?" Mac interrupted.

"When what?"

"When are you planning to do this?"

"Oh. June. I want to be a June bride. I want spring and gardens and—"

"*This* June? As in three months from now? We're booked solid."

"As if that matters." With a bright laugh, Linda whisked such mundane matters aside. "I'm your mother. Bump somebody. Now—"

"We don't bump clients, Mom. We can't ruin someone else's wedding because you want a date in June at the last minute."

Sincere—Mac knew it was sincere—hurt and puzzlement shone on Linda's face. "Why do you have to be so mean to me? Why do you have to spoil this? Can't you see I'm happy?"

"Yes, I can. I'm glad for you. I just can't give you what you want."

"You just want to punish me. You don't want me to be happy."

"That's not true."

"Then what? What is it? I'm getting married, and my daughter runs a wedding business. Naturally I expect you to handle it."

"We can't handle it in June. We've been fully booked for June for months now, nearly a year."

"Did you hear what I said? Money is no object. He'll pay whatever you ask. All you have to do is change something around."

"It's not a matter of money, or nearly as simple as changing something around. It's a matter of commitment and integrity. We can't give you what you want when you want it, but the basic reason is because someone else already has it."

"And they're more important than me? Than your own mother?"

"Somebody else has already booked the date, ordered their invitations, made their plans. So, yes, in this case they're more important."

"We'll see about that." Temper sharpened her voice, her eyes, turned them both into hot little knives. "Everyone knows it's Parker who runs this business. She's the one who calls the shots. You'll fall in line when she tells you to."

Linda stormed to the door, spun back. "You should be ashamed for treating me this way."

Weary, Mac walked to her workstation, picked up the phone after her mother slammed out. "I'm sorry," Mac said when Parker answered. "I want to say I'm sorry first. My mother's on her way over to see you. I'm afraid you're going to have to deal with her."

"All right."

"She's getting married again."

"Well, I'm shocked!"

Mac laughed even as tears stung her eyes. "Thanks. She wants it here, this June."

"She can't have it. We're booked."

"I know. I told her, but apparently you're the boss of me. Of all of us."

"I'm always saying that. I'll deal with it. It's no problem."

"It's my problem."

"Seeing as I'm the boss of you, I'm making it mine. I'll call you back."

In her office at the main house, Parker rose, walked to a mirror. She checked her appearance, smoothed a hair back into place, freshened her lipstick—and smiled because it felt like girding for battle.

She looked forward to it.

She took her time walking downstairs, even when she heard the bell ring insistently, repeatedly. She paused to adjust a rose in the vase on the foyer table, then fixing a cool smile on her face, opened the door.

"Hello, Linda. I hear congratulations are in order."

"She didn't waste any time." Linda breezed in, took a quick glance around. "It must be odd opening your home to strangers, for money."

"Actually, I find it very satisfying." Parker gestured toward the drawing room. "We can sit in here."

Shrugging out of her jacket, Linda crossed to a sofa. She tossed the fur negligently over the arm, sat, then leaned back, crossed her legs. "I realize I should have come to you first, but sentiment took me to my daughter. I wanted to share my happy news with her."

"Of course." Parker took a chair and, mimicking Linda's pose, sat and crossed her legs. "You must be very excited. That's a gorgeous ring."

"Isn't it?" Pleasure gushed again as Linda lifted her hand to admire it. "Ari is so thoughtful, and romantic. He's swept me off my feet."

"I think Mac mentioned he lives in New York. So you'll be moving."

"Very soon. I have a thousand things to see to first. My house, my things."

"And Eloisa. I'm sure she's excited at the idea of living in New York on college breaks when she's not with her father." Parker tipped her head slightly at Linda's blank look.

"Oh, Eloisa's ready to fly the nest. Of course we'll have a room for her when she visits. At least until she can get her own place. Meanwhile, I have a wedding to plan. I wouldn't dream of having anyone handle the details but you. Naturally we want the sort of affair that reflects Ari's position and status. He's a very important man, and—since we're talking business—has the means to afford the very best. I'll want to talk to the other girls about their end of things, but while I'm here I can give you a sense of what I'm looking for."

"Vows isn't going to be able to handle or host your wedding, Linda. We don't have any dates open in June. In fact, we're booked through the summer and fall."

"Parker, you're a businesswoman." Linda spread her hands. "I'm offering you a major event, the sort that will bring this business of yours a great deal of attention, and certainly future clients. Ari knows important people, so I mean *major* clients. As I've got my heart set on having the wedding here, in the home of an old friend—one I still miss—we'll compensate you for the short notice. How much do you estimate it would take to have a date open up in June. Say, the third Saturday?"

"You're right, I'm a businesswoman." Parker watched Linda smile in satisfaction. "I'm in the business of providing services for our clients. We have a client for the third Saturday in June. We've signed a contract with that client. When I give my word, I keep it. You really should consider having your wedding in New York. I can, if you like, give you names of other wedding planners."

"I don't want names. I said I wanted my wedding here. It's important to me, Parker. I want to be married somewhere I feel at home, where I have a connection, to have people I love and trust looking after the details. I want—"

"Tears won't work on me." Parker's voice turned cold as Linda's eyes filled. "And I don't care what you want. You're not getting married here. So." She got to her feet. "If that's all, I'm busy."

"You always thought you were better than us, looking down like you're so much more important. A Brown of Connecticut. What are you now, renting out your big house, scrambling around serving drinks and running other people's errands."

"I'm a Brown of Connecticut, following a time-honored family tradition and earning a living." She picked up Linda's coat, offered it. "I'll show you out."

"When I tell Ari how you've treated me, he'll put you out of business. You won't be able to run a kid's birthday party in this place. We'll ruin you."

"Oh, Linda, you have no idea how happy it makes me to hear you say that because it allows me to say something I've wanted to, for years. All the years I've watched you undermine and emotionally manipulate my best friend. All the years I've watched you alternately smother her or ignore her, as it suited your whims."

Shock leached color from Linda's cheeks. "You can't speak to me that way."

"I just did. Now I'll finish. You're not welcome in this house. Actually, you've never been welcome here, but tolerated. That ends now. You'll only be permitted to walk in this door again if Mac wants it. Now get out of my house, get in your car, and get off my property."

"And to think I wanted to do you a favor."

Parker stood in the doorway, watching while Linda slid into her car. By the time she'd driven halfway home, Parker estimated, she'd believe that. She'd tried to do them a favor. She waited until the car gunned down the drive, then grabbed a jacket for the walk to Mac's studio.

Mac met her at the door. "Parks, I—"

"Don't apologize to me. You'll piss me off." She glanced at the studio space, noted the backdrop, the floor pillows. "You've got the engagement shoot. Soon," she realized with a glance at her watch. "I'll be quick."

"How'd the consult go?"

"We didn't get the job."

"Did she cry or yell?"

"A little of both, with bribes and insults."

"It's amazing. She's amazing. She really believes everyone's world should revolve around her." Weary of it, Mac pressed her fingers to her eyes and rubbed. "Within the hour, she'll have turned this around to she was only asking as a favor to us, to try to boost the business. She was secretly relieved when we couldn't manage the job, probably because it was too big for our business."

"She was already on the way there when she walked out the door."

"It's a skill. Maybe it'll last this time. The marriage, I mean. It's pretty clear the guy's got money, and plenty of it."

"Bright side? She'll be moving to New York."

Mac paused. "I didn't think of that. That whizzed by me. That's a very bright side." Still Mac sighed and moved in to drop her head on Parker's shoulder. "Oh God, she tires me out."

"I know." Parker wrapped her arms around Mac in a hard hug. "Be okay," Parker ordered.

"I will."

"You want to come for ice cream after the shoot?"

"I might."

"There're the clients. I'll get out of your way."

"Parker? Even if we'd had the date open . . ."

"Oh, baby," Parker said with some cheer as she went to the door. "No way in hell."

With a shake of her head, Mac ordered herself not to feel guilty about that. At least not until after the shoot.

CARTER LOADED THE STACK OF ESSAYS IN HIS BRIEFCASE. THEY rode in the section that held a stack of test papers. His homework, he mused. He wondered if students had any idea how much homework the average teacher hauled away from the classroom every day.

On the board behind him he'd written the springboard for the essays he'd read that night.

*Explore and compare the attitudes and philosophies of Rosalind and Jaques on love, and why you think each holds them.*

The optimist and the pessimist, Carter thought, the melancholy and the joyful. His goal in the in-depth study of the play had been to guide his students under the surface of what might appear to be a light romantic comedy full of jokes and clever banter to the currents beneath.

Under all that, Carter supposed, his goal was to make his students think.

"Excuse me? Dr. Maguire?"

He glanced over at the woman in the doorway. "Yes. Can I help you?"

"I'm Suzanne Byers, Garrett's mother."

"Mrs. Byers, it's nice to meet you. Come in."

"I hoped to catch you before you left for the day. I won't take up much of your time."

"It's no problem."

"I couldn't make Parents' Night. I was down with the flu. I'd wanted to come, especially to speak to you. I guess you know Garrett didn't have a strong start at the academy last year. And he didn't come out of the starting gate with a bang this year either."

"He's made considerable progress, I think. Finding his stride. He's bright. His participation in class has taken an upturn, and so have his grades and test scores this last semester."

"I know. That's why I wanted to speak to you. His father and I had been discussing taking him out of the academy."

"I hope you won't. Garrett—"

"Had been," she interrupted. "We worked with him, threatened him, bribed him, tried private tutoring. Nothing got through, and we felt we were tossing away the tuition. Until a few months ago. It was like a light went on. He talks about books. He actually studies. He was genuinely disappointed when he got a B on his last paper in your class. I couldn't speak for ten minutes when he told me, with some heat, he was going to ace the next one."

"He could. He has the potential."

"He talks about you. Dr. Maguire says, Dr. Maguire thinks. His grades in his other classes are improving—not by leaps and bounds, but they're better. You did that."

"Garrett did that."

"You . . . engaged him so that he could do that. Would do that. He's talking about taking your creative writing course next year. He thinks he may want to be a writer." Her eyes filled. "Last year he barely passed. We had to meet with the dean. And now he's telling me about Shakespeare, and he thinks he may want to be a writer."

She blinked at the tears while he stood, speechless. "Dr. Maguire, according to Garrett, is pretty cool for a brainiac. I wanted you to know that whatever he does, whatever he becomes, he's never going to forget you. I wanted to thank you."

CARTER WALKED INTO MAC'S STUDIO WITH A LARGE PIZZA AND a light step. She sat on the sofa, her feet propped on the coffee table.

"Pizza," he said, walking into the kitchen to set it on the counter. "I knew you had an afternoon shoot, and I have a briefcase full of papers to grade, so I thought pizza. Plus, it's a happy food. I had a really good day."

She groaned a little and had him crossing to her with concern. "Are you all right?"

"Yes. Mostly. Pizza. I have a gallon of ice cream in my stomach. Possibly two gallons."

"Ice cream." He sat on the coffee table. "Was there a party?"

"No. Maybe. I guess it depends on your definition of party. Tell me about your really good day."

He boosted up to kiss her, then sat back. "Hello, Mackensie."

"Hello, Carter. You're wearing a very big smile."

"I had one of those very big moments, for me. I have a student. He's been a challenge, the sort who sits down and turns a switch in his head that takes him anywhere but the classroom."

"Oh yeah, I had that switch. It was handy, especially during lectures on the Revolutionary War, or tariffs. Tariffs hit the switch automatically. Did your challenging student do well today?"

"He's been doing well. It's about finding another switch, the one that turns on interest and ideas. It shows in the eyes, just like the turn-off switch."

"Really?"

"Garrett's the kind of student who pushes a teacher to work a little harder. And when you find that switch, it's intensely rewarding. He's the one who got a B on that paper I graded on Valentine's Day. Or the day before. I think of that as our Valentine's Day."

"Right. I remember. Good for Garrett."

"His mother came to see me today. The majority of the time when a parent comes in, it's not to bring an apple to the teacher. She brought me an orchard. She thanked me."

"She thanked you." Curious, Mac cocked her head. "That's an orchard?"

"Yes. It's not just about teaching facts and theories, or assignments and grades. It's about . . . finding the switch. I found Garrett's, and she came in to thank me. Now you have a very big smile."

"You changed a life. You change lives."

"I wouldn't go that far."

"No, you do. I document them, or at least pieces of them. And that's important, it's valuable. But you change them, and that's amazing. I'm going to get you some pizza. Which I can't share with you," she said as she rose. "Due to ice cream stomach."

"Why did you eat a gallon, or possibly two?"

"Oh." She shrugged as he followed her into the kitchen. "Greed."

"You told me you turn to ice cream in times of emotional upheaval."

She glanced over her shoulder as she got down a plate. "I sometimes forget how well you listen. Let's just say I didn't have a really good day. Or maybe I did," she considered. "It depends on the point of view."

"Tell me."

"It's not important. And you have Garrett pizza. Do you want a glass of wine with that?"

"Only if you're having one when you tell me. We can spend the next few minutes circling around it, or you can save time and just tell me."

"You're right. Circling around it makes it more important than it deserves to be." Another bad habit to break, she decided. "My mother's getting married again."

"Oh." He studied her face as she poured the wine. "You don't like him."

"I have no idea. I've never met him."

"I see."

"No, you don't." She laid a hand over his briefly. "You can't see how a mother could be getting married without her daughter at least being able to pick the guy out of a lineup. I doubt Eloisa's met him either, or that it's occurred to Linda either of us should. Anyway the Elliot/Meyers/Barrington . . . God, I don't know what her last name's going to be this time. The Elliot/Meyers/Barrington slash name to be determined connections don't have family dinners, so meeting this new one isn't a priority."

"I'm sorry it upsets you."

"I don't know what it does. I don't know why it surprises me. The last time I saw Linda was when she called here, hysterical at midnight, and I drove over there in a damn ice storm thinking she'd been raped or attacked or God knows."

"What? When was this?" He turned his hand over to grip Mac's "Was she hurt?"

"Oh, it was . . . that night of the parent thing at the academy, and no, she wasn't hurt. Except in Linda Universe. She was curled up on the floor *dying* because Ari—that's the new fiancé—had to fly to Paris on business and didn't take her. I was about to call the police, and an ambulance, then she's all boo-hoo Paris. I turned around and left. Points for me because the usual MO would be for me to, resentfully, calm her down, get her into bed."

"Why didn't you tell me about this before?"

"I don't know." With a shake of her head, she blew out a breath. "I really don't. It wasn't one of those proud mother-daughter moments, so I guess I tried not to think about it afterward. I walked out, and told her I wouldn't come the next time she called. I said very hard things and left."

"They needed to be said, and you needed to leave."

"You're right, both counts," Mac agreed. "And today, she whirls in here in her new fur and refrigerator-box-sized diamond as if none of it happened. Talk about flicking switches. She's getting married in June. Ari is forgiven due to fur, diamond, and proposal. And she expects us to do the wedding. June is like a parade of brides around here. We're booked. Much fury and anger ensues. Then she took on Parker. That was the good part. Parker shut her down, showed her the door. Then there was ice cream."

She took a sip of wine. "I like your day better."

"She had to know you'd be booked."

"No, not really. Honestly, that wouldn't have entered her mind. She doesn't see outside her own wants. Nothing else exists. And her anger and shock, even hurt, when those wants aren't met are sincere. They're genuine. She has the emotional maturity of a fruit fly, encouraged by a mother who indulged her every whim and taught her she was the center of the universe. She's a product of that."

"It doesn't mean she's allowed to treat you this way."

"She is. She's allowed to do as she pleases. I'm responsible for my reactions. And I'm working on them. Garrett and I are showing some improvement. She didn't get what she wanted."

"That's not the point, only a result. She'll repeat this cycle. She'll come back and hurt you again. And when she does, she'll have to deal with me."

"Carter, you don't want to take that on. It's sweet, but—"

"It's not sweet. She'll deal with me."

She remembered him taking a punch from an angry drunk. "I know you can handle yourself. But she's my mother, and I need to handle her."

"Sharing some DNA doesn't make her your mother."

Mac said nothing for a moment. "No," she agreed, "it really doesn't."

# CHAPTER TWENTY

THE SNOW STARTED LATE MORNING, AND BY NOON THE WORLD outside the studio was a storm of white. It fell, thick and fast, obliterating the brief end-of-February thaw. March, Mac thought, was coming in with the lion's fangs and claws.

The steady, spinning snow, the howl of wind that kicked it toward fury, made her want to curl up under a throw with a book and a pot of hot chocolate close at hand. Except for the fact they had a rehearsal scheduled at five. Apparently, Saturday's control-freak bride hadn't been able to work her will on Mother Nature.

Knowing the drill under such circumstances, Mac prepared to bundle herself and her equipment in protective gear, and trudge over to the main house. She packed her notes, opened a drawer for extra memory cards—and found the photo of her and Carter, along with his framed in the box.

"Yet to deliver on part three," she said aloud, and to please herself she set the photo she intended to keep on her workstation. "Reminder," she decided.

She headed upstairs to change into rehearsal clothes, then had to dash to answer the ringing phone. "Hey, Professor. Where are you?"

"Home. They cancelled afternoon classes. It's nasty out there. I needed to stop by here, get a few things, including the cat. I don't want to leave him here in case I can't make it back tomorrow."

"Don't." She carried the phone to the window to watch the trees whip and shudder in the violent lash of wind. "Don't go out in this again. Stay home—warm and safe so I don't have to worry about you on the roads. I'm getting ready to trek over to the house anyway. We have a rehearsal at five."

"In this?"

"We have contingency plans, which include the ritual sacrifice of a chicken."

"I could help. Except with the chicken."

"You could, or you could end up in a snowdrift, or skidding into a tree. All I have to do is walk a few hundred yards." She flipped through her clothing options as she spoke, settled on sturdy cords and a turtleneck. "Parker will have the head of the National Weather Service on the phone by now."

"You're kidding."

"No, only slightly exaggerating." She sat to pull off her thick, walk-around-the-house socks, then, cradling the phone on her shoulder, wiggled out of her flannel pants. "We'll do a conference call rehearsal if necessary, or a virtual one if the client has the computer capability. We'll shovel, plow, and clear. We've done it before. Barring genuine blizzard conditions, we'll have a wedding tomorrow. Maybe you could be my date. And bring the cat. That way the two of you could stay through the weekend."

"We'll be there. I'd rather be with you tonight than here grading papers."

She yanked up her cords. "I'd rather be with you than dealing with an hysterical, anal-retentive bride."

"I think you win. Try to stay warm. Maybe you could call me later, after you're done with everything. You can tell me how it went."

"I will. Oh, wait. Are any of those papers you'll be grading Garrett's?"

"As a matter of fact."

"Hope he gets an A. See you tomorrow."

She hung up the phone, then pulled off her sweatshirt, pulled on the sweater. She grabbed her makeup bag and a pair of dress boots should the bride insist on braving the elements.

Five minutes later, she hunched against the frigid blast of wind to trudge through the snow. It would take a miracle, she thought, if the storm didn't abate in the next few hours. Even with a miracle, the guest attrition rate would soar. It would take all her skill to pull any glowing bride shots of the client.

Or possibly liquor.

She dumped everything in the mudroom, stomped and shook away snow. She checked Laurel's kitchen.

Her friend stood, coating the second of three tiers with pale pink fondant.

"Wait. I have down the marquetry cake, white icing, pink and lavender flowers, traditional B and G topper."

"Changed to pleated, pale pink with nosegay of English violets topper. I guess you didn't get the memo—or honestly by the time we got to this, I probably didn't send one."

"No problem. I'll put it in my notes." Mac dragged them out to do just that. "How many guys do you figure she changed her mind about before she stuck with the one she's marrying tomorrow?"

"One shudders to think. Forecast is for twelve to eighteen."

"We can handle twelve to eighteen."

"We can. I'm not sure about the bride." She moved on to the last tier. "Parker's been dealing with her almost since the first flake fell. Emma's in her shop, dealing with the flowers."

"Is it still a pomander for the flower girl?"

"As of now. My mission was to match the fondant to the color of the roses." Laurel paused to pick up the bud Emma had given her, held it by the fondant. "I think mission accomplished. Now scram. I still have a couple acres of pink and white sugar paste to deal with before I even assemble this baby."

"I'll go help Parker."

In her office, Parker lay on the floor, eyes closed, talking in calm, soothing tones into her headset. "I know, Whitney. It's just so unfair. But . . . No, I don't blame you a bit. I'd feel the same way. I do feel the same way." She opened her eyes, looked up at Mac. Closed them again.

"I'm here for you. We all are. And we have a few ideas that may . . . Whitney! I want you to stop. Listen to me now. Stop and breathe. Breathe. Now, just listen. The weather is out of our control. Some things in life just are. It's what we do about them that counts, and one of the things you're going to do is marry the man you love and start a wonderful life together. The weather can't change that."

Listening with half an ear, Mac opened Parker's cabinet and got her friend a fresh bottle of water.

"Don't cry, honey. Here's what we're going to do. We're going to worry about today. At five, we're going to do a conference call with you and Vince and the wedding party, and your parents. We're going to go over every step of what's going to happen tomorrow. Wait, just wait. Today first. We're going to go over every step, as long as it takes. I know how much you were looking forward to the rehearsal dinner tonight."

With her eyes closed, she listened for several moments. "Yes, Whitney, but I agree with your mother, and with Vince. It's not worth risking the roads to try to get everyone here, or to the restaurant. But I've arranged, if you agree, for one of the caterers I know to deliver a wonderful meal to you. She only lives a couple of blocks away. She'll deliver it, and she'll set it all up. You can make this a party, Whitney, or a tragedy. I've talked to your mother, and she's thrilled with the idea."

Bending down, Mac tapped the bottle against Parker's hand. Parker took it, just held it.

"She'll have a houseful, and host a party with her daughter. You'll have dinner, wine, family, friends, a sleepover, a fire in the hearth. You'll have a rehearsal dinner that's unique and yours, and that makes something lovely and fun out of an inconvenience."

"Damn you're good," Mac whispered.

Parker reopened her eyes, rolled them. "That's right. Let me worry about tomorrow. I promise you, one way or the other, we're going to give you a beautiful day. And the most important thing, you're marrying Vince. Now I want you to relax, to enjoy yourself. We're going to have fun with this. I'll call you back. Yes. I promise. Go help your mother."

Parker pulled off the headset. "God!"

"I bet she's not worrying about pomanders now."

"No, she's too busy cursing the gods." As she sat up, Parker twisted the top off the bottle, took a long, long drink. "I don't blame her for being upset. Who wouldn't be? But a winter wedding means the possibility of snow. It's March in Connecticut, clue in. But in her mind, the snow is a personal insult aimed at ruining her life. Twelve to eighteen."

"I got the bulletin."

"We'll need the drive and parking plowed, the paths, porches, and terraces cleared." She drank again, and did what she'd advised Whitney to do. She breathed. "The road crews are out, so we'll have to trust them to do their part."

"Four-wheel drives?"

"The limo company can switch to the Hummer. The groom's

willing to forgo the limo and load up his SUV with his party. I've talked to all the subs. We shouldn't have a problem."

"Then I guess I'd better get a shovel."

By eight, with the snow slowed to a fitful trickle, Mac sat in the kitchen with her friends devouring a bowl of Mrs. G's beef stew.

"When is she coming home?" Mac demanded. "We're nearly out of provisions."

"First of April," Parker said, "as usual. We can make it. We'll make tomorrow, too. I just talked to a very happy, slightly drunk bride. They're having a wonderful time. They have a karaoke machine."

"We're plowed, forecast is for clear skies tomorrow, with a high of thirty-eight. The wind's already easing off. Cake's in the cooler and is a thing of beauty."

Emma nodded at Laurel. "Flowers are the same."

"The kids will be here first thing in the morning to shovel the path, clear the portico and terraces," Parker put in. "So that's cleared off our list."

"Thank God," Emma said with feeling.

"I've got the FOB taking pictures tonight at the rehearsal party with his pocket digital. I'll play with them, put something fun together in one of the small albums. We'll gift it to the bride. And now." Mac pushed up. "I'm going home, ease my aching body into a hot bath."

She walked home in the thinning snow, the path lights sparkling. It made her think of Carter, how he'd talked her into walking in the snow instead of wallowing.

She'd call him. Sink into that hot bath with a glass of wine, some candles glowing—and Carter on the line. She wondered how he'd react to phone sex, and heard herself laugh. He was always surprising her. She'd bet he'd be a phone sex champ.

She let herself in, listened to the silence. She liked the quiet, liked her space. Funny how he didn't disturb either by being there. He just seemed to make it more theirs. Their quiet, their space.

Weird thought.

She glanced at the photo on her workstation as she stripped off her coat. Maybe not so weird. They framed up together nicely.

It was good this phase they were in, she thought as she started upstairs. Not a holding pattern, not exactly, just staying in that nice, comfortable space. A kind of order and ease.

She walked into the bedroom, tossed the dress boots she hadn't needed after all toward the closet. She took off her earrings, dropped them on the dresser.

Then stopped, hissing out a breath as she looked around. She hadn't made the bed that morning. She'd tossed clothes on the chair. She'd dropped socks there, too. Her beautiful closet . . . It wasn't a disaster, she thought, but why had she put the gray shirt with the white ones? And the black skirt belonged in the skirt section, not in the jacket section. And that was Carter's jacket.

She'd fallen back into old habits, she thought in disgust. She had a place for everything now, so why couldn't she *put* it there. Control her own space, her own things, her own . . .

Life, she thought.

Because she was messy, she admitted. Because life was. Because Carter's jacket was hanging with hers, and what did it matter? Socks got lost, beds got rumpled. Your mother was a selfish woman, your father was careless.

And sometimes it snowed on your wedding rehearsal.

What had Parker said?

Some things in life are out of your control. You can make it a party or a tragedy.

Or, Mac thought, you could refuse to take the next step. You could refuse to take what you wanted most because you're afraid some day you might lose it.

She jogged back downstairs, picked up the photo. "He just happened," she said quietly as she studied how they looked, framed together. "He just happened into my life, and everything changed."

She looked up, saw the photo of three young girls under an arbor of white roses. And a blue butterfly over a clutch of wild violets and dandelions.

Her breath came out in a jerk that had her pressing a hand to her heart. Of course. Of course. It was so absolutely clear, if she just looked at it.

"Oh my God. What am I waiting for?"

WITH THE CAT WARMING HIS FEET AND THE MUSIC ON LOW, Carter stretched out on the living room sofa with a book and a short glass of Jameson.

He'd spent winter evenings like this before, he mused, with the cat and a book for company after work was done. It contented him.

He wished he had a fire. Of course, he'd need a fireplace first. But a fire would add a nice civilized evening-at-home touch. A kind of *Masterpiece Theatre* touch.

The professor and his cat by the fire, reading on a snowy evening.

He could almost see the portrait as Mackensie would take it, and the idea both pleased and amused him.

He wished she could be here with him. Stretched out opposite him on the sofa, so he could see her face whenever he glanced up from the story. Sharing the quiet of a winter night, and the imaginary fire.

One day, he thought, when she was ready. Part of him had been ready the moment he'd seen her again; there was no point in denying it. No sooner looked but he loved—to paraphrase Rosalind. And the rest of him caught up so quickly with that part of him. But she hadn't had that spark, that old flame inside her as he had, waiting to reignite.

Man for woman this time, not boy for girl.

He couldn't blame her for needing more time.

"Well, maybe a little," he said to Triad. "Not so much for needing more time, but for not trusting herself. How can a woman who has so much of it in her not trust love? I know, I know, Mommy Dearest, Absentee Father. A lot of scar tissue there."

So he'd wait. He'd love her, be with her. And wait.

He settled back into the book, letting the quiet and the journey of the story lull him. He lifted the whiskey, took a small sip. His hand jerked at the pounding on the door, so whiskey splashed on his shirt.

"Oh, crap."

Pulling off his glasses, he laid them on the table with the book. Triad protested when he pulled his feet free. "It's not my fault. It's whoever's crazy enough to be out on a night like this."

He got up reluctantly, then the thought struck that someone might've had an accident, and had come to the house for help. He quickened his pace, imagining skids and crashes on slippery roads. When he opened the door, his arms filled with Mac.

"Carter!"

"Mackensie." Alarm gushed into his belly. "What is it? What happened?"

"Everything." She turned her head, crushed her mouth to his. "Everything happened."

"The estate?" Fire leaped into his mind again. "Was there a fire? Or—"

"No." She clung. "You found me."

"You're cold. Come in where it's warm. You need to sit down. Whatever happened, we'll—"

"I forgot my gloves." She laughed and kissed him again. "I

forgot to turn on the heater in the car. I forgot to make the bed. I don't know why I thought that was important."

"Did you hit your head?" He pried her back to look into her eyes. They didn't seem shocky to him, but they were a little wild. "Have you been drinking? And driving in these conditions? You can't—"

"I haven't been drinking. I was thinking about wine and phone sex in the bathtub, but that was before I realized I hadn't made the bed or put my socks in the hamper." She sniffed. "But someone's been drinking. Is that whiskey? You drink whiskey?"

"Sometimes. It's a cold night, and the snow, and . . . Wait a minute."

"You see? You always surprise me. Carter drinks whiskey on a snowy night." She spun away from him, then back. "And he can take a punch in the face. He buys diamond earrings and laughs with his father in the kitchen. Oh, I wish I'd had my camera, so I could've stolen that moment and showed you. I need another chance at that, when I'm not fighting off nerves and envy. But I have another for you."

She dragged the box out of the deep pocket of her coat. "Third part of the gift."

"For God's sake, you drove all the way over here in this mess to give me a picture? You could've been hurt, had an accident. You—"

"Yes. I could've. Things happen. But I didn't, and I'm here. Open it."

He dragged a hand through his hair. "Let me get your coat."

"I can get my coat. Open it. Look." She dragged off the coat, threw it over the banister. "That's the kind of thing I do. Toss my coat somewhere. You don't even mind. You might some day. So what? Open it, Carter."

He untied the ribbon, opened the box. She smiled out at him, her cheek against his. It made him remember the kiss, her pleasure in his gift. The warmth afterward, and the feel of her face brushing his. "It's wonderful."

"It really is. I kept one of the kiss. You didn't know I took the shot. It's a great kiss, a great image. But this—this is us. Looking out, looking forward. Tonight, after the work, and the dealing with things that can't be controlled, can't be predicted—good or bad, happy or sad—and then the closet. I'd messed up my shirts, and your jacket was in there."

"Oh, I must've put it there when—"

"It doesn't matter. That's the point. It doesn't matter that my mother is my mother, or that things don't always work exactly the way you thought they should. Moments matter. I know that better than anyone, but I never let it apply to me. Not to me. People matter, how they feel, how they connect, who they are alone and together. All that matters, no matter how quickly the moment passes. Maybe because it passes. What matters is you're the blue butterfly."

"I'm . . . what?"

"Come on, Professor. Dr. Maguire. You know all about metaphors and analogies and symbolism. You flew into my life, just landed in it unexpectedly. Maybe miraculously. And the picture formed. It just took me a while to see it."

"I'm not . . . Oh, the picture. Wedding Day, the one you took when you were a girl."

"Epiphanies. I had one then, and I had one tonight. I want this." She took the picture from him. "I want . . . Here." She looked around, chose a spot on one of his bookshelves. "I want that. It looks right there, doesn't it?"

Something squeezed his heart. "Yes. It belongs there."

"It doesn't come with a guarantee. Why should it? It's not a car or a computer. It's life, and it's messy, and it breaks down. It's a promise, to try. I want to promise to try. Carter."

She walked back to take his face in her hands. "Carter Maguire, I love you."

As the fist around his heart clenched and released, he lowered his brow to hers. "Say it again, would you?"

"It's the first time I've said it to anyone—this way, I mean. I don't know why I thought it would be so hard. It's not. I love you. I love who we are together. I love who I think we might be. I'll screw up. So will you, you're not perfect. We'll hurt each other, and make each other laugh. We'll make love and we'll fight. I want us to promise to try not to let each other go. Trying's all we can do."

He met her lips with his. There was the promise, he thought. There was everything he'd waited for. There was Mackensie, and she loved him.

"I'm so glad you didn't make the bed."

Her laugh muffled against his lips before she tipped her head back. "That was one element of many that coalesced into a moment of absolute clarity. And I needed to tell you. I couldn't wait. You're the one who waits so well."

"It was worth it. Look what I've got."

"I want to tell you something. On Valentine's Day—our Valentine's Day—when it wasn't a ring in the box, part of me was disappointed. That's what scared me. I'm not scared now."

His eyes focused on hers, and what he saw in them had his heart leaping. "I want a life with you, Mackensie."

"I'm asking you to ask me."

Gently, he brushed his lips to her forehead. "I love your face, and your hands." He took them in his to press a kiss to her palms. "The way you look when you hold a camera, or hunch at the computer. I have dozens of images, pictures, and moments of you in my head. In my heart. I want a lifetime more. Marry me."

"Yes."

"Yes." He drew her to him, held on. "She said yes. Let's get married in June."

She pulled back. "June? We're booked solid. That's—" When he grinned, she narrowed her eyes. "You're a funny guy, Carter."

Laughing, he wrapped his arms around her once more. "I'll take the first open date, if that suits you."

"That's a deal. Speaking for my partners, let me say Vows is thrilled to provide its services, and promises to give you a perfect wedding."

"I've got you. It's already perfect."

She held him, strong and close, through the kiss. Then she laid her head on his shoulder with a sigh.

From the bookshelf their faces smiled out at her. Moments came and went, she thought. It was love that bound them together into a life.

She had love.

Keep reading for a special preview of
the next book
in The Bride Quartet
by Nora Roberts

# BED OF ROSES

From Piatkus

SINCE DETAILS CROWDED HER MIND, MANY OF THEM BLURRY, Emma checked her appointment book over her first cup of coffee. The back-to-back consults gave her nearly as much of a boost as the strong, sweet brew. Basking in it, she leaned back in the chair in her cozy office to read over the side notes she'd added to the entries for each client.

In her experience, the personality of the couple—or often, more accurately, of the bride—helped her determine the tone of the consult, the direction they'd pursue. To Emma's way of thinking, flowers were the heart of a wedding. Whether they were elegant or fun, elaborate or simple, the flowers were the romance.

It was her job to give the client all the heart and romance they desired.

She sighed, stretched, then smiled at the vase of petite roses on her desk. Spring, she thought, was the best. The wedding season kicked into full gear—which meant busy days and long nights designing, arranging, creating, not only for *this* spring's weddings, but the next as well.

She loved the continuity as much as the work itself.

That's what Vows had given her and her three best friends. Continuity, rewarding work, and that sense of personal accomplishment. And she got to play with flowers, live with flowers, practically swim in flowers every day.

Thoughtfully, she examined her hands, the little nicks and tiny cuts. Some days she thought of them as battle scars and others as medals of honor. This morning she just wished she'd remembered to fit in a manicure.

She glanced at the time, calculated. Boosted again, she sprang up. Detouring into her bedroom, she grabbed a scarlet hoodie to zip over her pjs. There was time to walk to the main house before she dressed and prepared for the day. At the main house Mrs. Grady would have breakfast, so Emma wouldn't have to forage or cook for herself.

Her life, she thought as she jogged downstairs, brimmed with lovely perks.

She passed through the living room she used as a reception and consult area, and took a quick scan around as she headed for the door. She'd freshen up the flowers on display before the first meeting, but oh, hadn't those stargazer lilies opened beautifully?

She stepped out of what had been a guest house on the Brown Estate and was now her home, and the base for Centerpiece—her part of Vows.

She took a deep breath of spring air. And shivered.

Damn it, why couldn't it be warmer? It was April, for God's sake. It was daffodil time. Look how cheerful the pansies she'd potted up were. She refused to let a chilly morning—and, okay, it was staring to drizzle on top of it—spoil her mood.

She hunched inside the hoodie, stuck the hand not holding her coffee mug in her pocket, and began to walk to the main house.

Things were coming back to life all around her, she reminded herself. If you looked closely enough you could see the promise of green on the trees, the hint of what would be delicate blooms of dogwood and cherry blossoms. Those daffodils wanted to pop, and the crocuses already had. Maybe there'd be another spring snow, but the worst was over.

Soon it would be time to dig in the dirt, to bring some of her beauties out of the greenhouse and put them on display. She added the bouquets, the swags and garlands, but nothing beat Mother Nature for providing the most poignant landscape for a wedding.

And nothing, in her opinion, beat the Brown Estate for showing it off.

The gardens, showpieces even now, would soon explode with color, bloom, scent, inviting people to stroll along the curving paths or sit on a bench, relax in sun or shade. Parker put her in charge—as much as Parker could put anyone else in charge—of overseeing them, so every year she got to play, planting something new, or supervising the landscape team.

The terraces and patios created lovely outdoor living spaces, perfect for weddings and events—poolside receptions, terrace receptions, ceremonies under the rose arbor or the pergola, or perhaps down by the pond under a willow.

We've got it all, she thought.

The house itself? Could anything be more graceful, more beautiful? The wonderful soft blue, those warm touches of yellow and cream. All the varied rooflines, the arching windows, the lacy balconies added up to elegant charm. And really, the entrance portico was made for crowding with lush greenery or elaborate colors and textures.

As a child she'd thought of it as a fairyland, complete with castle.

Now it was home.

She veered toward the pool house where her partner Mac lived and kept her photography studio. Even as she aimed for it, the door opened. Emma beamed a smile, shot out a wave to the lanky man with shaggy hair and a tweed jacket who came out.

"'Morning, Carter!"

"Hi, Emma."

Carter's family and hers had been friends almost as long as she could remember. Now, Carter Maguire, former Yale prof and current teacher of English Lit at their high school alma mater, was engaged to one of her best friends in the world.

Life wasn't just good, Emma thought. It was a freaking bed of roses.

Riding on that, she all but danced to Carter, tugged him down by the lapels as she angled up on her toes and kissed him noisily.

"Wow," he said, and blushed a little.

"Hey." Mackensie, her eyes sleepy, her cap of red hair bright in the gloom, leaned on the doorjamb. "Are you trying to make time with my guy?"

"If only. I'd steal him away but you've dazzled and vamped him."

"Damn right."

"Well." Carter offered them both a flustered smile. "This is a really nice start to my day. The staff meeting I'm headed to won't be half as enjoyable."

"Call in sick." Mac all but purred it. "I'll give you something enjoyable."

"Hah. Well. Anyway. Bye."

Emma grinned at his back as he hurried off to his car. "God, he is so *cute*."

"He really is."

"And look at you, Happy Girl."

"Happy Engaged Girl. Want to see my ring again?"

"Oooh," Emma said obligingly when Mac wiggled her fingers. "Ahhh."

"Are you going for breakfast?"

"That's the plan."

"Wait." Mac leaned in, grabbed a jacket, then pulled the door closed behind her. "I didn't have anything but coffee yet, so . . ." As they fell into step together, Mac frowned. "That's my mug."

"Do you want it back now?"

"I know why I'm cheerful this crappy morning, and it's the same reason I haven't had time for breakfast. It's called Let's Share the Shower."

"Happy Girl is also Bragging Bitch."

"And proud of it. Why are you so cheerful? Got a man in your house?"

"Sadly no. But I have five consults booked today. Which is a great start to the week, and comes on the heels of the lovely end to last week with yesterday's tea party wedding. It was really sweet, wasn't it?"

"Our sexagenarian couple exchanging vows and celebrating while surrounded by his kids, her kids, grandchildren. Not just sweet, but also reassuring. Second time around for both of them, and there they are, ready to do it again, willing to share and blend. I got some really great shots. Anyway, I think those crazy kids are going to make it."

"Speaking of crazy kids, we really have to talk about your flowers. December may be far away—she says shivering—but it comes fast, as you well know."

"I haven't even decided on the look for the engagement shots yet. Or looked at dresses, or thought about colors."

"I look good in jewel tones," Emma said and fluttered her lashes.

"You look good in burlap. Talk about bragging bitches." Mac opened the door to the mud room, and since Mrs. Grady was back from her winter vacation, remembered to wipe her feet. "As soon as I find the dress, we'll brainstorm the rest."

"You're the first one of us to get married. To have your wedding here."

"Yeah. It's going to be interesting to see how we manage to run the wedding and be in the wedding."

"You know you can count on Parker to figure out the logistics. If anyone can make it run smooth, it's Parker."

They walked into the kitchen, and chaos.

While the equitable Maureen Grady worked at the stove, movements efficient, face placid, Parker and Laurel faced off across the room.

"It has to be done," Parker insisted.

"Bullshit, bullshit, bullshit."

"Laurel, this is business. In business you serve the client."

"Let me tell you what I'd like to serve the client."

"Just stop." Parker, her rich brown hair sleeked back in a tail, was already dressed in a meet-the-client suit of midnight blue. Eyes of nearly the same color flashed hot with impatience. "Look, I've already put together a list of her choices, the number of guests, her colors, her floral selections. You don't even have to speak to her. I'll liaise."

"Now let me tell you what you can do with your list."

"The bride—"

"The bride is an asshole. The bride is an idiot, whiny baby bitch who made it very clear nearly one year ago that she neither needed nor wanted my particular services. The bride can bite me because she's not biting any of my cake now that she's realized her own stupidity."

In the cotton pants and tank she'd slept in, her hair still in sleep tufts, Laurel dropped onto a chair in the breakfast nook.

"You need to calm down." Parker bent to pick up a file. Probably tossed on the floor by Laurel, Emma mused. "Everything you need is in here." Parker laid the file on the table. "I've already assured the bride we'll accommodate her, so—"

"So you design and bake a four-layer wedding cake between now and Saturday, and a groom's cake, and a selection of desserts. To serve two hundred people. You do that with no previous preparation, and when you've got three other events over the weekend, and an evening event in three days."

Her face set in mutinous lines, Laurel picked up the file and deliberately dropped it on the floor.

"Now you're acting like a child."

"Fine. I'm a child."

"Girls, your little friends have come to play." Mrs. Grady sang it out, her tone overly sweet, her eyes laughing.

"Ah, I hear my mom calling me," Emma said and started to ease out of the room.

"No, you don't!" Laurel jumped up. "Just listen to this! The Folk-Harrigan wedding. Saturday, evening event. You'll remember, I'm sure, how the bride sniffed at the very idea of Icings at Vows providing the cake or any of the desserts. How she *sneered* at me and my suggestions and insisted her cousin, a pastry chef in New York who studied in Paris and designed cakes for *important* affairs, would be handling all the desserts.

"Do you remember what she said to me?"

"Ah." Emma shifted because Laurel's finger pointed at her heart. "Not in the exact words."

"Well, I do. She said she was sure—and said it with that sneer—she was sure I could handle *most* affairs well enough, but she wanted the *best* for her wedding. She said that to my face."

"Which was rude, no question," Parker began.

"I'm not finished," Laurel said between her teeth. "Now, at the eleventh hour, it seems her brilliant cousin has run off with with one of her—the cousin's—clients. Scandal, scandal, as said client met brilliant cousin when he commissioned her to design a cake for *his* engagement party. Now they're MIA and the bride wants me to step in and save her day."

"Which is what we do here. Laurel—"

"I'm not asking you." She flicked her fingers at Parker, zeroed in on Mac and Emma. "I'm asking them."

"What? Did you say something?" Mac offered a toothy smile.

"Sorry, I must've gotten water in my ears from the shower. Can't hear a thing."

"Coward. Em?"

"Ah . . ."

"Breakfast!" Mrs. Grady circled a finger in the air. "Everybody sit down. Egg white omelettes on toasted brown bread. Sit, sit. Eat."

"I'm not eating until—"

"Let's just sit." Interrupting Laurel's next tirade, Emma tried a soothing tone. "Give me a minute to think. Let's just all sit down and . . . Oh, Mrs. G., that looks fabulous." She grabbed two plates, thinking of them as shields as she crossed to the breakfast nook and scooted in. "Let's remember we're a team," she began.

"You're not the one being insulted and overworked."

"Actually, I am. Or have been. Whitney Folk puts the Zilla in Bridezilla. I could relay my personal nightmares with her, but that's a story for another day."

"I've got some of my own," Mac put in.

"So your hearing's back," Laurel muttered.

"She's rude, demanding, spoiled, difficult, and unpleasant," Emma continued. "Usually when we plan the event, even with the problems that can come up and the general weirdness of some couples, I like to think we're helping them showcase a day that begins their happy ever after. With this one? I'd be surprised if they make it two years. She was rude to you, and I don't think it was a sneer, I think it was a smirk. I don't like her."

Obviously pleased with the support, Laurel sent her own smirk toward Parker, then began to eat.

"That being said, we're a team. And clients, even smirky bitch clients, have to be served. Those are good reasons to do this," Emma said while Laurel scowled at her. "But there's a better one. You'll show her rude, smirky, flat, bony ass what a really brilliant pastry chef can do, and under pressure."

"Parker already tried that one on me."

"Oh." Emma sampled a skinny sliver of her omelette. "Well, it's true."

"I could bake her man-stealing cousin into the ground."

"No question. Personally, I think she should grovel, at least a little."

"I like groveling." Laurel considered it. "And begging."

"I might be able to arrange for some of each." Parker lifted her coffee. "I also informed her that in order to accommodate her on such short notice we would require an additional fee. I added twenty-five percent. She grabbed it like a lifeline, and actually wept in gratitude."

A new light beamed in Laurel's bluebell eyes. "She cried?"

Parker inclined her head, and cocked an eyebrow at Laurel. "So?"

"While the crying part warms me inside, she'll still have to take what I give her, and like it."

"Absolutely."

"You just let me know what you decide on when you decide on it," Emma told her. "I'll work in the flowers and decor for the table." She sent a sympathetic smile at Parker. "What time did she call you with all this?"

"Three twenty A.M."

Laurel reached over, gave Parker's hand a pat. "Sorry."

"That's my part of the deal. We'll get through it. We always do."

THEY ALWAYS DID, EMMA THOUGHT AS SHE REFRESHED HER living room arrangements. She trusted they always would. She glanced at the photograph she kept in a simple white frame, one of three young girls playing Wedding Day in a summer garden. She'd been bride that day, and had held the bouquet of weeds and wildflowers, had worn the lace veil. And had been just as charmed and delighted as her friends when the blue butterfly landed on the dandelion in her bouquet.

Mac had been there, too, of course. Behind the camera, capturing the moment. She considered it a not-so-small miracle that they'd turned what had been a favored childhood game of make-believe into a thriving business.

No dandelions these days, she thought as she fluffed pillows. But how many times had she seen that same delighted, dazzled look on a bride's face when she'd offered them a bouquet she'd made for them. Just for them.

She hoped the meeting about to begin would ultimately end the next spring with just that dazzled look on the bride's face.

She arranged her files, her albums, her books, then moved to the mirror to check her hair, her makeup, the line of the jacket and pants she'd changed into.

Presentation, she thought, was a priority of Vows.

She turned from the mirror to answer her phone with a cheerful, "Centerpiece of Vows. Yes, hello, Roseanne, of course I remember you. October wedding, right? No, it's not too early to make those decisions."

As she spoke, Emma took a notebook out of her desk, flipped it open. "We can set up a consultation next week if that works for you. Can you bring a photo of your dress? Great. And if you've selected the attendants' dresses, or their colors? Mmm-hmm. I'll help you with all of that. How about next Monday at two?"

She logged in the appointment, then glanced over her shoulder as she heard a car pull up.

A client on the phone, another coming to the door.

God, she *loved* spring!

EMMA SHOWED HER LAST CLIENT OF THE DAY THROUGH THE DISplay area where she kept silk arrangements and bouquets as well as various samples on tables and shelves.

"I made this up when you e-mailed me the photo of your dress and gave me the basic idea of your colors and your favorite flowers. I know you'd talked about preferring a large cascade bouquet, but . . ."

Emma took the bouquet of lilies and roses tied with white, pearl-studded ribbon off the shelf. "I just wanted you to see this before you made a firm decision."

"It's beautiful, plus my favorite flowers. But it doesn't seem, I don't know, big enough."

"With the lines of your dress, the column of the skirt and the beautiful beadwork on the bodice, the more contemporary bouquet could be stunning. I want you to have exactly what you want, Miranda. This sample is closer to what you have in mind."

Emma took a cascade from the shelf.

"Oh, it's like a garden!"

"Yes, it is. Let me show you a couple of photos." She opened the folder on the counter, took out two.

"It's my dress! With the bouquets."

"My partner, Mac, is a whiz with Photoshop. These give you a good idea how each style looks with your dress. There's no wrong choice. It's your day, and every detail should be exactly what you want."

"But you're right, aren't you?" Miranda studied both pictures. "The big one sort of, well, overwhelms the dress. But the other, it's like it was made for it. It's elegant, but it's still romantic. It is romantic, isn't it?"

"I think so. The lilies, with that blush of pink against the white roses, and the touches of pale green. The trail of the white ribbon, the glow of the pearls. I thought, if you liked it, we might do just the lilies for your attendants, maybe with a pink ribbon."

"I think . . ." Miranda carried the sample bouquet over to the old-fashioned cheval glass that stood in the corner. Her smile bloomed like the flowers as she studied herself. "I think it looks like some really creative fairies made it. And I love it."

Emma noted it down in her book. "I'm glad you do. We'll work around that, sort of spiraling out from the bouquets. I'll put clear vases on the head table, so the bouquets will not only stay fresh, but serve as part of the decor during the reception. Now for your tossing bouquet, I was thinking just the white roses, smaller scale like this." Emma took down another sample. "Tied with pink and white ribbons."

"That would be perfect. This is turning out to be so much easier than I thought."

Pleased, Emma made another note. "The flowers are important, but they should also be fun. No wrong choices, remember. From everything you've told me, I see the feel of the wedding as modern romance."

"Yes, that's exactly what I'm after."

"Your niece, the flower girl, is five, right?"

"She just turned five last month. She's really excited about scattering rose petals down the aisle."

"I bet." Emma crossed the idea of a pomander off her mental list. "We could use this style basket, covered with white satin, trimmed in baby roses, trailing the pink and white ribbons again. Pink and white rose petals. We could do a halo for her, pink and white baby roses again. Depending on her dress, and what you like, we can keep it simple, or we can trail ribbons down the back."

"The ribbons, absolutely. She's really girly. She'll be thrilled." Miranda took the sample halo Emma offered. "Oh, Emma. It's like a little crown! Princessy."

"Exactly." When Miranda lifted it onto her own head, Emma laughed. "A girly five-year-old will be in heaven. And you'll be her favorite aunt for life."

"She'll look so sweet. Yes, yes, to everything. Basket, halo, ribbons, roses, colors."

"Great. You're making it easy for me. Now you've got your

mothers and your grandmothers. We could do corsages, wrist or pin-on, using the roses or the lilies or both. But—"

Smiling, Miranda set the halo down again. "Every time you say 'but' it turns out fantastic. So, but?"

"I thought we could update the classic tussy-mussy."

"I have no idea what that is."

"It's a small bouquet, like this, carried in a little holder to keep the flowers fresh. We'd put display stands on the tables by their places, which would also dress up their tables, just a little more than the others. We'd use the lilies and roses, in miniature, but maybe reverse the colors. Pink roses, white lilies, those touches of pale green. Or if that didn't go with their dresses, all white. Small, not quite delicate. I'd use something like this very simple silver one, nothing ornate. Then we could have them engraved with the wedding date, or your names, their names."

"It's like their own bouquets. Like a miniature of mine. Oh, my mother will . . ."

When Miranda's eyes filled, Emma reached over and picked up the box of tissue she kept handy.

"Thanks. I want them. I have to think about the monogramming. I'd like to talk that over with Brian."

"Plenty of time."

"But I want them. The reverse, I think, because it makes them more theirs. I'm going to sit down here a minute."

Emma went with her to the little seating area, put the tissue where Miranda could reach. "It's going to be beautiful."

"I know. I can see it. I can already see it, and we haven't even started on the arrangements and centerpieces and, oh, everything else. But I can see it. I have to tell you something."

"Sure."

"My sister—my maid of honor? She really pushed for us to book Felfoot. It's been *the* place in Greenwich, you know, and it is beautiful."

"It's gorgeous, and they always do a fabulous job."

"But Brian and I just fell for this place. The look of it, the feel of it, the way the four of you work together. It felt right for us. Every time I come here, or meet with one of you, I know we were right. We're going to have the most amazing wedding. Sorry," she said, dabbing at her eyes again.

"Don't be." Emma took a tissue for herself. "I'm flattered, and nothing makes me happier than to have a bride sit here and cry happy tears. How about a glass of champagne to smooth things out before we start on the boutonnieres?"

"Seriously? Emmaline, if I wasn't madly in love with Brian, I'd ask *you* to marry me."

With a laugh, Emma rose. "I'll be right back."

LATER, EMMA SAW OFF HER EXCITED BRIDE AND, COMFORTABLY tired, settled down with a short pot of coffee in her office. Miranda was right, she thought as she keyed in all the details. She was going to have the most amazing wedding. An abundance of flowers, a contemporary look with romantic touches. Candles and the sheen and shimmer of ribbons and gauze. Pinks and whites with pops of bold blues and greens for contrast and interest. Sleek silver and clear glass for accents. Long lines, and the whimsy of fairy lights.

As she drafted out the itemized contract, she congratulated herself on a very productive day. And since she'd spent most of the next working on the arrangements for their mid-week evening event, she considered making it an early night.

She'd resist going over and seeing what Mrs. G. had for dinner, make herself a salad, maybe a little pasta. Curl up with a movie or her stack of magazines, call her mother. She could get everything done, have a relaxing evening, and be in bed by eleven.

As she proofed the contract, her phone let out the quick two rings that signaled her personal line. She glanced at the readout, smiled.

"Hi, Sam."

"Hello, Beautiful. What are you doing home when you should be out with me?"

"I'm working."

"It's after six. Pack it in, honey. Adam and Vicki are having a party. We can go grab some dinner first. I'll pick you up in an hour."

"Whoa, wait. I told Vicki tonight just wasn't good for me. I was booked solid today, and still have about another hour before—"

"You've got to eat, right? And if you've been working all day you deserve to play. Come play with me."

"That's sweet, but—"

"Don't make me go to the party by myself. We'll swing by, have a drink, a couple laughs, leave whenever you want. Don't break my heart, Emma."

She cast her eyes up to the ceiling and saw her early night go up in smoke. "I can't make dinner, but I could meet you there around eight."

"I can pick you up at eight."

Then angle to come in when you bring me home, she thought. And that's not happening. "I'll meet you. That way if I need to go and you're having fun, you can stay."

"If that's the best I can get, I'll take it. I'll see you there."